Distant (

by

David O'Neil

A-Argus Better Book Publishers, LLC

For information:
A-Argus Better Book Publishers, LLC
9001 Ridge Hill Street
Kernersville, North Carolina 27285
www.a-argusbooks.com

ISBN: 978-0-6158951-8-5
ISBN: 06158951-8-2

Book Cover designed by Dubya

Printed in the United States of America

Chapter One

In the stern-sheets of the dinghy, Lieutenant Robert Graham, RN, sat crouched forward, a club firmly gripped in his hand. As they neared the captured cutter, the tension mounted. He transferred the club to his other hand and wiped his sweaty palm on his jacket. He was worried, what if it was a trap and the French were waiting for them? Should they have tried to get away, perhaps stolen another boat and crossed to Dover. He could have let someone senior make the decisions.

He shrugged, it was too late now. The boat came alongside the cutter anchored in the inner basin. At the masthead the French Tricolour hung above the union flag, and the badly stowed sails added to the dejected appearance of the ship.

Reaching up to the transom rail, he peered along the full length of the cutter's deck. There was a man sprawled on a coil of rope, drinking from a bottle. A second man lay on the deck beside him. The semi-nude woman draped across him was actively involving the full attention of both men.

Robert rose silently to his feet and climbed onto the projecting edge of the deck and leaned forward. He reached out and took the bottle from the Watchman's hand and swung his club. Twice more the club rose and fell, leaving the three recumbent figures silent on the deck. Robert leaned over the transom and signalled the other two men in the boat to come aboard.

1

Now the action was under way Robert relaxed, followed by the others he went forward, at the hatch he started to go below. A movement caused him to hesitate, a voice spoke in French "Qui va la?"

In a quiet voice he answered "C'est Moi?"

There was the rustle of clothing and a man came into view, appearing at the foot of the stairs. He was below Robert. As he looked up he saw Robert's uniform. For a moment he just stood there, then he swore and started to turn back. Robert's backhand swipe with the club caught the man across the face and he fell back with a ruined nose, blood spilling down his shirt. Robert descended the rest of the way and swung through the door of the main cabin.

Inside a man was tied to the mast, it was the Captain. His back was torn from the lashed, and his wrists were bloody from his efforts to release himself. He was alive but unconscious. Robert left him to be attended by his companions and turned to the door leading to the crew accommodation forward.

The men imprisoned there began to murmur as he approached

"Silence!" Robert snapped in English, the tension of the moment and the shock at the sight of his Captain's condition combining to put him on edge once more. The murmuring stopped at the sound of a familiar voice. With the club Robert broke the hasp of the lock, allowing the door to open.

First out was Hansen, masters mate, the big Swedish volunteer from the cutter's crew. "Thanks Sir, I wass crowded in there." He was flustered and his English slipped a little in the circumstances.

"Bring the men on deck quietly," Robert ordered.

As Hansen opened his mouth to say something Robert put his fingers to his lips and whispered, "Later".

The men streamed out of the cabin and took their places on deck. Robert pointed to the swivel gun on the transom and the other mounted on the rail forward. The gunner's mate nodded, seeing the signal, and immediately went to the first gun and went to work on it.

To Hansen, Robert indicated the anchor. Midshipman John Williams, who had accompanied Robert in the boat, was already organising the men preparing to raise the mainsail. Three men grasped the chain and raised the anchor by sheer muscle power. There were guards on shore who wouldn't miss the sound of the pawl clicking on the windlass.

The jib was hoisted. With the anchor clear of the sea bed, the sail filled, the cutter started to move. As the mainsail rose up the mast the breeze caught and the cutter leaned and raced toward the open sea while the anchor was still being brought inboard.

Robert relaxed as they passed through the jaws of the inner basin, soon they would be clear of Calais and free to sail for home. A shout in French came from the harbour wall—followed by a musket shot—meant their escape had been discovered.

After a tense ten minutes, the cutter passed the outer marker into the open sea with no sign of pursuit. Robert relaxed once more and, having set a rough course for Dover with the lights of Calais a glow in the background, Robert was able to attend to his captain. Leaving Williams in charge on deck he hurried below to find Jones, the captain's servant, was bathing the savagely-wounded back with a mix of vinegar and water, before bandaging the lacerated flesh. Robert winced at the imagined pain; mercifully the Captain was still unconscious.

Leaving Jones with the injured man, Robert took the charts into his own cabin, he set the chair on its legs and cleared the small table with a sweep of his arm. From the mess they had made, it seemed they must have been looking for valuables. He grinned wryly at the thought

Seated in the cabin he paused for a moment to gather himself; so far so good, but he shuddered to think what might have happened if they had been caught. If the French prize crew had been still aboard, it would have been a different story. He had seen them go ashore, but suppose they had come back after dark? He straightened up and using the light of the hooded lamp within the cabin he studied the chart and worked out the direct course for Dover.

Back on deck, he gave the heading to the helmsman and for the first time began to relax.

"Mr. Williams, get the cook to find something to eat, I'm starving."

Williams ran below returning with a piece of bread and a bottle of wine, courtesy of their captors.

"Hot food will take an hour sir, the galley fire was out. Meanwhile?" he proffered the bread and wine. Robert took them both gratefully; he had not eaten since the previous day.

The bread was fresh and the wine drinkable, and the *Excelsior* was sailing comfortably on a course for Dover and safety. Masters-mate Hansen reported the anchor secured and the guns ready for action.

"Very good, Sven. Mr. Williams, sort the men into their watches and get the watch below clearing up. The

Captain's cabin is a mess but so is the Captain, so keep the men quiet."

Midshipman Williams nodded and turned and addressed the men giving them their duties.

The sea was calm and as Robert leaned against the stern rail he thought to himself of the journey that had brought him, Robert Graham, only son of a Devon squire, to his present position of Lieutenant in the Royal Navy. He was not old for a Lieutenant, but not young either. He recalled the pride he had felt when he first donned the uniform as a midshipman at the age of thirteen. He had strutted through the village letting all the people he had grown up with see that he was a man now, well almost. He remembered the looks he had received from some of the girls. Looking back he now had some idea of the meaning of those looks, though at the time it seemed just innocent excitement among friends. He recalled the comments made by his father, the local squire.

'Stand tall, Robert, you've chosen a man's career, see you remember all I've told you about being responsible, from now on it's others you'll have to think of first, that's what being an officer means!'

He could hear his father's voice in his head now. He turned with a start to realise he was being spoken-to by Midshipman Mathews, "Sir, we are in sight of the Dover harbour; signal from the flag, Captain to report on landing!"

The arrival in Dover was an anticlimax. Robert had not realised how the tension of the recovery and escape from Calais the night before had affected him. He watched the broken body of the Captain—Lieutenant Lionel Watts—be taken ashore to the hospital for treatment. The surgeon was

5

not too hopeful; it seemed the unfortunate man had been tortured as well as flogged.

As Robert prepared to report to the Port Admiral; he stood before the mirror in his room at the inn dressed in his best uniform. The reflection in the mirror was presentable, even to his own critical gaze. At six feet three inches, he was forced to stoop to arrange his fair hair; it was at last more or less in place. The face in the mirror was pleasant; the grey eyes were steady, clear and wide set; it seemed a face that would rather smile than frown.

He touched the scar that ran from his hairline to his ear remembering he had been just sixteen; it was the first time he had taken part in boarding an enemy ship. The French officer facing him on the deck of the prize was laughing at him as he fought for his life with his heavy cutlass, frantically parrying the expert fencing of the Frenchman. His opponent's sword was a proper blade flicking from side to side. When he tapped the clumsy blade to one side Robert felt the touch on the side of his head and stumbled, falling on his back. He remembered the blood running and the Frenchman laughing, drawing back for the final thrust to end it all, and the look of surprise on his face as the pike plunged into his chest. The towering figure of Sven Hansen wrenched the pike from the fallen officer and hauled Robert to his feet. He remembered glancing at the body sprawled on the deck, then wiping the blood from his face he plunged back into the fight.

The Frenchman's sword hung behind the door now, his prize from the action. He could still hear the voice of the Captain as he handed the sword over, "This is a good sword and it nearly cost you your life. Learn to use it well and it may save you next time!"

He smiled at his thoughts and hooked the sword to his belt, touching the polished scabbard as he turned to leave picking up his cocked hat on the way. Having been temporarily in command of the cutter *Excelsior*, he now was summoned to discuss his report on the incident and receive his orders for the future.

The room in the Admiral's Headquarters was warmed by the fire blazing in the elegant white marble fireplace. There were two men seated at the table with the Admiral, and they all three listened to his verbal report of the incident that led to the capture and recapture of the cutter *Excelsior*. He told them everything in order as it happened.

"When I was told to assess the defences and acquire as much information about Calais as I could, it was obvious I would need to go ashore. I was accordingly dropped off in a dinghy with a seaman Will Eckerd, a Dutchman, and Midshipman Williams. We left the dinghy on the beach or 'plage' as it is called in the area, placing the boat among the many small boats always to be found there. Mr. Williams and I then took a look around the harbour, and the inner and outer basins."

"Was it not a risk, just openly walking round the harbour?" The civilian asked.

"The seaman was a French-speaking Dutchman, many of whom can be found in Calais. Je had money and was sent to wander about and pick up whatever he could while we were there. I thought that on his own he would have a better chance than we. I speak French fluently though Mr. Williams does not, and we walked around the harbour and basins checking on the facilities and the defences, only stopping for the lunch period in the middle of the day when too many idle men would be about. Otherwise the fact that we were openly walking about in uniform was never questioned. We carried our hats in a bag with jackets undone. The difference between French and British Naval uniforms consists mainly of the Tricolour which we each had wrapped round our waists.

"It was during the early evening that we noticed the *Excelsior* being brought into the inner basin as a prize. We watched and we could see the crew were still aboard, apparently held below; and concluded they were being kept overnight. It was then that we decided that there was a good chance we could take the ship back so we made plans accordingly.

"After collecting Eckerd, we took one of the many dinghies tied up in the inner basin; our own was still lying on the plage. We waited for darkness and saw a boat from the cutter rowed over to the quay.

"We followed the man to the shop on the quay where he bought wine and bread. He then went up to the Place d'Armes and had a short discussion with a woman who was apparently a prostitute known to him. He struck a deal with her, and she accompanied him back to the anchored cutter.

"We gave them time to settle down and then rowed out to the cutter where we boarded and we managed to release the crew. I questioned the Frenchmen on board; apparently Captain Watts had been interrogated by the captain of the corvette, the ship that had taken the *Excelsior;* a man named Guilleme Artois. Captain Watts had been badly beaten and tortured by this Artois, who had a reputation among his own men for brutality. The French prisoners taken on the *Excelsior* asked to be brought with us rather than be left to face their captain's wrath. We sailed unchallenged out of the harbour. The rest you know."

He paused, and then added, "From the few words Captain Watts was able to tell us, Artois was trying to find out why the *Excelsior* was there and who were we trying to contact in Calais."

The Admiral and the two men sat quietly in thought before the Captain, who had not introduced himself spoke, "We know of this man Artois, captain of the corvette, *Revenant*, he is a former privateer, hated in France as well as here for his cruelty. If ever the chance arises you have my full permission to kill him if you can."

The civilian who had finally named himself as Mr. Smith coughed at these comments, Robert had the impression that this was one of those people who preferred death to be at arm's length, something to be read about in reports rather than faced. Personally having seen the method of questioning used by Artois he had no hesitation in agreeing with the still anonymous captain.

The Admiral rose to his feet, "Gentlemen I will leave you at this point. Mr. Graham, orders placing you in command of the *Excelsior* will be waiting you when you leave here; these gentlemen will be issuing you orders for your next task. I will confirm them before you leave."

When he had left the room the two visitors conferred, while Robert sat and absorbed the fact that he had been given his first command. He couldn't help feeling the thrill however briefly, as the two men who had been talking in undertones turned back to Robert.

It was Mr. Smith who mentioned the next task they had for the *Excelsior*, "We wish to have an agent placed on the French coast in the vicinity of Dieppe. I have Le Treport in mind." He looked at Robert inquiringly.

Robert's reply took both men aback. "Sir, with respect, I will of course be happy to accept your orders but, with your agreement, I shall discuss the location of the landing with the agent. It will make it completely discreet and there will be less chance of betrayal."

"Are you suggesting we cannot be trusted?" The captain was quite indignant.

Uncomfortably Robert replied. "I am not, sir! I am suggesting that were you in my position you would expect to use your expertise in a matter such as this, not rely on the possibility of being caused to risk the life of the agent and imperil the ship by using a landing site that may have been selected by a clerk with a pin."

The captain looked at Robert in amazement, astonished at this outspoken statement from a mere lieutenant; then he smiled and broke into a laugh.

"You're damn right, young man; and by the way, congratulations on your first command. We tend to forget that it can be critical to make your decisions based on experience and local knowledge and, on occasion, even on the spot. Things change, and as you say picking a place on a map may be convenient for communication and for other reasons but completely wrong for safety."

The civilian gentleman coughed and uncomfortably spoke, "Of course, advance arrangements can be betrayed. The agent will identify himself to you when he presents himself on HMS *Excelsior* tomorrow. You can decide your movements then."

The Captain rose and held out his hand to Robert, "Can you confirm that your ship is ready to depart promptly tomorrow evening?"

Robert shook the hand extended to him. "The ship is ready now, sir. Thank you and with your permission unless there is some other matter to detain us, I will take my leave and study my charts for the area."

***

The light at Phore de Ailly could be seen to port as the cutter silently approached the beach at St Aubin du Mer; on board, Robert arranged for himself and the agent he now knew as Rene to be rowed ashore.

The beach was deserted and quiet, so they left the boat with the seaman and set off up the road to the darkened village. It was only a short distance and the agent quickly sought out the inn that was also dark though it was only 9 o'clock.

Rene knocked at the door, and when the door opened carefully and a face appeared the agent said in French "Vive le Roi"—Long live the King.

The door was flung open wide, "Ah, Rene, mon brave. It has been too long."

Robert followed the two men into the Inn where a fire was still burning in the hearth. Wine was poured and the three men seated themselves; a conversation in French commenced between Rene and Albert the innkeeper.

Robert drank his wine then rose to his feet and said in English. "I will leave you two to reminisce and get back to the ship; good luck, Rene."

As he stood the innkeeper protested that he stay and enjoy more wine. Robert however was uneasy and he politely refused, pleading the dangers of being off a strange shore. He opened the door carefully and made sure there was no one about and then set off down the track to the beach.

Halfway there he heard voices. He hid behind the hedge at the roadside as three men in uniform approached, pushing the sailor from the beach before them. They were laughing among themselves. The sailor was not bound or shackled in any way so Robert took a chance and straightened up and donned his hat. Stepping out from the shadow he snapped at the three soldiers in French. They immediately sprang to attention. To the seaman who couldn't believe his eyes, he snapped in English, "Well, go on. Hit him."

The seaman swung round and with all his strength smashed the nearest Frenchman on the jaw with his fist. The soldier dropped as if he had been pole-axed, while the others stood still stunned by what had happened; Robert hit the second man with the butt of the pistol he carried while the sailor tackled the third man, grappling him for the musket he carried. They fell to the ground wrestling for possession of the weapon. Robert, his man unconscious, stepped forward and clouted the third man with his pistol. He subsided beside the others.

"What happened?" He asked the man. "Barlow, isn't it?"

"Yessir, they just came out of the dark and called out in English, I thought it was you, sir."

"In English? Then they knew we were here. Tie them up quickly and follow me to the inn. I must warn the agent." Robert rose, turned and ran silently back the way he had come.

At the inn there was a light showing through the side window. Robert checked the priming on his pistol and cautiously approached the building. Peering through the window he saw a stranger, a civilian, standing looking at Rene who was seated on a chair in the centre of the room. The Innkeeper was tying his wrists to the chair. Robert noticed the pistol in the stranger's hand. It was down by his side now the agent had been tied up. Robert took a quick look around the building, checking for other people, but there was no one in sight. Making a swift decision, he banged on the front door of the inn and ran round to the back. As he guessed the Innkeeper went to the front door, the stranger was looking that way as Robert entered through the back door, his pistol raised and pointed at the stranger.

In response to Robert's curt command, the stranger placed his pistol on the floor and stood up. The Innkeeper returned and stood looking apprehensive, appalled at the changed situation.

Robert gestured to the agent; the Innkeeper shrugged and untied the ropes. Rene then tied the Innkeeper and stranger together.

"Who is he?" Robert gestured at the stranger.

"I don't know, but I do know they are waiting for someone else."

"Any idea of how long?"

"Soon I think, from the way he spoke."

The seaman appeared at the door, "All tied and gagged sir, but there is someone else coming down the main road, I can hear hoof beats"

"Well done! Now, Barlow, get back to the ship, as quick as you can." He wrote quickly on a scrap of paper from his pocket. "Give this to Mr. Williams and bring the party back quickly and quietly now. Go!"

Barlow left running.

Robert closed the curtains carefully and he and Rene settled down to wait; both with pistols ready.

When the French party arrived, there were six men. The leader walked straight to the front door of the inn and banged on it. Rene went and opened the door and the leader entered, leaving the other men outside with the horses. Before the door closed, a pistol was put to his head and he was ordered to sit down. After tying him up and gagging him with the others Robert slipped out of the back door to meet the men from the ship. Hansen the master's mate arrived quietly with six men. Robert whispered instructions and Hansen and his men circled round the inn. The five remaining Frenchmen, all dismounted and standing, chatting quietly, were captured without a struggle.

Inside the building Robert and Rene had discussed the situation, Robert deciding to take the entire party back to England with the agent electing to carry on with his task.

Mounted on one of the horses from the new arrivals, he made his farewell and rode off northwards. The other horses were placed in the Inn stables out of sight. When the sound of the hooves of Rene's horse were out of earshot the little party made its way back to the beach herding the prisoners before them, and from thence to the ship.

The entire operation from the first landing, to the final departure took three hours, and it was just after midnight that the cutter left the vicinity under full sail to return to Dover. When the *HMS Excelsior* reached Dover once more Robert reported the events surrounding the landing of the agent. He faced the same Captain and Mr. Smith, his civilian companion, who drily remarked "It seems the enemy got the word despite your precautions!"

"Since the landing place had only been selected during the day of departure, and advised to your staff at that time, the news must have been leaked here regardless of your belief to the contrary. I spoke with no one and we did not even mark the chart once we decided where we would land."

He took the proffered chair and continued, "Whoever betrayed us must have sent the message to Calais and had the ambush arranged, using the French semaphore towers to contact the people in the area."

The enigmatic Mr. Smith was displeased with the suggestion but agreed he would certainly investigate. Meanwhile he received the prisoners enthusiastically at Dover Castle, and congratulated Robert on his quick thinking.

Robert returned to the *Excelsior*, now tied up alongside in Dover Harbour. In the absence of other orders he reported to the Port Admiral's office for orders, hoping to be released from the detachment in Dover to return to their home port of Plymouth for reassignment. He was not surprised, however, to be instructed to remain available in Dover until further notice.

The enforced delay at Dover gave him a chance to replace some of his uniform, which was getting a little frayed around the edges. He was delighted to hear that the recovery of the *Excelsidor* from the French at Calais entitled Midshipman Williams, Seaman Willem Egberk, and himself to prize money. Even after the Admiral had his portion, Robert's share was over £300.00.

Chapter Two

The days at Dover passed slowly and quietly. It gave Robert the opportunity to keep the crew up to the mark and train them in his own way. He was aware that he would be watched by the men but that was part of command. His insistence on the men actually demonstrating their expertise and practicing it was at first unpopular, but as they got used to the idea, they took pride in showing what they could do.

Robert had always considered that in a small craft everyone in the crew should be interchangeable, thus 'top men' learned to man the guns and gunners learned sail handling, and all did their turn at the helm. Especially popular were the days when they assumed the death of the captain and the middy took command, then the master's mate, finally the bo'sun. While these events were staged the officers watched and were available for criticism afterwards, this kept the crew on their toes.

They found the time to have the small repairs that were always 'to be done next time', actually done. The main problem was that eventually boredom set in, and the restlessness among the crew caused Robert to approach Mr. Smith with the request that they be given a real job to do. The resulting series of patrols off the French coast allowed the crew to settle down into a regular routine once more.

The weather in the channel could never be reliably predicted and when expected fine weather turned out to be fog regular sailors shrugged their shoulders and got on with life.

HMS Excelsior was scudding along to a fresh breeze, the sun had broken through the overcast and was glinting off the wind driven whitecaps. Robert was standing beside the wheel when the cry came from the forward lookout, "Boat ahoy, starboard side." The lookout pointed to the boat, low in the water now visible from the deck.

The open boat had four people lying in the bottom, two men and two women, none showing any sign of life.

Robert gazed down into the boat saddened by the sight, guessing that they had lost their bearings and had carried on rowing in circles until they were exhausted. When the bodies were recovered from the small craft it was found that the two men had both been shot, one of the women, just a girl, was dead, probably from exposure. It was only then that Hansen, who was passing the bodies up, realised that the other woman was still breathing.

Having searched the boat, recovering several small boxes and bags from under the seats, they abandoned it after punching a hole in the bottom to ensure it sank.

The young woman was taken into Robert's cabin where the carpenter, a middle-aged married man with several children, stripped her clothes off and rubbed her dry with cloths. Then he wrapped her in blankets to warm her up. As he bathed her lips with a little brandy he was rewarded with a gasp and a cough, followed by the regard of two steady blue eyes.

He called the Captain.

Robert faced the girl and spoke to her in French, "How do you feel?"

"Thirsty and hungry" She replied.

After a little food and hot drink she sat up in the bunk and introduced herself as Mariette, Comtesse D'Valle. The others in the boat were her brother the Comte and their friends Robert Chaumade and his daughter Felice. They had been hidden by loyal servants for several weeks until they were forced to flee when their protectors were denounced by a neighbour and taken to the Bastille.

Mariette D'Valle shuddered, and in excellent English explained, "We arranged to meet a boat to take us to England and left in the small dinghy to row to a rendezvous off the Calais light. We saw the craft we had arranged to meet and were signalled to approach. When we reached her side the men on board took our extended hands, we thought to bring us aboard, but instead they pulled the rings from our fingers. Then others got down into the boat and took the other baggage, hitting the two men when they protested. The things in the boat had been missed because the alarm was raised as another ship came near. They were discussing taking Felice and I on board to use and then dispose of, when my brother recovered his senses and pushed off away from the side of the ship.

"The boat drifted clear while they were arguing, my brother the Comte and Chaumade who had also recovered paddled the boat with their hands to escape from the thieves, the men on the ship laughed as we tried to get away and they began shooting at the men paddling. The oars had been lost so they could make little headway. Both were hit and my brother died then and there, but we were now drifting over shallow water and the ship set sail and abandoned us. M'sieu Chaumade died later in the night."

Mariette stopped and composed herself; she took a drink and continued.

"There isn't much more to tell, Felice and I clung together for warmth but it was so cold and our other clothes had been in the bags stolen by the crew of the ship. I got the coats of my brother and Robert and wrapped them round us, but we could not get warm enough. We had escaped, but without oars the boat was at the mercy of the wind and tide. Felice lost heart and despite my best efforts she succumbed to exhaustion, and quietly drifted off."

She sank back exhausted, so Robert tucked her in and let her sleep.

Mariette woke once more before they reached Dover, and she sobbed when Robert reminded her that her companions were all dead. In Dover she was immediately gathered into the system already well established by earlier émigré families.

Anticipating with some regret that he would see her no more, it was only seven days later Robert was pleasantly surprised to receive an invitation to a reception for the Free Society in Dover Castle as a guest of the Comtesse D'Valle.

It was a glittering occasion and, Robert, arrayed in his best dress uniform, felt quite overshadowed by the gold braid and fine clothes of the men and the sparkling jewellery and colourful silks and satins of the ladies.

He was greeted at the entrance by the Comtesse and her uncle Armand, a man of middle years; tall, slim and elegant, dressed in the rather more showy fashion that was becoming popular with elements of the Beau Monde at that time. He had escaped to England three years before. Both seemed pleased to see him, and as he bowed over the hand of Mariette she whispered to him to wait and escort her after the guest's reception.

Armand D'Valle was most grateful for the part played by Robert and his men in rescuing his beautiful niece, and surrendered him to the attentions of Mariette with a smile.

The two made a handsome couple as they strolled through the rooms and helped each other to the variety of food displayed. The mild evening air encouraged Robert to invite her to see the gardens, and both enjoyed the summer evening stroll among the roses laid out in formal beds.

She questioned Robert on his fluent French, and he explained that his mother was French and had insisted that they spoke French every day within the house. When she died his father had engaged a French tutor to make sure that Robert could speak effortless French as his mother had wished. He added that his father, who was a keen historian, had predicted there would be trouble with France in future, and he thought it sensible for his son to have knowledge of the language in his future career in the navy.

The evening passed all too soon for Robert who was enchanted by his lovely companion.

Though Mariette was no older, in many ways she was far more mature than Robert. The life of the French aristocracy was geared to a rather racier pace than that of provincial England. When they parted late that evening she had invited him to call upon her at the house occupied by her uncle, in Dover. She was staying there until her eventual move to London could be arranged.

It was a week before Robert was able to take advantage of the invitation; his note requesting permission to visit had been promptly returned with an invitation to dinner. It was still with a certain amount of trepidation that he approached the door of the imposing house located in what was seen as the better part of Dover.

The lights beside the door were lit even in the early evening and the door was answered by a lofty looking manservant, who was expecting him. Robert passed over his hat and sword, and was ushered into the drawing room where after just a few minutes the doors burst open to admit Armand. He entered in a rush, full of apologies for his lack of courtesy and the fact that he would not be able to join them that evening. It seemed that Armand, having become the Compte D'Valle succeeding his nephew to the title, was required to move in a different social circle, forcing him to accept the Prince de Conde's invitation to cards. His comment "An all night invitation to lose money to the old goat, I fear." He departed leaving Robert to be faced with the vision in a flowing blue gown; his hostess Mariette.

The thrill of excitement that the sight of his French hostess evoked was still with him as he returned to his ship.

When Midshipman John Williams observed his captain returning to the *Excelsior* at seven am the following day still dressed in his best uniform although a trifle dishevelled, he grinned at the bo'sun who was also enjoying the morning air. Neither said a word as both stood to attention and touched their hats in salute as their captain came aboard.

***

The *Excelsior* made three more trips to drop and collect agents while Robert was in command

His association with the delightful Mariette was sadly discontinued when she departed Dover for London.

When the announcement of Mariette's wedding came to a fellow emigré of similar social rank, although it was no surprise, it was still painful for some time.

The year of Robert's first command finally ended when it was decided that the *HMS Excelsior* would be handed over to the Preventive Service for anti-smuggling duty. When she was handed over the crew were returned to Plymouth for re-appointment to other ships.

For Robert it was a summons to London, a call at the Admiralty for his appointment to a new ship. His activities in the channel had been noted and he found he had been the subject of an entry in the Gazette, which was a surprise and a help perhaps for his future career.

He was informed of his appointment as first Lieutenant on the ship/sloop *HMS Witch*, Midshipman John Williams and Masters Mate Sven Hansen joined the ship at the same time.

The *Witch* was refitting in the dockyard at Plymouth so Robert was able to see her for the first time out of the water; he was impressed with her clean lines. Her Captain, Commander William Dawson was a Dorset man from Broadway, three miles out of Weymouth. He was old for his rank, perhaps thirty five, and still spoke with the burr of Dorset in his voice. At five foot ten he had to look up to Lieutenant Graham.

HMS Witch was teak built in Bombay for the East India Company, but as happens on occasion, she was seized by the navy on the grounds of greater need. Designed on the lines of a French corvette captured and used for many years on the coast of India, her design gave her speed that made her compare favourably with many of her peers in the fleet. A little longer than her corvette origins, her greater length allowed for taller masts and, balanced by the weight of armament, she was quicker than the English built sloops of the same class.

Her task in the present conflict was mainly confined to the service of the fleet; despatches, scouting, and the interception of convoys. Though rated a sloop she was virtually a small frigate, her broadside of eight 12 pounder guns plus two 24 pound carronades made her a formidable opponent and with the two, long twelve pounder guns mounted as bow chasers and a similar pair at her stern, she was well suited for the task of convoy escort, or for attacking convoys if required.

The days of fitting out were busy but there was time for Robert to visit his father in the Manor House, at Greyland the village where he was the local Squire.

Robert had not seen his father for over a year, and it was with genuine pleasure that he greeted the tall, austere man who welcomed him at the door of the big stone house. The entire household were there to greet him and he was swept into the embrace of Mr.s Wharton, his nurse of long ago, now housekeeper to his widowed father.

He took the chance to ride out over the farms with the stable hand, Tom Rivers, whom he'd known all his life. But it was the time he was able to sit and talk of grown up matters with his father that he treasured most.

When he left home to join his first ship he was a boy, and although he had returned on three occasions since then, it was only now that he was mature enough to enjoy spending time with his father, on a man-to-man basis.

They had sat together in the study and discussed the state of the world, of Napoleon and of life in general.

Squire Graham was a well-informed man and he spoke of Napoleon with gravity "That man may have captured Europe and may possibly spread his influence even further. Whatever happens, win or lose, the world will never be the same because of his influence."

The words came back to him on several occasions in the years to come, as the effects of the turmoil in Europe reverberated around the globe.

***

The crew of *HMS Witch* was mainly composed of local men; the master, Sam Callow, lived in the Half Moon inn with his wife, the owner. Located as it was on the hard in Plymouth, the Inn was the meeting place for the responsible members of the crew, just as the Angel was for the officers.

The stay in Plymouth gave occasion for a reunion for Robert with an old friend, Billy Beaufort, Lieutenant the Right Honourable William Beaufort-Robinson; Baron Brimpton; now serving as second lieutenant of the frigate *Hotspur*.

She had called in at Plymouth to collect despatches, and take on water before departing for the Mediterranean. Billy Beaufort found Robert on board *Witch* supervising the final array of the rigging with the help of Mr. Callow.

"Robert Graham, as I live and breathe, well met sir, will you come and join me in refreshment?" The arm smacked round Robert's shoulder, as Billy breezed in. As always his friend seemed to carry all before him.

Robert looked at Mr. Callow for whom he had considerable respect.

Sam Callow looked over at Robert, "Why not, sir? I've got this in hand; I'll be finished soon anyway!"

So the two friends went off to the Angel where they spent the rest of the day getting up to date since their last commission together as midshipmen in the *Argonaut* 74 five years before.

"Much though I enjoy your company," Robert observed "Do you not live somewhere in the vicinity?"

"Well remembered, young Graham, of course we joined here in Plymouth as midshipmen, you from the Manor in Greyland, and me from Hartwell Hall over the border in Dorset. Since I didn't have time to visit home, I decided to visit you. I would have called on you at the Manor but I heard at the dockside that you were here so here I am." He laughed at this comment. "I am impressed, by the way! I read of your deeds in the Gazette. When you get your command I will expect to be asked to join you as you're first lieutenant, in fact I am depending on it!"

"Rubbish—you'll be captain of your own ship by then."

The two carried on wrangling in the way of old friends until they separated, slightly drunk in the early hours of the following day.

When *HMS Hotspur* departed the following morning, both had sore heads. Robert, at least, felt every strike of the mallet throughout the day. Despite his discomfort he received scant sympathy from the other members of the crew, who had all at one time or another, been in the same situation.

HMS Witch sailed with the tide on the 14th of May, 1793. They had been ordered to the West Indies with three replacement officers for the West Indies Regiment, and an assortment of despatches. Captain Dawson confided privately to Robert that the underlying reason for the voyage, and their hurried departure, was the worry about the effect of the revolution in France.

The possibility of disaffection within the fleet was considered possible

Events at the Nore had thrown the entire country in turmoil. The unthinkable had happened, the fleet, the nation's defence, had mutinied. The flag of disaffection hung over several ships anchored off the Nore. Consequently the Admiralty had ordered as many ships as possible to sail in hopes of stopping the disaffection spreading.

The victory at Cape St Vincent in February had given the people a lot to shout about; the incipient mutiny that started in April was a shock to the nation and created something approaching panic in the hierarchy of the Navy. With the possible threat of revolution within the country ever present, some changes were won, but the resultant general mistrust in the air damaged the Navy more than defeat by the French, and it was believed that the repercussions would continue well into the nineteenth century.

For the *Witch* the voyage across the Atlantic was good for everyone. The weather was kind, and by the time they reached the Azores the crew were settled and everyone on board sported a tan. In most cases men stripped to shirt sleeves, rather than wear a heavy uniform. The guns were exercised daily; the crews were encouraged to compete in both speed and accuracy. The same was true with sail handling, the times for replacing sails, setting, reefing were all studied carefully every day as the voyage progressed, making time pass swiftly and productively. The Master attached a board to the bases of the mast showing a record of the best times for all to see. The crew were largely volunteers and the humour in the ship was good, Captain Dawson was a good captain popular with both officers and men.

For Robert, keeping the promise he made to himself eight years ago, there was daily exercise with fencing swords. He was more than proficient in the discipline and as a result he had been charged by the Captain with the task of taking a daily class in swordsmanship for the officers, this including the Captain himself.

It was a happy ship that anchored in Kingston harbour. The despatches once delivered and the passengers landed

Captain Dawson and Robert reported to Government House where the Admiral had a temporary office.

Up until now Dawson had not been given any inkling of what he would be required to do, and it was with a certain apprehension that he and Robert awaited the Admiral's orders.

"I see, Captain," said the Admiral, "that you have experience in a wide range of activities gained through your service in the Navy, and it occurs to me that we can use that expertise here in the islands, at least for a period. Our problem locally is that most of the ships that are sent here are of such deep draught that they cannot access the smaller harbours and lagoons. This has allowed the establishment of bases both for the enemy, Spain and France, and more pressingly, pirates.

"There are two tasks I ask of you. First, where opportunity offers, to map and sound every bay or harbour you enter.

"Second take or destroy every pirate or enemy ship or base you come across. The smallest ship of force on this station is a forty gun frigate, *HMS Warrior*; she will be available to back up any task you may find that needs it. The other craft I have do not have the sort of firepower needed, but I will allocate the *Hermione* to your command. She is an island schooner, fast and handy but with only six pounder guns, thus inadequate by herself." The Admiral sat back and studied the two men keenly.

"Written orders will be sent to you when you have victualled and stored ship. There is a Ball tonight, gentlemen; you will be expected to attend with your other officers, the ladies here become starved of company between the visits of ships from England."

Thus dismissed, the two officers left the shady precincts of Government House and stepped out into the raw heat of the late morning sun. In moments both were perspiring freely, and even the short walk to the town itself was enough to produce uncomfortable rubbing in inconvenient places. "Now I understand why people wear such light clothes wherever possible," Robert commented grateful for the relief provided by the sunshades of the more modish shops in the main street of town.

"Here," said his Captain, ducking through the door of the tavern overlooking the waterfront. The two officers sank gratefully onto cane chairs and called for chilled rum punch.

"Well, that was interesting" commented Robert. "Do you think we will get any prizes out of this? From the sound of it there has been little done for some time."

"Adjusting the charts for the area should be interesting at least," said Dawson, the burr of the relaxed voice matching the mood of the pair as they sat and sipped, gratefully at the cool sweet drinks.

"I was looking at the charts of the immediate area, sir, and the number of islands with inlets and harbours seems enormous. Have you been here before?"

Dawson took time replying. "I was here as a midshipman in '85 on *HMS Caister*, we were surveying the eastern area of the Caribbean among the Windward Islands. It rather sounds that we shall be there again shortly. Then it will be Barbados and Trinidad and up to the Leeward Island, Antigua, Saint Kitts and so on. It could be amusing, there are an awful lot of islands in the chain and several of them are held by the enemy. Well, let's wait and see. I wonder how Archer is getting on with the provisioning, our purser seems to be a bit of a broken reed."

He was referring to the fact that at least three of the barrels of beef had been like solid wood and uneatable. They had been used as bait to catch several sharks and a sailfish on the trip across the ocean, the purser had been advised that his advanced years were all that had saved him from a period in the brig for his sins.

The two men, fast becoming friends, returned to the ship where, tunics off, they got together to provisionally plan the forthcoming voyage and survey.

Lieutenant Archer wandered down the main street in Kingston, gazing at the goods on display, seeking some small memento to give to the young woman who occupied his thoughts at this time. He had spent the entire morning bartering with the local chandlers buying new provisions for the ships stores. The departure of the Purser who had succumbed to an attack of old age, according to the crew, had created problems for Lieutenant Archer. Required to replace a quantity of inferior stores that had been provided by the departed Purser, Archer had at last managed to negotiate a deal for stores and was free to shop for himself.

Midshipman Williams trudged along behind carrying the portfolio of charts collected for the task ahead.

He was looking forward to the Ball that evening because it meant that he would be fed well, a change from the disgusting food he had suffered as a result of the Purser's perfidy. In a dream, he bumped into the tall figure of Lieutenant Archer who had stopped suddenly having seen something suitable.

"Hold up, young man" Archer wasn't a bad sort but he did have the irritating habit of calling him young man all the time. He had only become a lieutenant a few months ago and he was not much older than Williams. "I'll just nip in here for a minute." He disappeared into the shop leaving Williams standing gazing around the colourful street.

The girl in the white dress with a parasol was descending from a carriage when her foot caught the edge of the step. John Williams saw what was going to happen and throwing the charts through the shop door he dashed forward in time to catch the young woman before she could hit the ground. The parasol fell to the ground but the girl was unhurt and her dress unmarked. They stood unmoving for a moment, the girl looked up into his eyes and smiled, "Why, thank you, sir, you saved me an embarrassing fall. Thanks for catching me, perhaps you can give 'me' back, do you think?"

John snapped out of his daze with a start. "Oh of course, are you all right?"

"Thanks to you, perfectly," she said taking her parasol now proffered by Mr. Archer, who had come from the shop carrying the chart portfolio.

John Williams remembered his manners, "John Williams miss, Midshipman, *HMS Witch* at your service." He bowed.

She curtsied "Jennifer Watson, Harray Plantation, Surrey, Jamaica. Will you be attending the Ball tonight?" She smiled sweetly.

"I certainly will." Midshipman Williams replied happily.

A grunt and nudge from behind him reminded John of his duty. "May I also present Lieutenant Richard Archerm also of *HMS Witch* sir, Miss Jennifer Watson."

The young lady smiled and said "Until tonight, gentlemen, thank you once more." Smiling again at John, she left them, taking John's heart with her.

The spell was broken for him rudely by the reminder from Lieutenant Archer that he was not a bloody pack pony and having the chart portfolio thrust at him.

"Come on, young Williams, back to the ship and the correction notices for you." They left walking down to the docks. Through the shop window Miss Jennifer Watson watched the polite young midshipman as he departed thinking how fine he looked in his uniform.

Chapter three

The sparkling blue waters of the Caribbean were painted with brilliant white smears by the leaping porpoises in front of the cutwater. The ship moved easily along the Windward channel between the green-swathed hills of the islands of Cuba and Hispaniola, sometimes called Haiti. The peaceful landscape showed no sign of the ongoing savage revolt of the slaves led by Toussaint L'Ouverture.

Here and there small craft passed along the shore and out to the ship offering to sell fish and fruit and the smoked (boucained) beef from the wild cattle that roamed the hills of Hispaniola. Lieutenant Archer had taken the trouble to inform Midshipman Williams in his loftiest most lordly manner that it was from the process of smoking the beef on a boucain. This was a local wooden grid that had given the name to the Buccaneers, the pirates of the area, so called because they had been drawn from the men stranded on the islands that had boucained the wild beef to survive.

Robert wiped his face with the damp cloth, having just concluded a session of fencing with Lieutenant Archer. Archer was well versed in the art of fencing but inclined to be a little impatient. Still a session with Archer was good exercise and kept him on his toes. He strolled in his shirtsleeves along the quarterdeck enjoying the breeze, thankful for the relaxed dress rule permitted by the Captain. He stopped in the shade of the sail, grateful for the shade it provided; passing his sword over to the wardroom servant standing waiting to take it below. He was thinking about the ball that had preceded the departure of the *Witch* on her present mission.

The ladies in particular had been interesting, dresses reflecting their taste for more simple material, muslin and tulle in deference to the heavy heat and humidity, made the best of their shape and form, flattering and titillating at the same time. He recalled the pleasure of dancing with the wife of the Deputy Governor, who was absent from the capital on duty. Her manner had definitely contributed to the indiscretions of later that night.

Young Williams seemed to be rather involved with the planter's daughter Jennifer Watson, whose dress illustrated her obvious claim to maturity beyond her years.

He had noticed the disappearance of the pair and had seen that their absence had not gone unnoticed by her father, though he seemed to be more interested in the attentions of a Spanish-looking lady visiting from St Kitts. Yes, it had been an interesting evening, especially in view of the enforced celibacy of his life since the separation from Marietta. The vigorous attentions of the Deputy Governor's lady had stretched his endurance almost to the limit. The pleasant tiredness that had followed the next two days of her husband's absence, had in turn been followed by the rush and bustle of getting under way once more. To be honest, it had been a relief to once again shoulder the responsibilities of his job and escape the pressure of the demands of the lady.

Midshipman Williams was in love, his evening with Miss Watson had opened his eyes to the world of adult romance. As Robert had guessed, the young lady was mature beyond her years and John Williams had been the lucky recipient of that maturity. The introduction to the delights of intimacy between man and woman had been at first humiliating and then incredibly satisfying. Jennifer

Watson, having decided to take his education personally under her tuition, ensured that he missed nothing of the benefits of her own education gained through the best efforts of an ageing visiting celebrity of the theatre with a taste for young girls.

The arrival of the Captain on deck disrupted Robert's pleasant daydreams and he reported the course and heading. As the ship cleared the Windward channel their course took them to the Spanish islands now dead ahead. Great Inagua and Little Inagua were at the beginning of the *Witch's* patrol area. The Caicos and Turks islands were beyond the horizon to the east but their course led past the southern shores of the Spanish islands. At dawn the day after leaving the Windward Channel the lookout spotted the schooner in the channel between Great and Little Inagua; she was sailing out across the path of *Witch* and had no chance of avoiding the sloop, which had cleared for action at the first sighting.

She was flying a Spanish flag, and was pierced for four guns each side but had definitely been caught napping. The bow gun from the sloop spoke, placing a shot across her bow. The schooner obediently backed her topsail and came up to the wind. Captain Dawson called. "Right! Mr. Graham, take the longboat and ten men; let's see what we have caught?"

As he was rowed across to the schooner Robert could not help noticing the clean lines of these local island ships. Named the *Christophe*, the schooner had the three raked masts of her kind, though he noticed she had a scruffy unkempt look and an unpleasant smell coming from her.

Robert boarded the schooner and was met by the Captain, a swarthy man with white teeth, presently bared in a smile. Ignoring the man standing ready to greet him, he scanned the deck for threats. Finding none, he turned to the waiting man, who bowed and introduced himself.

"Captain Juarez at your service, senor," he spoke in heavily accented English. "How may I assist?"

"Mr. Hansen, secure the ship. Your cabin, please, Captain Juarez!"

Below in the Captain's cabin Robert studied the papers produced by the swarthy man who was still smiling. "I see from your papers that you are carrying only food and wine?"

"Sim\, senor, just food and wine for the garrison at Porto Plata, Hispaniola." There was something about this little man that bothered Robert.

After a few minutes, there was a knock at the cabin door. It was Hansen. "Sir, have I your permission to knock down a door in the hold?"

Robert looked at Captain Juarez, who paled.

"I'm sure the Captain will be only too happy to open the door for you, Mr. Hansen."

"Oh, but sir, that door has no key. It is just a place where we throw the odd scraps of sail and timber. There is nothing there to see. You... you have seen the manifest there is nothing else in the cargo."

Robert stood. "Do you know, I am curious about this 'Glory hole' in the hold? Come, Captain, show me where you keep the junk on your ship."

Nearly weeping, the little captain accompanied Robert and the masters mate down to the hold, where two of the boarding party stood beside a solid iron hinged door with a large padlock.

"Break it." Robert spoke with a sharpness that reflected his suspicions. The heavy maul smashed down on the hasp and staple, breaking the staple and sending the broken lock from the door across the deck.

As the door swung open it revealed a long low ceilinged room with a several figures scattered on the bare deck. The smell was appalling and for a moment Robert did not realise that all the figures were women; white, black, and coffee-coloured. When counted there were thirty-two, all naked, crammed into the space.

"Why, what is this?" Robert took the captain by the scruff of his neck and thrust him into the doorway. From the woman a low growl came as they saw their captor. The Captain wriggled in Robert's grasp and tried to get away from the door.

"Perhaps you would like to visit the ladies for a while?" Robert suggested.

The cry of terror at this suggestion was all it took for Robert to drop him in disgust.

"Mr. Hansen, bring the crew below and strip them. Hold then in the fore part of the hold. Erect a screen round the companionway on deck and rig a seawater hose to the pump. Mount it over the screen. Then come and escort the ladies to the deck and start the pump. As soon as the ladies vacate this room, invite the gentlemen of the crew to inspect it, and incidentally, remount the lock." Robert returned to the deck and instructed that the Spanish flag be lowered and replaced with the British Ensign.

The women all came on deck—some being helped by others. The water showering the group had revived them and gave them the chance to clean themselves. A search of the ship revealed heaps of women's clothing; they were draped over the top of the screens for the ladies to help themselves.

After nearly an hour all had washed and dressed. The screen was removed and the food prepared for the ladies who it seemed had been kidnapped in Cuba and were destined to be sold to the garrison at Puerto Plata on Haiti. This was a practice that had been started when many of the civilian population had departed the Island following the worsening of the revolt by the slaves.

The schooner was, as suspected, a pirate ship and they had kidnapped the women from two small settlements on the north coast of Cuba, wiping out the men of the village on each occasion. The only two white women had the misfortune to be passengers on a coastal craft with their husbands when their boat was captured by the pirates. Their husbands had been murdered and the two women taken and kept with the other females captured in the villages.

The ships sailed in company to Grand Turk, and at the largest settlement on the island, the people of Cockburn Town received them with considerable excitement, Visits from naval ships were few and the small population of the area gladly offered their hospitality to the ladies. The balance of the population was woefully short of women and the addition of the rescued women would make a welcome difference.

So, to the relief of the *Witch's* captain, the ladies agreed to be settled in Grand Turk. Since they were without homes—their families were gone—they had nothing to go back to.

The Island's Chief Magistrate was pleased to hear the case for piracy and murder against Captain Juarez and his crew. *HMS Witch* delayed her departure while Lieutenant Graham gave evidence, and Lieutenant Archer surveyed the port and harbour, checking the existing survey figures. The ship stayed there long enough to see all forty pirates hanged.

A prize crew under Lieutenant Archer took the schooner sailing; at first in company with the *Witch* and the *Hermione*. Promising a return visit before the voyage back to Jamaica, they departed Grand Turk Island to continue on their mission.

The schooner *Hermione*, named for the wife of Pyrrhus, was known in the islands and her agility made her useful for searching out and reporting bays and harbours in use along the otherwise lonely coastlines.

The captured schooner *Christophe*, named—of course—for Christopher Columbus, was finally despatched back to Kingston. The delay in sending her, Captain Dawson confided to Robert; was just to make sure that Archer had everything under control.

Sailing to Puerto Rico—their next destination—they passed inside the series of banks that ran just offshore along the approaches to the northern coast; carefully navigating past the shoals until they were able to relax as the Navidad Bank dropped astern, leaving clear sailing to the north shore of Puerto Rico

The coast of the island provided a serious harbour on the north coast in which three ships lay. All were barques and all armed heavily with cannon. Such was the security of the anchorage; the biggest of the ships openly flew the black flag as she lay at anchor.

Having been told of the ships and the harbour by one of the fishermen that were contacted by *HMS Hermione,* the naval ships anchored in a deserted cove several miles down the coast. There they made plans to destroy the pirates and clear the harbour.

The crew of *HMS Witch* had been reinforced by men from the Kingston garrison under the command of Ensign Michael Grey, a likeable young man just eighteen years old with fair hair and a lively sense of humour; well-liked by his 20 men of the West Indies Regiment—smart in their red coats and armed with muskets and swords. The conference in the great cabin of the *HMS Witch* was attended by all the officers of both ships and the master's mate and bo'sun. *HMS Hermione* was detached to cruise offshore to warn Captain Dawson of any nasty surprises in the form of additional returning pirate ships.

Between the remaining groups, they devised a plan to infiltrate the harbour after a last reconnaissance by Robert and Hansen. Having arranged rendezvous and alternative pick up points, the two set out, being carried with their dinghy on one of the fishing craft that moved up and down the coast of the island.

The small boat ground into the sand on the shore in the small bay of Higuillar. The three pirate ships moored out in the bay showed lights, though it seemed most of the crews were ashore. There were several men lounging about the waterfront, but they took little notice of the two men, both dressed in the cast-off clothes of the pirates hung in Caicos.

Even the sword at Robert's side was the long Italian Epee formerly owned by the mate of the pirate ship. Hansen, wearing a headscarf over his straw-coloured hair, walked ahead; the big man clearing the way for Robert as they made their way up to the tavern overlooking the anchorage.

The room was packed with men and women; the air thick with the smoke of the many pipes being smoked around the room. The noise was loud and bursts of raucous laughter pierced the general hubbub.

At the back of the room sat the big man.

Robert thought, there was always a big man. This big man had a girl on his knee, her breast firmly gripped in his right hand and a tankard in the other.

He was surrounded by other men with the look of leaders in the same group, and when Robert asked the serving wench who they were, she said they were the captains of the ships lying in the anchorage.

The two men sat in the corner out of direct sight and weighed up the other men in the tavern. After a single drink the pair left and wandered idly around the bay. On the point they found a small battery of guns commanding the narrow entrance by the deep water channel. The islands scattered beyond the deep channel were separated by shoals and shallow water, useable for small boats in places but impassable for deep-keeled ships.

The battery was manned by a group of men sitting around drinking and smoking. Three women were keeping them company while they lay about. One man with a telescope was leaning against the front wall looking towards the village and commenting on the condition of some of the drunken men wandering about.

Robert and Hansen did not reveal their presence. As they withdrew Robert heard one of the men say something that made him stop and turn back to the group. The man . was saying "....he will be sailing tomorrow night because the bullion ship will be in the convoy, I don't know why we don't try for the bugger. Why should Cap'n Mace get all the loot? I know his ship is bigger but there are two of us, I'm sure we could manage if our pansy skipper had the guts."

"I know that's the drink talking, William, otherwise you would be a bit more close-mouthed. So just you shut up and keep your comments to yourself. I for one do not want to upset Cap'n Mace or his mate!"

There was a growl of approval from the others in the group and they all fell to playing with the women or the dice, some even sleeping.

The man who complained rose to his feet and began to open his clothes to relieve himself, the others seeing this yelled at him to bugger off into the dunes. Grumbling he wandered off, closely followed by Robert and Hansen. Still fumbling the man wandered away from the others and stopped and noisily emptied his bladder. He turned to go back and encountered the fist of Hansen, who caught him as he fell forward and, lifting him over his shoulder, carried him into the bushes down by the shore.

Splashing him with seawater they woke him up, "Wha…what happened." he said "Who are you? What are you doin to me?"

"Why, I'm just going to save the hangman a job." Said Hansen cheerfully, and he busied himself binding the man's hands together behind him.

"What do you mean? I've done nothin."

Hansen laughed "Why, you apology for a man, done nothing, raped women, killed men and women and children, I'll be bound, I'm sure you've done nothing!"

"Please. I don't understand who are you?" The whine in his voice put Robert's teeth on edge.

"Why, we're the nightmare you have now and then, when all your victims rise up to haunt you as you lie shivering in your hammock on dark nights. Now, who is Captain Mace? What ship?"

Thoroughly cowed, the man said, "He's the captain of the biggest ship in the bay the *Eagle,* 30 guns."

"Then who are the others?"

"They're Captain French and Captain Hollingberry, of the *Swan* and the *Black Boar*, both twenty guns."

"Do you all sail together?"

"Sometimes, but only when Cap'n Mace thin,ks he needs us. If he can manage on his own, he sails alone."

"How did he know about the bullion ship? They keep that a secret from their own people, so how would a pirate find out about that?"

"That I don't know but I notice that whenever he decides he will be sailing it's always after a small boat sails in; like last night. We sends the signal from here and he comes down and meets this handsome lady from somewhere and they go off to his house for a bit of you know what; she goes off and next day he sails after some juicy prize. Usually comes back with loot. Mind he'd better watch this time—there's a navy ship on the coast. She'll not be a pushover, I'll be bound."

"A Navy ship here? Where did you hear that then?"

"Fishing boat, I think it was, came through this morning."

Hansen turned to Robert, "Could you take a look up there behind us, sir? We don't want to walk into any trouble on our way out."

Robert turned and crept up the path towards the track along the point, watching for any movement as he went. Hansen caught up with him by the time he reached the path.

"What did you do with our friend?" he asked.

"Took pity on him, Sir; saved him a lot of grief." At Robert's raised eyebrow, he shrugged. "Fell into the water, didn't he? I cannot swim so I couldn't help and he drowned."

Robert looked at him disbelievingly. Hansen's innocent expression didn't falter. "He had a lot on his mind I think!"

Robert left it at that.

They returned to the jetty and took the boat out once more, only this time they rowed out between the other islands, having to drag the boat over a shoal before they reached the open sea once more. It entailed more hard work rowing but they eventually rendezvoused with the anchored *Witch*, just off the coast beyond the bay, a little further along the coast.

Chapter Four

Back on board the ship Robert drew the location of the three pirate ships on the chart and also the battery at the channel mouth. With the information they drew up a plan to take the place by surprise.

The party of soldiers under Ensign Michael Grey, with Hansen guiding them, would take the battery at dawn; a gunner's mate would accompany them and realign the guns to cover the ships in the harbour.

Assuming the *Eagle* would sail at dawn as suggested, the *Witch* would be ready with guns run out to support the battery if they were unable to stop the *Eagle* leaving. If necessary they should sink her in the mouth of the harbour and trap the other two ships within. The schooner *Hermione* was kept standing by to support *HMS Witch* if needed The overland party of soldiers set out for the battery that same night; a three-mile journey over a rough hill, it would need at least three hours to get into position. The *Witch* would sail at three, expecting to be off the channel by six in the morning.

At five thirty the hands went to quarters. The gun ports were opened, and the guns run out.

On shore the troops took the men stationed at the battery prisoner without a shot fired. The trussed-up pirates were laid out in a row and the guns swung round to command the three ships still swinging at anchor. At six am activity was noticed on the *Eagle*. Men appeared on deck and the anchor was brought up. As the ship began to drift the sails caught the wind and she swung towards the channel heading for the open sea.

From the battery the ranging gun fired and missed; the second gun was fired and it struck the *Eagle* at the foreyard, causing the yard and the sail to fall in a smother of canvas onto the foredeck. The *Eagle's* head fell off and the ship gently surged into the shoal on her starboard side. There was confusion on the deck as men ran back and forth until a roar from the quarterdeck stopped the panic. Captain Mace's voice gave orders and the men went to work clearing the wreckage from the foredeck and clearing the port guns for action. The four guns of the battery opened fire in a single volley that hit the portside of the *Eagle* with a crashing impact, dismounting two of the guns and creating havoc among the gunners. At the battery the gunner frantically drove his crew to reload all the guns, in time to pre-empt the broadside that he knew would be coming from the grounded ship.

It was no surprise to him that they did not finish in time and by the time the loading was complete three of the ships guns had been fired and the battery wall had be damaged, luckily without actually causing injury.

He carefully lined the guns up again and touched off the primer on each of the guns; his aim from the stable position on the ground was true. The impact on the *Eagle* made further hell on the gun deck strewing it with bloody ruin.

The *Witch* sailed into the channel and added her broadside to the battle and the mainmast on the *Eagle* fell causing the mizzen to fall in sympathy smashing the length of the deck with rigging and sails killing and maiming.

A flicker of flame appeared and the sails quickly caught, the charged guns sparked by the fire discharged one by one into the gathered canvas of the mainsail, causing even more fire, to add to the conflagration. The ready use powder by the guns exploded at intervals down the deck and the ship began to disintegrate. When the fire reached the magazine it was like the end of the world. The *Witch* had spun on its heel after the single broadside, and was protected by the first island, from the blast.

The noise had woken the crews of the other two ships, and signs of activity were seen on shore. A boat put out from the jetty to the *Swan*.

On the *Black Boar* men appeared on deck and began running about, preparing the ship for sea. Both ships were rocked and had taken damage from their exploding consort.

A few survivors struggled to reach the shore from the wrecked *Eagle*. There was literally nothing left of what was once a fine ship, the remaining keel section still stuck into the sand of the shoal and a scatter of pieces of wood and bodies floating all over the surface of the harbour.

The two remaining ships were now beginning to get in some sort of order. The gunner at the battery carefully sighted his guns and put a single shot across the bows of each ship.

The message was obvious. Move at your peril. The furnace for heating shot was well alight at the battery and the thin trail of smoke reaching up to the sky, the pirates would be well aware, indicated the danger of heated cannon balls prepared to be fired at their wooden hulls.

There was a hurried conference between the two ships, and the captains and many of their men went ashore to disappear into the tavern. The result of this gathering was the collection of a group of about 100 pirates armed with muskets, pistols and swords, assembled outside the tavern. Their intention was obvious; to march upon the battery and recover it, taking back control of the harbour.

Captain Dawson had other ideas. When the *Witch* had sheltered from the explosion behind the island he noticed that despite the shoaling on the landward side, the seaward side of the island was steep-to and the depth of water was ample for the ship to lie close. By using a hawser attached to a point on the island he could swing the ship across the entrance channel and sweep the harbour with her broadside. This would also allow the ship to give covering fire to the battery if, or rather when, the pirates got round to attempting to retake it.

Midshipman Abbot, the junior middy, was despatched to the battery in the longboat with two swivel guns and a supply of ammunition to use to help keep attackers at a distance. Robert went ashore on the island with a party of men carrying a heavy hawser, this they attached to a spear of rock that projected out of the folded strata that typified the shoreline. Letting out the hawser from the ship she drifted away from the shore and across the channel towards the mainland and the battery. At this point the bo'sun hurled a rope to the men of the battery with a shout to haul away, and a heavy hawser followed to be attached to a big tree, allowing the ship to be swivelled to cover every part of the harbour except the near shoals where the wreck of the *Eagle* still smouldered.

The pirate party were approaching the battery when they halted out of range and two men approached under a white flag. The Ensign Grey rose and stood in an embrasure and called. "Far enough, if you are surrendering just lay your arms down where you are and we will gather them up after we have taken you out of the way."

The leader of the two shouted back. "We have come to offer you safe conduct back to your ship, wherever she is?" The Witch appeared at that point swinging into position in the channel. Unbelievingly the leader saw her. As one, the two men dropped to the ground and a volley of musket fire shot above their heads and killed the young man still standing in the embrasure.

A volley of musket fire from the battery was followed by the heavier, whump of the swivel guns that sent their cargo of musket balls scattering through the bunched pirates in a hail of death. The screams of the dying and wounded caused a panic stricken scramble to retreat back to the security of the tavern.

The gunner did not hesitate, his carefully preset cannon fired and the charge of canister smashed through the tavern front wall causing the roof to collapse in a shower of branches, leaves and mud brick. The second round finished the demolition, the exploding shell destroying the back wall and scything the leaves from the surrounding trees leaving a dusty bald area where the tavern once stood. The pirates frustrated, howled at the destruction, and Hansen stood up in the battery and with Midshipman Abbot by his side called upon his party of soldiers and sailors who had come with the swivel guns. "Boarders away!" and the soldiers with swords fixed to their muskets and the sailors with their cutlasses advanced on the retreating pirates, their bloodlust high and revenge for their popular murdered officer in mind.

Captain Dawson took one look. "My God, they've gone mad! Mr. Graham, man the boats with all the men that can be spared from the guns. Master gunner, grape shot if you please, target the mob while you can."

Robert had two boats in the water and filled with armed men in a few minutes, they rowed for the shore directly, as the ships guns fired, he changed his mind when he saw the effect of the grape shot was having on the pirates ashore. He called to the other boat. "Mr. Callow, take the *Black Boar*,"

Callow waved and the boat swerved to come alongside the first pirate ship, Robert came up with the *Swan* and with the yell, "Boarders away!" He led his men over the bulwarks of the pirate ship, skewering the first man he saw.

As he anticipated most of the crew were ashore and the skirmish was short and bloody; no quarter offered or given.

The flag on the *Black Boar* was hauled down; as her crew were overcome and when Robert turned his attention to the shore he saw Hansen and his party surrounded by dead and dying men, and the remainder of the pirates disappearing into the forest.

On the *Witch* the lookout cried, "Sail Ho," from the maintop, "It's the *Hermione*" he added,

"She's being chased." There was a pause as the lookout studied the distant approaching ship; then concentrated on another sail clearing the horizon "There's another ship, looks like one of frigates."

Captain Dawson heaved a sigh of relief. He called up to the lookout "Can you identify her?"

"She's *HMS Exeter,* sir she was moored in Plymouth after her refit when we sailed."

As Dawson confided to Robert afterwards "For a moment I thought that the *Hermione* was being chased and we had more trouble than we could deal with."

The arrival of the 40 gun *Exeter*, under Captain Walker was a relief; she had been encountered by the

Hermione en-route to the Mona Passage. Captain Walker had been only too pleased to divert to the assistance of *HMS Witch* after an uneventful trans-Atlantic voyage from Falmouth.

Though the frigate had to anchor offshore the extra men on board were sufficient to take the two prizes back to Kingston permitting *HMS Witch* to continue her voyage.

Captain Walker had served in the West Indies earlier in his career and was saddened by the demise of Captain Mace.

Mace was apparently an ex-naval officer whom he would have like to see hang. His mutinous seizure of *HMS Garland*, renamed *Eagle*, and subsequent pirate activity had been a bitter blow to his fellow captains. He was sanguine about the fate of the runaway pirates, "They will not survive long in the jungle, the people only tolerated them when they were powerful and provided extra wealth to the community. Without their ships and with so many dead, they will be seen as victims and treated accordingly."

HMS Witch got under way once more two days after the defeat of the pirates. The village had been flattened, the battery dismantled and the guns stored in the hold of the *Swan* for return to Kingston. *HMS Exeter* resumed her voyage to Kingston with the two prizes in company.

For the *Witch* Lieutenant Worthing and six extra marines were provided by the *Exeter* to replace the unfortunate Ensign Grey and the other casualties.

They voyaged onwards to the Virgin Islands and, having inspected St Thomas and Tortola, put into English Harbour in Antigua to water and provision before sailing onward.

The Dockyard at the harbour was helpful, and they were able to replace cordage rotting in the humid climate. The crew were given some time to enjoy a swim and to relax. It was the encounter with the French frigate that caused some anxiety and it was indirectly the reason that the current cruise had to be completed early.

***

The *La Rochelle* was a thirty-six gun frigate, but she had been in the tropics for eight years and was in less than ideal condition. Her Captain was suffering from recurring malaria and many of the officers who had come from France in the beginning were now either dead, or transferred to a more salubrious post. With the passing of the last hurricane it had become apparent that *La Rochelle* would never survive another. Her timbers were working and it was now necessary to pump the bilges every six hours just to keep up with the present leaks.

Wearily, Captain Maurice Anders wiped his brow with the already wet cloth, and swore that he would leave the service and settle down as his mistress suggested. The only drawback was that if he did that he would need to live with his mistress and, much though he enjoyed her favours, he could not face the idea of having to face her temper for the foreseeable future.

Better his bitter wife than that. At least she was quiet, having refused to speak to him since she discovered the identity of his mistress. Whilst still contemplating his gloomy future, the report came of the sighting of a sail. "Oh damn," he thought aloud. "A sail, so what! A sail, everywhere you look in this accursed ocean there are sails, all sorts of sails big ones small ones, squares jibs spankers…" His mental tirade was brought to an abrupt end when the first lieutenant came to the cabin door.

With a sigh Maurice looked up. "What is it this time, the inter-island schooner from Martinique?"

"Pardon, patron, I think this time is trouble!"

Marvelling as always at the man's ability to garble every message with his Island patois; Maurice asked the question. "Well, what is it this time?"

Lieutenant Ambrose Charlet was a mulatto from Guadeloupe, and had been recruited from the local customs service to fill a vacancy in the crew of the *La Rochelle*. After three years he still found it a problem dealing with his captain, whom he admired.

"Patr…Sir I believe we have a British ship approaching; a warship!"

Captain Anders looked up sharply at this. "How far, can you tell?"

"She has just cleared Dominica and is heading for Martinique, I think"

"I will come on deck and see for myself. Call the hands to clear for action."

***

HMS Witch had checked and surveyed the ports and inlets of the Guadeloupe islands and was heading for Dominica when the frigate came into view.

Captain Dawson snapped the telescope closed. "She's bigger than us, 36-38 guns, I reckon; we could have our hands full!"

Robert grinned savagely, "French, eh, well we will give her something to think about. Now would be a good time for the *Essex* to appear, don't you think?"

"Oh, ye of little faith," Dawson replied "Just when things start to get interesting, you start thinking of negative things. Alter course 10 degrees starboard, call the men to action stations; stand by, boarders."

The beat of the drum was insistent, and the sounds of the crew, the guns being moved and run out made the next few minutes' pandemonium.

The comparative quiet that followed was a relief as they stood-to while the sun relentlessly beat down on the drama below.

"Port guns first" the Captain called, as the French ship approached.

On *La Rochelle* the pumps started once more. The guns were run out and one of the gun carriage wheels sank through a soft part of the deck stalling the gun immovably. With much shouting the crew tried without success to move the gun.

The First Lieutenant was heard, "Leave the gun!" The rest of the gun crews reported ready. The cry "Fire" echoed along the deck, Captain Anders aghast saw the gun captain of the stalled gun from habit, applying the match to the touch hole, His voice rose desperately "Noooooo......" The gun captain looked round but it was too late, the gun fired with the rest and the ball smashed into the bulwark taking the rigging stays for the mainmast and recoiling through the weakened deck to drop onto the men working the pumps below. There were screams and further crashing as the heavy barrel careered through the 'tween decks carrying all before it. The rest of the broadside gave the *Witch* some trouble but not enough to prevent her own broadside from causing havoc in the French ship.

Captain Anders knew it was all over, he could feel it in the way the ship staggered with the impact of her own gun, the main mast teetered, the starboard stays flapping unattached, the mast groaned in agony as it swayed with the roll of the ship. Two carronade shells blasted *La Rochelle,* hitting at almost the same spot as her self-inflicted wound. It was too much. With a final shriek the fore and aft stays broke and the mast fell. The hull split at the point of impact and *La Rochelle* commenced her last dive to the sea bed. The worn and rotted timbers separated as she tiredly gave herself up to the waters she had proudly commanded for so long.

Captain Anders clung to the taffrail with tears in his eyes as his world disintegrated around him.

Lieutenant Charlet grabbed his captain by the collar and hauled him into the boat. Charlet had shown unusual speed and ingenuity cutting the boat loose from its stowage on the main deck. It floated free as the frigate sank and was handy for the rescue of several of the crew, and now the captain.

The *Witch* had been damaged by the broadside from *La Rochelle*, but she stopped and picked up as many of the struggling crew as she could reach, including the boat with Captain Anders and his lieutenant. However there were repairs needed which would require a dockyard. So the *Witch* set sail for Kingston, leaving her assignment to be completed at a later date.

The officers and crew enjoyed a certain amount of celebrity following the success she had enjoyed. The prizes were welcomed in the port and scheduled for purchase to supplement the local fleet. The sinking of the frigate that

Robert privately felt was actually equivalent to it shooting itself in the foot was also well received. Notwithstanding her condition, she had always been regarded as a threat, and its removal had released shipping from one of its major curbs.

When *HMS Witch* had been made seaworthy once more she was ordered to escort a convoy to England. As to her role in the anti-pirate campaign, the recently acquired prizes would assume that task when their refit had been completed.

The docks at Kingston were able to carry out the repairs the *Witch* needed, mainly the replacement of a rib timber, smashed partially by one of the French 18 pound cannonballs.

As William Dawson commented to Robert, when money, especially profits are involved, little is allowed to interfere. The plantations had piled up large stocks of sugar and coffee for shipping, it having been delayed for lack of a ship of sufficient force to escort it. *HMS Essex,* recently returned from England, could not be spared for a three month absence, and the other ships in station were not deemed suitable.

The convoy was spread out downwind of *HMS Witch* as she nodded gently in the light wind three days out from Jamaica, The last of the small islands of the Turks and Caicos group were just disappearing from sight from the deck. For the first time since they had sailed there was no land in sight, and the kindly weather had encouraged a festive atmosphere among the eighteen ships of the convoy and the three escorts, The *Black Boar*, renamed *HMS Surrey* after the Jamaican Province, was up wind on the far side of the convoy and the *HMS Fleetwood,* a cutter was ahead of the ships, ready to give warning of any danger in their path.

As the winds decreased the convoy was reduced to drifting aimlessly and this gave the opportunity for communications between ships to be simplified, invitations were issued and social activities arranged.

It was with some amusement that Robert remarked to his junior, "I presume young Williams will be calling on his lady friend Miss Watson, while we are becalmed?"

Archer replied with a chuckle, "Oh I don't think so. It seems she has found another beau while we were chasing pirates. When we returned young Williams was no longer her preoccupation, it was one of the new Subalterns who sailed out with us who had taken over, closely followed by another plantation owner's son, who it turns out had been engaged to the girl for the past year."

Both were careful to avoid the subject when Williams was around, however the Captain was unaware of the situation, and he commented that Williams had not been invited to the gathering on the *Elephant,* the ship owned by Watson himself, who was sailing with his family in the convoy. He was hastily advised by Robert of the situation, "Wondered why he has been looking so gloomy" he observed, "Normally a good humoured lad, too."

The captain and Robert made the trip to the *Elephant,* though Robert returned after a short while to allow Archer to enjoy the party.

Chapter five

As the flirt of wind caught the sails of *HMS Witch* she heeled sharply, the wind dropped and then came again. The other ships were still becalmed, but as the fluky wind caught the *Witch* once more, a cry from the masthead "Sail Ho, ahead to starboard, coming towards."

"Can you make out what she is? Or what flag?"

"Reckon she's a frigate, sir, can't see too well."

"Williams, take the glass; up with you."

Williams ran up the rigging carrying the telescope carefully. *HMS Witch* was scudding along to interpose herself between the stranger and the convoy.

"Abbot, signal the *Elephant*. Sail is in sight. I am carrying the wind." The convoy was still becalmed and Robert did not dare heave-to in case he lost the wind.

"From the *Elephant*, Sir, Carry on and intercept. Good luck!"

Robert swung his own glass and saw his Captain wave from the deck of the *Elephant*.

The ship approached within range of the William's telescope and he identified it as an enemy immediately. The Tricolour was visible standing out from the rigging as the ship moved nearer the wind steady. At this point Robert realised that the Frenchman was being driven by a wind at variance with that driving the *Witch*. He called for a reduction in sail and brought the ship round to intercept from the Frenchman's port side. "Clear for action, starboard side guns run out."

Though the order was clear and confident, Robert was aware of the risk he was taking; there was a sick feeling in his stomach. If he was wrong about the wind he would be facing the frigate's broadside full on his starboard side and with the heavier guns the frigate would make a real mess of his ship. He was depending on one of the peculiarities of the Doldrums in this area. The winds that sprang up would be steady for a while then drop, a fresh wind would rise and blow for a while, then the breeze would drop immediately leaving a ship helpless in still air while the fresh breeze continued onward. Then it would drop and rise again on a different bearing.

As the ships closed the distance Robert gripped the rail and willed the wind for the other ship to drop. It did!

As the *Witch* closed the distance to the French frigate, he steered to pass across the front of the ship at a distance of just less than a cable. As they passed the guns fired one by one raking the frigate the full length of her deck, front to rear, the bow guns of the enemy ship both fired but they were already under fire from the *Witch* and both balls went astray. The carronades fired last smashing the bowsprit causing the foremast to sway alarmingly before falling with a crash taking skeins of the rigging with it. With the wind still abaft the starboard beam the *Witch* came about and beat back towards the convoy.

On the French frigate there was frantic activity as they worked to clear the wreckage of the foremast. After keeping the wind for a distance of three miles the wind dropped, still a half mile from the convoy. Robert immediately dropped all the boats with hawsers to tow the sloop nearer the convoy ships. The convoy had not shifted much but Robert noticed that the armed merchantmen and the two other naval ships he been pulled into line so that their guns would bear on any ship approaching from the direction of the Frenchman. Meanwhile the ships boats hauled the sloop closer to the convoy and swung her broadside to the potential danger if the frigate came in to the attack.

The afternoon passed slowly. The French ship was still in sight and the work to replace the foremast was progressing as Robert observed through his telescope. He hoped that the work would not be completed in time to take advantage of any wind that arose; and he prayed that there would be wind, for the convoy before it reached the enemy.

The Captain had returned on board and taken over command once more. He was well pleased with Robert's performance against the Frenchman. Like Robert, he too prayed the wind would come in time to give them the advantage over the enemy.

As it was the wind when it came caused all the ships to reef and the French frigate disappeared into the haze of spume and spray that enveloped the entire convoy as well.

They didn't see the French ship again or any other, until they spotted the sloop *Adventure*, scouting for the Channel Fleet off Ushant.

The rest of the voyage was fairly straightforward apart from the usual scattering of the ships for no apparent reason, an event so regular as to cause little comment other than the oath's rendered with frustration by the escorts. The last hours of the convoy seemed to be deliberately conducted to extend the life of the group as long as possible. Finally at dusk after nearly five weeks, with a sigh of relief, Commander Dawson saw the last of the ships safely moored in Falmouth roads. He turned the bowsprit of his ship to the east and sailed off along the Cornish coast to her home port of Plymouth once more.

It was eight months after leaving Plymouth that the *HMS Witch* dropped her anchor once more in the harbour, and the sails were brailed up for the last time on this cruise.

The threat of mutiny had gone and the trusted members of the crew were given the chance to see their loved ones once more.

For Robert, restlessness took him to the Manor and out into the countryside, riding the wild country up towards the high moor. It was while he was seated on a rock gazing through his pocket telescope at a buzzard soaring over a high Tor in the distance that the laughing voice asked him if he was stargazing in the afternoon. He caught the mood and answered the voice without turning, "I'm looking for the love of my life."

"Well you won't find un there." The local music in voice with the moorland accent was soft and happy, and he hardly dared look round. It was strange; he knew she would be a great disappointment but he had to look nevertheless. He turned and his eyes met a pair of dark, laughing eyes that shone from a pretty, heart-shaped face. Tanned by the sun, her bare arms were holding a basket filled with mushrooms obviously collected from the moor around them. She was slender and shapely and he called to her and invited her to share his lunch, packed for him by the cook at the manor.

"You're Polly Chadwick, are you not?" he was not quite sure, the last time he had seen her had been while he attended the village school. At that time she was the small sister of one of the boys in the upper class, and rumoured to be part Gypsy.

"I am indeed and I would be delighted to accept your kind invitation, Mr. Lieutenant Graham."

"You know me then."

"I would not consider your invitation did I not!" She answered tartly and reached out and took a leg of chicken.

He glanced at the basket of mushrooms, she saw the look and said "I collect them to sell in the village; the vicar is very partial, as is your father, the squire."

They both ate without further conversation until the cook's offering had been cleared. Then Robert lay back and looked at the white clouds wandering across the blue sky. He realised that he was at peace, for the moment at least. There was a thump beside him and when he opened his eyes he realised that Polly had lain down next to him and was gazing at the sky with rapt attention. She pointed to a cloud "That looks like the sails on your ship," she said, "When you first sailed off in her."

He looked round in surprise, "You were there when I left Plymouth in the *Witch*?"

She blushed. "I happened to be passing at the time." She observed.

"I didn't realise you noticed me when we were younger. I always thought you would have the pick of the boys, you were so pretty." He stuttered at that point "You still are, of course!" he said hastily, realising what he had said.

She turned and put her finger on his lips. "I think you'd better stop there before you get yourself in trouble." She laughed, "So you think I'm pretty, do you? Well, I think you are the best-looking man around here, and I always thought that you didn't even notice me, so how about that then?" She laughed, just a little embarrassed at her boldness.

He laughed in turn and turned towards her to answer, somehow the words died on his lips and he was kissing her, and more importantly she was kissing him. They lay with arms around each other whispering and touching until they found their bodies entwined making love. The afternoon faded and at last they rose and adjusted their clothes, both reluctant to break the spell.

Robert spoke "Can we meet again, tomorrow perhaps?"

Once again Polly put her finger to his lips. "Tomorrow I will be wed to Jared Pierce, who has his farm down by Wheal Gern in Cornwall; it's been arranged for the past six months. When I saw you here I knew that I had to find out if you were the man I imagined you were. Well, I found out. If you had known about Jared you would not have made me happy. I knew we were never destined to be together, our lives are too far apart. I will make Jared happy and he is a good man, I will be a good wife. Who knows?" she said with a smile "I may already have our first child on the way."

Robert was completely abashed "But ....but..." For the third time Polly put her finger to his lips.

"I always fancied a tumble with you. I thought I would never get the chance. Today I was lucky, and I hope you feel that way too because I enjoyed every minute of our little get together, I will remember it with joy always." She darted over to him and reached up and kissed him.

"Goodbye, dear Robert Graham, don't forget me!" Picking up her mushroom-filled basket she ran off through the heather and down the hill, dropping out of sight, the echo of her laughter seeming to hang in the air.

Robert sat, once more gloomy for the moment, at meeting and then losing the delightful Polly. At last he burst out laughing at himself. Polly was right; there would have been no future for him there with her, however much they enjoyed each other. They lived in different worlds with totally different lives.

His horse lifted his head and snorted at his wry laugh, before returned to its grazing. As he stirred once more preparing to ride back to the Manor, it occurred to him that his restless mood had gone.

The ship was being attended by the master Mr. Callow who was directing the necessary replacement of ropes and fittings. Men were over the sides in the dry dock, scraping and painting, and there were several panes of horn being replaced in the stern windows. As the Captain remarked dryly, "Perhaps we would be well advised to open the casements next time we go into action." Horn was expensive.

The work progressed over the next two weeks and several replacements were found for the crew members lost on the last voyage. Christmas passed and the annual festive board at the Manor was graced by the presence of Commander Dawson. The Commander was resigned to the fact that he was not destined to make Post Captain, he was content with his lot; at thirty six his position as Master/Commander kept him in reasonable comfort and since his wife had died giving birth to their only child, he had found contentment in his job. The child had been given to his brother and his wife who brought him up as their own. His family lived in Dorset near Weymouth and he would normally have been with them, but snow and ice dictated that the roads were not suitable for safe travel and he had gratefully accepted the invitation of Robert's father to join them for the Christmas feast.

At the Manor, the Christmas was an annual event for the village. The Squire, Robert's father, provided a repast for over one hundred people from the village and some of the surrounding farms.

They all gathered after church and walked to the Manor, the barn beside the gate was dressed and set up for the party and all the guests brought their own contribution to the event. The food, prepared by the Manor cook with the help of several of the village ladies, was brought to the long tables where everyone seated themselves to be served by the Squire and his son, this day joined with great good humour by Commander William Dawson. The meal was followed by music and dancing that carried on to the morning of the following day. The recovery from this party was normally accomplished over the next day.

By common consent the work of the area recommenced by that time and the dreadful recovery period lasted almost to the New Year.

The New Year began with a harsh wind that clawed its way into every nook and cranny. As soon as the chance arose the ship was re-launched and the final re-fitting completed.

They sailed on the fifteenth of January and set course for the Channel Fleet somewhere off Ushant. The beginning of a three-month period of sail changes rough seas and wet clothes.

The sea was running in long swells, lifting the sloop and causing it to pitch with a jerk, a most uncomfortable feeling for the hands currently lying out on the foreyard. The setting of the main had caused some problems as the sail had been furled whilst wet during the morning watch. A cringle had started, requiring re-stitching and the sail had not been cleanly stowed. Midshipman Williams standing in the Main-top cursed the sail-making crew in his high, half-broken voice.

On the deck below, Lieutenant Robert Graham, the first lieutenant, muttered impatiently at the delay, and turned to the bo'sun and expressed himself in no uncertain terms on the subject. Eventually the sail snapped out to the wind, bellying out until the sheets were snugged home and the sail was drawing properly. Satisfied, the tall young lieutenant resumed pacing the quarterdeck of the ship-sloop *HMS Witch* close hauled closing the Spanish coast, 60 miles to the east.

"That damned sail could have been a real problem if we had been caught out this morning!" the soft voice was calm but the admonition was there.

"My fault sir," Robert apologised. "I should have checked last night when the sail was stowed."

Dawson looked keenly at Robert as he stood in front of him, and still quietly said "I know what happened, see it doesn't happen again." He mused; *It was so typical of Robert Graham to just accept the blame for things that happened on his watch. I hope he had a word with young Williams.* His eyes swept round the horizon noting the build up of clouds to the South West.

"We'll need to take in sail shortly, there's dirty weather on the way," he nodded towards the building clouds.

A cry from the masthead jerked both men's attention from the impending weather.

"Sail Ho!" The masthead lookout called.

"Where away?" Robert called.

"Starboard bow, hull down!" The lookout replied.

"Mr. Williams, take the glass, and see if you can make her out!"

The lieutenant handed the telescope to the young midshipman, who took the glass and leapt into the port rigging and scampered up expertly to the maintop, from there up the topmast shrouds to join the lookout. He hooked an arm round the mast and lined the telescope up to the horizon and started a slow sweep from either side of the bearing indicated by the lookout.

He caught the scrap of white, the topsails of a ship and steadied the telescope. As the sloop rose on the swell the ship came into sight; he took a deliberate look before calling below.

"Looks like a French corvette by the cut of her sails. She is standing in across our course heading for the Spanish coast." He took another look on the next up roll and then reversed his upward journey, sliding rapidly down to the deck to report more fully.

"Well! Mr. Williams, what have we got?" The captain quite liked the young middy; he always seemed to be where he was wanted with a smile on his face.

"I think she is a corvette, sir, she had three masts like our own, but she lies low to the water. She either has not seen us, or she thinks we also are French. She showed no sign of avoiding us."

"How far away is she?" Graham interjected.

"I think perhaps 12-13 miles sir, she was at the limit of sight, sailing across our course. Perhaps she is running for shelter from the weather." He indicated the building clouds with his thumb.

"Well done, lad, back to your duties." The Captain dismissed him.

"My cabin, Mr. Graham. Join me for a glass." He turned and strode below, followed by Robert, who on his way below, called to the master, Mr. Callow, to keep the deck.

In the stern cabin, Dawson poured two glasses of Madeira, and handed one to Robert. The two stood swaying to the movement of the ship, each guarding their wine being careful to prevent it spilling, Dawson raised his glass. "Death to the French!" He said and drained his glass. Robert raised his own glass in turn and drank the sweet wine in one.

"Now, this corvette of young Williams, what do you think?"

Robert considered for a moment before replying.

"She should be hull up before nightfall so we will be able to confirm her nationality. Mind you, she should also be more heavily armed than we!"

"True, but our men are well drilled, and I would wager we can fire two broadsides to his one, but let's wait and see how things go. He may turn away, or even towards. Meanwhile, let's get sail off her and batten down for a blow. That storm is going to be a real snorter, to my mind."

Robert stood back. "With your permission, sir?"

At Dawson's nod, Robert strode back to the deck and roused all hands to secure the ship for the coming storm.

The second lieutenant, Richard Archer, joined him on the main deck and took over the supervision of the double lashing of the guns, Robert grinned as he heard the cultured tones using the sort of language normally associated with the gutter. Archer cheerfully drove his men to greater efforts. The men liked him, despite his upbringing. He had the knack of getting the best out of them, of that there was no doubt. He was also a good friend of several years standing.

Robert watched with envy the slim young man, six foot tall, with the thin aristocratic good looks, a rebellious curl of black hair lying on his forehead, to be brushed aside every few minutes. Others would say he had nothing to be envious of. Robert stood six-feet two inches in his stocking feet, with broad shoulders and wide-set grey eyes set in a pleasant face, his fair hair was not quite long enough to conceal the scar that went from his ear into his hairline above his left ear, relic of a boarding action as a midshipman five years before.

As the storm approached, the work was completed and Archer joined him aft. They strode up and down studying the approaching storm and chatting idly until Robert's servant brought his oilskins. Archer went below and the Captain joined Robert on deck.

"Nasty!" He said in his soft accent. "The corvette has shortened sail; she'll not be with us until tomorrow, that's for sure. It will be a long night; so you'd better get some rest. I'll stand with Mr. Callow until Archer takes over."

Despite the increased motion of the sloop Robert fell asleep as soon as his head hit the pillow. Dawson was still on deck when Robert took over the first dog watch, he passed the time with a grunt and clutched the mizzen stay as the sloop lurched in a cross sea.

It was near morning when the big wave hit catching the sloop plumb on the bow, the crew on deck hung onto the safety lines for their lives. Robert was standing by the wheel when the wave hit. The midshipman of the watch was Hardy, a rather stolid lad but dependable enough, he had just rung four bells and the first splinters of light were appearing as he saw the wall of water rising ahead of them in the faint light. He called out a warning and grabbed hold of the wheel ropes. He held on determinedly as the bow rose seemingly endlessly until it seemed the sloop must be upended. She lurched sickeningly on the crest, shaking loose three of the men from their handholds. All three were swept overboard by the surge of water as the ship raced down the back of the wave into the turmoil of broken water. With a loud crack the mizzen-staysail split and in moments was ripped to ribbons by the wind. The ship shook off the tons of water that had buried her, and Robert called for hands to strip off the torn sail and rig a replacement. The men on the wheel were fighting to keep her head to the wind under the pull of the storm jib alone.

Robert became aware of Midshipman Hardy tugging his sleeve. "Sir, please! The Captain."

He turned; Dawson had been caught by the wave and flung into the scuppers below the mizzen shrouds. He lay not moving, looking broken to Robert's eye. He plunged over the pitching deck, shouting for the surgeon.

Dawson's eyes were open, as Robert leant down he heard him say in a faint voice, "I cannot feel my legs or arms. I am gone. Look after the ship, Robert. She's yours now." He gasped, and his eyes closed.

Chapter six

Commander William Dawson died where he had spent most of his life; on the deck of one of His Majesty's ships of war. They had straightened the twisted limbs and placed him on a stretcher and carried him below.

With an effort Robert forced himself to put aside the sorrow at the loss of his Captain and friend and concentrate on the ship, it was now all down to him. He had dreamed about his first command but he would have rather not have earned it, however temporarily, in this way. He called the carpenter and sent him below to sound the well and set the bo'sun to check and repair the rigging damaged during the storm. The weather was settling down rapidly, the front having passed the veil of spray and cloud parted revealing the vast area of broken water around them and the French corvette.

Unlike the sloop, she had obviously suffered severely during the storm, or more likely, Robert thought, it was the wave that followed it that had done the worst damage. Her foremast was lying across her bows and men were busy chopping away the wreckage. In addition the mainmast looked unsteady, although it still carried a topsail.

"Beat to quarters and clear the decks for action, get the storm lashings off the guns, Mr. Callow, have plain sail set, let's get some speed for manoeuvres."

Men leapt to the shrouds, whilst others cast off the gun lashings. The rat-tat-tat of the drum underscored the frantic explosion of activity. A boy dashed about scattering

71

sand on the deck, while others ran below to bring shot and powder from the magazine.

The colours were raised and *HMS Witch* bore down on the Frenchman. Robert inspected her through his telescope, he observed she was pierced for fourteen guns, in the Royal Navy she would be rated a frigate, he also noted that she was frantically running out her guns, while still clearing the raffle of gear from her foredeck. The Tricolour flew from her mizzen stay.

Lieutenant Archer, now acting first lieutenant, was stationed on the main deck in command of the broadside guns. "Gun Captains, watch your aim, we will be crossing her bows and I want every shot to count."

Robert turned to the crew of the stern chase guns, "Load canister and fire as you bear."

"Aye, aye, Captain." The gunner touched his forelock and passed the orders to his gun crews.

The ship swooped down and as she crossed the bows of the corvette her guns spoke, one by one, to be immediately cleared, reloaded and run out once more. The effect on the Frenchman was shattering, the first cannon ball tore through the bow, smashing the bowsprit and ripping along the main deck with a shower of splinters, strewing broken men and guns in its path. One by one the guns spoke, creating their own trails of destruction.

As the ship cleared the bow of the Frenchman, the stern chaser fired when the sloop came about, the canister spreading its lethal contents across the fore deck causing even more mayhem among the crew of the battered ship. The corvette only managed to reply with scattered shots from her starboard guns; she was lying rolling badly in the troughs of the waves. Many of her guns were blocked by the fallen mast and sail. She had fired as the *Witch* drew away, one of the shots hitting the port side of the sloop and dismounting one of the twelve pounders; the gun crew were strewn dead and dying across the deck. The ship heeled as she came round to bring her starboard guns into action, the name of the corvette, *Le Vent,* was now visible on her stern.

The wind cleared the gun smoke, revealing the terrible damage done by the *Witch's* guns. Men were milling about trying to serve the guns while others were pulling the bodies of the casualties out of the way. As the broadside guns came to bear they spoke, one by one. Only two of the French guns managed to fire back and both balls missed. Fired on the down roll, the shot glanced off the water and skipped over the deck of the sloop without causing any damage. The mainmast of *Le Vent* started to lean forwards towards her bows, it stopped, caught by the tangle of sheets and shrouds, precariously balanced, swaying to the movement of the ship.

"She's struck!" Archer shouted pointing as the Tricolour was brought down to the deck.

Robert called to the first lieutenant. "Lower the longboat, Mr. Archer; take Williams, the boat crew and eight marines and secure the prize. Mr. Callow, get the carpenter and check the damage. Mr. Hardy, get the chief gunner's report on the dismounted gun. If it can be, I want it remounted as soon as possible!"

Hardy rushed off down the main deck, calling for the gunner in his high pitched voice.

As the boat pulled over to the French ship Lieutenant Richard Archer looked at the blood running from her scuppers and felt a shiver run up his spine; it could so well have been the Witch in this condition. He shook his head to clear it of the thought and leapt up to catch the port shrouds and haul himself aboard.

Followed by his boarding party he stepped over wreckage and wounded men to where an officer stood on the after deck with his outstretched sword. Archer took the sword and ordered Williams to take the carpenter's mate to sound the well. The marines assembled the prisoners. The sound of a disturbance caused Archer to turn to see one of the prisoners protesting at being pulled away from one of the wounded.

"What's happening?" He called.

"It is the doctor, he is attending the captain." The officer beside him explained in English.

"Sergeant!" Archer called "Leave the man be, he is the doctor, he may examine the wounded and do what he can for them, however give him an escort to help. Rogers," he called the big seaman standing by the group, "Give the doctor a hand, and keep an eye on things."

Rogers knuckled his forehead and nodded to the doctor. "Where's your bag then?" The doctor looked puzzled and returned to examining his patient.

Elsewhere the French seamen were being pushed into a group by the mainmast that was still precariously teetering as the ship rolled.

"Get those men working on the mainstay, brace up that mast first!" Archer found he had to be everywhere at once for those first few minutes, until the men realised what they had to do.

The carpenter's mate reported four feet of water in the bilges, and that the main mast stoppers had been knocked out of position. As soon as the mast had been braced up he would replace them. He rushed off to collect more tools.

The sloop hove-to alongside and the doctor went aboard to assist with the wounded. The bo'sun took charge of fastening a spare staysail yard to the stump of the foremast. A bowsprit was fashioned out of the trimmed end of the broken foremast which had now been cleared. The settling of the mainmast back into position—once stoppered in place—made the corvette seaworthy enough for the voyage back to England.

The quietening sea helped with the repairs to *Le Vent*, but it was three hours before it was deemed possible to raise sail once more. She had lost 28 dead and 22 wounded in the short action. The *Witch* had lost 5 killed and 2 wounded.

Under the command of Lieutenant Archer, *Le Vent* kept company with the *Witch* until she was ready to be released to sail for Plymouth manned by a prize crew.

The captain of *Le Vent* had succumbed to his wounds; the total loss to the Frenchman was now 29 killed and 21 wounded. In the hold they found eight prisoners from the crew of an English merchantman, captured by the corvette two weeks earlier. They were pressed into service on the *Witch* to replace the losses from the action.

The main prize from the events of the morning turned out to be the log book of the French ship. This listed her part as escort for a convoy of ships from the Indies. She had become detached from her charges during the night three days ago. Since the destination of the remaining ships of the convoy was La Coruna, the *Le Vent* had continued on her course hoping to join up with her missing charges.

Robert thought it was worth waiting for a day or so at least on the off chance that they could be in place to meet the missing ships of the convoy and perhaps obtain another prize or even two.

By retaining the *Le Vent* for the moment it should be possible to deceive any of the convoy ships into believing the *Witch* to be her captive. Providing, that is, any of the convoy had survived the storm. It was certainly worth a try.

Robert discussed the possibility with Lieutenant Archer who was entirely in agreement. Despite the damage she had endured, *Le Vent* was still in condition to give a good account for herself. The delay would also allow more time for the carpenter to effect repairs whilst she was hove-to.

The two ships lay-to with backed foresails as the burial service was read. Standing by the body of his captain, Robert felt an incredible sadness at the loss of the cheerful Dorset man who had shaped his career over the last two years. The wealth of seamanship knowledge gone in an instant, the kindness and understanding, shown by William Dawson would be sorely missed. As he doffed his hat to read the solemn words of the burial service, he could hear the soft Dorset words in his head as spoken by his former mentor on past occasions. Standing there he realised that this was what he had been trained for, and however difficult it may seem, it was upon his, Lieutenant Robert Graham's shoulders, that the responsibility for ship and men now lay. Donning his hat once more, Lieutenant Robert Graham. RN, assumed the burden.

It was just after dawn the following morning that the ship came into view. She was a fat East Indiaman with her sides painted like a man-o-war. Armed with a broadside of twelve guns she could give a good account for herself.

As she came up with the two warships *Witch* dropped the French flag that she had been displaying as did *Le Vent*, both ships raised the Union flag, and *Witch* fired a shot across the bows of the Indiaman. Under the threat of the combined broadsides of the warships the merchantman struck her colours without firing a shot.

The manifest of the *Coromandel* revealed her to be a true treasure ship, with a cargo of silk ivory, tea and gold bullion. Having placed a prize crew and marines on board under the Master, Mr. Callow, with the help of Midshipman Hardy, HMS *Witch* was left shorthanded, and it was for this reason Robert decided to accompany the prizes to Plymouth.

Sailing up the channel, the small convoy encountered the blockading fleet off Brest; where Robert reported to the Admiral on board the 80 gun Flagship *HMS Orient*. He was thrilled to be piped on board ship for the first time, while at the same time sad at the reason it was happening. He was received in the Great cabin lit by the windows that overlooked a gallery around the stern of the ship.

Sir Walter Keith, KB, Rear-Admiral in Command of the blockade squadron off Brest, was a sturdy robust man with a well-fed look. As Robert handed over his report, he spoke.

"I'm sorry to hear of the passing of William Dawson, he came from my part of the world, and he was with me in the Levant five years past. An enterprising and dependable officer, he will be sadly missed."

He shrugged. "Now your report." He turned to his servant. "Mason, some wine for Captain Graham. Take a seat sir," he indicated a chair and settled down to read Robert's report.

Mason brought a silver tray with two glasses of red wine, one of which he served to Robert. While Robert waited and sipped his wine the Admiral read with an occasional grunt and at one point a smile. Eventually he finished, picked up his wine and drank it straight down.

"Mason, more wine, man." As Mason hurried to refill the glasses the admiral turned to Robert, looking at him keenly, he spoke. "This report will go to the Admiralty with my covering letter; I suspect it will appear in the Gazette. God knows there is little enough good news at the moment. The corvette *Le Vent* should make a fine addition to the fleet, we are always short of frigates.

"Though I am not in a position to promise anything; I have little doubt you will advance, I can however, and will advance Lieutenant Archer as well as young Williams, who will become acting lieutenant. I will write orders for you to report to the Admiralty immediately. You can carry my own despatches with you."

He stood and held out his hand. Robert hurriedly climbed to his feet and banged his head on the deckhead, flustered he took the hand extended to him.

"Well done, lad!"

Robert stammered his thanks and left the cabin to the Admiral, who was already calling for his clerk.

Back on board his ship, Robert sat for a few moments still a little stunned at the way things were going. It seemed that events had begun to flow over the past few weeks, one thing after another without any effort on his part. He breathed deeply, once, twice, and then not able to sit still he leapt to his feet and went up on deck.

"Mr. Williams! Attend me!" He passed his hat to the master, and to the astonishment of the watching crew members stepped over to the port side and mounted the rigging to the maintop climbing round the futtock shrouds avoiding the lubber's hole. Williams arrived diplomatically at the same time as his captain.

"You have to do better than that, John," said Robert with a grin. "Even an acting lieutenant should be able to beat the Captain to the maintop!"

"It could be the quickest way to stop being an acting lieutenant," the tongue in cheek reply drew a chuckle from Robert.

"Touché, Mr. Williams. However I am happy to inform you that you are now officially acting and will be required to attend an examination board, probably in Plymouth, as soon as one is convened."

John Williams suddenly realised what his Captain had said. "You mean....so soon....I must get down to my books." He started to climb down; realised Robert had made no move and stopped reddening with embarrassment. "I beg pardon sir, have I your permission to return to my studies?"

"Congratulations John and off you go, just make sure you don't let us down."

He was smiling as he watched the young man sliding down the stay to the deck. He remembered his own board of examination, the nerves and the desperate wait while the board decided his fate. The relief had been incredible; he remembered the stiff-legged walk to the deck of the flagship in Gibraltar, the waters blue and calm. His sense almost of disappointment that the scene had not altered since he had entered the waiting room two hours before, and the handshake of the first lieutenant of the Flagship with whom he had served in a previous commission.

With a shrug and a last look round feeling a little deflated he descended to the main deck once more and accepted the proffered hat, the Captain once more.

***

A week had passed before the three ships sailed into Plymouth Harbour, saluting the forts according to tradition. The evening sky was reddening in the west as they came to anchor.

Midshipman Hardy, back on board once more, approached Robert. "Signal, sir, captain to report to the Port Admiral."

"Very well, Mr. Hardy, acknowledge if you please, and have the longboat lowered."

The middy turned and called for the longboat. The bo'sun had the lashings off in anticipation and the boat was being swung out before the acknowledging signal was sent.

Donning his boat cloak, Robert turned to the diminutive midshipman, "You have the ship, Mr. Hardy."

As he turned he caught the eye of the master's mate Sven Hansen, a steady experienced hand. He nodded to the man, who nodded back in understanding; he looked about the ship for what he thought might be the last time then descended over the side into the waiting boat. His servant Meadows had packed his luggage ready for his departure and he was waiting in the boat with the box and bags stacked around him.

At the admiral's port office he was greeted by Admiral Reeves, a grey and weatherbeaten old friend of his father, who had been helpful in getting him his first ship. The Admiral had been advised of his necessary departure for London and was therefore unfortunately unable to discuss the events of the latest voyage. He had however arranged for the London Mail coach to be slightly delayed, to send the young officer on his journey.

Once securely seated inside; the coach it set off with an impatient lurch; Meadows, Robert's servant rode outside, crouched in his oilskin against the wet weather.

It was a battered and weary Robert who descended from the coach after the eighteen-hour journey. He watched his sea chest and other gear taken into the Cock Inn by Meadows and the inn servant. The Cock was the preferred hostelry for sea officers visiting the Admiralty in London.

He was hardly through the door before he was greeted with a shout and buffeted by the strong right arm of his friend, Lieutenant, Lord William Beaufort-Robinson. Baron Brimpton.

"Here at last, Bobby, what kept you?" Billy Beaufort's usual robust, good humoured direct manner was like a breath of fresh air.

Robert looked at his friend. Billy's face was smiling and he looked well though a little pale. "I see you haven't changed, still the same old Billy! But what are you doing here? I thought you were still in *Hotspur.*"

"I was tagged in a scrap with a galley off Tripoli and came home with the mail to get repairs. They replaced me and now I'm fit as a flea and going mad in the Admiralty, trying to get back to sea. You have your orders, I suppose?"

"Yes, I must report to the Admiralty." Robert replied.

"It says forthwith does it not?" Bobby said tugging Robert's arm.

"But I need to clean up and change." Robert protested.

"You'll do!" Insisted Bobby, and dragged him through the door and called for a carriage, directing the man to the Whitehall.

On the way he demanded to be told of the action off the Spanish coast, and after hearing the bones of the story said, "You'll get a command, no doubt at all." Though Robert protested, he would hear none of it.

"I don't suppose you would consider finding a job for me to do. Perhaps you already have a first in mind?"

"You idiot, Billy, you know you would be my first choice if and when the chance arose. I think you are quite mad to presume that I will get a command. I have no influence and there are too many above me on the list to allow me a chance."

"Just wait, I will look forward to treading a deck again, under your command." Billy was quite confident about it.

At the Admiralty after handing in the reports and letters, they were asked to wait. The afternoon sky was grey and it was beginning to rain. Robert looked glumly through the window at the wet street below, he felt uncomfortably dusty and dishevelled.

"Lieutenant Graham, if you will?" The clerk called him and indicated the door being held open by Billy. Robert straightened his shoulders and walked through.

There were three men in the room, standing by the fireplace where a small fire did little more than dent the cool atmosphere. He noticed a slight figure in dark blue coat. He realised with a start it was Captain Nelson—no, he was Commodore Nelson—or was he? Confused, he turned to the figure seated at the table. The other standing man, still reading his action report; was Captain Sir Edward Pellew, whose actions in command of a frigate made him famous throughout England.

"Ah, Lieutenant Graham."

Robert straightened. "Sir" he acknowledged.

With a sigh the seated man shrugged and continued. "You do not call me sir, I am a civil member of the admiralty." Ignoring Robert's confusion, he continued, "I have to inform you that their Lordships have decided that in view of your actions in the matter of the corvette *Le Vent* and the merchantman Coromandel, plus the recommendations of your captain and that of Admiral Keith, you will be advanced to Post rank from this day.

"You are ordered to the command of the frigate *HMS Roister*, ex *Le Vent*, that has been bought into the service currently lying under repair at Plymouth. You are ordered to assume command on the first of the month, in ten days time. Do you have any requests for officers who may be available? I can tell you that newly promoted lieutenant The Hon David Ogilvie has been suggested as junior; though it is up to you whether you accept him or not."

Robert stood stunned for the moment; the civilian looked at him with the question hanging in the air.

"I would like Lieutenant Beaufort-Robinson for my senior and I would be happy to accept Lieutenant Ogilvie as junior."

"Good, you will of course choose whosoever you wish for second, and other normal appointments.

"Now...." He held up his hand to indicate he was not finished. "I note that you are likely to receive considerable prize monies for the purchase of the corvette *Le Vent* and the hull, and cargo, of the *Coromandel*." His eyebrows rose as he noted the estimated sum. "I suggest, only suggest mind you, that you place the handling of you funds in the charge of a reputable prize agent. As a frigate captain prize monies seem to accrue on occasion and it would be to your advantage to have a trustworthy agent to act for you. I believe these gentlemen will agree that Cox's have a reputation for fair dealing." He hesitated and both Nelson and Pellew nodded agreement, "But the decision is yours. That is all." He closed the book in front of him and stood.

"I would be honoured to shake your hand sir; you are a credit to the service!" He held out his hand, Robert surprised and touched took it and shook gladly. Both

Nelson and Pellew added their congratulations; Nelson said quietly. "Good luck, I'll look forward to seeing you again." He passed a package to the new Post-Captain. "You will need this!" He said with a smile.

Chapter seven

At the Cock Inn, after a wash and shave and a change of linen, Robert dined early with his new first lieutenant. The atmosphere at the meal was restrained as both men had much to think about.

It was Robert who eventually broke the silence when he said thoughtfully, "You'll need to take over the supervision of the refitting of the ship as soon as possible."

"If I may, sir, I will leave on the morning mail for Plymouth to take up my duties, I understand that the *Le Vent* took a certain amount of damage and I would like to ensure she is put together properly." Despite the casual manner Robert was well aware of the professionalism of his new first lieutenant and pleased that he was taking his new post seriously.

He looked at his companion keenly, "No socialising with your society friends this evening then?"

"Oh, we are expected at my aunt's soiree at nine. I must attend; the Countess has made me her heir. Besides she is one of the few relatives I have that I actually like. She insisted on meeting the gallant Captain Graham; I will have to attend to introduce you." He brightened, "With luck, 'Bootface' will be there. My sister Barbara," he explained hastily as Robert looked at him blankly. He rushed on. "You may not remember, she came to see me off when I joined *Argonaut*, where we first met?"

Robert repeated, "Bootface?"

Billy looked expectantly at Robert, who vaguely remembered a skinny blond girl; the one who had insisted on joining the boat taking the two new young midshipmen out to the second rate to begin their career in the navy.

Distracted, he nodded vaguely, "I think I remember; well, in that case we had better make a move." He said changing the subject. "My uniform should be pressed by now."

They rose and returned to Robert's chamber where his newly sponged and pressed dress uniform hung complete with the single epaulette on the right shoulder denoting his rank as Post Captain. When he had opened the package given him by Nelson he had found the single epaulette within, the note simply said, 'Wear it with pride' it was signed by both Nelson and Pellew.

At 27 years he would not be the youngest to achieve the rank, but it was not a regular occurrence at his age.

The carriage stopped outside the pillared front portico of the gracious house in Aldwych, servants waited at the door to help the visitors with their coats and cloaks. Inside the guests were received by Billy's aunt dressed in a plain grey dress elegantly cut to show off her still trim figure to perfection.

The Countess, Dorothy Beaufort-Robinson was a lady of middle years, perhaps fifty, perhaps sixty; her rather narrow face appeared flawless, rather like the Dresden figurines that were becoming popular at the time. Her autocratic appearance was belied by the broad smile as she greeted her nephew with a kiss, and turned to greet his friend.

"Captain Graham, how kind of you to make the time to come and call upon us," she held out her hand to him and he bent to brush it with his lips. As he straightened he saw the woman standing next to the Countess. She was wearing a dark blue gown that showed off her figure, tall with a smooth healthy skin, she was looking at him directly, her blue eyes smiling slightly as she observed the effect she was having on him. Robert found he was still gripping the Countess's hand and with a mumbled apology he released it.

The Countess laughed gently and turned to the blue-eyed lady, and taking her hand drew her round to face Robert. "Allow me to introduce Lady Beaufort. Barbara, this is Captain Robert Graham, your brother's new Commanding Officer." Lady Barbara dropped a small curtsey, then stood and held out her hand and shook Robert's hand like a man.

"We have heard a lot about you over the last few days, Captain, I expected you to be two feet taller, at least." Her tone was mocking but not unkind.

His reply was also mocking, "I have been hearing about you also, and I am happy to say the description I was given was equally inaccurate."

The Countess looked from one to the other and with a smile, taking her nephew's arm took him away to talk to the other guests.

"We appear to be abandoned!" Robert said "May I help you to something?" He waved vaguely at the buffet. He felt a strange excitement, a thrill on meeting this beautiful woman, a feeling of expectation almost.

"I don't think so," Barbara smiled. "Would you like to see the garden? It is at its most beautiful at this time of year." She took his arm as they went out through the open doors into the summer twilight. The servants were lighting the lanterns scattered around the formal lawns and hedges of the garden, casting bars of light and shadow along the pleasant walks.

"Please tell me about the taking of the *Le Vent*?" she asked keenly. "We read the Gazette but it gave a very impersonal picture of what happened."

Robert thought for a moment. "A battle of any sort is not for a Lady, the actual events would be most disturbing for a person of gentle upbringing to hear."

"Oh, stuff and nonsense! Billy and I both had the same upbringing and he can listen without coming to harm, and take part even. Because I'm a woman I must not be told the truth about the events that involve a brother or perhaps a husband?"

Robert looked at her with amused surprise. "I have just realised why your brother described you as he did."

She blushed "He called me Bootface, didn't he!"

He nodded. "But with great affection, and I now know it was no reflection on your appearance rather his recognition of you as an equal, a compliment I heartily endorse."

She looked discomforted but squeezed his arm, and he proceeded to paint a picture in words of the bloody scene on the decks of the two warships as the action occurred. She listened without a sound until he finished, by now they were seated on a bench on the terrace.

Their conversation become more personal as each retailed memories of their younger days, the times of youth in the country. For Barbara it was in the great rambling house surrounded by parkland. For Robert the squire's Manor house in the village where his father had exerted a firm hand and insisted on his being educated; not so firm as to prevent him getting up to mischief with the other boys of the village.

Too soon the evening drew to an end, though not before the Countess had obtained his promise to call upon her the following day, and Barbara had agreed to go riding in the morning.

The two young men returned to the inn in high good humour.

The Plymouth Mail left at 9.00am and Robert made sure to be in time to see his first lieutenant off. As they shook hands at parting, both knew that the easy, happy go lucky friendship they had enjoyed up to now would have to change; both accepted it was necessary but were saddened nonetheless.

Robert was not required to report to the Admiralty for seven more days and he used the time to his advantage. Having called on the prize agents, Coxes, as suggested, he was pleasantly surprised to discover he was a rich man. His captain's share of the two prizes would gain him close to £25,000, a huge sum. He invested £750.00 of the money in a house in Knightsbridge.

The popular village was growing rapidly around the barracks of the Foot Guards. He was able to move into his residence with the assistance of Barbara, who was happy to supply sufficient furniture from her aunt's house to allow him to live.

Thereafter, once again together, she helped select suitable furnishings for the permanent furnishing of the house. He invested in a cook/housekeeper and a manservant, to look after him, and to maintain the place in his absence.

He found Barbara's company exciting and the relationship between them unusual in that in addition to her desirability as a woman, her friendship was on a level normally he had only found on a man to man basis. They were able to discuss any subject and Barbara was well able to hold her own in many areas regarded as the province of men only.

Robert managed to see Barbara most days, and was happy to know that the Countess approved of their friendship. By the last day of his sojourn in London having received his orders from the Admiralty he called upon the Countess to thank her for her kindness and hospitality during his stay.

She was very sad at his departure and apologised for the absence of Barbara who had gone out early to Bond Street, for some urgent reason.

Disappointed and rather hurt, Robert returned to the Cock Inn to collect his belongings for the journey to Plymouth, to take up his new command. It was whilst he was finally checking his room to see that all his things were packed, that the maid announced with a smirk, a lady visitor.

Surprised he turned to find Barbara standing in the doorway. The maid left still smirking. Waiting until the maid left the room, Barbara stepped forward and put her arms round Robert's neck and kissed him firmly, if a little inexpertly on the lips. Getting over his surprise Robert warmly returned the favour. They parted, flushed and smiling, though there were tears in Barbara's eyes as she said.

"Oh I am sorry; I'm so glad I caught you. I should not have attacked you in that way."

With great daring Robert replied. "On the contrary, I cannot think of a better way to greet or say farewell to a future husband." As the words came out Robert was appalled at his own temerity, he could not believe he had revealed his thoughts in such bald terms. What would she think? But one look at the radiant face in front of him gave the answer. Once more she came into his willing arms and kissed him.

"Oh Robert, do you really mean it?"

"If you will have me, I certainly do. I will call upon your father as soon as I can."

"My aunt will be returning to Exeter next week, I know she will approve. Please find time to call before you sail, Plymouth is not too far from our estate."

"Depend on it, somehow I will manage to present myself during the next month. I am not due to sail until the 5th July." Outside the yard clock chimed. "Damn! Now I really must go. My post coach is here."

As they kissed once more she realised that the package she had brought was still in her reticule. "I nearly forgot! The reason I was late." She drew out a small packet and gave it to him. "Open it when you are on your way and think of me."

He tucked the packet in his pocket and left, clattering down the stairs to the waiting coach. She followed and stood waving as the coach departed, the coachman blowing his Post Horn to clear the way.

He remembered the packet when they passed through Kew, and opened the seal. Inside there was a small box, containing a gold hunter watch and chain and a letter from Barbara. He examined the watch, opening the front case, inside the lid was engraved the simple message.

Robert, 'God keep you safe' Barbara. The letter was also short and to the point,

Dear Robert,

I have been waiting, hoping to find someone to whom I could relate as an equal, not just as a lover, but as a friend also; my feelings for you became apparent to me the night we met at my aunt's house. I have felt us grow closer together daily since then, and I think that you feel the way I do.

I know you will be away from me for a long time, but I wish you to know that I will await your return impatiently.

If I am making a fool of myself so be it, I am confident that these words will go no further. If I am correct and you love me as I love you, I will look forward to seeing you before you depart for your duties overseas.

Yours, Barbara

Robert put the letter in his inside pocket. Thank God he had spoken to her before he left; at least she now knew he felt the same way as she did. With a glad heart he settled back in the coach to rest as much as possible during the long journey to Plymouth.

The hull of the frigate *HMS Roister* was looking clean, with her new copper reflecting the sun. She stood in her stocks in the dockyard at Plymouth, new timbers looking raw against the weathered paintwork of the undamaged sections of the bulwarks, new 'steps' had been placed in the keelson, ready for the installation of the masts when she was re-floated.

Lieutenant Beaufort reported to Robert that the ship would be ready for launch in two days; the stores were already being assembled. Robert had contributed to the paint for the hull plus gold leaf for the escutcheon for her name on the stern; it would not do to skimp on these things.

A second lieutenant had been found. Lieutenant Martin Walker, a former member of an ill fated mapping expedition captured by Barbary pirates. He had been rescued from slavery after five years captivity when the galley he was serving in had been taken off Tunis, the action in which Billy Beaufort was wounded causing his return to England.

Robert was aware that Walker was an excellent navigator but likely doomed to spend the rest of his service on the beach. He had been in the hands of the pirates for five years before his rescue and for some reason this seemed to prejudice his obtaining another post.

He had presented himself at the Angel Inn where Robert was staying whilst the ship was being refitted. He did not beg nor cajole. He came to Robert as he sat in the lounge before leaving for the dockyard, and asked for a position in the ship. Though he held rank as a lieutenant he would accept to sail as master's mate if there was no place for his rank. Robert had been thinking of possible candidates for the post. He had considered John Mathews who was, at present, in his first appointment, preparing to go to sea in the *HMS Witch* as third lieutenant under the newly promoted Commander Archer; so when Robert met Martin Walker he studied him keenly and decided he liked the look of the big man, who stood at least six feet six. He had to stoop slightly because of the low ceiling. His uniform was worn and fraying round the cuffs, but it was clean and pressed. When asked the question, he answered directly, detailing his experience prior to and during his capture by the pirates. He also explained that the Admiralty had been unable—or unwilling—to place him during the past lull in naval activity, and that he wished to get back to sea, where he belonged.

Robert looked keenly at him, "How old are you?"

"Thirty one years, sir." Walker replied.

"Married?"

"I was, sir, but it was annulled in my absence, I was reported dead and she remarried as a court-declared widow. She and her husband look after my son along with their own two girls."

"How old is your son?" Robert was curious.

"He will be ten years old in September, sir."

Robert thought for a minute, there was no doubt in his mind, Walker knew his business and had a good knowledge of the Mediterranean, and their orders were for Gibraltar.

"Come back this evening," Robert said. "I will be dining with the first lieutenant, Billy Beaufort-Robinson. Join us as my guest; I believe you have found a berth."

Walker bowed, "I would be delighted, sir. Thank you." and he left leaving Robert trying to remember where he had heard of Walker in the past.

That evening the three officers dined on the beef pie for which the inn was famous, and during the meal it was formally agreed that Walker would fill the vacant position of second lieutenant, thus completing the allotment of officers for the frigate. He agreed to report the next morning to take up his duties. The business over, the three men enjoyed the rest of the evening over three more bottles of red wine, telling yarns of their past service under various captains.

Whilst they were reviving old memories Robert noticed a man watching the three officers as they enjoyed the evening. The man was tall and dark haired, Robert had noticed him as he had entered the room. There was something about him that was familiar and the watchful way he had come in studying the clientele as he sat down hinted at something secretive in his manner.

He spoke to Walker. "Martin, the tall dark man seated by the window, do you know him?"

Martin looked discreetly and sat back with a wry grin. "We are drinking brandy supplied by his men. He is the most notorious smuggler on the Devon coast. Named Peter Tregarth, hails from Looe, in Cornwall, and is as crafty as a shipload of monkeys. For years he used to travel the countryside with a peddler's cart. Sharpening knives, mending pots, and discovering who and what could be found in the West Country. His father was a fisherman based in Looe.

"His father died and they had a problem with the local squire over the house occupied by their mother; the matter was not resolved until the squire fell off his horse and managed to spear himself on his own sword. There were no witnesses so, who knows?

"Suspicion made life difficult for Peter so he joined his brother with the fishing." He finished his story with a shrug. "The rest just seemed to happen. Supply and demand, plus a good knowledge of the coast here, and over the water, coupled with an unpopular import duty led to the so called Free Trade being born. The war has in fact fostered it."

Robert decided that he must have some vague memory from the days of his youth in the Manor house, but why should Tregarth be interested in him now? He shrugged, his future would take him far from here and unlikely to lead to further contact. He promptly forgot Peter Tregarth, having remembered where he knew the name Martin Walker.

He had made a point of visiting the home of William Dawson, at Broadway when he had arrived in Plymouth from London. He had made his way via the Channel Packet to Weymouth and hired a horse for the three-mile trip to the little village of Broadway.

The parents of William Dawson were very pleased to see him and most grateful for the gift of £100.00 contributed by the officers and crew of the '*Witch*'. Robert was not impressed by the son-in-law married to Dawson's sister. He suspected that much of the money would end up in his hands; he shrugged, there was little he could do. While there he was presented to Dawson's son.

At twelve years old he was a fine upstanding young man who obviously disliked his uncle intensely. Young Alan was cared for by the younger brother of William and his wife, but both had been killed when the coach to Dorchester had been held up. The driver had been killed and the coach horses had bolted, careering over the edge of the road at speed, leaving the passengers piled up in a heap of broken bodies. His uncle broke his neck and his aunt died of blood poisoning within three days. The ten-year-old orphan had been brought up since by his Grandparents.

Dawson senior asked Robert quietly if the lad could be taken on as a midshipman. The Commander had entered him on the books as captain's servant over two years ago so he could join as midshipman if a Captain would accept him. They could fund his uniform and such. Robert questioned the lad in private, not that he would not have taken him anyway, just that he wanted to hear from the boy how he felt about going to sea. He need not have worried,

Alan Dawson had been preparing himself for a career at sea ever since he was old enough to know what his father's profession was. Impressed with the lad Robert took him back with him on his return to the ship. Alan Dawson was appointed as Midshipman in *HMS Roister* the following day, with the creases newly pressed on his first uniform jacket.

***

Robert visited Barbara on several occasions during the refitting of the ship, and she visited the ship with her father the week before it was completed. The special sea cabinet for wines and glasses was now standing in his cabin, a gift from his prospective father-in-law.

The Marquis had been seriously delighted that his strong-minded daughter had found a man she would marry, and, what's more, one that he approved.

He was a bluff country gentleman who adored his daughter and thoroughly approved of her sensible outlook on life, noticeably more practical than her contemporaries from within the local hunting set.

He came of ancient lineage, and would often be heard boasting of the Viking origins of his Norman ancestors, and the bloody history associated with them. In view of the paternal way he regarded and treated his tenants, this caused some amusement to his immediate family.

Robert had ridden horses since he was big enough to sit a saddle. What is more, his riding instructions had been undertaken by a onetime farrier-Sergeant of the Life Guards. Once the Squire's coachman, Michael Green was now the village blacksmith. Robert's training had followed the program required for recruits to the Cavalry, and started with bareback riding and progressed from there. His father had always deemed it necessary for a gentleman to learn the accomplishments of gentlemen, and despite his relaxed upbringing nothing important had been ignored.

Visiting Hartwell Hall, Barbara's home required that he ride, usually on his one of his own horses; he now had several in the Manor stables. But as the sailing date drew near, Barbara and the Countess came and stayed at the Manor conveniently closer to Plymouth. Although their homes were only twelve miles apart as the crow flew, the different county roads entailed a much extended journey to cover the distance between the two properties.

This saved Robert the extra journey involved to see his fiancé. His father was hale and hearty and had over the past few weeks become acquainted with his prospective daughter-in-law, Barbara. They found an easy friendship between them. Squire Graham had lost his wife, Robert's French mother, when Robert was eight and he had never remarried. He found new friends at Hartwell Hall and he made sure that welcome awaited visitors from Hartwell when they came to the Manor.

The Countess and he became particular friends, finding many common likes and dislikes. Both were confirmed in their present lifestyles and the question of romance between them never arose; but she welcomed the visits, and enjoyed the lively discussions between them. At the Graham celebration of the betrothal she offered her services as hostess for the occasion and graced the event personally with great panache.

For Robert and Barbara the good relations' between the two families was a great boon. The social climate could have made things difficult, but the similar backgrounds of both fathers made the association of the two families easier than it might have been. As Lord Hartwell pointed out, the two crusty old widowers had a lot in common apart from their children.

The betrothal celebration at Hartwell was held during the last week before sailing, the ship being left in the charge of Lieutenant Walker while the others attended the celebration. Robert, torn between his new command and his love for Barbara found the period very trying.

When *Roister* was finally ready for sea, it was a relief to get back into the ship routine. Although the past few weeks had been among the happiest in his life, Robert was ready to resume his chosen career. The last three days were busy and when the eve of sailing day arrived, Robert entertained his fiancé, the Countess and both parents, in his newly refurbished cabin.

Since he was not aware of the full extent of his forthcoming detachment, his orders taking him to Gibraltar only, they were unable to decide when he would be available to marry, but the evening went well despite this uncertainty.

Chapter Eight

The surface of the water was grey and choppy, the wind whipping spray from the wave tops. Across Plymouth Harbour the anchored ships rocked and pulled at their moorings in the rising wind.

The orders for *HMS Roister* required them to carry a passenger to Gibraltar on behalf of the Foreign Office. They were still awaiting his arrival, and the timing was becoming critical if they were to make the tide. So it was with some impatience Captain Graham stalked the deck of his new command awaiting his passenger.

"How is the tide, Mr. Beaufort?" Robert said gruffly.

"It's on the turn now sir, we really should be away already." Beaufort was sounding worried, and with reason, as the tide, once it really started running, would be difficult to stem, even in the blustery wind.

The officer of the watch, Lieutenant Ogilvie called at that moment, "Boat approaching starboard side."

As he approached the ship in command of the gig, Midshipman Alan Dawson was thinking how three weeks in the ship had made a complete difference to his life. Always a natural on the water he had taken to the handling of the gig without a problem, his easy friendly manner had made him popular with the seamen of his watch. The fact that he was his father's son had also helped, and to Alan it seemed that he had come home. When he first arrived on board he had learned his way about so quickly it had gained him respect in the gunroom, it now felt as if he had been in *Roister* for years.

The gig rounded the stern of the merchantman lying to shoreward of the frigate, and with a flourish of oars ran alongside the Roister. The bo'sun called for the falls to be attached and had the boat and crew complete with passengers raised and swung over to drop neatly into the chocks on the main deck. Alan leapt out of his place to assist the passengers onto the deck. The two women thus helped out of the boat looked round in a bewildered manner at the sight of the seamen marching round the windlass, raising the anchor, whilst others ran around the rigging releasing the sails. As the sails cracked open in the breeze, the cry, 'Anchors aweigh,' came from the foc'sle; and the ship began to make headway, nodding her head into the waves driven by the tide.

Robert watched while the salutes were exchanged with the admiral's flag, and the frigate gained headway against the incoming tide. After watching their progress for a few minutes, he realised that they would be able to clear the headland and, with a relieved sigh, he turned to the waiting passengers.

Surprised in the first place that it was two people waiting to introduce themselves; not one, both women. The nearer dressed in men's breeches and riding boots, he had initially thought to be a man but now seeing her properly standing erect with the black hair cut close to her head and piercing dark eyes, he realised how mistaken he had been. Full five-feet six inches tall, handsome rather than pretty with a fine drawn face; he estimated she would be about thirty years old. The other, shorter than the first; pretty, fair-haired and blue-eyed, dressed conventionally in bonnet blouse and skirt, with a shawl round her shoulders, carried a carpet bag.

"We are expected, I believe?" The voice was throaty and cultured, with just a touch of something in the accent that made Robert think she may not be English.

"Of course," Robert said. "Though I was not told you would be a lady." He amended his comment. "Two ladies," he answered.

"I would have travelled alone, but convention demands that on a ship crewed entirely by men I must have a chaperone, hence my companion, Amelie. I am Charlotte Mansfield at your service." She bowed, inclining her head.

Bowing back to the lady Robert introduced himself.

"Captain Robert Graham at your service, Madam... er Miss....Mansfield."

"I am a widow, Captain. My friends call me Lotte. Since we will be together on you little ship, you may find it easier to address me as Lotte." She smiled, and her face lit up and he realised she was quite beautiful. She indicated the bags that were now placed on the deck beside her companion. "Perhaps we can be shown our accommodations so that I may get changed!"

"Of course, Madam – er – Lotte. Meadows, here man!" His servant appeared with two seamen to take the bags and the ladies to the captain's cabin. Robert had moved out to the first lieutenant's cabin, causing the first lieutenant to oust the second from his cabin, consigning Walker to the gunroom.

Out in the open sea the breeze freshened and the motion of the frigate steadied as she set course for Gibraltar down the channel and through the Bay of Biscay. The wind from the quarter allowed the ship to carry full sail, and she fairly flew across the blue water, flinging up a fine spray to spatter across the foc'sle and create a large damp area of deck. The passengers were both on deck standing by the starboard rigging. The companion Amelie's hair had escaped from her bonnet, so she had removed it and it streamed out like a blond pennant in the breeze. She was laughing from the sheer joy at the motion of the ship and wind in her hair. Lotte smiled, her own hair free to flick and flutter also. She was dressed today in a dress that clung to the contours of her body in the steady breeze.

The midshipman of the watch, young Robin Abbot, was standing as close to the two women as he could, ready to dance attendance on their slightest wish.

Concealing a smile, Lieutenant Walker, officer of the watch, called Abbot and gave him a navigation problem to work out. To his evident chagrin, Abbot left the deck to collect his journals and instruments to perform his task.

The ladies walked backwards and forwards on the after end of the deck, Lotte stopping to pass the time of day with Walker on the way.

During the first two days, the ladies added a new dimension to the lives of the officers and men of the ship. They had maintained smiling faces since they had boarded the ship in Plymouth. Their late arrival had been caused by the conditions on the road from London. Far from being the servant of Lotte, Amelie Parker was her colleague. Both, it seemed, were experts in their fields, though it was not readily apparent just what these fields covered. Robert was told in his orders to exercise tact in the matter and thus he discouraged discussion of the subject whenever it rose.

Whilst not as vividly handsome as Lotte, Amelie was a pretty woman, who seemed to be quite unaware of her good looks; content, it seemed, to stand in the shadow of her more dramatic-looking friend.

There was no doubt the crew admired them both, though they kept their distance. The ladies were particularly interested in the daily exercise of the guns, and both were happy to stand by the wheel whilst the gun crews ran out the guns and loaded and fired at targets flung overside for the purpose; mainly barrels or crates. The extra powder used had been provided by Robert for that purpose. The first lieutenant was well pleased with the speed of loading and the accuracy of the guns when fired.

He was himself very taken with the lady Amelie Parker and sought her company whenever it was possible. She, it seemed, enjoyed the attention though she took care to give more attention to the rather gauche conversational offerings of Lieutenant Walker and the midshipmen when they had the chance. David Ogilvie pursued Lotte to absolutely no avail. Lotte treated all with polite attention, encouraging none and offending none. She made it quite clear that she had no interest in men at the moment, though privately Robert had the impression that there were circumstances which could change her attitude.

The days of smooth sailing were all too short and soon Cape Trafalgar appeared to port and the ship had to make the turn to enter the strait and into the bay of Gibraltar.

The harbour was busy with ships, the Mediterranean fleet preparing to sail the next day.

They sailed into the harbour, firing the salute to the Admiral's flag, but as soon as they dropped anchor the signal for Robert to repair on board the flagship was made and acknowledged. He was rowed across immediately. He had to say farewell to the two ladies who were being taken ashore as he boarded the gig. Whilst he welcomed the use of his cabin once more, he would, like the rest of the crew, miss their cheerful chatter, and the softening effect on the atmosphere of the normally all-male society of the ship.

Rear Admiral Willard had a hard, sour, look and a reputation to match. He was temporarily in command of the Mediterranean fleet, and already overdue for relief.

It seemed he was not expected to live to enjoy retirement, the way he treated his captains, made them feel that he intended taking them with him. His orders were brief, the Roister was to patrol the North African coast and intercept, where possible, any ships found to be interfering with the free passage of the merchant convoys passing through the area. The orders were to intercept and take such steps as necessary to terminate the activities of these North African pirates. As Robert observed to Lieutenant Beaufort, orders like this can be interpreted in more than one way, and god help the captain that chose the wrong one.

One of the problems involved in carrying out their orders was the existence of an agreement with the Bey of Tunis, who had promised to stop interference with British ships passing his shores in return for a generous annual payment from the British Government. Unfortunately the Bey's orders were not always obeyed and several ships had been attacked and taken along the coast of Barbary.

***

The longboat crept carefully and silently into the harbour at Bougie. The North African night was like black velvet with the stars scattered across the sky, the immediate area was dark but the waterfront was lit up by fires along the shore and the sound of drums and pipes seemed to vibrate the very air.

In the long boat the men were packed together waiting for the order to be given. Lieutenant Walker was poised, ready to board the moored galley, one of three lying at anchor in the harbour. The other two were targets of the gig and the two jollyboats, commanded by Ogilvie and Midshipman Abbot and Masters Mate Hanson, the giant Swede, one of the volunteers in the crew, with Alan Dawson.

As the boats approached their targets, Alan Dawson turned to Hanson, "Do you ever get scared before a job like this?"

Big Sven smiled and looking across at the diminutive midshipman "Once the action starts all fear disappears, you are too busy surviving to worry about the ones you're up against. You'll see!"

Shipping the oars, and using rope fenders, the longboat came gently alongside the galley. Once the boat was stopped, held in place by several of the crew, Peter Morse, in the bow, crawled over the bulwarks of the galley and disappeared from view, Peter had been a poacher. Having been arrested he was given the choice, the Navy or the treadmill; having chosen the Navy he had fitted in with the top-men and become a valued member of the crew. When his head appeared once more he signalled the first group to board. Six men climbed quietly onto the galley; there was a brief scuffle and a strangled cry, then the signal was given for the others to board. On the stern deck, Walker raised the shielded lantern and opened the panel in the direction of the other three boats. He closed and opened it twice. Then, receiving an answering flash from the other boats, he ordered Abbot to have the lateen sails raised to sail out of the harbour with the offshore breeze. The slaves were stirring with the activity around them, and a murmuring rose from the benches. The six marines in the party cocked their muskets and strode along the walkway between the benches hushing the chained men. Walker spoke to the slaves in a language they obviously understood because they quietened down immediately.

From one of the other galleys came the sound of a shot, and at that point all need of quiet was forgotten. Whilst some of the men readied the stern chasers, the sail dropped from the yard and filled. The anchor rope was cut with an axe and the ship sailed free, followed by a spatter of shots from the shore. The other two galleys were also cut loose and the three ships sailed for the open sea.

Walker's was first through, despite starting from its place nearest the shore. As they passed the fort at the harbour mouth, the galley fired both its stern chaser guns at the fort, creating confusion within the walls. The second galley was nearly clear when the first of the fort's guns fired. The ball passed above the deck of the heeling ship, missing the ship but carrying off two of the boarders as they were securing the sail, causing the sail to flap and ship to lose way. The third galley received three hits from the fort, killing four of the boarders and wounding Mr. Hanson in the leg with a flying splinter. Four of the rowers were also killed as they sat still chained on their bench. The ball carried on through the side of the ship, and she began to take water as she heeled to the wind.

Hanson called for the helm to be brought up, raising the hole above the water line. The tethered slaves pushed out the oars and waited for the command to row. Hanson called to Alan his second in command. "Get a patch on that hole and get someone to beat time for the oars."

Alan, ordered men to drop the sail and use it to stuff the shot hole in the hull, he picked up the mallet himself; as he struck the drum a single beat the oars rose together and dipped into the water, he struck the drum again starting to establish a rhythm and the oars followed the beat, driving the ship through the choppy sea.

Seeing the effect of the oars, Hanson ordered the mast dropped and the galley swiftly made its way out to their ship waiting offshore with the two other galleys.

In the two days whilst at anchor in Gibraltar harbour, the ship had provisioned and taken on the latest charts of the Mediterranean, and the other inland seas. The two main pirate bases had been indicated. As Robert sat in his cabin studying the charts of the North African coastline, he smiled at the notation in the corner of the chart, 'Amended in 1793 by the observations taken by Lieutenant Martin Walker RN'. He recalled how the name had intrigued him at the time of Walker's joining the ship. Of course he knew the name. At the time of Walker's capture, Robert, as a midshipman had been responsible for amending the ships charts.

The city of Tangier was by far the most important to the west, but it was Bone to the east that occupied his attention. For some considerable time, the Bey who commanded the galleys that raided from the city had been creating havoc amongst the merchant traders of the Mediterranean. The *Roister* was under orders to stop the pirate activities from this area, using whatever means available.

The capture of the three galleys had been the result of a hasty decision on Robert's part, and he was still not quite sure what he could use them for.

The released slaves were at present camped several miles down the shore under the eye of Captain Ullyet and his company of marines. There were several sick men from the benches, currently under the care of the surgeon, John Sweet. Three of these men were not expected to survive the next few days.

Robert's biggest need at present was information. He had no knowledge of the layout of the city of Bone, and the slaves he had spoken to so far had not seen much since their capture. The one factor which could be of assistance was the deep and abiding hatred felt by the slaves for their former masters. All had volunteered to join in the fight against their former captors, but without information Robert could not take the risk.

His musings were interrupted by the arrival of the surgeon with his report on the condition of the released slaves and the crew.

"Give me the bad news, John." Robert was not feeling too confident.

"Sorry, sir, I can only give you good news at the moment. Of the crew, no problems; the splinter wound suffered by Mr. Hanson is healing nicely and apart from the odd case of rope burn and cuts and bruises, the crew are fit.

"The slaves have a wide variety of ailments but apart from my three serious bed cases, all are reasonably fit, and with decent food will recover fully in time."

A knock at the door interrupted the discussion and the figure of Lieutenant Walker appeared.

"Sir?"

"Yes, Walker, what is it?"

"Sir, I know one of the slaves in the surgeon's care."

"So what are you telling me?" Robert was puzzled.

"Sir, Carlo was the house slave of the Bey himself. He only came to the benches after he had displeased the housekeeper, I saw him only briefly before I was rescued as he was transferred to another galley. The important thing is that he knows the layout of the city and the routines of the Bey's household."

"Bring him here and we can create a map of the city."

"I'm sorry, sir, he is in the charge of the surgeon and is currently under treatment."

"Doctor, can this man Carlo be brought here?"

"No sir, at present he is exhausted, to speak with him I am afraid we must go to him; and even then he must not be tired too much as he is still in danger "

There was an assortment of skills among the freed slaves, though the majority were fighting men of one sort or another. Their origins were from several European countries, other North African areas, Nubia and Scandinavia, Greece and Venice. They were able to converse in a lingua franca, a local argot of the Mediterranean. Lieutenant Walker's past history as a slave meant he was able to converse with the freed slaves in the tongue he had learned whilst he had been on the benches himself.

All of the 180 men now added to the forces at Robert's disposal seemed eager to exact their revenge on their former captors.

A plan began to form in Robert's mind.

***

The darkness was profound and the party below the walls of the outer fort crept quietly round to the lower embrasures, the small noises of their passage covered by the sounds of the sea on the beach below.

Robert led the assault party, preceded by Peter Morse, who slithered over the wall which was crumbling and broken at this point. Robert waited and watched Morse rise up behind the figure of the sentry who was gazing across at the lights of the city around the harbour. The sentry died without a murmur; and the raiding group moved in after Robert, through the embrasure and into the fort.

The previous seven days had been taken up with planning the raid on the Pirate haven at Bone; Carlo the former slave had been invaluable and, having recovered from his exhaustion, was with the raiding party to ensure they did not get lost in the maze of streets surrounding the Palace of the Bey.

Two fishermen taken offshore had been able to confirm that the Bey was absent at the moment; discipline at the fort and among the other military in the city was slack.

Morse gestured to Robert, and the party swiftly followed into the central square of the fort. The second half of the party scattered as arranged to deal with the other lookouts. The whole operation was conducted in silence.

The garrison was housed in the rooms built into the walls in the courtyard below the gun platforms. The marines came forward to deal with the sleeping men, who made little resistance.

The few that tried were swiftly despatched, the others were crammed into a single barrack room and held there under guard.

The guns of the fort were loaded and where possible swung round to cover the city and palace.

Leaving Abbott in command, Robert raised the signal to the frigate to enter the harbour. With the tide such as it was making, plus the light wind on her quarter, she crept into the Bay.

Dropping anchor she swung until her broadside was opposed to the Bey's palace and its surrounding buildings.

The fort at the far side of the bay was out of range of the frigate, but as far as they knew it was out of use. The city was lit up with lights, mostly flickering firelight, The palace was outlined by the watch fires of the guards stationed around the building.

The shore party made their way to the slave quarters situated beside the quay. The watchman seated beside the big locked doors was sound asleep and fell unconscious from the offhand crack with the butt of a musket.

Walker led his group into the building, the guards, mostly only half awake were killed where they lay. The released galley slaves were not disposed to be merciful. The men scattered through the building releasing the captives and herding them into the central quadrangle.

Chapter nine

Walker himself, with the assistance of the bo'sun, released the women captives, keeping them grouped in what was the guard's common room. Among the released slaves were several European women, three of whom were English, recently captured from a merchantman carrying them from Livorno in Italy, fleeing homeward from the threat of an invading French Army.

The English were all of the same group, Lady Elizabeth Merrick, Countess of Newbury, her maid Flora, and her companion Mrs. Harper. The others were Spanish and Italian, captured from passing ships over the last few weeks. All had been detained ostensibly to be ransomed by the Bey. Howeverm Walker was of the opinion that they were more likely to end up in the Bey's Harem

From their comments it seemed they had been captured after the departure of the Bey who had now been away for several weeks, visiting the desert areas of his domain, accompanied by the members of his personal guard. The 150 strong party had been reported to be returning in two days' time. The separate detention of the English party was to preserve them from the unwanted attention of the other prisoners to ensure they are not spoiled in any way before the Bey has a chance to see them. In view of the blond beauty of the Countess, Robert doubted that the Lady would have progressed beyond the harem.

The Palace of the Bey was swiftly surrounded and the watchmen gathered up and lodged in the slave quarters with the other prisoners.

The third landing party under the command of Lieutenant Ogilvie, after a forced march from the town, established that the fort was indeed deserted and falling into ruin. It had been out of use for some time apparently, the guns standing in the embrasures were old and rusty, and the touch holes stopped with nails. He reported to Robert at the palace delivering seven more released slaves and nine new prisoners.

Walker came to report the finding of the treasury. "I've placed the place under lock and key and posted guards, sir," he reported. "There is a large amount of specie, both gold and silver. I've brought this chest to you, sir. It seems to be the container for some other valuables. There is an inscription I cannot read."

Two men lowered the chest to the floor in front of their captain.

At first glance it seemed quite ordinary, the inscription was Chinese and though Robert could identify the script he could not translate it. He guessed what its content would be and indicated to Walker to open it.

The gasp of disbelief from Walker brought a smile to his face. "The Admiral will be pleased with this!"

"As will the men," Walker commented, looking at the mass of jewels of all shapes, sizes and colour. "Place them in the strongbox in my cabin, and load the gold and silver. I'll have the ship rigged to look as if she has been captured. We will ambush the Bey and his men when they approach the palace."

***

The returning column wound its way through the city gates, the men unsuspecting and looking forward to enjoying the delights of the city after eating dust for the past few weeks. As soon as the last file passed through the gate, the trap was sprung. Robert's men rose all around the party, muskets up, locks cocked. Some few resisted and they were swiftly despatched. The majority surrendered, giving up their arms and allowing themselves to be taken and locked in the, now crowded slave quarters.

The Bey was conveyed to the palace where he was accommodated in the dungeon beneath the floor.

The box of monies carried back by the expedition to the desert stood unopened before the empty throne. When Robert received the Princess, sister of the Bey, he listened carefully to her application to assume the rule of the port of Bone.

He knew he had no chance of holding the port, so in this event, he granted her application and agreed to leave the Princess in charge.

The captured galleys were hauled up on the beach and burned. The extra men would be accommodated in the small fleet of xebec's normally trading along the coast, but currently lying alongside the jetties in front of the city. Having warned the Princess that he would be returning soon, *HMS Roister* set sail once more for Gibraltar, to report.

***

Robert wiped the sweat from his brow and cursed quietly when a drop fell on the page before him. He was finishing his personal comments on the final draft of the report on the incidents of the last four week cruise, and the action at Bone. He sipped water from the glass in front of him and returned to his labours.

HMS Roister was moored out in the bay beneath the loom of Gibraltar, and the sun had just cleared the rock. The full rays were now concentrated on the stern of the ship and the relief of the Rock's shadow was now denied him.

The report was delivered personally to the Admiral in the great cabin of the flagship. Robert stood before the desk studying his newly arrived commander. Rear-Admiral Lord Broughan-Midgham was a big man with a healthy farmer's open face, and as he sat reading Robert's report, the sweat ran freely down his plump cheeks.

"Damn it's hot!" He ran his finger round his neck loosening his stock, then "Right young Graham, I've read the words. Now tell me what you really think is happening." He fixed Robert with a steely stare, "Sit down man. Wallace, get some wine for the captain," this aside, to his servant waiting by the open door.

Robert sat as ordered, "Well, sir, I believe that we can control Bone, at least by allowing the Bey to carry on ruling the port but under our eye. By placing garrisons in the forts the city, palace and harbour would be under our control. The local people look to the Bey as their ruler and in my opinion he would be quite happy to resume his position under British rule, provided we do not prevent the people following their Muslim beliefs."

Robert sat back.

Broughan studied the young man seated across the desk, then "What of the Princess, the Bey's sister?"

"I am sure she would be much happier with her brother back in charge, sir. In the Muslim world women carry little authority on their own. I did arrange matters on a purely temporary basis."

"Very well, you will reinstate the Bey under our supervision as you have suggested, we probably have some sort of civilian who can act as the Bey's conscience, a High Commissioner or some such. I will send a company of infantry and a company of artillery to hold the forts. I'll have the orders sent over to you and arrange for a departure within the week." He turned to the austere looking figure of his flag captain. "See to it, Merrick, will you?"

At that he turned once more to Robert. "Right, Captain. You may prepare for this task and for an onward voyage to Sicily, with despatches for Sir William Hamilton, Ambassador to the King of Naples who is currently visiting Palermo. Off you go."

Thus dismissed Robert rose and returned to his ship and the privacy of his own cabin.

With his coat removed and his shirt open, Robert stood by the open windows watching the swooping sea birds diving on the scraps floating on the surface of the water. A light breeze gave some relief from the heat. He thought about Captain Merrick, husband of the lovely Elizabeth. At the thought of her, he flushed and recalled the sight of that beautiful body rising from the scented waters of the bath in the palace of the Bey, of the intensity of their lovemaking in the bedchamber cooled by the sea breeze through the open windows.

She made comment at his hesitation at the outset of their liaison; then explained her attitude to his suggestion that the outcome could be an embarrassing pregnancy. "Edward needs and requires an heir, he is an anxious and poor lover and it appears he cannot provide one, I must therefore make my own arrangements, however discreetly."

She made it quite clear that she would not be tied in any way as she had no intention of leaving her husband, of whom she was quite fond. At the same time she did find him Robert, a pleasant companion and a pleasing bed mate, whom she would readily welcome if circumstances allowed.

As Robert uneasily conceded afterwards, it was after all a gentlemanly thing to do, having done and said all.

When the *HMS Roister* sailed in convoy with seven merchantmen en route to Sicily; there was an additional sloop of war *HMS Jaipur* swiftly becoming known affectionately as the *Jampot*, Commander John Keith, under Roberts command.

The transfer of the garrison and the installation of the Bey went as anticipated without hitch, and Mara, the Princess, sister of the Bey, was most grateful for the relief from the complexities involved in the rule of the North African Territory. To Roberts's embarrassment she seemed to look to him for counsel, and it was with some relief he found that his First Lieutenant Billy Beaumont was only too pleased to take over the mantle of confident to the princess.

The remainder of the voyage to Sicily went without incident, though the ships found uncomfortable sailing with the onset of the Sirocco. The wind carried the sand from the desert and deposited it on every open area, and pushed dust throughout the interior of the passing ships.

Sir William Hamilton was a kind and interesting man; over dinner he discussed his archaeological findings in the historic area around Naples and here in Sicily. The society in Palermo was provincial but well suited to the nature of the area which was bucolic rather than cosmopolitan, and the easy manner of Sir William Hamilton was well in tune with the tenor of the place. Significantly his comments on the progress of the French incursion into Italy were prophetic.

By the time *HMS Roister* set out once more to return to Gibraltar both Robert and crew had happy memories of the warm and friendly welcome of the people of Palermo.

It was with some trepidation that Billy Beaumont approached his captain on a delicate subject.

The visit of *HMS Roister* to Bone on the return journey to Gibraltar had revealed that the relationship between the Princess and Billy Beaumont had resulted in an important development.

Despite their best efforts the Princess had become pregnant. This information had not as yet been conveyed to the Bey, were it to become known the Princess would by now have been put to death under the laws of Islam.

It was necessary to arrange passage for the Princess to a western port, beyond the reach of retribution; the matter was even further complicated by the willingness of Billy Beaumont to marry the Princess, by no means a simple matter in view of his position in society and the religious differences involved.

Having established that the Princess was quite happy to become Baroness Brimpton, Robert arranged passage on one of the merchantmen in the convoy, and their subsequent marriage in Gibraltar, where the legalities were arranged. At Robert's insistence Billy wrote a letter to Barbara to break the news to the family, he included the letter with one of his own.

Elizabeth Merrick, now obviously pregnant with her husband's child, was extremely helpful in arranging matters. Captain Merrick's manner had become much more relaxed with the expectation of an heir, and was arranging for his wife to return to England to have her baby at the family home and this gave her the opportunity to take the new Baroness Brimpton with her as company. It was thus arranged.

The work of a frigate in the Royal Navy was varied and the *Roister* was no exception to this rule. She was, according to orders, despatched to Odessa in company of the flagship, the 80 gun ship of the line *HMS Persephone*. At fifteen years old, the flagship had seen better days. Though she was still seaworthy, she could not be considered fast, thus both *Roister* and *Jaipur* assigned to accompany the *Persephone*, spent much of their time tacking to keep company with the ponderous Line of Battle ship.

The first sign of trouble came with the appearance of the Turkish ships. Though there was no official conflict between the Ottoman Empire and Britain, the tensions between the two fleets had always existed just beneath the surface. On this occasion the Turkish admiral decided he was senior to the British admiral, the salutes therefore became confused and insult was taken and Turkish Admiral was forced to retire with damage to his rigging, though thankfully without casualties.

This was not a good beginning to the expedition since the passage of the Bosporus would need to be taken once more on the return journey.

The Diplomatic mission to Odessa had been the result of the actions of the French States General in starting the revolution in France. The Kingdoms of Europe were all nervous that the seeds of revolution would spread so it was purely a move to reassure the Russians that the British were standing firm.

The whole expedition was a wasted effort as the Grand Duke despatched to Odessa by the Tsar failed to appear as agreed. Officially it was because he had been held back by bandit activity; privately it was because he was enjoying a quiet sojourn with his new mistress in his palace in Kiev, his wife being safe in St Petersburg at the time.

For whatever reason, the promised meeting did not take place and it was an irritated Admiral who was faced once more with the uncooperative Turks at the Bosporus. The appearance of the customs launch in the path of the flagship causing it to heave-to did nothing to ease the situation.

The arrival of three ships flying the flag of Naples was fortuitous and possibly prevented an incident of more serious proportions.

In *HMS Roister* the atmosphere was generally good-natured, the crew was now at full strength with the addition of the volunteers from the captured galleys, and the officers and men known to each other, and more importantly having served under fire, willing to depend on each other. Robert encouraged initiative and he was pleased to see the way men stood out in the situations they encountered.

They were at the extreme end of their covering beat when sail was sighted. When several more hove into sight it became apparent that at least part of the French fleet was out.

Robert signalled to Commander Keith in *HMS Jaipur* that the enemy were in sight, at least three of the line and possibly three frigates. The flag, in company with the Naples ships, signalled for *HMS Roister* to shadow and report. *Jaipur* was detached to assist.

It was late morning when the sound of the guns was heard. *Jaipur* reported the guns from the direction of *Persephone*, Robert immediately ordered the *Jaipur* to investigate. The French were apparently heading for Egypt. Having paced the deck for a good few minutes he made up his mind and gave the order. "Mr. Beaufort, bring her about and crack on all she'll carry, course for the flagship!"

"Aye Aye, Sir, Course for the flag. All hands to the braces, stand by to come about! Helm's a lee, sir" the master cried.

The men hauled in the sheets as the ship's head swung and the bow came round to retrace the course they had been following.

With the wind now on the quarter the ship flew, more sails appeared as the studding sails unfurled and the skysails bellied out to add their weight to the task, "Twelve knots by the log, sir," the master called. Robert stood by the port rail, ignoring the spray that soaked the deck around him. The deck trembled with the pressure of the mass of sail aloft, as the ship flew as she had never before, almost planing over the blue water.

Ahead *Jaipur* was also flying with all sail set including the spanker bending under the strain.

Still the cannon crashed ahead of the two ships. Topsails came in sight, three sets all ships of the line, as they watched the lookout called "It's the *Percyphone* and two Frenchmen." Then, "One of the Frenchies has lost her topmast!" The men on deck cheered.

HMS Persephone was laying shrouded in the smoke of her guns, the broadside from her starboard battery roared out, followed by the crash of the impact of the cannonballs on the French seventy four lying on her beam.

The reply came but the French guns were not all fired together and they lacked something of the timbre of the British guns. Her topmast was hanging across the stays of the main which was swaying as Robert watched. "She is going to fall," the voice of the master rang out as the mainmast of the French Man-o-war toppled slowly, carrying a raffle of sail and spars along with it. The portside guns of *Persephone* were still busy with the second French ship that was creeping closer, coming alongside the British ship. Obviously the French captain was attempting to board.

The guns of both *Roister* and *Jaipur* were already run out and as they neared the creeping French ship they roared out in reply to the French bow guns. The broadside from the *Roister* caused the bulwarks of the French ship to splinter, shattering into a lethal swathe of wood shards, slashing into the men crowding the fore deck of the ship. Reloading with canister, the next shots caused mayhem among the assembled boarders.

The two battleships came together and grappling irons flew from the Frenchman to the embattled British ship.

"Stand by to board!" Roberts cry caused the assembled men on the deck of *Roister* to rush to the deck lockers where the bo'sun issued cutlasses and pikes. The men were ready and as the French boarding party crowded onto the deck of *Persephone*; the grapples went over from *Roister* and led by their captain, they went into action. The *Jaipur* men joined the conflict from the stern of the French ship, her men clambering over the stern rails to tackle the quarterdeck party and taking over the wheel.

The action was bloody and Robert found himself hacking with his hanger at a small man with a big pike who was attempting to spear him. The slashing blade cut through the pike shaft causing the point to drop to the deck. His opponent stabbed at him with the broken end only to drop suddenly to the deck with blood pouring from a head wound delivered by the cutlass of Dawson.

Slipping and sliding on the blood-splattered deck, the combined force of Persephones and Roisters between them left the French boarders nowhere to go and the boarding stalled and then became a desperate rearguard action as they tried to get back on board their own ship. The fight ended in surrender by the survivors. Back on the French ship, the *Jaipur* party were just managing to hold the quarterdeck, but were hard pressed. The attack by Robert's men returning to the Frenchman took the pressure off and the hand to hand struggle was swiftly concluded with the surrender of the surviving French.

The other French Man-o-war was a sorry sight, the guns of the flagship had silenced those of the Frenchman and her flag had been lowered in defeat. As the smoke cleared it was possible to see the damage caused by the disciplined broadsides of her British opponent, the shattered holes in her side, the masts lying still cluttering the deck and hampering her guns, and the red streams of blood running down from her scuppers.

In the aftermath of the skirmish, as the admiral who had regained his good humour insisted on calling it, it had taken three days to clear up and had resulted in the flagship and the two prizes *La Provence* 74 guns, and the *Oberon* 80 guns, in company with *HMS Jaipur*, returning to Gibraltar for repair whilst *HMS Roister* continued in her search for the other French ships. The Admiral had explained that the Naples ships had parted company off Limnos, and as they disappeared behind the island, the French ships had appeared from the direction of Ayios Eviratios, almost as if they had been waiting in ambush. One of the lookouts swore he had seen the Turkish customs launch returning to the Dardanelles as they cleared IMros Island, but they could not be certain.

The hammering by the carpenter could still be heard two days later as he worked to complete the repairs from the damage that occurred during the short action.

The breeze was fresh and windsails rigged, diverting the cooling air throughout the frigate. Robert studied the charts puzzling over the whereabouts of the missing French ships. On their last observed course they appeared to be making for Egypt.

They did not locate the missing French ships, eventually guessing they had turned around and returned westward back to Toulon or even slipped by night through the Strait of Gibraltar out into the Atlantic.

Chapter Ten

HMS Roister herself was turned to the west, and following the North African coastline made her way to Bone, where she called for a visit and fresh water, before cruising onward to Gibraltar to make her report. At a meeting with the Bey, Robert was able to reassure him that his sister was properly wed to her English nobleman, and was currently with child back in England in her husband's palace. The result of this news was the gift of a jewelled and gold-hilted sword of Damascus steel to be presented as a gift to the young Prince when he was born. The Bey had no problem deciding that the baby would be a boy thus would require a suitable sword.

The voyage was interesting since it gave opportunity to give the men practice at musketry.

When fitting out in Plymouth the purser had slipped and fallen breaking his leg. Since they could not manage without a purser another was appointed.

Mr. Abel Jackson was an American-born loyalist whose family had moved up to Canada after the revolution. He had lost his family to Indians, and without ties came to England seeking a new life. Now in his thirties, he had worked in the dockyards on the supply side for three years where discreet investments had built up his finances to the point where he could bid for a purser's position. The chance of the post on *Roister* arose at just the right time.

Jackson had provisioned the ship with an eye to detail that caused dismay among the victuallers of the shipyard.

The water casks were the newest to be found, and every cask of beef came from recent stores. The victuallers bewailed the fact that the American not only knew the system, he used it against them, ensuring that the provisions loaded were in reasonable condition, with no ancient casks containing meat that had turned to wood, charged at full price of course. Jackson's philosophy worked on the principle of fair profit for fair quality.

Because the captain still held fencing sessions on deck whenever the weather permitted, the officers of the ship had all attained a proficiency in fencing well above average. The encouragement for the rest of the crew to develop their skills had resulted in permission for wrestling and some other activities being given.

It was however with some surprise that Abel Jackson, having established a good reputation within the ship then created a legend of another sort. He had appeared on deck several times to watch the fencing; he had actually taken part on a few occasions, showing a good level of skill in the art; but it was with a gun shooting at targets he really made an impression. He had his own weapon and ammunition and he shot at targets, mainly boxes and kegs thrown over the side. He was a crack shot. Lieutenant Beaufort was on watch on the first of these occasions, noticed and commented to the Captain on Jackson's skill and accuracy with the weapon. A discussion between Robert and Mr. Jackson resulted in the regular appearance of several crew members and the entire contingent of marines on deck for practice with the ship's muskets and, on occasion, with the weapon belonging to Mr. Jackson. His piece was a rifle which was capable of extreme accuracy when fired by a person trained to use it.

Fourteen men chosen by Mr. Jackson were selected for training with the rifle. Mr. Jackson was in turn charged with obtaining suitable extra weapons for the purpose. The guns would be purchased at Robert's expense when and how he could. Four German hunting rifles had been obtained in Odessa, luckily they were all of the same calibre and the ammunition moulds were available when the guns were purchased. Rifles were not popular in the army due to the time taken to reload and basically the use of firearms was generally in volley firing, where the accuracy of the gun was not so critical. Later in the French conflict it became a weapon of choice for the skirmishers of both armies.

Because of his experience of survival in the backwoods of America, Jackson had developed a drill for the reloading of his rifle that he taught to his trainees. Requiring at least three shots per minute from them and later four; a further six rifles were obtained from Bone when they called. The Arabs were happy with their own guns and treated the European weapons with disdain.

Among these new weapons were two Ferguson Rifles, breech loaders, invented by Major Ferguson and used in the American war by his men until his death. His successor had them stored since he personally favoured the muskets in use by the rest of the army. They had only recently been recovered and were now causing interest once more, though newer models had been created and were more favoured. The selected men now armed with rifles were four seamen and ten marines, and the competition between then was fierce, albeit friendly. All were now expected to hit targets up to 500 yards range, and considering the movement of the sea and the firing platform that was no mean feat.

As a sporting exercise the officers generally regarded the whole business as a diversion, small wagers being made on a favoured marksman. The remaining marines were trained to reload using the same system and all achieved the target of three rounds per minute and several could reach the four rounds standard.

Their captain however had a much more serious reason for the exercise. In action, the task of the marines in part is to shoot at the officers on the quarterdeck of the opposing ship. Whilst it could be effective using muskets, normally it was more of a matter of luck to hit or to miss.

With real marksmen in the tops, the odds changed and the consequent confusion caused by the loss of the officers during an action could bring an end to a battle with less collateral damage to men and ships.

In addition Robert had long felt that owning a gun was for the purpose of killing. Inept use of a gun was a waste of time and money, so by training his group of riflemen to shoot quickly and accurately he justified the ownership of the rifles.

As for the training of the marine detachment, since he had the expert available why not use him?

Abel Jackson had demonstrated his worth with the rifle and had passed some of his skill along to his trainee's, earning the respect of Captain Ullyet, who, in command of the marines, had been sceptical at first, accepted that their effectiveness had been enhanced by the training they received. The four marksmen armed with rifles gave the detachment flexibility not normally encountered in the Marine Infantry. *

The Marine infantry regularly carried on board ship at this time were not the formally recognised sea soldiers of present day. In many cases their duties on shipboard were menial and although they were expected to snipe at the enemy, their duties were largely protecting the Officers from the possibility of mutiny, and to impose discipline. In some cases they proved their worth when enterprising Captains used them in landing parties and to support the crew in boarding parties. As their worth became recognised their part in the ships company was formalised and the training and operation of the marines resulted in the essential role they now fulfil, and the honours gained reflect that. The flexibility of operation displayed by the modern service has been anticipated here, but why not? It had to begin somewhere?

Another aspect of the adaptability of their Captain was demonstrated by his acquisition of the field gun. Normally found bouncing along behind a team of horses, the six pounder and a supply of ammunition had been 'found' on the Hard at Gibraltar after a battalion of Horse Artillery had been embarked for England.

During the loading of the Artillery the gun had been mislaid due to the confusion of the assistant detailed to check the guns onto the merchantman. The completion of the loading was not until after dark, and the loadmaster had been flustered, causing him to miscount the number of guns and caissons taken on board. The ball rounds had been found when *HMS Roister* was rearming after the Bone expedition. The gunner had decided that there was no purpose having a six pounder gun without ammunition, the gun was therefore added to the inventory and ammunition acquired accordingly. When asked why his ship should have such a weapon, Robert would tap his nose and lower his eyelid in a wink, implying secret services, and leave it at that. To his surprise he found the system worked, suitably modified of course, even with senior officers.

From among the ex-Galley slaves a crew of gunners was recruited and trained by the master-gunner for whom the gun held no mysteries; the command of the gun, in deployment ashore was given to Captain Ullyet, who wisely kept his own counsel on the subject when in the company of Marine Officers in barracks.

Whenever a task was deemed worthy of a ship of the line in the navy, it seemed always to occur at a time when either none were available or suitable for the particular task. It would often require detached service, a most sought after situation, and despite the permanent shortage of frigates, the task would be handed to a frigate.

Frigate captains had acquired a reputation for dash and daring, often accomplishing tasks that they were ill equipped to perform. The history of the navy was enlivened by the exploits of such names as Pellew and Samaurez, thus it was decided that *HMS Roister* in company with the sloop *Jaipur* and a cargo brig *Dove* in which a battalion of the garrison troops had been embarked, would be given the task of recapturing the island of Djerba in the Bay of Gabes off the North African coast almost due south of Malta.

The island had become the base for a group of insurgents who had fomented an uprising against its ruler; the Emir of Djerba, who had been away, absent on the mainland at the time. It was not normally the responsibility of the British Government but the assistance of the French had been obtained by the rebels to keep control of the island. The Emir had no navy to oppose them; here apparently was where the third French ship of the line had hidden herself.

On the basis of mutual enemies making strange alliances, Captain Graham and his force had been detailed to recapture the island and hold it. If needed, a squadron of ships could be sent to deal with any French naval forces that the frigate and her consort could not themselves handle.

Though the island was joined to the mainland by a causeway of sand, the presence of the French ship prevented the Emir's forces from crossing. The task of the British force was to occupy the island and having subdued the rebels, construct a fort at the causeway to command the island end of the causeway, in conjunction with the mainland fort at the other end.

A major problem for Robert's assault parties was the lack of dock facilities. His men would need to land on one of the beaches, preferably one with easy access to the interior. It would give them a chance to manhandle the guns to the south-western end of the island where the main settlement stood, around the island end of the causeway.

In the Captain's cabin all the stern windows were open and the skylights propped ajar to allow whatever breeze there was to cool the group standing round the table. After examining the charts of the island Robert turned to Lieutenant Martin Walker, "You surveyed this coast, what can you tell us about this island?"

Walker scratched his chin. "Not too much, sir. I'm afraid the islanders were not pleased to see us at the time. Most of them being involved in piracy and smuggling. However we did sound the area on the northern side of the island fairly well." His finger indicated a beach area beside an unnamed headland.

"Here, Sir, is a sand beach with steep-to soundings; up to a fathom's depth to close on ten feet from the water's edge; ideal for boat landing. There was evidence that the beach has been used before and where the hill comes down at the eastern end there were several caves that had ashes of old fires, though that was some years ago now?"

"Very good. For want of a better choice, Ogilvie. you will take Mr. Abbot and the jolly boat to reconnoitre/ Captain Ullyet, four marksmen I think to accompany the party with their rifles, and they will stay if the place is suitable under the command of Mr. Abbot, whilst you return to report. If all is in order, I will send our artillery," he smiled as a chuckle went round the group at the mention of their 'found' six pounder gun. Initially it is easier to manoeuvre than the guns for the fort. He turned to the Colonel Sir Michael Baxter in command of the infantry battalion. "We will disembark your men at that point and they can prepare for the overland march to the causeway."

The Colonel nodded. "I think the wheeled carts would be better used for the transport of the guns, rather than for our baggage. If we find other carts on our way we can send them back to collect our gear; this would save delay in reaching our objective." He looked keenly at Robert. "You agree? This is a small island and news will travel fast."

Robert was impressed, the Colonel looked like a stuffed shirt; and there had been little contact on the voyage here, but obviously he was no fool. "Thank you, Colonel. I had not thought of that. I will have skirmishers out to collect whatever transport we can find as soon as possible."

He turned to the group as a whole. "Two men are already searching for information, and a contact with a local informant will be made tonight. If all is in order we will proceed as planned.

"Thank you gentlemen we will assemble again tomorrow evening when we are in position off shore of the beach."

As the party dispersed he detained Commander John Keith, the captain of *Jaipur*.

"All arranged for tonight, John?"

"Yes sir, I'll collect our agent at the rendezvous and bring him here; I will be prepared to return him before first light if necessary."

"Good, well! You'll stay for dinner I trust; the Colonel will be joining us along with Captain Reece of the *Dove*."

"Thank you, sir, I would be delighted. I will just go and confirm my orders to my people if I may?" With that he left Robert to return to his own ship.

As the young commander left Robert reflected, he had been lucky to have the support of Keith; he recalled the interview with the commander's uncle Admiral Keith, commanding the blockading squadron off Brest. His enthusiastic report to the Admiralty had helped his career; of this he had no doubt. The nephew was a real chip off the old block, ideally suited to small ship operations.

The *Jaipur's* longboat came alongside *Roister* at ten that night and the robed figure of the contact climbed agilely aboard, going immediately to the great cabin where the marine on duty knocked and opened the door when ordered.

The shadowy figure entered and the door closed firmly. The cabin was stuffy as the ship was darkened with curtains drawn. The informer removed the Burnous, revealing the trim figure of Lotte Mansfield. "Good evening, Captain Graham; we're well met, I think."

She was dressed in baggy silken trousers and a diaphanous top that did little to hide the shapely body beneath. There was no chance of mistaking her for a man in these clothes, thought Robert, who cleared his throat and bent over the outstretched hand and brushed it with his lips.

All business, she produced a map of the island and began to point out features with quick succinct comment.

Robert found that things were much as he had already gathered from his own spies. When she had finished her briefing she sat back looking weary.

"Can you stay?" Robert asked.

"I must I fear," she was hesitant, "the French were becoming suspicious, and though the agent in place was not sure, I am convinced he was planning on removing me anyway. I managed to slip away tonight leaving all my clothing behind, so I have nothing to wear but the clothes I stand up in. Until, that is, you successfully recapture the island of course." She looked at Robert and smiled. "We had little chance to become acquainted before; perhaps we will have more time on this occasion?"

The landing parties managed the initial stages with no opposition and little difficulty. The disembarkation of the Infantry went smoothly though the horses of the officers and the mules to pull the wagons took longer than anticipated.

The skirmishers and their field gun under the command of Captain Ullyet had disappeared completely before the Infantry and the train of guns were ready to move.

Lotte, now dressed in midshipman's uniform courtesy of Mr. Abbot, rode off alongside the Colonel at the head of the column. Robert had joined up with the advance party and was currently lying face down on the rim of the ridge to the north of the town situated at the end of the causeway. Through his telescope it was possible to make out the movements of the detachment of French soldiers landed from the 60 gun ship lying offshore.

There was no quay evident where a ship could tie up despite the deep water almost up to the tide line. This was obviously one of the ways that the control of the island was maintained from the mainland; unfortunately this was a disadvantage when the invasion came from the sea as the causeway was easily dominated by an armed ship.

Below the watchers the soldiers were directing the location of several guns that had been unloaded from the warship lying offshore. Parties of labourers were manhandling the guns on carriages in to position to command the Causeway approaches.

"Will our popgun reach them?" Robert asked. The master gunner who had placed himself in command of the gun team answered. "Not from here, sir; we'll need to get down to the edge of the houses." He pointed to a spot two hundred yards down the hill before them. "From there I can command their entire battery."

Robert studied the ground. "We'll need a cart then, or wait until nightfall, though I had rather hoped we could be in position by then."

The gunner looked at him pityingly. "Now don't you worry about it, sir; we'll managed in plenty of time." He turned to his gun crew, who were all dressed in nondescript garb. "Sling the gun, boys, and prepare the carriage."

The crew lifted the barrel of the six pounder field piece from its mount and laid it carefully on the ground. The wheeled carriage was dismantled and strapped on to the caisson carriage. Two broad planks were removed from beneath the caisson and set either side of the box. A canvas was lashed on top to cover the load and a purpose made crossbar was attached to the towing link.

At this point Captain Ullyet appeared. "Marksmen have all been placed, Sir". He reported. Four of his marines removed their Red coats and stowed them under the canvas with their rifles and took their places around the caisson/cart.

Taking hold of the slings round the gun barrel, the gunners with a collective grunt lifted it between them and set off down the road, the caisson following.

They appeared to Robert to look like any other bunch of workmen doing their work. He watched their progress holding his breath until he sighed with relief as they gained the concealment of the building selected. Nobody had appeared to notice. At a range of less than 400 yards the canister round would be lethal to the gunners at their positions without damaging the guns themselves. At least that was the theory, Robert thought.

The Colonel appeared beside Robert in his position overlooking the town. He produced his own telescope and studied the situation. Despite getting his immaculate uniform dirtied he seemed quite at ease lying on the ground and his comments made it quite clear that he would not be content to take reports from others when it was possible to see for himself. "Besides" he remarked "I am the only infantryman present who has been in action before, saving your presence, Captain Ullyet." He acknowledged with a nod to the captain.

Roberts respect for the colonel grew at this evidence of practical soldiering.

"May I ask where you have served, Colonel?"

"In the Americas, against the Huron Indians and the French and Spanish. The Indians and Pathans and their French allies in India," he continued. "I see no real problem here; as soon as our artillery opens fire on the gunners, my men will attack and take over the position, your gun crews will then take over the enemy guns and open fire on the ship, which by this time will be engaged with *Roister* and hopefully trying to make sail to defend herself."

With a final scrabble, Lotte arrived and joined the two men. "Mr. Abbot will not be pleased with me!" She said ruefully noticing a tear in her sleeve. "So, gentlemen, are we nearly ready? I wish to retrieve my wardrobe as soon as possible."

"All in good time, Madam! I will not allow my men to be hurried for the benefit of a box of frills and furbelows. You will have your chance when we are ready and not before!"

The no nonsense comment from the Colonel caused even the normally irrepressible Lotte to hold her tongue.

Robert smiled to himself, last night had been difficult. Lotte had decided that he should share his bed finally with her and he had needed the utmost tact to arrange for other matters to occupy his time, making the proposed coupling impossible, but it had been a near thing. It was not that she was unattractive to him but having succumbed to the amours of Lady Herrick, he already felt guilty enough. Facing Barbara would be difficult as it was, he did not think his conscience could stand the extra burden of guilt.

Leaving the Colonel in command, Robert took the Colonel's horse and rode back to the landing place, where

Ordering Lieutenant Beaufort to up anchor and make sail he collapsed into his chair and gratefully took the glass of wine proffered by his servant Meadows.

Chapter Eleven

Robert despatched Keith in the *Jaipur* round the western end of the island in search of the other French ship(s), still unsure of the number that had given them the slip several weeks before. They would rendezvous in three days' time at the new fort or offshore from the island in the event of complete disaster.

It was dusk when *HMS Roister* rounded the headland under full sail. The French battleship lay at anchor, tethered by moorings at bow and stern to allow her guns to command the causeway. He could make out her name, picked out in scrollwork on the stern, *Guerriere.*

Robert had depended on this when he made his plan of attack, knowing that he could fire upon the Frenchman with no chance of an immediate reply even if the French ship's guns were manned, an unlikely event at this place and time.

The signal for the land assault was his first broadside into the tethered French ship, and for the occasion he had called for the port guns to be double-shotted to increase the impact of this first stage of proceedings. As *Roister* came up to her bearing, the 14 twelve pounder guns with their double shot and the two 24 pound carronades, making her full broadside fired as one. The flash and roar followed by the billow of smoke echoed off the hills to be immediately followed by the puny sounding crack of the field gun firing its lethal shower of pistol balls among the gathered gun crews at the waterside battery. The lively scene by the water's edge turned immediately into a bloody hell of torn

139

and bleeding bodies screaming and crying for aid. The second round from the field gun left the battery without gun crews and the first wave of infantry accompanied by the assigned gunners swept down to the battery and commenced swinging the guns to point at the moored French Line of Battle ship.

On the *Guerriere* there was a scene of frantic activity but little action against the frigate standing offshore. *Roister* came about smartly and fired her second broadside into the stricken French ship, which had at last managed to cut her bow mooring line. The ship swung to her stern line the current bringing her in an arc towards the causeway. The stern line parted but too late and the ship buried her bow into the sand and stuck fast her bowsprit projecting halfway across the spit.

The force of her impact caused the main and foremast to lean forward, the sound of the breaking foremast a loud crack heard over a mile away.

The advancing infantry doubled down the causeway to the ship and began to board, meeting little resistance. The Flag fluttered down to the deck and the crew assembled in sullen silence.

Doctor Sweet from the frigate and the medical officer from the infantry set up a hospital on the beach to deal with the wounded that were mostly French.

The army of the Emir crossed the now open causeway, the column spitting into sections and searching the houses for the rebels who had dispersed and gone to ground. The Emir reclaimed his palace and at a reception that evening thanked Robert and the Colonel for their efforts in regaining his lands, and suggested that now the country was secure once more, there were no doubt many other matters for them to attend to. As the Colonel commented to Robert, a diplomatic hint that their presence was no longer needed.

The sight of the *Guerriere* afloat in the bay caused Robert great satisfaction, the French crew had been put to work digging around the bow of the stranded ship until the combined pull exerted by the bower anchors laid out astern with the help of the extra tug given by the towrope attached to the stern of *Roister* succeeded in hauling her offshore once more. The repairs were nearly complete, the two dismounted guns had been remounted and the foremast replaced, the bo'sun's crew crawling round the rigging even now replacing ropes where needed.

The sloop *HMS Jaipur* had done a complete circuit of the island seeking the other French ships without success. Meanwhile, proper embrasures had been built and the guns of the new fort ranged in and tested, the thin line of smoke indicated the location of the forge which doubled as the site of the furnace to heat cannon balls for anti-ship action. The French guns were remounted covering the causeway, allowing for additional cover for the approach from the south.

The regular thump of the ranging shots from the cannon went on throughout the day as the Master gunner trained the local gunners in their new jobs. Beside each gun, scratched into the stone of the embrasure were the ranges and elevations required, as each gun was proved.

Billy Beaufort groaned and held his head. "Damn all gunners and their stupid exercises!" He moaned, "My head is splitting!"

He received scant sympathy from the other officers assembled, as they stood awaiting the captain, currently meeting with the Emir in the great cabin. The first lieutenant had been entertained by the army officers at their temporary barracks in the main fort, a farewell feast to mark the departure of *Roister* with her prize, under the command of Lieutenant Beaufort, his prize crew made up of members from *Roister*, *Jaipur* and released prisoners from the French occupation of the island. These men, being mainly merchant seamen captured by the French during the dash through the Mediterranean Sea earlier in the year, were competent seamen and therefore a welcome addition to the strength of the little fleet. The non-seamen and women were carried on the Dove with the exception of Lotte Mansfield, now reunited with her luggage and respectably dressed once more.

There had been nearly two hundred men found toiling on the works being built by the French. They had been replaced by their former captors who, apart from their officers, were being held on the island.

As they sailed, Robert looked over his small fleet with some satisfaction. The *Guerriere* was a fine, newly-built vessel of 60 guns, she would be a formidable addition to the fleet. Whilst still a little short-handed, under the command of her temporary captain she should be able to make it to Gibraltar without trouble. *Roister* had a full crew. Though partly made up of released prisoners, they would soon settle in. *Jaipur's* Captain Keith with similar crew replacements was equally confident. The *Dove* completed the group, keeping up well with her escorts. Under full sail the little fleet was making good progress westward. Robert was pleased to see the gun ports of the prize opened once more for gun practice, and was not surprised when Lieutenant Walker, acting first lieutenant, approached for permission to exercise the guns. There was no sign of a reduction in the vigilance of the men despite the comparative ease of the last operation.

Robert was under no illusion, had the French not been taken completely by surprise there could have been a different end to the mini invasion, just completed.

***

The fleet lay at anchor in the bay, overshadowed by the great looming rock. The prize lay awaiting the decision of the prize court, sitting at present in Government House. There was little activity on the other two ships, *HMS Jaipur* sitting above its reflection creating hardly a ripple in the waters about her.

On *HMS Roister* Billy Beaufort yawned and stretched, he was restless, awaiting the decision of the Prize Court as were all the other officers and men of the expeditionary force. The original members of the crew had been returned to the ship after the transit east from Djerba Island. The little fleet had experienced an untroubled journey, much to the regret of the first lieutenant who had fancied the opportunity to take the *Guerriere* into action, "Now we wait, we seem to be always either sitting around or rushing about!" Walker, who had just come on deck in time to hear the comment, smiled

"You youngsters are too impatient by far, relax and enjoy the quiet times, there will be plenty to occupy ourselves with when the French come out!"

"It's all very well to say that, suppose the war ends soon, there will be no chances for promotion in peace time and I'm not getting any younger." Beaufort strolled along the quarterdeck to the stern rail. Looking down into the blue water he could see the fish swimming just below the surface. He stood upright and shook his head. "Sorry,

Alastair, I'm missing my lady and it's making me moody I just wish we were busy doing something rather than sitting around, it's easier to bear the separation."

A shadow passed over the face of his friend, and he was immediately contrite. "I'm sorry, Alastair, that was thoughtless of me; I should have remembered your family. Please forgive me?"

Walker shrugged, "I now realise that in some ways I am very lucky, my son is well looked after by a father who is always at home rather than roaming the world. He and my ex-wife are not wanting anything and let's be honest, they hardly knew me, I was at sea when my son was born. I saw him when he was two, then back to sea for one year. I then saw him for one month, we had just got to know each other when I was off again this time for two years in the Mediterranean where I was captured and enslaved for five years. When I came home, I was a stranger; my home belonged to another man as did my wife and son. I shall now admit that I could have been diverted by Miss Mansfield had she glanced in my direction, I suppose that is a sign of something. Yes, I think I have decided that the past must remain in the past, and look to the future. After all, if their lordships decide in our favour I could be comparatively wealthy. Perhaps I will be able to afford new uniforms?" He looked ruefully at the frayed cuffs of his jacket and the tarnished braid of the trim.

The two men were interrupted by the call of the lookout. "Deck boat in sight, It's the Captain, Sir."

"Bo'sun pass the word, man the side for the Captain!" The order was given quietly and, observed Walker, confidently. The crew moved about smoothly and there was no wasted time rushing to and fro, the men knew what to do without shouted orders. He suddenly realised that Billy

Beaufort, for all his casual light-hearted manner, had like the rest of the ship's company become part of a team. The men, well led, worked together. There was no carping and no use of the lash. He had not even noticed that the lash had not been used, not since he had boarded this ship in Plymouth Dockyard. Looking over the assembled side party waiting the captain he realised what the difference was, the men were willing and proud, of their ship and of their Captain in a Navy where most of the crews were pressed men and ex-felons. He was suddenly aware that he also was proud, of the ship the ship's company and of his Captain. He straightened as the pipes rang out shrilly, welcoming Captain Graham aboard. 'I'm a part of it he thought.'

In the stern cabin, Robert called his officers in to hear the orders. "First, I know you will be pleased to hear that the *Guerriere* will be bought into the service, the prize court decided today."

As the murmur of approval and congratulation died down he continued. "We are ordered home to England in company with the *Guerriere* for duties in home waters, whatever that means. It does mean that we will get the chance to see our families, and I know that will be mean a lot to some of us anyway." He joined in the chuckles that greeted this comment, as Lieutenant Beaufort blushed.

"The *Guerriere* will sail under the command of Captain Merrick. You may recall, gentlemen, that Lady Merrick, the Captain's wife, was one of the ladies recovered from the action at Bone last year.

"We will be sailing in two days time so there is much to do!" he stood and the group dispersed. He stopped the first lieutenant, "Billy." He said. "We will be sailing without our friends on *Jaipur*. I will be entertaining Captain

Keith tonight. How about the other officers, do you think the ward room is up to it?"

"Of course, sir, we will miss *Jampot* and her company. I'll be delighted to entertain them, tomorrow. And, if it's in order, would you care to attend as our guest?"

"Why thank you Billy, I would be honoured."

***

The fog was thinning slowly as the *Roister* made her way through the grey waters of the English Channel. On the portside could just be seen the outline of the nearest ship still in company the brig *Dove;* astern the two East Indiamen clung to the fringes of visibility, though the clearing fog allowed more of the surrounding area to be seen almost like the withdrawing of a curtain. The Lizard Point appeared to port as the group of ships opened Falmouth bay, several fishing boats came into view in the clearing weather.

"Our first view of England," Lieutenant Beaufort commented, raising his glass to scan the area, "Anything to report?" He called to the masthead lookout, as the lookout made his cry "Land ho, port beam!"

"Stay awake up there, or I'll find you something to occupy you!" Billy Beaufort was not pleased.

"Sorry, sir, I was watching the sail on the starboard bow, she's a wrong–un I reckon."

Beaufort swung his glass to locate the sail in question in time to see the ship, a racy looking schooner, turning back into the fog towards mid-channel once more. "What did you make of her?" Beaufort asked. "Here, Dawson, take my glass and get aloft, see what you can see."

As Dawson ran up the rigging, glass slung round his neck, the captain came on deck. "How's the lad managing?"

He indicated Dawson scrambling through the rigging.

"He's doing well. The others already here are struggling to keep up with him in navigation; and practical seamanship seems second nature to him. I think with the right backing he'll go far. Nice lad!"

"So what's all this fuss about?" Robert waved his hand towards the boy in the tops.

"Looks like one of Peter Tregarth's pals either late or early for a delivery." Billy explained about the schooner that had reversed its course back into the fog when they sighted *Roister* and her companions.

"Any sign of her?" He called aloft.

"Sorry, sir, she's out of sight, the fog is still thick to the south, there's no sign of her now!" Young Dawson slid down the backstay and returned the glass to Beaufort.

"Log the incident, Billy. Either the smugglers are getting slack or perhaps they have too many friends; whichever, I am not happy to see British seamen trading with our country's enemies."

***

HMS Roister lay alongside having her rigging renewed under the eagle eye of the master, Mr. Callow. Beside him stood the quartermaster Abel Jackson; the two had become good friends during the time they served on the ship. Both were anticipating a run ashore that evening.

Mr. Callow's wife Elizabeth was an excellent cook and her neighbour and good friend Judith would be joining them for the meal in the comfortable quarters behind the 'Half Moon' Inn, owned by the Callow family and run in

Sam's absence by Elizabeth. Judith helped in the Inn on the occasions when it became busy on market and feast days. She was the widow of an Excise man, shot by smugglers during a raid over the county border into Cornwall. Three officers died that night on the cliffs above St. Austell Bay.

Judith was a fresh-faced country lass of slender build, 27 years old, and she had liked the look of Abel Jackson from the moment she had first seen him in the inn. As for Abel, he was looking forward to furthering his acquaintance with the lady.

As he stood on deck beside his friend Sam Callow, his face broke into a smile that lightened his rather stern angular face. "Why, Sam, I must say I'm looking forward to Elizabeth's cooking tonight, she does have a way with that Stargazy Pie."

Sam looked sideways at his friend. "You're not fooling me, Abel Jackson; my Lizzie's pie is great I grant you, but 'tiz Judith that brought that smile to your face!"

"Well I do admit, she does stir up this old man's blood, but not to detract from Lizzie's pie. The both together are enough for any red-blooded man, you mark me!"

Mr. Callow turned, spotting something that did not please him. "Watch that sheet, you great lummox, you got it twisted through the sheave. Get it straightened out before I come up and box your ears!" This was to one of the workmen on the rigging who incidentally was twice the size of the diminutive Mr. Callow. "Aye aye sir," the big man grinned and straightened the rope as ordered, much to the amusement of Abel Jackson. He was made aware once more of the respect the dockyard workers had for his friend.

That night in the snug quarters behind the Inn the four friends enjoyed a convivial evening, and Abel Jackson made up his mind. However, before he could raise the subject, Elizabeth Callow—with a straight face—asked him when he would like to have the party.

"Party? What party?" Abel was puzzled.

"Why, your betrothal party, of course. Am I the only one here who knows then?" She asked innocently with a sweet smile.

Abel spluttered, Judith blushed and Sam roared with laughter and said. "She got you going there!"

"But I haven't asked her yet!" Abel said.

"Well, you better get on with it, you silly man. We can't all wait forever, you know!" Lizzie' could hold it in no more and she collapsed into the arms of Sam and the pair dissolved completely with laughter at the dumbfounded faces of their two friends.

Abel turned to Judith sitting next to him. "Will you?" he said hesitantly.

"Oh I suppose so, yes." She replied and flung her arms round his neck and kissed him soundly on the lips.

"Am I to understand that I am not the only member of the crew to be getting married while we are in England?" Abel heard the Captain behind him and turned hastily from checking stores being unloaded to enable the ship's hull to be fumigated.

"Why, yes sir," he stammered, blushing in his embarrassment. "I am proud to say that my proposal has been accepted. We are to be married two weeks hence on the Saturday, in the church down by the Hard. All are welcome."

"Why, thank you, Mr. Jackson, I will bring my fiancé Miss Beaufort if I may, and if you are here at the time I would welcome you and your lady to my own wedding, one month hence in the Church at Hartwell Hall. You shall receive an invitation from Miss Beaufort direct."

Robert made a note in his cabin and sent a note to Barbara to change the invitation to the wedding from Mr. Jackson and friend, to Mr. and Mrs. Jackson. In addition, he advised her of their invitation to attend at the church in Plymouth for the wedding of the Purser and his lady.

The preparation for the wedding was left to the efforts of the Countess and Barbara. Between them they recruited Squire Graham and the Marquis, both of whom were only too pleased to assist.

It was the efforts of Mrs. Callow of the Half Moon Inn, and Mrs. Wharton from the Manor that made the difference. The cook at Hartwell Hall was accomplished but for the local delicacies, the two ladies excelled themselves, leaving the trained chef at the Hall open mouthed in admiration. As Mrs. Callow told her husband, he had asked for, and received the recipe for her Stargazy Pie, for future feasts at the Hall.

The Chapel at Hartwell Hall was cleared and decorated for the occasion and bridesmaids from the local gentry invited and clothed. By the time Robert and Billy stood side by side before the altar, waiting for the appearance of Barbara and her father, it could be said that all that should be done had been done.

The entrance of Barbara on the arm of her father was dramatic and heart-stopping as far as Robert was concerned. She was stunning in a white dress of fine muslin, styled like that of her mother's when she married the Marquis. The bouquet of red roses made a splash of colour against the pale gown. The Marquis, in a blue coat with his star and decorations of his rank, looked proud as they strode down the aisle.

To Robert the rest of the ceremony passed in a moment and it seemed that they were exchanging the rings while he was still taking in the promises they had made. The crowd assembled outside the Chapel was huge. The couple were well liked in the area and many of the guests came from London and even further afield.

The couple led the ball that lasted until the following morning, though by then the happy couple were well on their way to the London house.

Chapter Twelve

Baron and Baroness Brimpton were giving a reception at their Berkshire home when Robert's new orders arrived. Robert and his new wife Barbara, as guests of honour, were dressing for dinner when the courier from the Admiralty came with the package for Captain Graham of HM frigate *Roister*. The happy smile on the face of his new wife was replaced by a rueful grin that quickly became a broad smile for his benefit. Observing this Robert took her hands in his. "I always knew how lucky I was when I found you, whenever I look at you I think I could not love you more, its then that I discover I do!"

He bent and kissed each of her hands. She put her hands on either side of his face and looked into his eyes.

"I knew you were likely to be called away for much of our lives together; I married a naval officer after all. Just keep coming back to me, my love. Now read your orders and we will make our arrangements for the future."

He opened the packet and read the documents within.

"I am to report to the Collector of Customs in London in two days time to discuss strategy to stop the illegal import of goods from France and Holland. The ship is to be careened to clean her copper and give her the speed to catch the smugglers' ships that are causing havoc amongst the revenue cutters presently engaged.

"It seems they do not have the speed or the armament to tackle the smugglers effectively, especially the two schooners that are operating in the Western approaches to the channel; both are apparently armed with 9 gun broadsides probably as heavy as 12 pounders, certainly 9 pounders. The cutters 6 pounder popguns don't have a chance against them. I will be stationed at whichever of the channel dockyard ports that I find convenient. So, my love, it may not be a long separation after all."

News of Admiral Nelson's victory at Abukir Bay had been gazetted to tumultuous celebrations by the people of England.

After the victory at Cape St Vincent last year the stock of the Royal Navy had been high, but the disaster of the Mutiny at Spithead had quickly changed things. Now most of the action in the war was confined to the land. The king of Naples, having captured Rome, was evicted from there and had lost Naples as well. It seems that Napoleon was unbeatable on land at least.

The lull in enemy activity at sea at the time was largely due to the blockades being maintained at the major French ports containing the bulk of the French Naval forces. The boring trudge to and fro keeping the entries and exits of the enemy ports sealed was a soul destroying business, but it did release some of the hard pressed fleet to perform other tasks. The rising number of attacks by privateers on merchant ships, and smugglers, in both directions, combined with the disaffection among the sailors of the fleet through sheer boredom and harsh discipline was all having its effect on the morale and efficiency of the service."

The Collector of Customs wore the uniform and held the rank of Rear Admiral. Viscount Malmby KB was a spare man with as dry manner but a twinkle in his eye. He lifted the walking cane he carried and indicated on the wall a mounted chart of the south coast of England, a series of places on the coast of Kent and Sussex, Dorset, Devon and Cornwall. "You may be surprised to learn that, though we are enemies, officials on the other side of the Channel are also concerned at the trade that is being conducted between our countries."

He held his hand up to prevent Robert interrupting. "Wait! We do not have a dialogue between us on the subject, but we are aware of the attitudes of our opposite numbers, simply based on how they go about things and what sort of things they punish and so on. Obviously both sides used smugglers to deliver spies; now neither side does, since betrayal is a way of life to these people.

"As far as you are concerned, I require a flagship to head the fleet which you will assemble over the next four weeks. You may be interested to know that the recovered galley slaves from the Bone raid have been kept together, rather than dispersing them through the fleet. The Lords of the Admiralty decided that they would be more efficiently employed if kept separated from the general service for the present. They have been placed under your command and are held on a hulk in Portsmouth dockyard.

"In addition a call for volunteers to serve under you has been conducted throughout Dorset producing another one hundred and eighty men."

The Admiral smiled, "You look surprised, Captain; you cannot be unaware of the influence of your name in the county. The opportunity to serve with the illustrious 'Lucky Bob' Captain Graham of *HMS Roister* is a certain crowd puller." His wry grin re-appeared briefly as he stopped to take a sip from the glass of wine at his side, raising his hand once more. "Let me finish. There are several smuggling ships and boats held, and I can give you a fast

Dutch brig-sloop recently taken from a cutting out raid at Dunkerque. She has sixteen guns and a shallow draught. Currently she is lying at St Katherine's dock. She is fast and is now crewed by Channel Islanders who know their waters intimately. The Captain is a Guernsey man who lost his family in a raid on St Peter Port by a privateer; he has subsequently made his career in the Preventive service. He previously served as master's mate in *HMS Marlborough* at the Battle of Ushant, and was made lieutenant for his bravery in the action. It was whilst he was on his way home that the raid on his family was carried out. He commenced his service with my Department at that time.

"In this package you will find a list of the ships and men available. If there is any problem with dockyards or suppliers let me know."

***

"Well, Billy, what of Admiral Viscount Malmby KB?" Robert waited, head on one side to hear what his friend had to say.

"I have nothing to say, I had not heard of him until today!" Billy was quite put out; he prided himself on knowing all as far as the hierarchy of the Navy was concerned.

"Obviously that is what this post is all about, closed mouths, Billy, closed mouths. Too many people depend on the goods smuggled into the country to allow us to confide in anyone at all. Please make sure that no one finds out what *Roister* is doing. I would rather the privateers and smugglers discovered the hard way.

"Remember that smug Peter Tregarth in Plymouth? He had a network of spies from the Assize Judge to the local fishermen, and I'll bet his wine and Brandy is drunk at Hartwell Hall."

"I'll not take that bet, though it won't be because it were bought from Tregarth, t'will be sold through the local wholesaler as part of the provisions. We will need to be very discreet in our enquiries back home!"

There was little said of the meeting on the journey to the docks, and as the carriage passed the grim bulk of the Tower of London the silence between them reflected their awareness of the importance of their new mission.

The masts of the brig-sloop towered over the smaller craft contained in the dock. The challenge as they approached the ship was sharp, the sentry awake and alert.

Robert stepped under the light at the foot of the gangway. On seeing the uniform, the watch called below and with a rush of feet men poured onto the deck to form ranks to welcome the officer aboard. Graham and Billy stepped onto the deck of the ship and both touched their hats to the quarterdeck. No pipes shrilled as Robert called out. "No pipe" The Captain saluted and led them down to the stern cabin.

He introduced himself as Lieutenant Jean Leclerc, Captain of the sloop *Delft*. He was a tall, slightly stooped man with a fine aristocratic look about him. His dress was neat and clean, and he looked confident. The men they had encountered so far had been smart and well trained; all indications of the efficiency of the ship and the respect given to the Captain.

Robert introduced himself and his first lieutenant and passed over orders to Leclerc, and they all seated themselves. Leclerc called for wine and opened the orders and read them. They sat for a few moments while Leclerc digested the orders again, then Robert asked.

"Are you ready for sea?" At Leclerc's nod he continued. "You will sail with the tide tonight and allow yourself to be seen at Hythe and Newhaven; from there I would like you to patrol the waters between the Isle of Wight and the French coast. My ship will be ready for sea by the end of the month which means we should be able to rendezvous south of the Needles in two weeks' time. I realise you have just taken over command of this ship; by the time we meet again I expect you to be thoroughly familiar with her and ready to take her into battle if needed. Now what can you tell me about the private trade and the smuggling at this end of the Channel?"

For the next hour Leclerc told them in his faintly-French accent exactly what he know of the current situation in the Eastern Channel. He also mentioned on three occasions the name Marc Charles, and once Peter Tregarth.

At the end of his dissertation Graham mentioned what they knew of Tregarth.

"We have several small ships at our disposal which I intend shall only be seen as commercial ships. Mark this, I do not want them seen as part of our force. I have a list here of three cutters and two pinks. I am told all can fly; none have more than a few popguns as main armament, either 6 pounder or the sort of swivel gun found in the maintop or used to repel boarders clamped to the taffrail of a ship. They have hand weapons of course, but their best defence is speed and secrecy.

"We will arrange a series of message points on the shore where they can communicate with the bigger ships, to pass on information. If necessary they may cover their true purpose by cooperating with the smugglers. My intention is to clear the channel of the privateers and large scale smugglers in the first place. So let's concentrate on them. I do not wish you to hazard your ship against impossible odds but you will have to decide just what that means. Remember, you have men depending on any decision you make. Am I making myself clear?"

Both Beaufort and Leclerc nodded at the serious faced Graham.

"Very well, carry on, Captain Leclerc; we will meet south of the Needles in two weeks at grog issue time, God Willing!"

***

The sharpshooters from *HMS Roister* were brought ashore to the barracks occupied by the Marine Infantry. The area offered ample ground for the instruction of the men in woodcraft and concealment. As a result of discontent among the other members of the marine detachment, this instruction was given to the entire company, and for this purpose the slop chest of the ship was scoured for suitable civilian clothing for the men to wear whilst training. The other development was the opportunity to obtain one hundred of the discarded Ferguson breech-loading rifles, still stored since the death of Major Ferguson in 1780. By now those Ferguson's already in use had enabled the most skilled to fire ten rounds per minute.

Colonel Stewart, in command of the barracks, had been a friend of Ferguson's during the American Campaign, and was a firm supporter of Ferguson's attempt to get his rifle accepted as a standard weapon for the British army. He was also discreet and co-operated in keeping the training for Captain Ullyet's men separated from the regular training area. He placed a building at their disposal which had been disused for several years for the rifle drill with the breech-loader.

Captain Ullyet took pride in the way his men responded to their training. The uniformed training with muskets was conducted with all the proper pomp and ceremony expected, and it appeared with an extra snap that brought complements from the Garrison Commander.

The 180 men detained in the hulk at Plymouth were gradually infiltrated into the training programs run for the crews of the *HMS Roister* and the other Preventive ships of the company. From these men they chose a company of horsemen; volunteers who could ride and were capable of training in swordsmanship, to complement their skills in marksmanship. Robert found Preventive men who had been officers in the service and were ready and willing to lead these two highly mobile companies to support ambush officers when swift reaction was required. All were kitted out in naval jackets, dragoon breeches and boots. The remainder of the men were brought into the service as additional crew for the fleet, using other recovered boats to enhance the present numbers available and cover more territory.

Abel Jackson took an important part in the training in woodcraft, and the former poacher Peter Morse was an able assistant in teaching silent movement through the wood and gorse lands of the Devon moors. Throughout the ship, the enthusiasm of the men for the training given by Mr. Jackson grew and more and more of the seamen applied to undertake the training. Billy Beaufort suggested that they were only interested because it gave them skills they could use for poaching when they left the sea. Robert was a little more charitable being of the opinion that the chance to get ashore away from the ship whilst they trained had something to do with it.

Regardless of why, the number of men capable of quiet movement through woodland and field grew to form a large part of the crew. The number of trained riflemen grew in proportion. The additional Fergusson rifles were soon allocated. The relaxed discipline required for the crew members of *Roister* were remarked by the other Naval officers stationed in Plymouth, and Robert was required on several occasions to point out that the work they were doing needed trustworthy men and he was personally prepared to vouch for them each and every one.

Without the cooperation of Colonel Stewart they would never have succeeded, but because of his help it was possible to infiltrate selected men from the crew into the local underworld, and this led to the capture of a series of wanted men, and the death of the most notorious highwayman in the south west of England.

He called himself Lord Gilbert and he was a ruthless outlaw who killed rather than leave witnesses; his treatment of victims was divided between gallantry and cruelty. He had been known to rape the female passengers on one coach, and return the jewellery of a lady on another.

Young Alan Massie, nineteen years old, and a valued topsail hand, suitably dressed for the occasion as a sweet maid and the cause of much hilarity in his Mess, was placed as passenger on the mail coach to London. The purpose of the subterfuge was to establish a link between a known smuggler and the squire in the village of Bramwell on the London Road.

Young Alan had been given a message apparently from the smuggler to the squire to arrange a meeting, where the squire would be arrested and charged with smuggling. The cold weather gave reason for the muff he carried, and his disguise was sufficient to cause him concern from the attentions of one of the male passengers. Between Buckfastleigh and Ashburton Lord Gilbert appeared, pistols raised. and stopped the coach by shooting the guard before he could use his blunderbuss. He called the passengers to leave the coach and line up alongside.

Noticing young Alan, he retrieved the purses of the other passengers and ordered them back into the coach. He then turned his attention to Alan, ordering him to strip. Alan just grinned at the man, who raised his pistol to hit him. According to the other passengers Lord Gilbert was furious at being defied by this chit of girl, and they all expected Alan to be knocked to the ground. Instead Alan drew out his pistol from within the muff and shot Gilbert through his open mouth. The unknown girl became famous throughout the South West.

The reward for the removal of the highwayman was paid discreetly into the *Roister* prize fund. The identity of the girl was never revealed to the public. The link between the Squire and the smuggler was not established at that time, though both were caught in the end.

The Half Moon Inn had become a useful listening post for information on the local smuggling scene. The absence of certain people at certain times indicated when a run was being made, and it soon became apparent who were the members of the smuggling gangs, and who weren't.

The other sources of information were the local members of the Preventative service. Up until now there had been occasions when they could not attempt to interfere with a landing because of lack of numbers. The reinforcements from the sharpshooters, whose numbers were increasing daily with the issue of the rifles to the marine detachment, made interception possible in all events.

The weather for the past month had not helped the campaign against the smugglers; however it was becoming obvious that the intelligence service operating on their behalf was aware of the new blood in the Preventative Service. The use of Dragoons had often resulted in betrayal in the past; since Robert's men had been used there had been no surprises.

Warning of reprisals against any who betrayed the 'Gentlemen' were broadcast, throughout the Devon and Cornish countryside. There was frustration in the Custom House in Plymouth, as it seemed that nothing was going to happen whilst the watch was so efficient.

In the waters off the port of Calais, however, the cutter *Brilliant* spotted one of the known Privateers, *Corbeau Noir,* preparing for sea. The weather had caused ships in convoy to scatter and several were now beating up channel, still being rounded up by their harried escorts.

The *Brilliant* spun about and dashed down channel to rendezvous with the *Delft,* catching her in mid-channel off Newhaven. Leclerc sent the *Brilliant* on to meet *Roister* off the Needles whilst he took the *Delft* direct to Calais to intercept the Frenchman.

It was evening when the Masthead lookout on the *Delft* spotted the *Corbeau Noir* leaving the Guet at Calais. *Delft* was to the east of the harbour and the privateer was outlined against the dying daylight to the west. Leclerc ordered full sail to catch up with the French ship which was an armed schooner of 12 guns, and a large crew for the boarding operations that they would anticipate.

The chase went on through the night, the lights of the privateer displayed without attempt at concealment as she crept along the French coast, well inshore and clear of any patrolling British ships, unaware of her shadow.

As the dawn light started to creep into the eastern sky the sloop cut in to the shallow waters between the *Corbeau Noir* and the shore, her shallow draught allowing her to enter water that the deeper-keeled ships would not dare. As the light strengthened, the masts of the frigate *Roister* appeared to seaward. The reaction on the *Corbeau Noir* was immediate and she started to come about to escape the enemy frigate. At that point the Delft, unnoticed until now, opened fire with her bow chasers.

"Across her bows Master gunner." The high voice of Captain Leclerc rang out. The ball raised a column of white water across the turning bow of the Frenchman. As she continued to turn the bow was exposed to the broadside of the sloop, and Leclerc had no hesitation in opening fire. "Starboard broadside, fire as you bear!" Leclerc's voice was without emotion.

The crew of the *Corbeau Noir* were running to her guns to get the ship prepared to defend herself, the cannon balls from the first broadside caused mayhem along the crowded deck. *Delft* spun about, her starboard gun crews reloading their guns for a second broadside.

Meanwhile the port guns got their chance and poured fire into the French privateer, which was looking the worse for wear with holes in her bulwarks and her mainsail ripped where a ball had smashed the boom on the main mast. The bow of the *Corbeau Noir* fell off the wind, with her mainsail flapping. As the third broadside from the Customs sloop roared out, the schooner struck an underwater sandbank and her masts toppled. The waves were still quite high from the bad weather, and the panic that broke out on the French ship caused the launching of the surviving boats to become a disaster; both spilling over as they descended to water level. The area around the stricken ship became carpeted with the heads of the abandoned crew.

At that point the waters were too shallow for even the Dutch sloop to approach and, as Leclerc declared afterwards, he was not prepared to risk launching a boat and place his men' lives at risk in those troubled waters.

Except for seven hardy members of the privateer's crew, who managed to swim to the next sandbank and from there by degrees to the shore, the entire ship's company perished.

Leclerc made his report to Captain Graham on the *HMS Roister* later that day, when they rendezvoused in mid-channel.   As Robert observed to Billy Beaufort afterwards, Leclerc did not seem too upset at the loss of life in the shipwreck.

The first lieutenant replied "It's possibly because of the brutal murder of his family by privateers. In the circumstances I would probably feel the same way."

The loss of the *Corbeau Noir* caused a stir on the French side as the crew came largely from Calais and Sangatte. Over 150 men died that day, a loss mourned over the whole area. Significantly, news of the part played by *Delft* was not known until the survivors came home; and the identity of the mystery ship was still unknown apart from the fact that she flew the hated British flag.

***

Back in Plymouth, Robert was enjoying living at home when ashore. The new home of the Graham family was on the bank of the Tamar River opposite Saltash, one of the many properties that came as part of the dowry of his titled wife. Tamar House stood beside the river and the harbour west of Plymouth looking over to Cornwall.

At the meeting held in the drawing room of Tamar Manor, many of the Law officers of the two counties were present.

"I have called you here together to inform you that the time has come to stop the smuggling that is prevalent in our area. We are all aware, I am sure, of the identities of the leading members of the smuggling gangs and I am sure you will all agree that the lawlessness that these operations are responsible for must cease." Robert stopped and looked around at the group.

"I have been given the task of clearing up matters in this area, and I am calling upon you all as leading members of the Law Administration of the community to assist in any way that you can." Robert sat down, yielding the floor to Sir Arthur Murray, Lord Lieutenant of the County of Cornwall.

"Gentlemen" he started, and then turning to Barbara and inclining his head "and Lady Barbara of course. I have been made aware of the problem of smuggling in this area for many years, and though I have tried on many occasions to stop it, I have never managed to do more than slow it down.

"In achieving even this small success; twelve officers in the Preventative service have been killed over the last ten years. What solution can you propose, that has not already been tried and, up to now, failed?" He sat to a chorus of agreement from others in the room.

A small wiry man, Captain Willet in command of the Customs Service in the local area, rose to his feet from the back of the room and said bitterly.

"In the past whenever we planned a raid we were betrayed. Too many of the wealthy in this area find it convenient to have a source of cheap Brandy; aye and other things hard to come by in this damned war. As Sir Arthur said, twelve of my Officers have died trying to do their work for King and Country, only to be betrayed and killed by their own countrymen.

"When we caught that Senior Magistrate in possession of Brandy and tobacco enough to stock and supply half of Cornwall, what happened? All a mistake they said, he didn't know the goods were untaxed. Fined him £50.00 and seized the goods.

"They transported his Housekeeper for actually buying the goods on his behalf and the seized goods were auctioned off to his friends at knockdown prices. How can we fight that?"

Robert rose to his feet. "Barbara, gentlemen, I propose that we elect a committee here and now to study this problem. From there we will create an operation group who will keep all plans within the group. If betrayal occurs we will know it is within the group, and any action will then be taken by the group who will be responsible for any outcome. I suggest the group be comprised of Captain Willet of the Preventative Service, One senior Law Officer, Sir Arthur perhaps, a Magistrate;" his eye swept the room settling on the well-fed figure of Rebus Gowan, squire and Justice of the Peace for Kingsbridge, "….and a landowner, can we call upon Sir Charles Wellworthy of Dartmeet. I will act as Chairman and in conjunction with Captain Willet, will provide the armed arresting parties. Can I ask those gentlemen to remain after this meeting?" Robert seated himself as the buzz of conversation that followed his short speech filled the room.

Barbara leaned over to him. "You didn't give them much choice?"

"If I allowed them to choose we would still be here at midnight, and the whole business would have descended into the sort of muddle that has been the problem in the past.

"Secrecy, keeping the smugglers guessing is the answer to the failures in the past. Using information from local informants we can make a difference, and providing we keep our sources protected, we will get cooperation. The bigger problem we are up against is indiscretion, innocent revelation of our plans and sources."

***

Two weeks later, the five men comprising the committee sat around the table in the dining room of Tamar House. The second meeting of the action committee was in progress.

Captain Willet said, "Since we are agreed, gentlemen, I will be ready to act as soon as we get the date and time of the next run. It's time to crimp the operations of the Tregarth family."

The meeting broke up and the members dispersed to their homes in the carriages lined up outside the colonnaded porch.

Rebus Gowan sat with a sigh in the heavily-cushioned interior of his coach. The matched bay horses pulled powerfully up the long hill leading out of Plymouth to the East and his home in Kingsbridge. His thoughts were concerned with getting information to his associates without making it apparent that he had betrayed his colleagues on the committee. By the time he reached the gates of his house he had made a decision. Rapping on the roof he called his coachman to take him to the Samphire Inn at the riverside. The coachman steered the coach carefully through the gates of the Inn yard as dusk fell, and hurried to assist his master to descend from the coach.

Chapter thirteen

The portly Magistrate brushed past his coachman and entered the inn by the side door leading to the snug, the small room kept for special friends of the landlord. The three men within the room looked up at his entrance then returned to their conversation as Gowan subsided gratefully onto the large chair reserved especially for his bulky figure.

A glass was placed before him and he drank deeply then addressed the gathering as his glass was refilled. "Well, boys this had been a fruitful day, in fact I would say a very fruitful day. The committee has decided to concentrate on the Tregarth family which means we can breathe easy for a week or so. Good time to run a cargo 'eh. Ted?"

Ted Moult sneered. "And when, Rebus Gowan, did you decide you could start ordering me about? Tis enough we have to cut you in on our fair gained profits. Would you now expect us to jump to your tune?" He drank from his tankard of ale and called for another.

Rebus Gowan thought for a minute before he replied. "If you wish to carry on trading in this area perhaps you would like to remember that you operate here through my good offices, I could replace you in a moment, so it's in your interest to listen when I tell you something, do I have your attention?"

The three men wriggled with embarrassment then nodded, Ted Moult was thinking maybe he had had a little too much to drink; he could not afford to upset the old bastard. As Magistrate he had the power to deport him to Botany Bay if he wished, but one day...

Rebus spoke. "Perhaps you could consider what I am saying here for a moment. I think if we ran the next cargo soon, landing at Womwell Beach rather than the river here, we could keep the trail away from me. As long as I remain unsuspected I can bring information to keep us in business. Can you all understand what I am saying. I know where the Preventive men will be every night, so we can run cargo whenever we will!" He sat back with a sigh and drank from his glass.

The other three men thought about this and eventually Ted Moult answered for them all. "Right. That makes a lot of sense; I have to meet the brothers off Start Point at nine. We'll be using your fishing boat, Bill." He turned to the taller of his two companions. "We're bringing in ten o' brandy and four kegs of Baccy, silk, lace and spice. If we land at Womwell Beach we need to make sure that the pack animals are there ready by half past eleven. It's easy to unload on the beach but the moon'll be with us by twelve-thirty so we'll need to get a move on. Store the stuff in the Dolphin Inn in Kingston Village; if we run into trouble we can we can use the passage down to Wiscombe to get the stuff out by sea again. Any questions?" Since nobody had anything to say, he sat back and finished his drink.

Rebus arose from the comfort of his chair and said good night, he walked outside and boarded the waiting coach. "Home!" he bawled at the driver, who set off down the road once more for the house on the outskirts of the town.

In the Half Moon Inn, Robert sat quietly discussing things with Captain Willet. He sat back for a moment and looked directly at John Willet. "Who do you think is our traitor?"

Willet studied the content of his glass for a few moments. "If you want proof, I can't help. My opinion is Rebus Gowan's the informer and I'd be willing to bet that he's involved in the business up to his neck. Why? Because he comes from a shore cottage at Bigbury, his Ma took in washing from the fishermen after her husband died at sea. She died at the tub they say and that idle bugger never lifted a hand. He had left home to work for the local vicar who taught him to read and do figures. From there he went to the clerk's office in the Court House; made a name for himself keeping the books and lining his pockets doing favours for folk. His mother never got a penny from him. Like I say, she died still scratching a living while he was already beginning to lord it around Kingsbridge. He wed the daughter of the Draper in town and took over the books and the business when the old man died. He was made a Justice of the Peace when the post came vacant. Nobody dared run against him. They reckon half the town was in debt to him by this time so he could do as he liked.

"That was when he decided to join the gentry. That was when he found out that it took more than money and position to be a gentleman. I don't think he's given up the idea; just put it to one side until he becomes rich enough to bribe his way in."

"That's it, then? You think it's him because you don't like him?" Robert was not entirely convinced.

"Lord no. I think he's involved because he holds private meetings in the Samphire Inn in Kingsbridge with the biggest smuggler in that part of the county, Ted Moult!"

Robert grinned, "You don't think he is trying to get information for the Committee then?"

"If he is, he's forgotten to tell us that there is going to be a pick-up off Start Point at nine o'clock tomorrow tonight, landing at Womwell Beach by eleven thirty."

Robert looked at John Willet, "Tomorrow? Landing at eleven thirty tomorrow night?"

John Willet nodded. "My man listened to the entire conversation while they sat in the snug bar. Only my man and the landlord know of the spy panel behind the settle in the snug, and my man—when he saw Rebus come—slid into position before Rebus was seated and heard the whole conversation.

"Seems Rebus thinks he's the king of the local smugglers, telling them what they may do or not do. Ted Moult don't like it one bit. I reckon one day he'll save us all trouble by 'arranging' Mr. Rebus. That is, if Ted can stay out of prison after tomorrow night."

"How many men do you need? They're sharpshooters you know?"

Willet thought for a few minutes. "Ten should be enough if you can spare them."

"Good, you concentrate on the smugglers when they come ashore; we'll go after the ships after we stop the shore side. I'll be at sea with Leclerc in *Delft* off Looe. We're putting pressure on Tregarth wherever we can; we are working to get them jittery so that they make mistakes."

The two men left the inn and walked down the dark street towards the Docks.

The attack came as they passed the entrance to one of the many yards along the seaward side of the street. John Willet heard the scuff of shoe against the wall, he immediately grabbed Robert's arm in warning and both drew their swords. There were five men altogether and they rushed out, brandishing clubs. Robert slashed the nearest across the face with the edge of his blade and finished the stroke with a stab in the chest for the man behind, both reeled back and out of the fight, John Willet had his back to the wall and was fighting off two men as the third circled looking for a way into the conflict. Robert shouted at him and cut him on the arm with the cutting edge of his sword.

He felt a fierce pain in his left shoulder and swung round to face his second victim withdrawing his sword to strike again. Almost casually Robert ran him through, his sword entering just under the ribcage of his attacker, who fell, coughing blood, to the ground.

John had despatched one of his opponents and the other seeing himself outnumbered turned and ran, leaving his four companions groaning on the ground.

The man with the slashed face staggered to his feet and ran off holding his ruined cheek together. The other three were still on the ground, the one Robert had run through was now obviously dead. The others were moaning and clutching their wounds. "Leave them to sort out their own!" John growled. "They are hired thugs."

Seeing Robert lean against the wall he was immediately concerned. "Are you all right, did they get you?" He ran over and supported Robert as he began to feel the effect of the stab wound in his back. He helped Robert back to the Half Moon and banged on the door. The door flung open.

"What is all thi.... Come in! Lizzie, the Captain's been hurt, quick now!" They hurried the wounded man into the parlour and Lizzie appeared and took the cloak from around Robert's shoulders. The bloody area where the blade had penetrated was high in the fleshy part of his left shoulder. The men took off his jacket and tore the shirt away from the wound that was still bleeding; it was quickly staunched by Lizzie putting pressure on the wound using the torn shirt.

"Sam, fetch hot water and some fresh cloths and bring my bag of possibles, quick now. Captain John, nip into the bar and get a bottle of the good brandy."

The men ran about their errands, Sam returned quickly with a bowl of water from the stove. When the brandy arrived Elizabeth soaked the clean cloth brought by Sam with the spirit and cleaned the area round the wound, causing Robert to wince. From her bag of possibles, she removed a needle and thread. John looked at these items dubiously. "Should I call the Doctor?"

"No, the quicker this is done the better." Elizabeth was firm and proceeded to plunge the needle into Robert's back and stitch up the wound with a series of neat loops. With a pad she covered her handiwork. Only a little blood was now seeping from the wound as she finished off with a bandage to hold the pad in place.

"Now just you lie back and relax, sir. Here's a drop of brandy to settle your stomach. Out, you men! Leave the Captain to rest." She ushered the men from the room while Robert sank back with a sigh of relief.

Outside the room Elizabeth gave her orders: to Sam to send a message to Tamar House to say the Captain would be sleeping at the Inn; to Captain Willet, go to the ship and fetch Doctor Sweet to the Captain to make sure all was well.

The Carriage arrived within the hour and Barbara came into the Inn with a flurry of skirts and a waft of Lavender. Taken to Robert she was immediately reassured that he was feeling only slightly the worse for his wound.

The Doctor then arrived and examined Robert's wound, pronouncing Elizabeth's work to be first class. Robert was then permitted to rest once more while Barbara and Elizabeth sat and drank tea together, chatting quietly about the general situation.

The morning brought a rather sore Captain Graham to the quarterdeck of *Roister* having boarded at daybreak and despatched Captain Willet's party of sharpshooters by the cutter, *Relentless* to be landed after dark on Wiscombe Beach, down below Kingston Village. The short cross country march would bring them to Womwell Beach where the landing was due to take place.

As long as the men were concealed in time the surprise should be complete. The shore party under Captain Willet would gather above the beach staying concealed while the smugglers brought the pack animals down.

Under the command of Captain Ullyet the riflemen would not show themselves until after the challenge was made by Captain Willet. If the smugglers surrendered to Captain Willet, the rifles would remain quiet and out of sight. Robert did not wish to publicise his secret weapon too soon and as long as the presence of the rifle detachment stayed secret, the smugglers would be unprepared to counter their threat.

The outline of the masts of the lugger stood out against the skyline. The clear, starry night was light enough to betray her as she anchored off the beach at Womwell. She stood off a good half cable from the shallow shelving beach, which here swept round to the point in a great arc of smooth sand at the mouth of the River Erme.

A group of pack horses meandered down the path to the river side, thence onto the soft sand that seemed to absorb the sound reducing it to a shuffle made by the hooves in the soft surface.

At the water's edge three boats could be seen being dragged up onto the firm sand below the high tide mark. The group of men manhandling the boats were making hard work of shifting the heavily laden craft.

A voice called to bring the horses, and the shadowy men with the animals started to move them towards the water's edge. No one seemed to notice the flurry of movement among the men with the horses as Willets men replaced the horse holders, successive thuds was the only indication that the horsemen had been replaced, the dark shapes of the unconscious men concealed by the bulk of the advancing horses. A late arrival came running down the beach and stumbled over one of the unconscious men, his call of warning went unnoticed until he cocked his pistol and fired a shot.

At the boats the men immediately started to push the boats the other way, but they had done too well bringing them in and the advancing horsemen scattered the animals and lined up with muskets raised and called on them to surrender. There were eighteen men in the beach party of Captain Willet, the twelve smugglers were in no state to resist. Two ran into the water and struck out for the Lugger, the others raised their hands and were pinioned by the officers. Several shots were fired at the escaping swimmers but with no success.

As Willet reported to Robert next morning, they had captured ten men, all local to the Kingsbridge area, and the three longboats loaded down with contraband. His men were delighted and were quite happy to share the bounty with the riflemen, who were not revealed but were there if needed. The cargo valued in excess of £2500.00 meant that each man involved would receive close on ten pounds, nearly two years' wages, a fortune to the men involved.

The three longboats were owned by the Moult family, and though Ted Moult had not been seen or identified at the scene, no claim of theft regarding the boats had been made. Thus the boats were seized and disposed of along with the smuggled goods.

Word the success of the operation spread rapidly throughout the area, and the illegal movement of goods slowed down temporarily to a trickle. The Schooners were glimpsed on three occasions but the presence of the frigate scared them off before they could be approached.

Robert discussed the situation after dinner in the great cabin of the ship. It was over a week since the raid and Robert was concerned about his campaign losing its impetus.

"Everything seems to have stopped, and I am worried that by the time they resume, my men will be lulled into a sense of complacency, and when new events occur they will not be ready to react as they should!"

John Willet was confident that things would begin again soon enough. "They cannot afford to leave it too long. Their customers will be crying out for goods, you mark my words."

Barbara, who was present, interjected. "At the Hall my father said that the Housekeeper was complaining that her local supplier was unable to bring certain items owing to a temporary shortage, do we presume they're part of the regular trade?"

"I'm afraid we must assume so. Obviously the imports have become a routine part of the local economy. So if we have reached that stage we had better prepare for some diversion. With the patrols all along the coast and our increasing network of informers we must have a good chance of stopping some of them for good!" Robert sat back feeling a little better.

Seated around the table were the assembled officers of the ship plus Barbara and Captain Willet, but it was Midshipman Abbot who hesitantly spoke next, it was a tribute to the relaxed atmosphere on the ship that Abbot dared open his mouth in such exalted company, but after several months of being encouraged to speak if he had something of worth to say, he made his suggestion. "In my home in Boscastle, the 'Gentlemen' have an easy time because they have things organised with their customers. The main trader has a legitimate business as a general supplier of virtually everything. He delivers his 'trade goods' alongside his legally obtained items, so local folk can turn a blind eye to how some of the goods are obtained. In addition, in a warehouse full of a variety of goods picking out contraband can be virtually impossible."

Willet interrupted. "We know all this, it happens here."

Not put off Abbot continued. "But integrated with this trade is the trade in poached venison and other game and fish from the local estates. In many cases people are supplied with their own deer and grouse, and salmon from their own rivers. Of course the local landowners do what they can to stop the poaching, but they still accept smuggled Brandy and tobacco, and whatever other exotic goods are offered. Our local officer was like us, frustrated, and he thought up a way to trap the smuggler. Contacting the local poacher he convinced him that he was being used by the smugglers to cover their own operation, they had been right on the heels of the smugglers when they had been led to the poacher's smallholding where they had discovered contraband goods concealed behind the hay in his barn. The officer had convinced the poacher that he had not arrested him because he was aware that it was a set up!" Abbot paused and looked around; his audience were silent waiting for the end of the story. "The poacher had supplied people prior to the entry of the smuggler into the business, he had resented the way he had been forced to deal with the General Trader, he was also upset to find that his personal cache of contraband had been located, and quite content to allow the officer to assume the goods had been planted to implicate him."

Abbot concluded. "The next time a cargo was being run by the smugglers, the officer was there with his men, and such is the greed of these men, the owner of the General Traders was there and caught in flagrante delicto. His protests that he had been lured to the spot by the poacher fell on deaf ears, and the threat of hanging soon caused his men to give him up anyway. They cleared up the entire crew and the local community mourned their passing."

Barbara asked. "What happened to the poacher?"

Abbots answer caused great amusement. "My uncle was shot in the backside with rock salt whilst fulfilling an order for the local landowner; his wound was inflicte, by the same local landowner! Uncle James no longer supplies anyone other than the family nowadays.

"The officer is now working out how to catch the new local smuggler. It appears that the contraband trade has become a regular part of the community trade."

Willet spoke up. "What the lad says could be the answer. If we could convince Ted Moult say that he had been betrayed by the Tregarth brothers who want to take over his trade."

He and Robert spoke together 'Rebus Gowan!'

Willet continued. "When we meet tomorrow, a slip of the tongue, a mere hint should be enough. He's no fool, he will pass it on surely."

The meeting of the committee was held at the home of Sir Charles Wellworthy at Dartmeet on Dartmoor. During the meeting the news of the successful raid at Womwell beach was given and as the congratulations were being given there was a mention that it was a pity that the Tregarth brothers had not been the subject and their capture not achieved. Robert laughed and tapped his nose, knowingly. "Peter Tregarth can be helpful on occasion."

"What does that mean?" Sir Arthur asked.

Robert merely said. "I'm saying nothing. Information comes from more than one source, and you cannot discount it wherever it's from." Noting the alert look of the normally semi-comatose Rebus Gowan, Robert reckoned that the message went home. Later at the Samphire Inn, Captain Willet's spy confirmed that Rebus Gowan had told Ted Moult that the raid had been because of betrayal by Peter Tregarth.

"I'll be 'avin a word with that Tregarth feller." Ted's voice was even angrier than usual on hearing this news."

"No you won't." Rebus Gowan's voice was cold and his face was like stone. "Seeing the man would just confirm that we have a spy in the committee. You will let me know when he is going to make a run and I will fix him for you. Understand?"

Ted recoiled from the sheer viciousness of Gowan's tone of voice. He had never heard him quite like this. It occurred to him that perhaps that was how he had obtained the position in life that he now occupied.

"Do you understand what I am saying?" Gowan repeated.

"Yes, I understand," Ted said aggressively. "I'll keep my mouth shut this time, but...."

Leaving the comment unfinished he sank his nose in his glass. He had not intended speaking to Peter Tregarth, it was just bravado, but they didn't need to know that.

On Willet's orders a close watch was kept on Rebus Gowan over the next few days to make sure Ted did not pass anything on to Rebus without Willet knowing; and it was on the fourth day that their watch was rewarded. At a brief meeting in the Samphire Ted told Rebus that a landing had been arranged on the Saturday, in two days, a big cargo at Cawsand Bay before moonrise. At approximately nine-thirty, the schooner would come close in where the shore sloped steeply, the goods in kegs would float ashore, a boat would only be required for the people. It seemed that there were several people coming across from France on this occasion.

Delft crept in towards the cliffs in Cawsand Bay. The vague outline of the schooner under topsail alone was ghosting in towards the small village of Cawsand. The subdued rumble of her anchor was heard followed by the sound of oars as a small boat carried out a stern anchor to keep the ship steady. The squeak of blocks then followed as the cargo was hauled out of the hold followed by the splash of the kegs hitting the water. On shore the men allocated by

Robert and Willet gathered themselves as the reception provided by the smugglers prepared to unlash and load up the precious cargo. Before the cargo was half unloaded a cry from the deck of the schooner warned the smugglers they were under observation. At the cry the bow gun of *Delft* crashed out and the schooner shuddered with the impact.

"Stand fast in the Kings name." Leclerc's voice through the speaking trumpet rang out across the bay, raising an echo along the cliff face. Ashore the smugglers rushed to remove the goods already landed and the small group of people landed from the ship were hurried to the track through the cliffs. Lanterns were suddenly lit all round the village and on the road out. The armed men seemed to be everywhere, a pistol fired and a man fell crying out in agony, the clash of steel followed briefly, then it was over. The ambush was successful, the shore party was arrested and the schooner seized, and carried into Plymouth dockyard under the guns of *Delft*.

Chapter fourteen

Sunday was normally a quiet day in the Dockyard; this day was different. The schooner *Amy* named for the wife of Peter Tregarth lay alongside the quay being unloaded. The stack of goods in kegs on the quay grew as the remainder of the cargo was stacked, then the empty ship was stripped by the customs men searching every nook and cranny for anything missed. Once they were satisfied the ship was handed over to the shipwrights to repair the damage caused by the cannon shot from the night before. The cargo was loaded onto carts and taken to join the rest of the contraband taken the previous night at Cawsand; all stacked in the customs house on the quay. Provisionally valued at £15000.00, the worrying element was the cases of muskets and ammunition consigned to a house in Princeton where the French prisoners of war were accommodated.

Among the people taken were a French Holy Father and a family of Émigré, fleeing from France. They had been hiding for two years from the authorities. All were being closely questioned by a quietly dressed group of men who appeared out of nowhere. They were joined by a face familiar to Robert, Amelie Parker, though she made no sign of recognition. The local prisoners included both of the Tregarth brothers, Peter on board ship and Adam on the shore.

Present at their first interview Robert was surprised at the indiscretion of John Willet who let slip that the information about the landing had come from a

Kingsbridge smuggler. No names mentioned but a week later Willets' spy in Kingsbridge reported that the carriage carrying Rebus Gowan had broken a wheel and gone over the cliff at Bigbury, killing Rebus and Ted Moult, who was riding with him; of the driver there was no sign.

The *Amy* was taken into the customs service, the crew drawn from the pool of men that included the remaining ex-galley slaves.

Further down the coast there was a serious fight between the Romney marsh smugglers and the Preventive men who found a great hoard of goods concealed in the Church crypt. The smugglers led by the local Priest fought vigorously and the death toll amounted to eight men, five smugglers and three Customs men. Several others wounded.

The hanging of the survivors sent a message to the brotherhood that while it didn't stop the smuggling it certainly slowed it down.

Robert took Barbara to London whilst he toured the various outposts of the service around the south coast; she used the opportunity to complete the decoration and refurbishment of the house in Knightsbridge under her charge and had finally created a presentable establishment for entertaining to her satisfaction. Her aunt was pleased to stay in the temporary absence of Robert, who was detained in Dover. The repercussions to the efforts of the Preventive men in the Kent area were considerable, and the hanging of the Dymchurch smugglers was a cause celebre for the less lawful of the area. As was pointed out, the hanging was not for smuggling but for the killing of the officers making the arrests.

The local officer's spy network had brought word of a mysterious new figure in the smuggling world, new at least to the Kentish Officers, though the man Marc Charles was known to Leclerc.

The new man in the Kent trade was French. His ship was rigged and armed like a ship of war, and rumour had it that the Captain and crew were in fact French Naval personnel who were smuggling and doing a little piracy on the side. The ship *Le Corbeau* was brig rigged and quick, she also carried a broadside of 8 guns, nine pounders at least. The cutters and pinks of the British Preventive Service had no chance against her, so it became the task of *Delft* and *Roister* to hunt her down.

In the crew of *HMS Delft* were several French-speaking Channel Islanders and Leclerc landed three of these men in the Calais area. They found the location of the ship in her regular base on the outer wall of the inner harbour at Calais. Her berth allowed her to put to sea at all states of the tide, depending of the wind of course.

This information was passed to Robert and discussed at length and, when a plan was devised, Leclerc asked to lead the cutting out party. He explained to Robert that *La Corbeau* was the vessel that had raided his home in St Peter Port, Guernsey.

"If we can come close enough to Calais to land the men, we could cut out *Le Corbeau* and add her to our little fleet, she would make a useful asset, and at the same time we would be ridding the channel of a serious problem."

Leclerc thought for a while, then he suggested. "If our trained men could be placed at the seaward end of the quay, it should be possible to steal the ship without too much trouble from the crew. The big problem would be the forts at the Harbour mouth." He sat back as Ullyet spoke.

"As far as I'm aware, sir, the men, once landed, should be able to subdue the forts, at least until we get the ship out. In effect, the forts are both basically batteries manned by men billeted in the city. They have no garrison as such, and therefore the personnel would consist of the gun crews only. They would be vulnerable to infantry. Holding the position would be more difficult but not impossible. Once the ship was out there would be no further need to hang on and the landing party could be uplifted."

At the end of the discussion the plans were made providing for the cutting out of the ship—or her destruction—to take place at the next dark of the moon, in two weeks time. Meanwhile a watch would continue on the movements of the shipping in Calais.

"How does he get out of the harbour to raid and smuggle while we have a squadron of ships supposedly blockading Calais?" The question was from Captain Ullyet.

Leclerc chose his words carefully in replying.

"The seas off Calais are difficult to patrol. There are shallows and tidal currents that can trap a ship of draught easily. Over the years the waters have been surveyed by many different chart makers, however still ships are trapped. A knowing captain can leave Calais under the eyes of the fleet and still elude capture merely by using the correct state of tide and slant of wind. Using the *Delft,* we have the best of both worlds, a ship of shallow draught and big enough to carry the men needed. Also she is Dutch and they are regular visitors to Calais; this is all in our favour."

From the stores of the frigate, uniforms captured from the French were produced to outfit a platoon of men. They would form the escort for the balance of the 120 men who were to be 'prisoners of war' under escort, wheeling the carriage with their weapons and ammunition along with them. The escort was commanded by Leclerc himself.

The men would be carried to the outer quay by *Delft* where they would be lined up and escorted to the building works being carried out in the inner harbour. As they passed the fort on the quay they would take their weapons and take control of the battery. Half the men would then board the supply boat kept to communicate between the forts. They would cross and assault the other fort and take control.

Once the forts were taken the cutting out party would be escorted round the harbour wall to the moored French ship where they would take over control of the vessel on the inner quay as quietly as possible. The ship would be brought round to the outer quay and take on board the landing parties as it left Calais.

***

The dark water swirled past the hull of the *Delft* as it made way in between the arms of the harbour entrance at Calais, the lights of the fort at the eastern side, showed faint through the mist that had risen following the warm day. The men crouched on deck were silent as they waited for a cry of warning or challenge but none came. The ship slid alongside against rope fenders and men leapt ashore to secure the ship alongside.

The landing party silently filed ashore and lined up. The carriage was swung on to the quay and the party gathered round and prepared to push it along between them. The uniformed men formed up, rifles at the port and the whole party moved off openly chattering and murmuring as they marched down the quay to the port battery. The tramp of feet and the noise of the creaking of the carriage warned the sentry at the battery, who came out of the guard room to challenge the party.

Leclerc spoke to the guard, explaining that they were supposed to be working on the repairs to the dock but the ship's captain refused to sail any further in the poor visibility, so they had to walk round to the building site. The party moved on while the conversation took place and as they came abreast of the embrasures, the covers were whipped off the carriage and the 'prisoners' armed themselves and poured through the entryway into the courtyard behind the guns. The gun crews were sitting round the tables set out beside the magazine eating and drinking and playing cards.

The surprise was complete, and the gunners quickly lined up without a fuss and pushed into the storerooms that formed part of the enclosure behind the gun platforms.

"They haven't even got slow matches alight, or ready use ammunition by the guns!" *Roisters* gunner's mate was disgusted, and he immediately set about preparing the guns for action if required.

"Second party; man the boat and take the other battery. Lively now!" Leclerc's voice was low but the snap was there and the party under Captain Ullyet boarded the boat lying alongside, with one of the Guernsey men to translate if needed. They set off, rowing on a compass bearing across the water to the other battery.

The cutting out party set off down the quay to the point where they could board the French ship. As they approached, the shadowy outline of the masts stood out against the lights of the city, quietly both the bow and stern parties ranged alongside the ship in their allotted places. At the call they boarded the ship swarming over the bulwarks and overpowering the deck watch.

The noise roused the rest of the crew and a pistol fired and the clash of steel signalled a general melee on the crowded deck. It was lucky that many of the crew were ashore in Calais; otherwise the outcome could have been different. As it was the ship was secured quickly, and with the sails raised the ship gradually gathered way. The Leclerc called for the sweeps to be deployed and the long oars were pushed through the ports provided and the men laid on the sweeps driving the ship forward; at the wheel he directed the helmsmen to swing the head of the ship round to enter the channel.

The noise began as a distant roar but it increased as the moving mass of figures waving torches came walking on to the end of the quay. There were ranks of soldiers marching six abreast leading the way, followed by a mass of civilians waving weapons of various kinds at the hated English raiders.

Leclerc's voice rose above the growing racket, calling to the men in the battery to form up on the quay. Whilst the gunner spiked the guns the remaining men formed two ranks across the quay facing the approaching enemy "Front rank load!" The order rang out and the ten men in the front rank loaded their cartridge "Rear rank load!" The second rank loaded their rifles. "Front rank, volley, fire!" The ten rifles fired as one and the front row of troops collapsed. The second volley caused the entire column to hesitate, stumbling over the bodies of the injured and dying men in their front. By the time the third and fourth volleys had been fired, the column came to a complete stop and the men pushing from behind suddenly realised that the forward ranks were being killed at an astonishing rate.

There must have been over twenty men lying bleeding and dead on the quay, and the volleys were still coming every ten seconds.

Once started, the panic quickly began to spread and the column melted away; the civilians and soldiers running back towards town to escape the terrible slaughter.

"Cease fire!" Leclerc called. "Retreat to the ship." The men gathered their equipment and dashed to the ship, now alongside the seaward side of the quay.

The gunner ensured that all guns had been spiked. He had also placed a barrel of gunpowder under each of the ten guns, and stacked the rest around them and laid a fuse. "They'll not be using these guns again, nor the embrasures" he chuckled, touching the slow-match to the fuses gathered on the ground before him. His report to Leclerc was breathless and he recommended immediate departure before the charges blew.

"Right; all aboard lively now, is everyone here?" All the men were aboard including the wounded. So *Le Corbeau*, sails filling, made her way across the to the other battery to collect the remainder of the raiding party. Having created a similar arrangement of charges, the Gunner's Mate gathered his party and followed Captain Ullyet and his men on to the ship. As they sailed out of Calais to rendezvous with *Delft* the first battery exploded with a tremendous roar, the second blew as they passed outer channel marker.

"I reckon they'll remember our visit." Captain Ullyet commented quietly to Captain Leclerc with deep satisfaction. "The men and the rifles performed well."

"They certainly did, now let's see what fish we captured with this ship."

The prisoners were lined up on deck between two lines of marines. There were four who were obviously officers, all trying to make themselves inconspicuous among the other men. Unfortunately for them, the other men were not cooperating and they were all four isolated from the men around them.

Puzzled, Ullyet asked Leclerc why the men were not helping their officers. "It is because they are French navy. The men resent their officers because they do not share fairly when they take a prize, and many do not like the way the officers behave in action. They say the officers do not want prisoners so they kill any they take. The men say that if they do this, what happens to us if they are taken prisoner? They do not wish to die.

"Is the captain here?"

"Yes, he is Captain Marc Charles, that man standing over there." He indicated a tall man isolated from the men around him, dressed in a black coat with the leather baldric still over his shoulder, the empty scabbard swinging at his side.

"Is this the man you were looking for, Leclerc?"

"It is. The man, who raided Guernsey, murdered my family; and burned down my home."

In the later questioning it was interesting to discover that the so-called 'rule of the people' boasted of by the leadership of the French people, was anything but.

At his meeting with Robert following the cutting out expedition, Admiral, Viscount Malmby KB was quite seriously clear on the subject.

"We have been aware that the movement in this country towards egalitarianism has taken a severe blow since the last series of executions in Republican France;

and the declaration by Napoleon Bonaparte of his ambitions to the Chair as First Consul of France; has been a serious blow to the republican fraternity. They are becoming persuaded that their great experiment is not working.

"As to the captive Captain Marc Charles, his piratical cruise through the Channel Isles was part of the official efforts of the French to impress us, to convince us that they still had some influence in the Channel waters.

"It was of course a wasted gesture that we have swiftly demonstrated was futile. You may tell Captain Leclerc that Captain Charles has been convicted of piracy and is destined to hang this week for his crimes. He made the plea that as a French naval officer he should be treated as a prisoner of war; however the court decided that his conduct, and the fact that the raid was carried out under a neutral flag, placed him outside the protection of the rules of war and he will hang beside several others of his crew also individually convicted."

Malmby walked over to the bureau and poured two glasses of Madeira, one of which he passed to Robert. "I suppose you are now wondering what happens next?"

Robert cleared his throat but, before he could speak, Malmby raised his hand to stop him, and spoke himself. "Your crew made quite an impact on the French, I understand they fired six times in one minute, and I hear that the efforts of your purser have been put to good use training men in field craft?"

"Yes but......."

Stopped once more Robert listened to the Admiral. "Lord Mills has become interested in you and your crew of ruffians, he will be joining us shortly so I will take this opportunity to caution you. Lord Mills is a very dangerous man; he has the ear of the high and mighty both in government and at the Admiralty, plus a close relationship with Horse Guards. This means that he can make or break virtually anyone at the snap of his fingers. I suggest a long spoon sir, you understand? A long spoon...." He tapped his nose, looking at Robert keenly.

Robert nodded "I understand, sir, but what does he want with me?"

Malmby shrugged "Who knows? All I can tell you is that he has made it known he wishes to speak with you in secrecy, hence the meeting here rather than in some public place where it may be observed."

A knock at the door put an end to the Admiral's comments and a neatly dressed man of middle height entered, waited until the door was closed, and then introduced himself as Lord Mills. He was thin-faced and gave an impression of repressed energy, like a wound clock. After a few conventional comments back and forth the Admiral asked to be excused and withdrew from the chamber.

As the door closed the visitor clasped his hands behind him and walked over to the window overlooking Tower Hill. Robert noticed that he did not stand in full view of the window remaining where he could see without being seen. Mills spoke.

"You will be wondering who I am, and why I am here? Am I right?"

Robert nodded.

"Well to take things in order, I am the country's first line of defence, I occupy no known position, and I can do virtually what I like to whomsoever I like. I am here to possibly recruit you and your ship and crew to perform some tasks that are difficult to discuss for various reasons.

In a nutshell I am in charge if intelligence gathering and I run a network of spies throughout Europe, two of whom you have already met."

"Lotte Mansfield and Amelie Parker!" Robert blurted out.

"Precisely," Mills cut him off. "Now, listen, I understand you have—some say misguidedly—trained your marines to perform a range of activities not normally associated with sailing a frigate. Rifle skills, field craft and the murderous methods employed by the American Indians and the woodsmen of that country to dispose of their enemies.

"Not only the marine detachment, but the seamen also; my men are expected to fight hand to hand on deck against enemies, they are required to assault land targets as well. I consider they should have the best training I can give them. The rifles were discarded by the army, I have merely put them to use, and—in fact—if I can, I will obtain more so that the entire crew can become proficient in their use."

Chapter fifteen

Lord Mills looked at him in astonishment. "Do I understand that all your men are trained thus, what of their officers?"

"The officers also, I myself can now shoot accurately with the rifle and I can fire six shots within a minute sometimes seven!"

"And the field craft—you have the officers crawling about in the undergrowth too?"

"I certainly do. There is little point in training my men to be silent in approach if their officers cannot keep similarly silent."

There was a period of silence while Mills walked up and down the room, digesting this information. He stopped suddenly, turned to Robert and said. "Captain Graham, from what you have said it appears that I will need to rethink my plans. Please return to your ship and continue you activities with the Customs service. I believe that you should commence training Captain Leclerc to assume your current sea duties.

"You will remain under the nominal command of Admiral Malmby but you will be directly responsible to me, this will permit me to keep you and your ship in the area and prevent the Admiralty from snatching you off to some distant part of the world for months on end. Do you understand?"

"Yes sir, but what of the normal promotion for my men? This is normally an Admiralty matter."

"You and your men still come under the command of Admiral Malmby. If promotions are merited or due, he will ensure they are awarded. Anything else?"

"Yes sir, the rifles! I will need 100 more with the required ammunition of course."

"Very well, I will arrange it immediately. I will be in touch through the Admiral when I need your services; no word of this to anyone except you immediate deputy."

With that Mills, rather limply, shook hands and left abruptly.

It was with some surprise and amusement that a puzzled Abel Jackson reported to his captain ten days after the discussion with the mysterious Lord Mills.

"Sir, I have received a consignment of materials from the Admiralty, 10 cases of Fergusson rifles two cases of ammunition 1 case of maintenance equipment, and 24 bales of uniforms. I confess I expected the rifles but uniforms?

Robert reassured him. "I have a memo from Lord Mills. 'In view of the possible employment of the crew of *Roister* as irregulars, it has been decided that they be issued with suitable dress to ensure there is no suggestion that they be mistaken for outlaws or guerrilla forces. The uniform has been designed to be inconspicuous; the shade of green has just been suggested for a regiment of riflemen to be formed for the army. When operating on land as troops, the company will be designated Naval Infantry, part of the 1st Regiment, of the Rifles whatever they are called when formed. These uniforms should only be used overseas!'"

In the precincts of the training base at Plymouth the crew tried out their uniforms amid great hilarity. The green tunics with their twin rows of dull black buttons and the black naval infantry badges with the large one superimposed, looked quite smart, and with the small pill box hat, also green with two black bands, the complete uniform from overall trousers to hat, the men looked like soldiers at least.

Captain Ullyet, wearing the green jacket with his Marine badges suitably blackened, stood in front of his marine company—who stood at ease—demonstrating to the naval crew how the uniform should be worn, and how to conduct themselves when wearing it.

Each man thus fitted, the suitably marked sets were gathered and packed in boxes and returned to the ship.

The duties of the customs service still required the maintenance of patrols and it was whilst the freezing weather of November covered the moors with a white blanket that the news of the escape of the two Tregarth brothers was reported. The task of arresting them after their escape was for the law officers but their contacts in the smuggling fraternity made their escape a definite problem for the Preventive men.

Since Captain Graham was able to depend on the men he provided; the success rate of arrest was formidable. The Tregarth brothers were known to have sworn to get Graham and his family for his part in their capture. Barbara was in London visiting friends and preparing for the birth of their first child. For this Robert was grateful. When the news of the escape became known he sent a letter telling Barbara to remain in London until the men were retaken. The letter passed Barbara as she travelled homeward by the mail coach in the opposite direction.

Peter and Adam Tregarth had managed to elude pursuit so far, both crouched shivering in the ditch beside the London road a mile north of Bovey Tracey. Peter carried the musket taken from their escort when they broke away from their guards between the Assize court and the prison in Exeter.

The Judge taking the Smugglers Circuit was an old customer, but he had not been friendly and he had been severe in his judgement. Despite Peter's plea for his nineteen-year-old brother Adam, making it clear that he had not imperilled any lives, the Judge had still ruled that both men hang for their crimes. These included the murder of three Preventive Men and an unknown number of civilians, killed at sea and to keep their mouths shut on land.

When they ran, the crowds had helped, interfering with the troops trying to recapture the escapees; unfortunately the people of Exeter were not willing to shelter the two men and that was why they were crouching shivering by the roadside.

Peter was worried about his young brother Adam; he had picked up a fever in jail and was shivering badly despite having Peter's coat on as well as his own. They had to get to shelter soon or Adam might not survive the night.

The lights of the mail coach from London appeared across the moor, the jingle of the harness a cheerful sound against the rumble of the wheels grating and sliding over the sometimes slippery uneven surface. Almost without thinking Peter rose from his position in the ditch and pointed the musket at the driver. "Stop now!"

The driver hauled the rains back and pulled the horses to a standstill. He looked down at the bedraggled man at the road side. "And what might you be doing here at this time of night waving that useless piece of artillery about?" The driver was a former soldier and was fully aware that the musket was soaked in the rain and would not fire. Peter felt a wave of helplessness wash over him, dropping the musket he said. "Please help my brother, he is very ill." He indicated the crouched shivering shape in the ditch.

At that point Barbara leaned out of the coach and saw what was going on. "Well, don't just sit there, driver, help the man get his brother in the coach. And wake up that drunken guard to assist you. Come on, man, move!"

The hastily awakened guard and driver lifted the shivering Adam into the coach, Peter climbed on top and the coach moved off once more.

Within the jolting vehicle Barbara stripped the outer clothing from the feverish man, she turned to the other people in the carriage. "We must keep him warm or he will die, please pass over your spare blankets and coats."

The other passengers—a farmer and his wife and a young Ensign in the Dragoons—hastily passed over a blanket and the Ensign's cloak. The man lay on the floor of the jolting coach until it started to rumble over the cobbles of the streets of Plymouth.

Looking at the man, Barbara made her decision. "Coachman", she called. "Drive straight to Tamar House, this man must be helped immediately!" She turned to the others. "It is not far and I will be pleased to entertain you to refreshment at the house before delivering you to your destination."

The farmer's wife beamed. "Why no trouble, my Lady, we're only too glad to help. I'm sure this young man would not be put out either, would you sir?" The Ensign, who had sat admiring Barbara for most of the journey, stammered his agreement and the coach diverted to Tamar House and deposited the passengers and their luggage before clattering off into Plymouth once more.

The Ensign helped Peter carry the sick man into the house while Barbara called for a room to be prepared. The housekeeper was swift to arrange things and the shivering man was dried off by the footman and put to bed in one of Robert's nightshirts. The bed was warmed with hot stones wrapped in cloths, and a fire lit in the room. By the time the doctor came the man had begun to sweat.

Peter stood, steaming, in front of the fire in the drawing room; the rum punch sent a warm glow through his body, and he relaxed for the first time that day. He shook himself, he must decide what to do. Adam was ill, and as long as he was not recognised he would be safe here. The doctor was not from the Cornish side and was unknown to them both, but anyone from over the river might see and recognise them, and that would mean the noose.

The Ensign and the farming couple left in the carriage provided by Barbara with her thanks.

In the drawing room she faced Peter. "I know who you are and I know you for a smuggler and a murderer. I also know that your brother was a fisherman and was only dragged into the trade because of you. I believe he is no killer."

Peter replied. "He is no killer indeed, that judge would not listen, I take my chances and if I hang 'tis because I earned it, but Adam is no killer, and he does not deserve to hang. It's why I took the chance to run, better the bullet than the rope."

"Leave your brother here, he will be looked after. I will make sure he escapes the rope, but you must take your chances, you cannot stay, you are too well known and my husband would have to arrest you and return you to be hanged. Without you, your brother has a chance of life; with you he will assuredly die. Do you understand?"

Peter Tregarth bowed. "I will leave the country and take my chances, perhaps America? Thank you, Lady Barbara, for everything." He turned, put down his glass, and walked out of Tamar House and his brother's life.

Barbara turned and walked through to the study. Robert was standing by the fire, smoking the long pipe kept there. He raised his eyebrow in query. Barbara nodded. "He has gone; perhaps to America, perhaps elsewhere. I believe he has gone for good."

Robert nodded, put down his pipe and held out his arms, Barbara snuggled up close.

"I'm glad to be back." She kissed him. "I knew you would let him run."

"You know me too well. I should have arrested him, but I don't like the hypocrisy involved in this smuggling trade. The sooner I get back to proper sailoring, the better. Will the young man survive his fever, d'ye think?"

"I believe the Doctor thinks so, he certainly has a chance here."

"Good! I've an idea that young man could be saved, away from the influence of his brother. Let's go to bed."

Barbara giggled. "Who do you think I am, sir, some doxy to be......" she saw his face and ran out of the room laughing.

***

HMS Roister was scudding along across the small waves under a blue sky spotted with small puffs of white cloud. The foc'sle was occupied with hands enjoying a make and mend.

The feeling of relief throughout the ship was reflected in the skylarking on the foc'sle and cheerful smile on the face of the master, renowned for his habitually lugubrious expression. Even the midshipmen grouped around the master were happy to be back at sea, as he explained some of the arcane mysteries of solar navigation. At the lee rail Abel Jackson was conducting a class in the finer points of deflection whilst shooting at moving targets; the occasional crack of the rifle punctuating his lecture.

The surgeon John Sweet came on deck and walked over to Robert. "May I have a word, sir, in private?"

Robert nodded and stepped below to his cabin. "What can I do for you, John?"

"Its Adam Tre.-Tamar." He blushed and apologised. "He is ready to take his place in the crew; I am happy he has recovered completely from the fever and is fully fit once more. I would suggest he would be better occupied on the quarterdeck rather than in the rigging. He raised his hand, I know he was a fisherman, but he is educated, he can read and write.

?I think he would be wasted as a seaman, he would be useful as a clerk or using his sailing experience as an officer of some sort, perhaps master's mate, he is too old to be a midshipman." He stopped and took the seat offered while Robert looked thoughtful.

After a few minutes Robert spoke. "Do you know who he is, or rather was?" At the surgeon's nod he continued. "Now we are away from that damned Preventive work what you suggest is actually possible. I would not have recognised him, and apparently the crew haven't, so I think I will take your advice and be guided by your recommendation, what shall it be?"

John Sweet smiled. "I think fresh air is what the lad needs; master's mate, it is. I'll send him down with the master."

"Send the master first please, Doctor." Robert opened his Journal and made a note.

The coast was visible as a line of white surf to port. The ship sailed through the passage between Belle Isle and the Presqu'ile de Quiberon; it was nearly midnight though not really dark.

Roister crept towards the beach at St Guildas-de-Ruys and backed her sails less than a cable offshore. The longboat was lowered and commanded by Midshipman Dawson who whispered to the waiting men to give way. Alan Dawson had filled out, his fair hair had been tamed and trimmed and his bronzed face had thinned and matured over the past few months.

As the boat neared the shore the men rested on their oars and waited while a lantern was shown briefly; on the beach the reply was seen and the boat resumed its progress. The figures from the beach waded out and boarded the boat, carrying their bags.

On the ship the two visitors were brought below to Robert's cabin

The taller man introduced himself to Robert. "I am Henri Duvall and I work for Lord Mills." He held out his hand and showed a small badge. Robert took it and examined it curiously. He had been told about the badges but had never actually seen one. The engraved falcon was surmounting an escutcheon with the letters M of D standing for Mills of Dee, Lord Mill's family seal. He returned it and sat down, inviting the two men to take the other chairs in the cabin. Lieutenant Billy Beaufort stood swaying easily to the motion of the long swell.

Henri spoke. "I have bad news. One of our most important agents is about to be arrested in Vannes. My source tells me that she has come under suspicion, having been seen by a visitor who believes he recognizes her from Paris under another name. The agent has sent for proof from Paris. When it arrives, Honore will be arrested; I cannot reach her to warn her, since she is being watched by the secret police who will recognise me."

"Can I help in any way? Perhaps if I send a file of soldiers—can they be guided to her location? We can appear to arrest her and carry her off, bringing her here of course, or some other place of safety.

"Whatever we do will have to be decided quickly; I have to move the ship out of sight before morning."

"Pierre could guide a group, but soldiers?" He indicated the other man. "Pardon, this is Pierre, he does not speak English, he is a staunch Loyalist and he hates the rule of Napoleon."

"Mr. Beaufort, send for Captain Ullyet, please." Robert turned back to Henri, "I can supply soldiers, how many would be suitable for this purpose?"

Henri thought for a moment. "Perhaps twelve, with an officer."

As Ullyet came into the cabin he gave his orders. "Captain, I will need twelve French infantrymen and one officer who speaks French."

The uniforms captured in the earlier action at Djerba Island were still held aboard and Ullyet swiftly produced eleven soldiers and one sergeant, himself. "I don't speak French, sir," he said.

Across the room Lieutenant Beaufort spoke. "I do, sir."

"Very good, Mr. Beaufort. Get dressed and report on deck in ten minutes. Carry on, Mr. Ullyet."

Ullyet turned to the Frenchman "Right. Mr. Duvall, perhaps you could tell me where we must go."

The squad of soldiers marched through the flickering lights of the flambeau placed along the main streets of Vannes. The tramp of the marching feet echoed from the walls of the ancient citadel, their shadows black against the red walls following the troops growing bigger and smaller as the light breeze caused the flames to flare.

The civilian in the long cloak leading the party held up his hand and the officer called the men to halt. The civilian accompanied the officer through a doorway in the otherwise smooth wall. There was a wait of several minutes, the officer appeared once more and beckoned the sergeant, after a few words the sergeant gave instruction to the first two men, who passed their weapons to the men behind them and followed their officer into the building. They emerged a few minutes later carrying several bags and bundles, followed in turn by the civilian and the officer similarly loaded; a lady heavily cloaked completed the group. The whole party reversed their direction and marched back to the harbour with the lady in their midst and boarded the longboat awaiting them at the quay.

The crew of the longboat stepped the mast and, raising the sail, they began threading their way between the islands of the Golfe de Morbihan, gradually making for the Pointe de Kerpenhir and the open bay.

The channel between Belle-Ile and Presque-Il-de Quiberon lay ahead. Though by now it was daylight; the mist that covered the bay area still concealed their progress.

They did not see the guard boat until it was quite close. The challenge called on them to stop and through the mist they saw the cutter lying in wait for them, Billy Beaufort in command of the party whispered to Ullyet. "Guns loaded, I hope?"

Ullyet's dry reply brought a smile to face of the sergeant sitting beside him. "My rifles are loaded and ready for action, as always!"

Unconcerned, Billy nudged the civilian sitting beside him. "Tell him we are taking a prisoner to Lorient for interrogation. The road is full of traffic moving the grand army to St-Nazaire and it is quicker to sail."

The boats drifted closer and the crew of the cutter relaxed when they saw the uniforms of the men in the boat. The longboat crew had dropped the sail and it was out of the way of the riflemen as the boat bumped alongside of the cutter. The men in the longboat rose as one and boarded the cutter. There were no shouts, or shouted orders, just the sudden appearance on deck of twelve men pointing rifles at the cutter's crew, swiftly followed by the crew of the longboat and the civilian with their lady passenger.

The surprise was complete and the small warship was taken without a shot being fired. Lieutenant Beaufort took command, the prisoners were sent below under the charge of the marines, the longboat was trailed from the stern of the cutter. With the course selected they made for the open sea and the ship awaiting them beyond Belle-ile.

The sea sparkled under the sun, porpoises leapt and played ahead of the two craft as they carved twin white paths through the blue water. *HMS Roister* and her recently acquired consort, the cutter *Morbihan*. In the great cabin on the frigate Robert sat facing Honore—who it turned out was Amelie Parker—as well as Pierre and Henri Duvall, Captain Ullyet and Billy Beaufort. All had coffee cups in front of them.

Chapter sixteen

"What you are saying is that there is a column of British prisoners being moved to Lorient from St Nazaire to be used for the building of a new dock in the port. With the escort for that same column will be three wagons carrying gold and silver bullion from the Americas plus a coach carrying a secret agent who has caused more trouble for us than any other.

?He is believed to be an English nobleman but—not surprisingly—his identity has been kept a closely guarded secret by his French paymasters, and is referred to only as the Ferret. He obviously has access to men in high places in the British Government and, since he is above suspicion, is trusted with information vital to the conduct of our campaign.

"What size would the escort for this convoy be? Have you any information?"

"So far we know of a squadron of Heavy Cavalry, about one hundred men in all, plus a platoon of infantry escorting the prisoners directly." Amelie was quite specific. "The prisoners will be chained at the wrist but not at the ankle to make it easier to march, they do not expect any escape attempts. There should be one hundred and fifty prisoners in the column, being guarded by twenty-eight Infantry."

Captain Ullyet rose to his feet. "The journey is about 120 Kilometres in all. I estimate at least six days march; the nearest place to the coast is Muzillac." He pointed to the village on the map pinned up to the bulkhead. "I would normally suggest another place but in view of our means of escape by sea we have to consider it. I would prefer Plouhinec, here." He pointed out another village close to Lorient. "But it is close to Lorient and I think they may opt to travel through Merlevenez. Here on the main road."

Lieutenant Beaufort interrupted. "Just a minute, what about the Grand Armee? Are they not travelling through the area during the next few days? Surely the escort commander will wish to avoid the main roads while they travel through?"

A slow smile spread across Ullyet's thin face. "I underestimated you, Mr. Beaufort. You are quite correct. With the army passing through, they must take the side roads and that gives us a distinct advantage for an ambush." He went on to detail how the ambush would be laid. "The main question was who do we concentrate on, the bullion or the prisoners."

"Prisoners first, I think." Robert's voice was firm. "That is unless there is some other reason, for the sake of the operation, that we have to dispose of the bullion first?"

"I agree the prisoners are the easiest target and we can get to them easier in the first instance,

"The way I understand the column to be formed is with the bulk of the cavalry stationed around the bullion wagons, the supply wagon forms part of this section, certainly there should be 50 troopers close escort, 20 in skirmish order scouting ahead for accommodation and camp areas, and the balance, perhaps 20 rearguard while the remainder patrol the entire column, outriders and so on. Remember this part of France has its share of loyalists and there is always the threat of ambush for the unwary. While this makes our job more difficult, it is not impossible. Since we have French infantry uniforms in our stores, we should first concentrate on replacing the foot soldiers escorting the prisoners.

"We can actually release the prisoners discreetly, hopefully without revealing our presence. Our main company, in our Green Jackets, will prepare an ambush for the troopers and wagons.

"For this reason I suggest we attack late afternoon or early morning, when the sun will blind them, and while they are either jaded and tired or perhaps still only half awake. They will be confident in their numbers that they are safe from attack anyway so we should be able to take them completely by surprise. I do stress that we must make every shot count. The Grand Armee will not be that far away and confident though I am about our abilities, I do think an entire French Army may be too much, even for us."

Ullyet sat down in silence as each of the assembled people absorbed what had been suggested. Finally, Robert spoke. "Thank you, Captain, I think you have laid out the situation clearly. Please prepare detailed plans so that the various parties can be informed of their part in the matter. On this occasion I will command the operation myself with you as second. Please suggest any other officers or men you will particularly need so that we can make proper arrangements."

He rose to his feet. "Thank you, lady and gentlemen, we will meet again tonight for a final discussion. By the time we have the ship in position, we should be ready for the operation in two days, by which time our target should be in the right place."

The people of Maguero were unaware of the creeping progress of the cutter that landed the platoon of soldiers just past the lagoon where the road on the coast turned inland. The entire platoon landed and formed up, and left unnoticed. The five-mile march to the crossroads at Plouhinec was accomplished in just over one hour.

The prisoners were lying huddled together round the signpost in the centre of the village. Six soldiers were wandering round, two were smoking pipes, the others stamped their feet to keep awake. Whilst they waited, a file of soldiers marched up, and the senior guard came to attention and called his comrades to fall in. The newcomers, led by a sergeant, halted and the sergeant ordered his men to take up position. He didn't bother with the relieved guard, who, having gathered themselves together, shambled off to their billet in the village hall.

At the village hall the remainder of the platoon were all awake and as the relieved guards entered, several spoke up in disgust.

The incoming guards were relieved of their weapons and ordered to strip off their uniforms, which were added to the pile obtained from the others. The entire platoon were bound and gagged and seated against the wall of the hall. The leader of their captors, Captain Ullyet, had the bundled uniforms placed on a handcart and wheeled down to the assembled prisoners who were beginning to awaken. Ullyet spoke to the nearest prisoner and asked him in English, who was in charge among the prisoners, the man pointed to a big man, still asleep.

"Ee's a master from an Indiaman captured three month ago. Ee looks after us all and can talk to the frogs in their own lingo."

Ullyet walked over to the sleeping man and roused him by shaking his shoulder. The keen blue eyes stared at him for a moment. In English Ullyet quietly spoke to him. "Get the men up and go with the guards down to the shore please; outside the carpenter will unlock the main chain, I'm afraid you'll have to wait until we reach the ship to get the cuffs off."

"Aye sir, with a will." He rose to his feet and went round rousing certain men and talking quietly giving his instructions, the men started to form up, exclamations were hurriedly stifled. As the column started off back along the road towards the sea, they were flanked by two of their replacement escort. The carpenter, dressed in uniform like his companions, broke the long chain that ran through all the wrist cuffs so that as they marched away the long chain remained on the ground, to be gathered up by four of the men and dumped over the wall of the blacksmiths shop located by the green in the village centre.

The remainder of the platoon formed up and Ullyet told Pierre what he had in mind, using the services of the Dutchman Eckhart. The men marched off towards the Chateau on the other side of the village. It was here that the wagons and the carriage carrying the Colonel of the Cavalry and the spy were housed overnight. By this time, Captain Ullyet was making things up as he went along.

The troopers and their horses were camped on the lawn in front of the Chateau. As the platoon arrived at the gates, the two men on duty at the gate moved their horses to bar the way. Pierre, dressed as the infantry captain, ordered them aside. The troopers, with the arrogance of cavalry in the presence of infantry, were slow to comply but they did give way. With a whack, Captain Pierre laid the flat of his sword on the haunches of both horses causing them to rear up and jump aside, with the troopers frantically trying to control their mounts. He muttered "Cochons!" and stepped forward through the gates

The platoon followed—laughing at their discomfort, but rapidly calming down under the icy glare of their officer—through the gates and into the grounds beyond. The small party marched over to the wagons and the captain roused up the drivers and ordered them to harness the horses and prepare to move. Thoroughly cowed by the fierce manner of the officer, they set about their task. He then strode over to the tent occupied by the senior cavalry officer present. The Colonel was being housed in the Chateau with his guest, the English spy.

Major Curtain the 2nd in command was shaving when he was interrupted by Captain Petain of the 1st Regiment of Foot. "And who the hell are you?" He said impatiently.

"Sir, I am Captain Petain, in command of the prisoners escort. I have to report that my platoon has been relieved of their prisoners and ordered to ride the wagons for the rest of the march as close escort. There has been a report of partisan activity in this area."

The Major was disgusted. "I have 150 troopers under arms here, what do they worry about."

The captain shrugged his shoulders and sighed, as if to say, 'so what's new'? The Major also shrugged and thought, 'bloody amateurs' and turned to the Captain. "Very well, fall your men in close escort to the wagons; I'll inform the colonel when he appears. Carry on!"

The Captain saluted and turned and left the tent. As he crossed to the men, he sighed with relief and reported to Ullyet the success of his plan.

Ullyet spoke quietly to Midshipman Dawson, "I want you to contact Captain Graham." He showed Dawson the map they had made of the area pointing out where their

Captain should be. "Tell him that we are in command of the wagons. As soon as the ambush occurs, we will turn the wagons and make for the beach. If he concentrates on keeping the cavalry occupied, we should manage the rest." He walked with the young man down to the gate and past the two disgruntled troopers who glared at them but let them through. He sent the boy off and turned to the troopers. "Captain Petain, oh ho!" and shrugged his shoulders and returned to the wagons.

Alan Dawson put his rifle over his shoulder and trotted down the road towards Lorient; he stopped, studied the map and looked about at the local area. He climbed the bank beside the road on the left and from the top of the bank he called out in a clear voice, "Captain Graham, Sir?"

A green-jacketed figure rose from behind the hedge, and pointed down the road towards Lorient, "Should find him just before the corner, Mr. Dawson!" He touched his hat and sank down once more.

Dawson ran down to the corner and found the captain. He explained to Robert the developments regarding the prisoners. Robert sent messengers down the line both ways to warn the riflemen to avoid the wagons and carriage and ordered Dawson to remain with him to act as messenger if required.

The camping arrangements had taken them by surprise, however it had simplified matters. That they were able to get the prisoners out of the way unharmed left the field clear for the rest of the operation on the road after the column left the Chateau. The infantry men were ideally placed to support the ambush party if necessary; otherwise they were well situated to escape to the beach while the cavalry were otherwise occupied.

The wagons and their drivers were lined up ready to leave by the time the colonel and his guest came out of the Chateau. Ignoring the trooper's formation, they boarded the coach and the cavalcade moved off through the gates for the final ten mile stretch to Lorient.

The long column stretched out on the country road, the leading unit out of sight round a bend and the skirmishers as much as a mile ahead of the train. Two of the infantrymen dropped back to march beside the carriage, dropping back until they were beside the rear wheels as two more took their place either side of the front wheels. Nobody commented and for another half mile the march continued without incident.

Suddenly a cry was heard from near the front of the column and the entire party shambled to a halt. There was shouting from further up the road and a galloper came to report to the Colonel, a peasant's hay cart had broken a wheel, blocking the road where it went out of a cutting. Men were moving it now, it would be just a few moments.

The front section of the escort was well ahead by now unaware of the incident behind them. A volley of shots rang out and several troopers fell around the peasant cart. The men immediately in front of the wagons suddenly found themselves under fire from both sides of the road. Seventeen men fell at the next volley.

The sound of the shots brought the rearguard pounding forward to support the section under fire, leaving the defence of the wagons and carriage to the infantry platoon. Drawing their carbines ready, they ran into a fire storm of bullets fired with extreme accuracy from both sides of the road. The steady volleys shattered the ranks of the beleaguered troopers, who were watching their comrades fall on all sides. Their discipline was not sufficient to stand this sort of fire and they broke, scattering in all directions. Under the command of Captain Ullyet, the wagons and carriage turned and retreated back the way they had come. The colonel and his companion were flung about inside as the driver whipped the horses to escape the flying bullets that were murdering the cavalry.

The soldiers marching alongside the carriage jumped up and clung on for dear life riding the steps of the vehicle while holding onto the window frames, the soldiers with the wagons climbed frantically onboard and clung on for dear life.

Back at the Chateau gates, the carriage stopped and the Colonel and his companion got out. They were tousled and furious. As the Colonel opened his mouth to speak, Captain Ullyet appeared on a trooper's horse, and ordered them both back inside the carriage. He emphasised his order with a levelled pistol. The wagons caught up and the whole party together once more made their way back to the beach.

As they approached the beach, the boats had just begun ferrying Green Jackets who had been sent down direct from road out to the frigate. The cutter was close inshore, awaiting the wagons; groups of men were there to help with loading the small boats waiting on the beach.

The Colonel was released from the carriage and he and the civilian were taken under escort out to the frigate. As the loading progressed, the sound of horses was heard from the woods above the beach, Midshipman Abbot in charge of the beach party signalled a warning to *Roister* even as Captain Ullyet and his riflemen deployed in cover along the beach edge, rifles ready.

As the first of the cavalry broke cover, rifles cracked, and the three troopers dropped from their saddles. No others showed themselves; though several shots were fired from within the trees.

The loading was now completed; all the contents of the wagons had been taken on board so Ullyet's riflemen retreated down the beach in groups of three. When they reached the water's edge, a signal to the ship was followed by cannon fire from the ship causing the trees to shudder with the impact of the hail of shot from the grape charge. The retreating men piled onto the waiting boats and were pulled out to the ship passing swiftly out of range of the trooper's carbines.

Robert greeted the Colonel of cavalry and the civilian in his cabin, the Colonel handed his sword over with the comment that the party would not get far; he would be reclaiming it shortly! Robert sent him to join the other prisoners and turned his attention to the civilian.

As the two ships sailed past Ile-de-Groix, sails were spotted downwind—two ships, both under topsails. The signal to increase sail flew up to the yard of *Roister*, and the top-men raced up through the rigging to set the sails, the ship moved appreciably faster in response to the extra sails set. On the cutter she set her trysail and a spanker below the long bowsprit. Both ships settled slightly in the water, and the race began in earnest.

It was soon apparent that the cutter would not be able to keep up the pace, despite her best efforts she kept dropping behind. *Roister* slowed, easing her sails to keep company.

Astern the pursuing ships began to gradually increase in size as they closed the range.

It is often the case that when things look as if they are going well, it could be time to look over your shoulder.

Captain Graham went on deck and spoke to the master Mr. Callow, "How soon will they be with us?"

"Not until after dark, we should have a chance to lose them in the dark, but with Quimper off to starboard we have to turn to port and they will know that."

"I think the blockade fleet should be in the area of Brest, and we will be up to there shortly, so what I think is we will take advantage of the prevailing wind here and turn in to the bay of Brest whilst it is still light, then out past the Ile Beniguet as soon as night falls. Since we have not seen the blockade fleet, I would guess they have sailed out beyond Ile d'Ouessant and will be returning with the dusk. If I am wrong, we'll fight." He shrugged and went below to question the spy.

In the cabin the civilian from the carriage was seated on the bench beneath the stern windows, his back to the light, he appeared relaxed and rose to his feet when Robert entered.

The man walked over and seated himself in the chair opposite Robert's desk. "The window seat is a pleasant place to sit in your little ship." He drawled the words and seemed perfectly at ease.

Robert looked at him gravely. He was a tall man, perhaps 6 feet even, with black hair swept back and held by a black ribbon over the collar of his neat jacket, also black. Robert did not recognize him, which was not that surprising, since he did not move in the exalted circles of government or society. Amelie however did know him, and when she appeared through the cabin door the stranger blanched.

For the first time Robert spoke. "Who are you, and if you would please explain why you were being entertained by the French military?" There was a lengthy silence while the stranger struggled to think of an answer that would be accepted.

Amelie spoke. "Perhaps it would be easier if I opened proceedings with a little background!

To Robert she said. "This is Lord Charles Wade."

Robert looked up sharply at the name, although he did not know the face, the name was familiar to most people in England.

Amelie continued "Lord Wade is a confidant of our foreign minister and regularly is called upon to advise Horse Guards on our military strategy. His lordship comes from an Irish landed family of considerable antiquity but questionable ethics. Over the centuries they have suffered from a succession of extravagant descendants. The family holdings have been progressively sold off until at this present time they consist of a semi-ruined castle in the west of Ireland, and an empty title.

"Like many of his forebears, Lord Charles has had to depend on his wits to live in the manner he feels is appropriate. Spying for the French provides an income."

The silence following these damning comments extended until finally broken by the subject.

"I find that the politics of the European nations are all driven by greed. The so called rule of the people in France is a sham, and Napoleon will no doubt soon declare himself as King. The Royal family in Britain comprises weak, sick, self-indulgent Princes; one a buffoon the other a stuffed shirt. Their father shows no sign of interest in either. I enjoy a better standard of living playing one against the other, and why not? For me there is no loyalty due to either side, their financial contributions to my living have been earned with the impartial transmission of information in both directions."

He sat back with a smug look in his face, expecting that he had explained himself in a satisfactory way. The proceedings were interrupted by a knock on the door. On being told to enter, the bo'sun saluted and said "I've rigged the noose from the yardarm for the spy, sir! It's all ready when you are."

"Very good bo'sun, I'll let you know when we're ready."

There was another lengthy silence when the bo'sun withdrew, and it was a very shaken Lord Charles who broke the silence. "What is all this about hanging?"

"Why, that is the sentence for spying under British law, and added to that is the charge of treason against the crown, which also carries the death penalty. By hanging you now it saves you having to anticipate being hung for the next few weeks, gets it all over quickly." Amelie said brightly.

Lord Charles looked appalled, "But... but" he stuttered "I have to be tried in court, there are explanations I can make information I can help with...." He trailed off and buried his head in his hands.

Amelie was relentless "By hanging you now we will save a lot of time and expense, and in the circumstances the Captain of a Naval ship at sea has the right to try and sentence enemies of the crown, they call it summery justice in law!"

Robert looked up on hearing this, and for the first time began to understand how clever this pretty woman was. Whatever else happened there was no way that Lord Charles would hang on this ship, he had neither the power nor the right to arrange that, but Lord Charles didn't know that!

Meanwhile Lord Charles was telling Amelie everything he knew including a list of sympathisers in the hierarchy of the war department and the admiralty, evidently one of the reasons for the frustration of several operations over the past few years.

He called for his clerk, and having seen him settled with pen and paper, left the cabin to Amelie, her broken informant and the clerk, and returned to the clean sea air of the quarterdeck.

Some of the things that seem to be trouble can suddenly become a benefit. So it was with the chasing ships, far from threatening capture the chasing ships were in fact two of the frigates from the blockading fleet, returning from a sweep down coast. By the time Roister and her consort made contact with the flagship the two frigates had rejoined the fleet.

Chapter seventeen

Admiral Keith was anticipating retiring from active service with the Navy and, when Robert reported, he was in high good humour. "I was considering having you transferred to my command." He said "But as luck would have it I did not need to bother. When I arrive home I will be taking over command of the Preventive service from Admiral Malmby, I understand that you are still under his command and I will in fact take you over with the rest of the department.

In Plymouth, while the ship stored, Robert established contact with Captain Willets.

The *Morbihan* sailed on direct to Dover to report to Lord Mills, with Amelie Parker and Lord Charles. They anticipated that the cutter would join the fleet operated by the Preventive service.

For Robert the chance to see his beloved Barbara and his new son David was appreciated. Normally in the regular service he could have been away for up to a year at least. As it was, just over two months had elapsed since he had sailed.

The regular gathering at the Half Moon inn was enjoying a convivial evening when the door burst open and Alan Dawson burst in. his uniform was torn and there was blood on his face. Elizabeth cried out when she saw him and rushed over in time to catch him as he staggered and almost fell. "What is this?" she cried "What has happened?"

"It's Adam Tamar. We were walking down to pay a call here when we were attacked by a bunch of ruffians who seemed to recognise Adam, I did what I could but there were too many for us and they are carrying him off to the fleet they said."

Sam Callow turned to Judith, "Run round to the Anchor and call Sven Hanson. Tell him help needed at the Fleet inn. Tell him it's Adam Tamar in trouble; he'll know."

Abel Jackson came through with his pistols and a Hanger clipped to his belt. "I'm ready, Sam."

"Let's get going. Stay here, Alan, we'll take over from here."

Sam and Abel left the Half Moon and strode off through the dark streets. As they passed on the way to the Fleet Inn they met Peter Morse and two of his mates, who joined them as soon as they heard what was happening.

The bar of the Fleet Inn was not a pleasant room at the best of times and fwas ull of a crowd of smoking, drinking men, who smelt trouble and were ready for it. The moment the group came in from the street carrying the struggling figure of Adam Tamar, the air became electric with the taste of suppressed violence.

The crowd looked on expectantly waiting to see what would happen.

Adam was tied to a chair whilst his captors called for drink. He sat testing his bonds while blood ran down his face from a wound in his hairline; the bruises on his face were purple patches against his tanned skin. There was fire in his eyes as he swore at the men who had attacked him and brought him here.

"You have made a mistake, Dan Creedy. I always knew you were a coward, took you six men to take me; you never were man enough by yourself."

The door of the inn opened and Sam Callow walked in followed by Abel Jackson. A hush fell as the two men were recognised. The crowd parted as the two men made their way to the seated figure of Adam Tamar.

Dan Creedy, a big bulky man with his friends all around him, stood to bar their way.

"Stand aside Creedy." Sam said mildly.

"Who'll make me?" Creedy was confident.

The back door of the inn opened and Peter and his two shipmates slid in while the attention was on Sam Callow and Creedy. Peter strolled over to Adam and sliced through the ropes binding him to the chair.

It came as an unpleasant shock for Creedy to hear the voice right behind him say, "I will." The hand that spun him round by the shoulder was not the hand of the sick young man who had sailed away three months ago. It was the hand of a man who had hauled sheets in the wind and rain and learned to reef in a gale as he learned his trade as a master's mate.

The fist that followed the hand made him aware that it could be more trouble than he had anticipated. A big man, he was confident he could deal with this and he reached out to grab Adam and draw him into a bear hug. He found he was grabbing air and, as he leaned forward off balance for a moment, a fist hit him on the nose and broke it, bringing tears to his eyes and a stream of blood down his chin. He spat and shook his head, spraying blood everywhere. He threw a punch that caught Adam beside the head and threw him against the crowd behind him. They thrust him back towards Creedy, who advanced ready to grab the young man in front of him. Once again that fist came out of nowhere and hit his already broken nose. Creedy cried out in pain, grabbed blindly at Adam and caught him. Clasping his hands behind Adam's back he crushed him against his chest. Adam was wearing shoes and when he felt the arm start to crush him he lifted his foot and scraped the sharp edge down the shin of his opponent and crushed it on the instep with all the weight he could muster. Creedy howled in agony and released the young man, who stepped back and smashed his fist into the broken nose once more. This caused Creedy pain beyond bearing and he fell to the floor sobbing holding his ruined face.

This proof of his cowardice caused a moment of shocked disbelief as the men in the crowd watched their leader grovelling on the floor. Then the door opened and big Swede Hanson came in with a group of *Roisters* and all hell broke loose.

***

There was a subdued air in the Half Moon inn as Sam and Abel ate carefully next morning. Lizzie and Jessie were pleased that the young Adam had been saved, but neither felt that their men needed to be involved in the brawl that followed. The regulars at the Fleet inn were basically smugglers. Creedy aside, most were hard drinking, hard living men. Disgusted with the shaming of Creedy, they had been determined to demonstrate that they would not be pushed around, especially by Preventive men. The role of *HMS Roister* being now known, the town divided in their attitude to the men who manned her. To the men of the Fleet Inn they were the enemy and the bloody conflict that resulted was a vicious attempt on both sides to pay off scores.

Both men winced when they moved in response to the bruises they had received during the melee. Despite the contrition both had expressed to their wives, secretly they had enjoyed the fight and were happy that they had demonstrated to the other crew members that they could still hold their own in a fight.

What they were not aware of was that their wives were also secretly proud of the fact that they had stood by their crew and despite the bruises they had demonstrated their manliness in an appropriate way. For the moment they would be made to suffer. After all they were mature men not boys and they needed to be reminded of their responsibilities.

On board ship, Adam Tamar and Alan Dawson, already friends were drawn even closer by their survival of the sticky situation on shore. The younger Dawson, though junior by nearly eight years, had been educated to a level that placed him in a position of equality in many ways with the older Adam Tamar. Adam had hardly had a youth. He had been expected to do a man's work from an early age and in Alan he had found a friend willing to help him with the schoolwork needed for his navigation study and an undemanding companion who didn't pass judgement on his past, which by now was known throughout the ship. Added to this was the fact that Alan was tall for his age and Adam was not, in fact they were both five-feet six inches tall, though the younger lad was destined to become taller.

Alan tended to lead the way into and out of mischief, but he was quick witted and looked after both of them. He was wiry and agile without an ounce of fat, but he was muscular and though not in full growth he was getting there.

Adam on the other hand was content to follow, not as quick to act as his friend, tended to think things through before he acted. He was fit and in the full strength of manhood. He had taken to the life on board ship to the manner born. Both could only see their future in the navy.

The meeting with Lord Mills was short and the substance was that Robert would be kept in London and *HMS Roister* would be commanded in the interim by Captain Willet. The task for Robert in London was to find and capture the network of agents that were being operated as a support group for Lord Charles. They had all dispersed as soon as word of the capture during the raid at Quiberon was sent through their secret channels.

Using a house in Park Lane, Robert was to operate in plain clothes with the assistance of Sergeant Walter Smith, a man of experience in the game of espionage.

When Robert arrived at the Park Lane house he found it was not on the lane at all. In fac,t it was in the Mews behind one of the houses halfway down. An apartment above a carriage house, currently unoccupied, and it was an extremely comfortable dwelling. Sergeant Smith had made himself at home in the accommodation and was prepared to use the premises as combination office and quarters for the duration of the enquiry at least. He was a widower and found no hardship changing his abode from the cottage in Deptford owned by his wife, and now given over to his daughter and her husband.

He was near six feet tall with friendly-looking brown eyes and a rather battered face. Robert discovered that his appearance was a result of his earlier career as a successful bare knuckles fighter. Having joined the army when his wife died he had found a place with the then Major Mills who recognised that the man he used as a bodyguard had a natural talent for espionage and was an astute investigator.

When Mills left the army he took the sergeant with him. They had worked together for the past five years.

"Welcome to this humble abode Captain Graham, my name is Walter Smith at your service.

"Since we are supposed to work together I think we should forget the titles." Robert was, not surprisingly, wary, though he liked the look of his partner.

"If I may suggest, Sir, I appreciate the gesture but our differences in status make it impossible for us to appear in public as equals. May I suggest I take the posture of bodyguard/assistant in public and call you sir and in turn you call me Smith? In private I am happy to be informal, I am known as Walter." He held his hand out and Robert took it with firm grip.

"My name is Robert, as you please, and I am pleased to meet you, sir."

The two men sat down and went over the information already gathered by Lord Mills' organisation. Broadly it was divided into two sections: known haunts of the agents and, where known, the areas where they operated. The main problem was actually identifying the people themselves.

Walter briefed Robert on what had been done so far. "I have enrolled you in the Academy of Arms in Vauxhall; you are brushing up your swordsmanship in the expectation of returning to the colours at some time in the future. If questioned on the subject be vague, undecided. You will also be able to brush up you pistol shooting, as they have a target range on the premises. The Academy is run by a French Master named the Compte D'Valle."

Robert stopped him at that point "I have met the Compte D'Valle. I rescued his niece off the coast of France in '94. I met him just after he acquired the title."

"That's odd, the man calling himself the Compte D'Valle came here last year. Je said he had only just managed to escape, the man who died in "'94 had been an imposter." He tapped his teeth reflectively.

Robert said "We can easily check, Mariette D'Valle can identify him for us!"

"I'm afraid not, she apparently went off to visit friends in Ireland with her husband shortly before D'Valle arrived and has not returned since. We do not know where she is."

"I see. Tell me, am I entered into the Academy under my own name?"

"Good lord no, sir... Bob we had linked the two names to start with. We could not allow that to happen. You are listed as Sir Robert Lindsey, from Dunnire, in Scotland. Educated here at Oxford, living in the Albany." He passed over an address, "You will be recognised and received by your sister who shares the apartment."

Robert raised his eyebrow in enquiry. Walter answered the unasked question; "Mistress Amelie Parker, your widowed sister." He said this with an absolutely straight face, though he was obviously aware that the two were known to each other.

"When do I report for training, and do I take my own weapons?"

"Tomorrow I would suggest, and take your sword in the first place so that the master may assess your requirements for training. Meanwhile, may I suggest a little supper and then sleep; there is much to do tomorrow" He indicated the table already laid with a cold collation and wine and the room beyond with a bed made up already.

The following day was busy as Walter suggested it might be. Robert reported to the Salle d' Armes with the sword given him by his father when he began fencing as a young man. It was unpretentious as swords go at the time but a sound practical weapon. He was greeted by the assistant Master as his employer was absent at the time. The man introduced himself as William Bain, late of his Majesty's Dragoon Guards. He was regarded as an expert in the art of duelling, having written a text book on the subject. Whilst waiting to be received, Robert had been able to read the details of the Masters in notices displayed in the foyer of the Salle.

While he understood that Robert wished to brush up on his swordplay in general, he would be happy to advise him on any matter of the art that he could assist with.

Dressed for fencing he took care measuring Robert and his sword in hand, before pronouncing himself satisfied that the two would work well together. Then, with foils provided, he proceeded to work Robert almost to exhaustion, fencing relentlessly for nearly one hour.

"You are very competent, sir," he commented. "You are certainly in much better condition than I expected you to be. Few people could have survived nearly one hour of combat as you have done. May I ask have you been serving his Majesty over the past few years?"

Having detected the trace of Scotland in the man's accent, Robert had an answer ready. "Every day for years my father made me train with a Broadsword, fencing with the local strongman, who had fought in the rising of '45. He was fifty-five years old and he beat me until he was sixty; from then on I beat him." I also served for a short period in the Yeomanry." He said no more, and Bain was convinced.

Later that night when he discussed his day with Walter he explained. "Made the mistake of answering his challenge. I'm sure it was deliberate, testing me out."

"He is a duellist, it would be second nature."

"I realised that I had been able to hold him far too long for an amateur, and then I recalled that I was supposed to be Scots, I can still hear my father talking of the wild Highlanders that came through England in the '45 wielding their broadswords. Heavy weapons to play with, I suggested that I had been forced to train with the broadsword as a young man, and he found it believable. At least I think he did?"

Walter walked over to the cabinet by the wall and flung open the door, exposing a selection of swords in a row, above which were a rack of a variety of pistols. From the selection of swords he found a double-edged broadsword—similar—though not the same as the famous Highlanders sword. He threw it to Robert and said "Downstairs with you."

Robert went downstairs into the carriage room below followed by Sergeant Smith who had selected another sword of similar weight to Robert's.

The carriage room was a surprise to Robert, he had not been shown it when he came to the Mews. In the centre was a square rope ring, and hanging from the joist above was a large punch bag.

"I like to keep fit!" was Walters's muttered explanation. "Now help me clear the floor."

Between them they took the ropes away and made space.

"You need to prove you know what to do with a heavy blade. Have you used one before?"

"I've used a cutlass and a hanger, both heavy...." He was interrupted by Smith who threw the scabbard of his sword into the corner.

"Both of those swords are single-edged; to use a broadsword effectively you must remember that there is a wounding strike on the backhand, using the length of the sword from the hilt to the point." He retrieved the scabbard and demonstrated on the punch bag.

By the time Robert fell in bed that night, he was exhausted. The sergeant was relentless, "You may not attend the Salle tomorrow, but the next time you do, you must be able to prove your skill with the broadsword or be proved a liar; and that would defeat out purpose!"

The following morning Robert called on his sister to establish his presence physically and to ensure he knew where the house was.

Amelie was pleased to see him and they discussed their past adventures over a polite and proper tea taken in the drawing room. The little house was just the sort of place that suited the attractive widow; and the handsome bachelor brother who would be expected to only use the house when he was not involved in amorous pursuits elsewhere.

He confirmed that he would stay at the Mews with the sergeant as it was more central and allowed him to be within a short walk from the Salle where the action seemed to be centred.

For three days Robert practiced with the sword and at his suggestion, Walter Smith took the opportunity to show

Robert some of the techniques of the fine art of wrestling, as he pointed out the streets of London could be a hazard to the unprepared.

It was with some trepidation that Robert returned to the Salle d' Armes, making the excuse of a visit from his parents for his absence.

He was introduced to the Master, Comte D'Valle, who had returned during Robert's absence.

"I understand, Sir Robert, that you have some acquaintance with this weapon?" He produced a broadsword used by the army. Robert smiled, "I am afraid not, sir; this weapon had a single edge. I was accustomed to a double edge in my youth, though the weight seems right.

At the request of the Master, Robert demonstrated the various cuts and thrusts associated with the broadsword before being given his practice in the art of gentlemen's fencing for the morning.

He noticed during the morning several people seemed to come and go. Some merely seemed to bring a message; others stayed and drank coffee with the Comte. Among these was at least one lady, whose presence was a surprise in this place so exclusively male.

He reported the events of the morning when he met Walter later at the Mews. The main things he had noticed was that the Comte had a room that was kept locked, and that some of the visitors had spent time in the room with D'Valle who opened the door with a key each time.

Robert concluded "Two things occur to me; one is that I agree with you the Comte is not genuine and I would like to know what happened to Mariette and her husband, and her uncle Armand. The other is there seem to be very few émigré members of the Salle. I find that strange in view of the number of other clubs in London with many émigré members. Can we find out if they are encouraged to join?"

With the funds provided by Lord Mills, the sergeant had built up a team of watchers and informants throughout the area surrounding the Salle d'Armes, and because the visitors to the Salle had been assiduously followed by these watchers, the pattern of interest spread from Bayswater to Wapping.

South of the river there was one suspect, in the Chatham area, who worked in the dockyard, though his place in the scheme was not apparent. The northern area of Highgate appeared to be the home of the lady visitor, the house being set back from the road and surrounded by several acres of parkland. All this information was gradually forming a pattern that the two investigators were finding increasingly suspect.

It was during the next week that they realised they were being watched. The first inkling Walter had was when watching Robert returning to the Mews one day, he observed someone ducking behind the pillar at the gateway to the area. Robert looked round before approaching the door, but the watcher was out of sight by then. When Robert came up stairs, Walter pointed out the watcher who was now leaning against the wall, puffing on a clay pipe.

Chapter eighteen

"Let's have a word with him, shall we. If you would like to wait at the door for him, I'll send him round." The sergeant was quite jocular as he jogged down the stairs, to disappear to the back of the carriage room.

Robert stood behind the carefully opened door waiting. On hearing running feet, he flung open the door and stepped out into the path of the running man, who had abandoned his pipe to run. He saw Robert and tried to avoid him. As he passed, Robert's fist shot out and hit him in his side below the ribs. He folded and tumbled to the ground, ending up on his back with his legs up against the side of the house wall opposite the mews apartment. The sergeant cantered up and, between them, they carried the man inside and closed the door. Robert looked out to see if there was any sign of trouble, but it seemed that nobody had noticed the scuffle.

Tied up to the punch bag, the watcher was a sorry sight. His face was grazed where he had hit the cobblestones; he was conscious but stubbornly silent.

"What's your name and what were you doing following me?" The first innocent question was from Robert.

As he spoke Walter appeared, Robert's eyes opened wide. The man was stripped to the waist and wearing thin leather gloves, the muscles rippled over the broad shoulders and torso of a true athlete.

235

He towered over the trussed figure who looked positively terrified.

"I'll ask you again your name, and what were you doing following me?"

After licking his lips and glancing nervously at Walter, who was now tapping the other side of the punch bag, he spoke. "I'm Nolly Ward, I was asked by this geezer to keep you in view, said you was her fancy-man and she reckoned you could be visiting."

Walter translated for the puzzled-looking Robert. "A lady asked him to follow you, since you are her man friend and she suspected that you might have another lady friend tucked away somewhere."

"Who was the lady, what does she look like?" Robert tried to look menacing but with Walter there he didn't need bother.

"She didn't give her name, she was tall as me and had black hair, dressed lady-like and went off in a carriage with some badge on the side." He was still looking at Walter as Walter began hitting the bag causing it to jolt and throwing him off balance.

"Come on, lad, did you know the lady? Did she pay you to follow my friend? Speak up, lad, my arms are stiffening up. I'll need to give them some work to loosen off properly." With that he hit the bag hard, causing the man to lose his footing and swing with the force of the punch.

"Oy, I'm doing my best, give over." He was sweating badly "No, I don't know the lady. I was told to wait outside that French place and I would be give a job by someone. No names just lean on the wall and smoke my pipe. She come out and called me. 'You want a job'? I said yes, she said 'follow that man I think he is a cheat'. She slips me a quid and says more if I tell where you go."

"Where have you arranged to meet her, and when?" Robert was becoming excited, but he tried to keep his voice calm.

"Same place – outside the club place at half past ten tomorrow."

"Now tell me, laddie, was she English or what?" Walter's voice was deceptively quiet.

"She had an accent, bit foreign like." It seemed if anything Walter's quiet manner seemed even more frightening to the man tied to the bag.

Leaving their victim they went upstairs to discuss this latest development.

"I think the lady needs to be followed by us to find out exactly where she lives, I do not like the absence of the real Comte D'Valle and of Mariette and her husband. It smacks to me of the work of the French agents. I have the feeling they have all three been abducted or in fact killed to keep them quiet. What do you think?"

Walter Smith scratched his chin reflectively, "You're probably right, and the lady's house sounds just the place to keep them out of sight, and if they have been killed, a nice quiet place to bury them somewhere in the grounds. What about our little man Nolly?"

"He seems to me to be just what he says he is, a runner for a gang, earning a little extra on the side."

The two men discussed the situation and finally decided to let their victim go and hopefully keep his appointment tomorrow. With a little encouragement he might be persuaded to follow the lady to her home and report back.

After leaving Nolly Ward for a little longer to think about things, they let him go with the offer of a little work for them. Neither was surprised when he agreed.

He left after peering both ways to see if he was being observed.

There were several pairs of eyes on the entrance to the Salle the following day, and it was with a grim smile that Mr. Smith pointed the fact out as Robert passed on his way to his morning training session.

Within the chambers he swiftly changed and donned the protective clothes for his fencing bout. When he walked out into the long room he was surprised to find he was the only person dressed for combat.

The Master came over to him also dressed for fencing. "I understand from Master Bain that you have shown great application and that you are our most accomplished student. I have arranged to fence with you as an examination of you progress, Master Bain will fence my best student, and the others will look on and hopefully learn."

Robert nodded shrugging, thinkingm 'what is this? Is this a way of getting rid of me perhaps?'

The two men took their places on the mat and saluted, they took stance and the bout commenced.

The Comte had a light touch and the blades slid sibilantly counter and thrust, feeling each other out. The pace increased and it became more and more difficult to avoid the dancing point. D'Valle stepped back and dropped his point, and signalled a break. As he lifted his mask, the watchers applauded the two men. Surprised Robert saw the Master bow to the watchers and realised that the applause was for his efforts as well and bowed in turn.

Master Bain came into the Salon with another fencer and they went through the ritual of salute and started to fence.

D'Valle took Robert to one side.

"Sir Robert, I must tell you that Master Bain is correct, you are a truly excellent swordsman, as good as any I have seen here certainly. I do not think there is any more we can teach you. Just keep up the exercises and you should be a worthy opponent for anyone. I will have your account sent to your home in Albany?"

"No more practicing then?" Robert asked.

"No more, Monsieur, au revoir." He bowed, turned and joined the polite applause for the efforts of the other student, in his match with Master Bain.

Thus dismissed Robert changed and prepared to leave quietly. He was interrupted by Master Bain who came in still wearing his fencing garb.

"A word Sir Robert, I have said nothing to Mr. D'Valle, except to let him know you are a natural, I am aware that you are a practiced and skilled swordsman and I presumed you had a reason to come here. I know nothing of any matter other than my teaching, but I am uneasy and I will not stay. Good luck with your enquiry!" He left the room as swiftly as he had entered.

Mr. Smith was intrigued but not concerned at Robert leaving the Salle d'Armes. As he pointed out, they knew who used the place and Nolly Ward had reported the address of the mysterious lady who was known as Madame Therese Clos. Northwood Manor, Highgate.

The local traders reported that she paid her bills promptly, and she placed generous orders for food and drink, indicating that there were several peopleliving at the Manor.

***

It was three days later that having secured the assistance of several members of the Bow Street Runners Sergeant Smith placed them around the boundaries of Northwood Manor grounds with instructions to stop anyone from within escaping. The Runners were well acquainted with this sort of operation and neither Smith nor Robert had any doubt of their skill and effectiveness. Accompanied by only two of Smith's associates Robert and Mr. Smith quietly entered the park, climbing over the gate with a thoughtfully provided ladder.

At the gate house, they found the back door unlocked, and on entry found the gatekeeper and his wife, in bed.

The two unhappy people were passed over to the Bow Street party through the now opened gate while Robert, Smith and their two helpers walked quietly alongside the gravelled drive, on the grass verge to the front of the rather impressive Manor House.

Guessing once more that the rear would probably give the easier access they made their way round to the tradesmen's entrance at the back of the house. The kitchen door was only on the latch and there was a light showing through the window. Though voices could be heard, no one was in sight.

Opening the door, Smith poked his head through and took a quick look. He withdrew his head and, putting his finger to his lips for silence, he opened the door wide and stepped in closely followed by Robert and their two men.

The lobby was empty but sounds through the partly open kitchen door made it clear there were at least two men and one woman within.

Looking carefully round the edge of the door, it was possible to see not only two but three men, one was sitting eating quietly, the two others were laughing at some comment made by the little woman who was obviously the cook.

Robert heard one say in French that he would enjoy giving the cook something to really worry about; he made a rude gesture grabbing his groin and laughing. His companion grinned and suggested she would eat him alive. The cook obviously didn't understand the words but she got the message. The knife she waved under the man's nose made it quite clear what she thought of his humour.

She spoke sharply to the other man, "Take this tray to the Comtesse quickly, she has had nothing since mid-day. Move yourself, you lazy great pillock."

The man addressed understood the tone if not the words and with a surly grunt picked up the tray and left the kitchen.

When he closed the door, Smith stepped in. He was carrying a truncheon like those used by the Bow street runners. As he stepped in, he almost casually smacked the laughing Frenchman across the side of his head, causing him to stop in his tracks and fold over and collapse to the floor, like a closing book.

The seated man stopped eating and sat mouth agape until one of the Smith's men stuck a pistol in his face, while his partner tied and gagged the man.

The cook calmly looked at the intruders, crossed her arms and said, "About time, too. What took so long?" she shook her head in disgust muttering "Walk about with their eyes shut half the time!"

Robert took a guess. "Where will we find Madame?"

"Where she always is at this time, resting before a light supper in the Drawing room, at the front of the house."

"And the prisoners?" Robert continued.

"The Countess is upstairs in the first bedroom; the master is in the cellar with the Comte and his servant."

"And who are you?"

"Who do you think? I'm the cook and nothing to do with this bunch of foreigners. They keep me here to feed them, but they make sure I can't get out or I would have had them taken long since. Satisfied?"

Robert held his hands up in surrender and, looking at Smith, nodded and together they went into the hallway. There they split up. Robert and one man went upstairs and Smith and the other went through to the front of the house to the drawing room. Robert heard voices from the first room at the top of the stairs, a man and a woman. The man's voice sneering, the woman's raised in protest. The door was ajar, he heard the man speak and laugh. "Come on, then, give me a kiss and I'll let you see your husband. He won't last long anyway!"

"What do you mean?" The woman was anxious.

"We've just about finished here, so it's either the Guillotine in France or a knife here for him. I might save you if you are friendly to me."

Robert pushed the door open, the man from the kitchen stood in the centre of the room. To one side, by the table on which the tray had been placed, stood Mariette.

She saw Robert and her eyes lit up with hope. Sensing something was wrong the man turned and Robert hit him with all the anger that had built up as he'd listened to the conversation, The baton hit the man across the jaw, distorting his face with the force of the blow.

He dropped like a stone, his face distorted, teeth spilling from his ruined mouth; he hit the floor and did not stir. Mariette ran into Robert's arms and clung to him. "Oh, Robertm thank God at last. I prayed someone would come, and it's you of all people. Tell me, are my husband and Armand all right?"

"Let's go and see shall we? Quiet now!" They went down the stairs quietly, meeting Mr. Smith coming from the drawing room, Madame was walking, hands tied, between Smith and his companion. As one they turned down the stairs to the cellars below.

The room below was a stocked wine cellar with an annexe to the right. It was within the annexe they found the three men. Armand was tied upright to a tall rack fixed to the wall. The other two were bound hand and foot and lying on the floor.

Mariette ran to Armand, calling, "Please, a knife; cut him down, he is not well!"

On the floor one of the men raised his head, and seeing the group, wept with relief, He nudged his companion, "We are saved, mon ami, saved!"

The other looked at the rescuers blankly, not quite understanding what was happening. The men were released from their bonds and sat trying to get the circulation .going in their limbs that had been constricted for far too long. It was painful process and while the attention of the rescuers was distracted Madame made her escape up the stairs, slamming the door at the top.

Smith ran up the stairs in pursuit to find the door locked. Exasperated he kicked it, them shrugged and turned to return to the party below. As he came down the stairs the door opened again and Madame stood in the doorway, swaying, before tumbling in a flurry of skirts and petticoats to the foot of the stairway. The little cook appeared at the top of the stairs with the rolling pin in her hands. "She was no lady, whatever airs she put on." She turned and disappeared from view.

Smith twitched the disarrayed skirts to cover the exposed limbs of the lady, and said. "Let's clear up, shall we? We still have the others to collect."

A watch kept on the Manor disclosed no visitors through the night so at dawn the following day the party reconvened to place a discreet cordon around the Salle d'Armes.

Captain Robert Graham and Sergeant Walter Smith, dressed in full uniform each with sword and pistol, waited patiently in the premises of the tailor on the other side of the street, with a clear view of the Salle. To the rear of the establishment were stationed a group of Runners covering the back door.

The premises were opened by Master Bain at nine. He was followed by the servants who cleaned and took bookings and assisted generally. Finally D'Valle appeared accompanied by three friends known and recognised as regular visitors by Robert.

As soon as the group entered Robert and Smith crossed the road and followed them in, their two companions on their heels.

Inside the group were standing while D'Valle opened the normally locked office.

Not recognising Robert in uniform D'Valle said "I'll be with you in a moment, gentlemen," and flung open the door for his friends to enter.

It was while doing this his eyes met Robert's and recognised him. He took in the uniform and his hand dropped to his sword hilt.

"Don't do it!" Smith's pistol was raised. Just then someone opened the door behind him and jogged his elbow. The pistol went off with a bang and the bullet went off into the air. The man, who poked his head through the door, hurriedly withdrew but the damage was done. Using the distraction, D'Valle drew his sword and leapt at Robert with a snarl of anger. Robert managed to draw in time to beat off the blade, but the space was too small to do other than defend himself any way he could. He flung the small hall table at D'Valle to give room and put him off, and lunged, causing D'Valle to step back, thus making space for Robert to swing his sword more effectively. The blades clashed and sparks flew. These were not fencing foils with buttons attached; these were the real things, killing weapons, and both were intent on doing the other harm.

D'Valle, seeing Robert as the enemy he hated who had discovered his secret; Robert with the thought of the betrayal of his friends and the attempt to hurt his country. He fought with a cold anger, ignoring the fact he was fighting a fencing Master.

The door to the fencing Salon burst open and Bain appeared. He saw what was happening and stood aside as D'Valle backed through. As Robert passed, he called out "Watch his hands he fights with both."

Robert nodded and pursued the spy through the door, catching his opponent's sword hilt and flipping the weapon out of D'Valle's hand. Without stopping D'Valle reached up and tore a rapier from its wall mount and engaged Robert's sword once more. Never was Robert more grateful for the training he had persisted with all his life, the sword he was using was the cause of his own scar and it had served him well for many years. He thanked god for the hours of practice that had made the sword comfortable in his hand. As the two squared up and the blades clashed Robert was aware he was fighting for his life. The rest of the group were battling the friends who had been joined by two others who entered when the first clash occurred.

For Robert the fight had become personal the moment Robert had found Mariette and her Uncle.

Back and forth, round the salon, the fight continued, neither prepared to give quarter. For D'Valle, it was a shock to discover just how accomplished Robert was; for Robert this was like any other battle, to be fought and won, and that was part of the determination that gave him an unthought-of advantage.

As Bain had warned D'Valle picked up his lost sword in his left hand, and started weaving the two blades into the clash with Robert. In turn Robert picked up one of the single sticks from the rack on the wall, and used it to parry on occasion. Robert slipped on the edge of one of the canvas covered zones used for fencing bouts, as he staggered slightly. D'Valle lunged with his left hand sword, at the same time lifting the right hand sword to parry Robert's cut. Robert swung round, allowing D'Valle's blade to pass between his body and his arm. Lifting his arm to clear the blade he did a complete turn gaining his balance once more and smashed the singlestick down on the left arm of D'Valle, causing him to drop the weapon to the floor. The single stick broke with the force of the blow and Robert threw it away. The fight seemed to have gone on for hours, though it was only a few minutes in fact.

The fury of the engagement made it deceptive. Now D'Valle was favouring his left arm which Robert hoped was broken, but it had not stopped the man and he caught Robert during the next flurry of action with a cut to the ribs that he could not quite avoid. The fight ended suddenly, and bluntly. D'Valle dropped unconscious to the floor, having been struck from behind by a truncheon wielded by the intrepid Mr. Smith.

"Sorry to spoil your fun, Captain, but the lessons are over for today.

Sergeant Smith turned to Bain, looking him in the eye, "Well, Sergeant McBain, what have you to say for yourself?"

"Hullo, Walter, it's been a while since we last met. " He held out his hand and Walter Smith shook it. "Given up the Donkey Wallopers (an Infantryman's Reference to a cavalryman) have we?"

"Left the Dragoons after we returned from Portugal, took up this to pass the time and make some money. I was intending to leave and mebbie return home."

The gather of people from the Salle d'Armes was regarded by Lord Mills as most satisfactory as he informed Robert before allowing him to rejoin his beloved ship. His parting words were that he was, "no longer needed at present!"

As Robert told Barbara when they were together again "I seem to have been released by that impossible man but I can never be sure. He has the irritating habit of popping up when I least expect or want him to!"

He had been chastened by Barbara who had not been told about the events of the past two weeks until his return. His wound, though it was minor, was another cause of dissention, Barbara's contention being that if it was such a small affair how did he get injured. His explanation that there was an accident at the Salle d'Armes he was attending did not go down well.

***

Elsewhere in London things were happening, Admiral Malmby still in residence was pleased to have the *Morbihan* added to the Preventive fleet. With the return of *Roister* he was hoping she would undertake more work for the Service. He was unaware of the part the ship had played in Quiberon Bay and therefore had no idea of the possible plans Lord Mills may have for the ship.

He was also looking forward to the handover of his post to Admiral Keith, who was due to return from his current posting in the blockade off Brest.

Chapter nineteen

For Robert, the events of the past two years had made him a rich man. He was restless despite the variety of jobs they had undertaken over that period. Things were happening in the world. Napoleon had declared himself First Consul of France, in essence King. Now the news of the recovery of Malta from the French, and here he was kicking his heels in London waiting for the world to wake up and recognize that he and his perfectly good frigate could be involved somewhere actually doing something.

His irritation must have been observed by the Admiral, who suggested that while Lord Mills was away it would be an idea for him to contact Captain Leclerc and get up to date on the current situation in the channel.

They met at Dover Castle in the officer's mess, conveniently placed at the disposal of the Preventive officers stationed in Dover. The artillery men stationed in the castle were a friendly bunch and Leclerc had integrated well. In fact, he lived in the bachelors' quarters when he was ashore.

In the corner of the great ante room, the two men were undisturbed as they sat over coffee discussing the activities of the past two months. It was while relaxing after they had been talking for over an hour, that Robert heard that Marc Charles was dead, hanged at Tyburn like the other convicted pirates in history.

Despite the chapter being closed, Jean Leclerc was not feeling any better. It was taking time to sink in, but he now had only himself to think of. If he was going to make a future for himself he was going to have to consciously put the events of the past two years behind him. He could no longer live for revenge.

"So what will you do?" Robert liked the taciturn Guernsey man and had noticed his restlessness; it was this that spurred him to invite him to London for a few days.

Leclerc surprised himself by accepting and one week later found himself dressing for dinner in a guest bedroom of the house In Knightsbridge.

His share in the prize money for the cutting out of the *Corbeau Noir,* and the arrest of the Tregarth brothers and their ship, had made money little problem. Added to the fact that his social life had been suspended since the loss of his family, meant that financially he was well off.

At the table he found himself seated between a rather pompous Lieutenant of the Life Guards, and the cheerful wife of the adjutant of the Grenadier Guards battalion currently stationed at the barracks across the way. The party consisted of twelve people evenly divided between six ladies and six gentlemen. Opposite Leclerc was sitting a rather grave-faced lady he judged to be 25-27 years old. She wore a ring and he recalled she had been introduced when he had come down for dinner, but he could not recall her name—just that she had no husband present. He spoke to her on two occasions during the meal and received a very civil reply on each occasion; it was after the men rejoined the ladies in the drawing room that he found himself standing next to the young lady.

He introduced himself formally and learned that she was the widow of Captain the Honourable Michael Yorke, of the Lancers who died in service under General Sir John Moore in Holland just over a year ago in 1799.

Margaret Yorke herself demonstrated a lively wit and Jean noticed her face lit up when she relaxed and smiled. The fact that she made no effort to remove herself from his company was noticed by Barbara, who had arranged the meeting in the first instance. Even Robert was unaware that the party had been organised specifically for the benefit of Leclerc. Hearing Robert's comments on his meeting with the Guernsey man, and having met and been impressed by him in Plymouth. Barbara took it upon herself to arrange the party.

Margaret Yorke had been a friend ever since the house in Knightsbridge had become their London home. Barbara had found Margaret a charming companion when she was left alone in town whilst Robert worked. Pragmatically, she thought Margaret's widowhood a challenge, one she kept strictly to herself.

The introduction of Captain Jean Leclerc to the scene created the ideal situation. As she mentioned to Robert that night, the two people seemed to suit each other very well! When Robert mentioned the coincidence of the two meeting, Barbara pointed out that a good hostess has to arrange for suitable balance of people at the table for dinner. Having invited Margaret she had to find a detached male to make up numbers. The visit of the Captain to London was fortuitous. At this comment Robert smiled to himself. He liked Margaret and also Jean Leclerc, so why not?

The call to the Admiralty came after three weeks, and after a meeting with the secretary, he left with orders to form part of the convoy to India.

"Being in all ways prepared for departure you will rendezvous with the convoy in three weeks time and report to Commodore Hillard on *HMS Beacon* 74."

"You will open your second orders when you arrive at Capetown, and pass the enclosed envelope to Commodore Hillard."

The days before the sailing date were all too short. For Robert and Barbara the time was taken with arrangements for the long separation.

For the rest of the crew of *HMS Roister* provisions had to be ordered, barrels scoured and washed with vinegar water, selected casks of beef and pork stowed and at the last minute, nets of limes taken aboard.

Billy Beaufort had the gun ports raised, wind sails rigged and the entire 'tween decks scrubbed down, giving the ship a fresh smell for a day or two at least. Powder was sieved and tested and stocks renewed and the entire arsenal of round shot was lifted from the hold and cleaned off, removing the rust patches that were produced by the damp atmosphere below decks. The boxes of fine powder for preparing cartridges for the rifle arsenal were carefully stacked away behind the felt curtains of the powder magazine. The Pre-prepared cartridges, well packed in their sealed boxes, also found their way to the Magazine, to ensure they would not get damp.

Preparing a ship for a long voyage was not the work of a moment, and though three weeks seems quite a long time, for the purser it's all too short, Judith scolded him because he returned each night exhausted but she was aware of how important it was for him to do his work as he saw it. The scolding was for his benefit and she loved him none the less for his disregard of her comments.

When all was finally ready, the ship sat laden with stores, the final touches were being made to the paint and gilding work, otherwise all was ready for sea.

Robert sat with Barbara in the drawing room at Tamar House, the child David had been put to bed—still too young to understand the ways of grown up's, Barbara was writing a note to Margaret Yorke, inviting her to stay for a few days in the coming month. Robert was smoking the long clay pipe, that lived on the rack on the over mantle. "It will be at least three months, if not considerably longer. You have sufficient funds and if you need more speak to Mr. Fisher at Cox's."

Barbara chided him, "Please, Robert, I have plenty of money and I will certainly know what to do if I need more." She rose and went to him, sitting on his lap and hugging him. "I am more concerned about you, I will miss you terribly. So far we have been lucky; you have not needed to be away for long periods of time. I fear our son will not recognise his father if you are away too long."

Robert wrapped his arms round Barbara. "As long as you remember who I am, we'll manage. I have your picture beside me at all times on the ship and I'll write whenever I can."

The knock at the door interrupted their personal moment. The butler announced a messenger to see Robert.

The messenger had a package from Lord Mills. Asking the man to wait, Robert told his butler to see the man had refreshment and broke the seal on the package.

The documents within were divided into two sections. The first section was a simple directive to sail with the India convoy as far as Capetown, from there to the Indian ocean island of Madagascar, and at Tamatave on the east coast a man was to be uplifted. He would identify himself with the badge. The passage from there should be made with the intention of reaching India in the fastest time possible.

The second package was marked personal and to it was attached a note to Robert. '*Open this packet only if you feel unhappy with the instructions given by your passenger. I trust you to make the right decision and I will back whatever decision you make*'. It was signed Simon Mills.

Astonished he passed the instructions over to Barbara. He rang for the butler, and when he came he instructed him to tell the messenger there was no reply to be taken.

***

As the ship reached the softer weather south of the Bay of Biscay, the men became bronzed with the increasing sun. They abandoned the heavy oilskins and for three days the ship seemed to be surrounded by a cloud of steam rising from drying clothing. The first lieutenant permitted the clothing to be draped around the deck and lower rigging while the windsails were rigged to clear the fetid atmosphere below created by the foul weather encountered since leaving Plymouth.

The convoy stretched out to the West, as the frigate covered the possibility of interference from the African coast, clearly visible to the east.

The trade winds coming abaft of the port beam, made easy comfortable sailing and despite the irritation of having to herd the recalcitrant merchantmen back into position each morning; the task made few demands on the frigate.

Robert had been at the gathering of the Captains at an uncomfortable rendezvous on the flagship in the English Channel off Ushant. The flagship with her greater bulk and size was much steadier than the smaller ships of the convoy tossing about in the channel chop. The naval officers present made a stark contrast to the civilian dress of the merchant captains. The Commodore himself was a bluff senior Captain given the rank for his present command, probably his last in service. *HMS Beacon* was not the newest ship of the line in the fleet, but her sailing capabilities were adequate with the assistance of the other escorts. Apart from *Roister,* their old friend *Jaipur* was there and the frigate *Penelope* 36, the two other sloops, the *Ajax* 22, and the brig-sloop *Richmond* 20. The cutter *Mavis* had been added for swift communication throughout the large convoy.

The Captain of *Penelope*, Charles Grayson, was the senior after Commodore Hillard. Robert was quite happy with the arrangements which allowed him to concentrate on the training of the crew in their alternative role as riflemen. The crew was given their training by watches, the competition was fierce but the men were all encouraged to support each other, and through the easy sailing area of the north east trade winds the drills went well.

Robert was pleased to entertain Commander Keith of the *Jaipur* along with Lieutenant Ward of the cutter *Mavis* to dinner during the gentle weather. He was surprised to discover that the *Jaipur* was under sealed orders to detach from the convoy at the Cape. His further orders were to be opened at that time.

As the winds died and the temperatures rose in the doldrums, Robert requested permission from the Commodore to launch his boats, and to mount the small taffrail cannon in the long boat in case of attack by galley from the African coast. The ships were in the grip of the Guinea current which ran south and east following the West African coastline.

Using the opportunity of the moment, Roberet had the boats manned and the crews competing in sailing and rowing. The Commodore, who had presumed that the boats were launched to keep the seams tight, was amused and entertained to the extent that a competition was arranged between the escort ships, and a light-hearted regatta was held. The spectators spent most time in the rigging of the competing ships as the boats would disappear periodically in the long Atlantic swells.

Despite the frustration of the doldrums, the voyage progressed, stopping at Freetown to water and take on fresh fruit, dried fish and meat.

By the time Table Mountain hove into view, the convoy had settled to a routine that it seemed would go on forever; but anchored in Table Bay, the whole scene altered.

Robert delivered his orders to Commodore Hillard, who was upset at not having been informed beforehand.

The ship re-provisioned and a round of farewells was made. As he had suspected, the *Jaipur* had been placed under his command for a specific task that would take them to Madagascar and India in the first place, thereafter who knew?

"Well, at least we won't have to battle the Mozambique current to get there, and from Tamatave north the currents should help." John Keith nodded and drank his wine. They were discussing the orders in Robert's cabin.

"I have strict orders to place *Jaipur* and my crew at your disposal, I am not sure why but I also have a separate sealed order to opened only if I am out of contact with you without orders for more than a month. Do you know what that is all about?"

"Sorry, John, I'm afraid I have no idea, and unless I am forced to open my own sealed orders I will never know. Now I think it's time we were on our way. If you keep to a course parallel to mine but just over the horizon perhaps people won't realise that we are together. I suggest you sail as soon as possible and I will sail tonight."

The friends shook hands and arranged to rendezvous one degree south of Tamatave in a week's time.

Robert was ashore in Capetown when *HMS Jaipur* sailed as he stood on the veranda of Government House discussing the progress of the war in Europe with the Governor and Commodore Hillard. The India convoy was waiting in Capetown for a complete week before sailing on to Bombay.

The Commodore had been unhappy to receive his instructions from the letters carried by Robert and Commander Keith, but he had to admit the two ships were not really required for the escort of the convoy; though he was convinced that the presence of the two ships had discouraged any interference on the journey so far.

The Governor had mentioned that there had been reports of a strange ship seen off the coast recently. She had not been identified as she showed no colours, but all the reports had stated that she was pierced for at least 36 guns, and she avoided contact with other ships.

When *Roister* sailed it was without formal signals or other ado. The anchor was raised as quietly as possible and she equally quietly sailed away. To most she disappeared without trace.

They sailed due east for two days before turning north following the Eastern shore of the great island of Madagascar. Keeping well clear of the shore they sailed north along the 50 degree line of Longitude to the meeting place on the 19 degree line, where the topmasts of *Jaipur* were spotted as she awaited their arrival.

Contact established, Robert was interested to hear that *Jaipur* had spotted the mysterious ship in the distance, 'on the rise', the expression used when two ships can be in sight because both rise on the waves at the same time allowing a brief sighting if you happen to be looking in the right direction at the right time. The mystery ship seemed to be following a course to the east parallel to the two naval vessels.

The entrance into the harbour at Tamatave was tricky at the best of times, and the politics of Madagascar Island were questionable always. The French had several trading posts here and the township Tamatave was one of the largest settlements on the east coast; based around the import-export operation of the major trading establishment. The Island itself was ruled by a warlord society, its history riddled with a succession of rulers from Arabs in the eighth century to Pirates in the eighteenth.

The forts at the entrance to the harbour were currently unmanned as the French who had designs on the Island had just moved out, trouble in Mauritius requiring their presence.

The two warships sailed unhindered into the harbour and dropped anchor, dominating the township under their guns.

Robert, accompanied by Abel Jackson, was rowed ashore by armed men who waited at the quay until John Keith joined them. The three men made their way to the big store that stood on the hill at the head of the street up from the docks. Within the building Abel made his way to the counter and spoke with the tall, stooped man waiting there.

They were almost immediately in deep conversation haggling over the price of the goods Abel was ordering. At the tables off to one side the two friends seated themselves and Robert called for a bottle of wine. Several others seated around the dark room resumed their conversations.

A stocky man carried a tray over to the table for the English officers. He placed the bottle on the table and returned to fetch the glasses. As he put the glasses down, he slipped a coin on the table and went back to the bar. Robert drew silver money from his pocket and counted it on the table lifting the coin placed by the waiter with his change. He inspected the money in his hand. The coin was marked with the M of D sign identifying the man as the agent they were sent to collect.

Abel Jackson came to the table, reporting that he had arranged for fresh water and fruit to be delivered to the quay. Glancing at the waiter he signalled to pay for the wine and the waiter came over. He accepted the money passed to him including the Identifying badge. As he leaned over to pick up the dirty glasses he said in a whisper he would board tonight before midnight.

***

The long swells lifted the ship in smooth surges that in turn, revealed and concealed the accompanying sloop. The lookouts had reported the sighting of the strange sail at first light, the tops being revealed against the dawn sky. To Robert this meant either their shadow was unaware he had been spotted, or intended that they know. He felt uncomfortable with the realisation that he was being manipulated by Lord Mills, and his meeting with his agent did nothing to ease that feeling.

The ugly little man had been taciturn to say the least. Having established his bona fides on his boarding the ship he had merely said, "We need to get to Bombay as quickly as possible." He would say no more until the ship was at sea.

Patrick Micah Carter came on deck and stretched in the morning sunshine, short, five-foot five inches to be exact, his stocky figure showed not an ounce of fat. Dressed in a simple loincloth he walked over to the seawater hose that was pouring water on to the deck whilst the men were holystoning. With a sigh of pleasure he raised the hose above his head, hooked it to the shrouds and allowed the water to wash over him scrubbing himself with some sort of soap and a brush. Finishing with a sluice down he stepped back brushing the excess water from his skin and stood allowing the sun to dry him off.

The officers and men on deck at this time looked on in astonishment.

Ignoring the effect his performance had on his audience, Carter went below once more to the gunroom where he proceeded to dress in a thin cotton shirt and loose trousers. Slipping sandals on his feet, he came back on deck and approached Robert. "We must talk!" The voice was quiet and cultured with just a trace of the brogue of Galway.

"Please join me for breakfast." Robert said formally, and turned to Ogilvie. "You have the deck, Mr. Ogilvie, rifle practice at four bells."

"Aye sir, I have the watch!" Lieutenant Ogilvie squared his shoulders and strode over to the wheel where he checked the course.

In the great cabin below Robert faced Carter "Now perhaps you will acquaint me with the instructions you have to pass on?"

"My instruction is to get to Bombay as quickly as I might and to do whatever is necessary to aid and assist our agent there. I understand the agent is currently in the stronghold of the rebel party that is based at Daman, north of Bombay on the Gulf of Cambay." The soft almost gentle voice coming from the ugly man was almost incongruous, but then the piercing blue eyes seemed also out of place. This strange man seemed to be a contradiction, one moment unmemorable, the next unmissable.

"How do you know all this? It has taken weeks for this information to reach England, how did you find out?"

"I sent the information in the first place by courier overland. I then came by Dhow to Madagascar to meet you. If you had not arrived by next week I would have returned and done what I could to rescue our agent. You see, I could not get the authorities to act by sending troops. I have no authority in the east India Company nor am I officially recognised by the Governor and his troops. It was necessary to get an official presence into the area to get the forces needed to deal with the rebels and rescue our agent."

"What sort of force had you envisaged; I mean how many soldiers would be required? A platoon, a company or are we talking of an army?"

Carter looked thoughtful, "I had perhaps a company in mind, maybe about one hundred and twenty, would do it. A gun would be useful, yes that would help." He looked keenly at Robert. "Do you think you can arrange that?"

Robert rang the bell on his desk and his servant appeared. "Call Captain Ullyet and bring coffee and breakfast for three." Mathews, his servant disappeared and returned to announce Captain Ullyet and delivered the coffee and bread, fruit and cheese for their breakfast.

To save time Robert outlined Carter's request for a rescue force, and while he did so had Carter draw a diagram of the rebel camp layout as he knew it.

Ullyet studied the diagram and commented. "I see no real problem here, the camp is laid out almost traditionally, I would almost suggest the leader is a military man, and like many soldiers he is thinking in terms of either undisciplined tribesmen, or formal infantry, with red coats and muskets. Using our riflemen, the base is vulnerable. We don't need to approach by open roads, nor do we need to group to fire effectively. Our cannon would be useful to tickle up their artillery; I notice you have shown the magazine behind the breastworks. It would be difficult to reach from the main gate but not from the surrounding jungle. I don't think we need bother the authority, sir, we can manage on our own."

Carter listened with disbelief. "You have no idea what you are saying. I have seen there are only 20 marines on this ship. You are not suggesting using sailors for this task? Gopal has trained soldiers at his disposal, they'll slaughter your untrained seamen, you'll be sending them to their deaths, and achieve nothing!"

On deck four bells struck and almost immediately the crack of rifle fire woke the already disturbed population of sea birds sending then screaming into the sky from their perches through the rigging.

"Perhaps a turn round the deck would be beneficial." Robert rose to his feet and, followed by Carter and a smiling Ullyet, went on deck to watch the rifle practice.

Carter stood open-mouthed at the sight. On deck under the eagle eye of Peter Morse, Abel Jackson's deputy trainer, six men armed with rifles stood. Off the beam streamed a line with a raft attached. The raft had a fixed sail the caused it to keep abreast of the ship towing it. On the raft was a rack with six targets. Not surprisingly the raft was rising and falling with the waves. As he watched Carter saw the first rifle rise, hold, then fire. The midshipman of the watch had his telescope trained on the targets, "Top Inner" he cried. The watchers nodded in approval, meanwhile almost without pause the second rifle fired, "Upper Bull!" the Middy shouted, a cheer went up from the watchers. Carter noticed that the first riflemen had already reloaded; the other four shots were taken with varying results, though none missed their target. All had reloaded before the next round of shots was taken. After five shots were fired by the group the targets were retrieved and examined closely by the marksmen and their supporters.

"Well, Mr. Carter, what do you think now?" Ullyet's voice broke into the stunned realisation of Carter that this was a most unusual ship.

The whole exercise had taken less than five minutes. Twenty-five aimed accurate shots within five minutes, five round a minute, the words went round and round Carter's brain.

"These must be your best marksmen, I presume?" Carter had regained his senses and was all business once more.

"Oh no, these men are average for the ship, our best can fire and hit the target ten times a minute."

"How many riflemen do you have on the ship?" Carter's next question was natural, but the reply was difficult to believe.

"The entire crew can shoot, that includes the Captain. Of the crew, 178 are marksmen; the remaining men are fair shots. We also have a field cannon which we have deployed in the past. The entire crew have practiced field craft and satisfied the training officer with their competence.

"Our trainer learnt his trade evading and fighting redskins in the forests of the Americas. He is the man who set the standards for shooting. All the personnel on the ship have the use of a Fergusson breech-loading rifle. All can fire a minimum of four rounds per minute, most can exceed that rate. When I mentioned the competence of the crew, I include all the officers." Ullyet completed his dissertation with a wry smile. "My marines are the best trained in the Navy, and they all compete regularly with the rest of the crew, and train alongside them. I pray that this information will not be passed to my masters. They have a jaundiced attitude to diverse training among their units."

"Your secret is safe with me, and I now see why Mills sent you and why you think this exercise is within your scope."

Chapter Twenty

The smooth sailing was replaced by stormy weather for the next three days. The heat did not diminish and the humidity made tempers short and the work seem twice as hard.

The battering of the wind kept everyone but the most intrepid below decks as much as possible. However the benefit of the high winds was the ground covered and by the time the storm blew itself out, they had made good time covering over 700 miles during the three days of the storm.

The temperatures rose daily now and the clothing disappeared and the outrageous washing arrangements of Carter were adopted by most of the crew. The sight of a whole group of the crew standing and capering naked under the water pipe became a regular feature of the voyage. The menu was varied by the fishermen in the crew who caught several sharks using scraps of the gristle left from the beef rations.

The main benefit of the smooth sailing weather was the chance to dry the ship, clothing and try out drills for the land side, using the uniforms and learning hand to hand fighting.

Here the expertise of Patrick Carter came into its own. Having learned to use his fists as a young man, he discovered when he set out into foreign parts that his fists alone were not enough. He had been lucky to be teamed with an Oriental, who—though small—always appeared to be able to come out of hand to hand fights unscathed, regardless of the size and strength of his opponent.

Patrick had marvelled at the way he was able to use the other man's own power and weight to defeat him.

The stranger on the ship, Carter, had—apart from the washing episodes—intrigued the crew with his regular morning session of poses, steps and sharp actions. Punching objects that were not there was how Billy Beaufort described it. Every morning at the same time during the morning watch at six bells he would appear and begin a series of poses, followed by kicks and strikes with open hand and closed, punches and chops with the edge of the hand.

He sparred with the foc'sle's best mauler, and caused the big Cornishman to give up exhausted, having not laid a hand on him. The two became friends and Carter taught the big man some of the moves that made him so difficult to hit. He also taught him how to fall without hurting himself. At these sessions he always had an audience, and it was not surprising that several of the men joined in.

Alan Dawson was very intrigued and managed to persuade Carter to teach him privately, during the dog watches. As an officer he could not practice with the men as the penalties for striking an officer were severe. And the risks of a disgruntled seaman taking advantage of the training to hurt an officer were too great.

Being an officer did not make the training easier. His fitness was the first lesson to be learned, and he soon discovered that there was more to being fit than the ability to run up the rigging and back.

His progress was marked by running fast and moving slowly. He learned to push against himself, stressing one muscle against another. He learned to fall from most angles, and he had the bruises to prove it. Mostly he learned self discipline, and it was here that the training paid off and he began to understand what the science of the fighting was all about. Adam Tamar was mystified; he could not understand why his friend should put himself through the torture of learning this discipline. They remained friends but he was discovering that there was more to the lad than the lively companion of the past. In addition, Alan was filling out and growing up; during the last two months he had grown taller and his jackets and breeched had shrunk.

Robert had observed the changes, and thought the additional fighting skills had given the young man a much more adult outlook. It seemed his studies had also benefited, an improvement that had been shown in Adam's work as well.

The voyage north had been good for the relationship between *Roister* and *Jaipur*, both ships had been able to work together and practice manoeuvres together. The friendly rivalry between the ships was tested in the boat races during the days of light winds that occurred during the voyage.

The sightings of ships became more and more common as they sailed north. Ever since they passed through the Laccadive Islands they had encountered traders both from the East India Company and privately owned ships, all were wary until the two identified themselves, and it was not until they reached the waters of the city of Goa that they encountered any serious problem.

The winds had been dropping slowly for three hours when it disappeared completely, leaving the ships becalmed with unmoving sails. As they drifted half a cable apart boats were seen putting out from the shore. Robert had ordered the long boat and the gig to be launched, to allow swimmers to enjoy the warm waters of the Indian Ocean. Riflemen were stationed on deck to keep an eye out for sharks.

On the quarterdeck Billy Beaufort lifted his telescope to watch the boats coming out from the shore. He thought at first they were coming to sell fish and fruit to the stationary ships; then as he looked over the leading boat he caught a glimpse of metal, and noticed there seemed to be a lot of men in the boat.

"Call the Captain!" his order was urgent. "Recall the boats, now and pipe action stations."

The shrill calls resounded through the ship. In the water the swimmers were splashing their way back to the boats and being hauled unceremoniously aboard, Robert arrived and, seeing what was happening, called for the warning to be given to *Jaipur,* lying on the seaward side of *Roister*. The sound of the pipes from *Roister* had been noticed and the *Jaipur* had called her boats to take towlines to give her the chance to move and bring her guns to bear.

On *Roister* the swivel guns were mounted on the taffrail and the port and starboard rails, and the men began lining up to receive their rifles and ammunition pouches. They were ordered to keep their heads down. Robert intended that the raiders would be given a nasty surprise.

The boat parties had collected their swimmers and, on being given instructions, came round to the seaward side of the ship where they were reinforced with the boat swivel guns and ammunition and rifles. Additional men swarmed down and joined them for the action.

The shore boats came nearer, approaching at an angle avoiding the broadside guns which were run out but would not bear. The bow chaser spoke with a roar and splashed the rowers who had carelessly moved within range, they hastily adjusted their approach and with no attempt at concealment began screaming abuse and firing muskets at the exposed crewmen, who began running about in apparent panic. There were seven boatloads of men approaching, Ogilvie estimated one hundred men at least. Three of the boats were making a wide berth around *Roister* obviously making for the *Jaipur*. At the starboard bulwarks of the *Roister* crouched forty riflemen, prepared to give the boats their full attention. Alan Dawson, in charge of the starboard rifles, waited until the range was right then gave the order to fire. As one, the forty rifles cracked. Out of sight as they were from the main force of boats, the terrible effect of this volley was not seen by the main force.

The bullets did dreadful damage, each of the three boats stopped in their tracks as several of the rowers fell bloody in their places. They were quickly replaced but the second volley was equally destructive, then the swivel guns from the rail of the *Jaipur* took their toll, and the waters around the three craft turned red with the blood of the dead and wounded.

The bows of the first boat had been smashed by a swivel gun loaded with ball, and the boat was sinking. That was when the sharks appeared and the screams of the men thrown into the water were added to the cries of the wounded. The other two boats turned round to escape from the slaughter but the swivel guns spoke once more and so did the rifles pouring deadly fire into the raiders.

The panic spread throughout the boat crews and the oars waved about as the leaders tried to get the men organised to escape. The third volley was the breaking point and men from the boats leapt into the water to escape the hail of death from the rifles. Alan had heard of the feeding frenzy of sharks but it had in no way prepared him for the sight before him now. The next volley was fired as a mercy for the survivors in the water, struggling to escape the voracious jaws of the growing gathering of sharks.

On the other beam the approaching boats were unaware of the havoc, having heard the firing of the guns and possibly the screams the assumed it was the intended victims not their own men.

The boats had reached the point where all were in range. Robert gave the signal and as one the men rose from behind the bulwarks and fired. The bullets cut a swath through the four boats, the second and third volleys were equally devastating and the leader—not expecting the second and third volleys—recoiled in shock. The intended assault melted into confusion, as once more the waters around the boats turned red with blood and the sharks gathered. The volleys continued and more and more of the would-be pirates fell dead or injured in the overloaded boats. One of the nudging sharks driven by the scent of blood managed to roll a boat over and several of the wounded and dead fell into the sea. The sharks went mad, and the screams of the victims added to the rapidly growing panic.

The leader tried to regain control without success and the four boats milled around without getting anywhere, while the relentless volleys of rifle fire slashed into the packed men.

Sickened by the slaughter, Robert signalled for the men to cease firing. The longboat pulled round from behind the ship and began herding the bloody ruins of the attack fleet towards the ship's side where nets were lowered to help get the survivors aboard. The thirty-four survivors included the local chieftain who had led the raid. He was wounded. Though not seriously, he insisted on being treated separately from his wounded followers. To the surgeon all wounded are equal and he paid scant notice of the shouting man; treating him in turn when he was brought in.

Questioning the survivors brought the fact that the ships were attacked in response to a suggestion by the Captain of the French ship *Rivage* which had called four days ago. The French Captain, Clemente Chavez, was a regular visitor to the coast and had on occasion refitted his ship in the bay beside the village. The *Rivage* had sailed north after leaving the villag; they did not know where.

Chapter Twenty-One

Robert had all the boats except one sunk; the dead were consigned to the sharks, the living loaded into one boat which was towed to the shore at the village by the longboat. The disastrous attack had been witnessed in part from the shore and the beach was lined with wailing women and children. Before the longboat pulled back to the ship. the remaining boat was stove into prevent her immediate use. The crew regarded it as suitable punishment in the circumstances.

Carter was very thoughtful on hearing of the French captain's name and he was not a little troubled by the fact that the *Rivage* had sailed north. He confided in Robert later that day.

"To the north there is only British territory up to the north of Karachi. There are ships trading and warships cruising through the entire area. Either he is going to disguise his ship and bluff his way through or he has a destination in mind that can provide protected anchorage. I suspect a combination of disguise; a little piracy, perhaps, and a haven in the Gulf of Cambay—our own destination. If that is indeed what he has in mind, we could have more trouble than we can cope with."

"Surely no white man would conspire with the natives in that way?"

"You think not? I am sorry to say the French revolution has produced unspeakable cruelty and a massive increase in treachery. Morals have become degraded to the extent of child informing on parent, sister on brother and vice versa. There is no right and wrong in the accepted sense, merely is it to my benefit or not? Sadly, self comes first, others a poor second!"

The voyage north continued the two ships called into Bombay to store and allow the crew a chance to relax after the lengthy time at sea.

Sam Callow and Abel Jackson took the chance to explore the exotic city on the edge of the ancient continent. The heat and the smells of the streets soon drove them into one of the many tea houses where they sat and sweated in the shade of the awning cutting out the direct rays of the sun.

Sam, who had visited India before, suggested they take things easy until the late afternoon, then perhaps they could walk through the brass and cloth markets and perhaps find some presents for their wives. They accordingly spent the rest of the hottest part of the day in the gardens beside the fountains where the mist of water kept the air slightly cooler and the shade of the palm trees made it possible to doze through the heat of the day.

Alan Dawson, with Adam Tamar, was enjoying a different day. First—the tailor's shop suggested by one of the locally based Midshipmen on the Port Admiral's staff. Alan's uniforms were woefully inadequate with the cuffs failing to reach his wrists and his breeches handed down from Mr. Ogilvie, but still too small for the fast-growing young man.

It was a pleasant surprise to find that the tailor was able to find a fitting uniform jacket and breeches in lightweight material. He changed into his newly purchased garb, feeling much better about roaming the streets of the city in fitting uniform. The tailor took back for resale the uniforms made for growing midshipmen and thus kept a supply to suit most stages of growth during the awkward years before full maturity. He was also able to measure and promise delivery four dress uniforms made with a little further growth in mind. The arrangements for delivery to the ship were made for the next day.

The two young men were free to explore the city for the rest of the day. It was while they were exploring the intriguing lanes near the central market that they noticed that they were being followed. Adam saw a face that was familiar, he realised that he had seen the man outside the tailor's shop. Realising he had also been where they had stopped for tea, he pulled Alan into a doorway and whispered, "Wait! We are being followed."

Alan stiffened. "Followed? How do you know?"

"I recognised a face that I've seen before; not once but at least three times today. He tries not to be seen but he is too slow. And he has friends; two at least."

"Perhaps we should ask him what he wants." Alan put his hand on the dirk at his waist.

"Yes, I agree, but not here. Let's find somewhere a little more private."

The two set off down the lane and turned in the main street towards the gardens along the shore of the bay. Sure enough, the followers were still with them; definitely three men. They all were dressed in native garb but they had the look of soldiers, not normal market thugs.

Adam and \Alan waited in a small clearing where the bougainvillea was showering down from a ring of trees, the clearing shielded from the view of the other people in the garden.

Their followers appeared one at a time from the concealment of the bushes. They spread apart and walked slowly towards the two young men.

The apparent leader of the three stopped when Alan asked if they wanted something. He smiled and said "First your money, then we will see." There was no emotion in his voice and his face betrayed no feelings.

"Would you like to deal with me first?" Alan stepped forward, causing the leader to step back.

"I don't think I will give you any money, I had to earn it, you have done nothing to earn from me."

The man stepped back, obviously surprised, then he jumped forward aiming a blow at Alan's face. The next few minutes were a painful experience for all three men. Adam stepped forward and sank his fist in the midriff of the man facing him. Alan turned sideways as his assailant tried to hit him; he grabbed the offered arm and turned it over his shoulder and threw the man over his shoulder in a way that Mr. Carter would have approved of. The man landed in an untidy winded heap on the hard ground. His neighbour recovered from his shock and drew a knife from his belt. Alan's hand slashed down across his exposed wrist wringing a cry of pain from him as his wrist bone broke and the knife dropped on the ground.

Adam had followed up his first punch with an uppercut to the jaw laying his man on the ground stunned; he turned in time to hit the leader across the throat with his rigid forearm, sending the man gasping for breath to the ground once more. Adam's first opponent had jumped to his feet and fled. The man with the broken wrist also ran.

The leader was rising still gasping from the ground with the knife that had been dropped by his departed accomplice. Alan feinted with his left hand, flicking his fingers towards the eyes of the man. The knife followed the move and Alan reached out and plucked it from his unprepared grip.

"Now why are you following us?" He casually played with the knife tossing it up and down in his palm. The man looked at them without comment. "You understand English, I'm sure," he flicked the knife to within an inch of the man's foot, causing him to jump back in alarm. Adam retrieved the knife. "You are really out of practice." He addressed Alan "This is the way to do it." He flicked the knife to land beside the man's big toe, touching the skin and shocking the man into crying out in protest.

"What is your name?" The question brought a response this time.

"Amin Raj!"

"Who do you work for?"

"I work for myself...." He stopped as he saw the knife raised in Adam's hand. "Ram Das," he growled.

The answer meant nothing to either of his questioners.

"What did he want with us?" Alan pressed him.

"I don't know, I was told to get help and then rob you both; if possible, bring you to his house for questions."

"Where does he live?" Alan persisted.

"On Vasai Creek, outside the city; he has a big house in the old summer palace of the Mogul Prince. He is a powerful man and I dare not fail."

"It seems you have failed Amin Raj, your master will not be pleased."

"Master?" Amin Raj spat on the ground. "He is not my master; he is a cruel mean man who lives for money. I carry out his orders or I die. No one is allowed to live in the area without his permission. When I returned from service with the Company I wished to set up in business and find a wife. I was foolish enough to ignore his demand for a share in my leather work shop. It was burned down with all my stock. I have been scratching a living since then; this job is the first I have had in three months."

The two friends listened to the story in silence.

Then "You know the city?"

"Like my own hand."

"You were a soldier for the Company?"

"For seven years I soldiered with the infantry. I was a Subadar in the 2nd Bombay Foot," he said proudly.

"Do you know the area round Daman?" Alan was inspired to ask the question without knowing why.

"Scum!" the word spat out and Amin Raj, stood back from Alan. "If you have anything to do with the people of Daman, I want nothing to do with you; they are the scum of the earth, lower than the meanest beggar in Bombay. They are murderers and rapists, and they killed my family, stole my sister. Raped and murdered my mother.

?General Parlavi is a mongrel pig who was born in the slums of Karachi. His father was a soldier for Clive, his mother was a Persian prostitute. He learned his trade from the pirates of the coast of Malabar before he transferred his attentions to the Arabian Sea and the Gujarat lands in the north. He allied himself with the French when they were driven out of India. The French pirates keep them supplied with slaves and transport them on raids along the coast."

Alan and Adam were taken aback by the vehement outburst of the man; it was Alan that realised that this man would be of interest to his captain and Mr. Carter.

"If you are hoping for a way to get revenge for the murder of your sister and family then I suggest you come with us to the ship. If you board after dark we can keep it secret from any spies in Bombay. We can also keep it secret from Ram Das which will be good for you. We can possibly visit Ram Das after we return from Daman.

It was late evening when the boat pulled alongside *Roister*. A whispered conversation took place and Amin Raj climbed to the deck and met Patrick Carter.

With the tide running the ship ghosted up the coast to the Gulf of Cambay creeping into the shoaling waters of the Gulf.

Coloured dirty brown, the sluggish waters of the Sabarmati River ran out to the sea, creating an enormous stain on the otherwise blue Arabian Sea. The Gulf was nearly 200 kilometres across at this point. *Roister* and her consort *Jaipur* needed to get within a few miles of Daman to mount their attack. With the help of Amin Raj, a plan had been devised to land a company of Riflemen in the ship's boats, and while the ships then proceeded to the town itself, the Rifles could approach the back door.

Robert had decided that their best chance of rescuing the agent was with a direct approach—with the Rifles in reserve—on the landward side. If the French ship was already there, he would sink her.

Privately he thought that he was taking a chance, presuming he could sink a frigate of unknown size, manned by a crew of unknown quality. Such was his faith in the abilities of his men; he decided that the risk was acceptable, especially since *Jaipur* was with him.

With the help of Amin Raj, they had managed to modify the map of the town showing all the important places and highlighting the headquarters of the General. With its embrasures and fortifications, the General's HQ was a formidable challenge.

There was a tension on board as the ship neared Daman, the troops were despatched under the command of Captain Ullyet, with Lieutenant Ogilvie as his second in command. The field cannon and gun-crew accompanied him. The entire company wore their green jackets for the operation, as much for identification as anything else.

When they landed they were faced with a 10 kilometre march through rough country, so Robert had decided to give them a three hour start to get into position.

The two ships sailed on towards the port of Daman, rounding the point the bay before the town came into view. Sitting above its reflection, the French frigate *Rivage* made a pretty sight, her gun ports open with the guns run out.

The two British ships were equally prepared, separated by sufficient water to enable them to catch the Frenchman between them. As the *Roister* entered the anchorage, she fired a twelve gun salute from her stern chasers. The fortress/palace answered and the ships dropped anchor to seaward of the *Rivage*.

A boat put off from the quay and approached *Roister*. She carried a banner and two elaborately uniformed men. Robert welcomed them on board with the usual formalities, the pipes sounding shrill in the heavy tropic air.

The officials welcomed the ship and conveyed an invitation to the Captain to a reception at the palace that evening. They also offered the facilities of the port, for provisions.

Robert accepted the invitation and having been offered tea and refreshment, refused graciously by the visitors, they returned to the shore making no mention of the French ship in the anchorage.

Billy was intrigued; the first lieutenant commented to Robert that the Frenchman was flying a flag he did not recognise.

"It will be the flag of the Warlord, the local Rajah." Robert suggested. "It saves them the embarrassment of being tackled by us the moment we appeared."

The purser approached.

"Yes, Mr. Jackson, what can I do for you?" Robert addressed the American with a raised eyebrow.

"I would like permission to go ashore to purchase fresh provisions and arrange for fresh water if it is possible?"

"Very good, Mr. Jackson, take the jolly boat and call for the long boat if you need it. Mr. Abbot, convey Mr. Jackson ashore, Find two extra hands to assist him; wait for him at the quay. Take weapons concealed just in case. Carry on, Mr. Abbot."

Abel hurried off to arrange his funds and collect his lists; the shore visit was important so that contact could be made with the shore party, who would be in position soon.

The town was typical of the west coast of India, a sprawling assembly of shops and houses scattered along the shoreline. The general ship suppliers and chandlers lay behind the quay that stretched out like a finger into the bay. Adam and his two helpers strolled into the market area and he haggled with several of the fruit merchants, sending their bearers down to the boat with their burdens while he progressed through the town. He observed several European men about the area, though none approached or attempted contact in any way.

Amin Raj made an appearance and wandered casually down to the quay, seating himself apart from but near enough to the boat to speak to Midshipman Abbot. He reported that the company was in position and awaiting a signal before opening fire on the palace. He then departed to the area of the Palace to nose around and locate, if possible, Mr. Carter's agent before returning to Captain Ullyet. Amin Raj had to be careful, if he was recognised he would be dragged before the Rajah. If that happened, he might as well cut his own throat. It would be less painful than any punishment given out by the Rajah. Taking his time and wandering from stall to stall, he gradually worked his way to the Palace wall

Amin Raj had a pretty good idea of where the agent would be found: if undiscovered, he would be close to the Palace; if already discovered, he would be in the prison behind the Palace.

Enquiries among the stall holders elicited the information that there were three Europeans in the prison. One had been there for several months, the others only two days.

The reception at the palace that evening was a grand affair. Robert arrived with Midshipman Alan Dawson in all his new finery. The pair were greeted at the gates by an elegantly dressed servant who spoke impeccable English and who escorted them to the reception room. The guests were introduced to the colourful throng assembled by a major-domo in a loud voice. As Robert was heard to comment, it was all terribly English.

Despite the best efforts of the punkha-wallahs, the air was still humid and the crowded room was quite uncomfortable at first.

With the arrival of the Rajah, all that changed. He made his entrance through huge double doors that opened onto the veranda overlooking the sea.

The opposite end of the room had appeared to be as solid wall, but it was pushed aside on runners revealing the green forest rising up the hill beyond the palace grounds. The opening of the doors at each end of the room allowed the sea breeze to pass through the room, cooling the air within.

The Rajah himself was not a striking figure though Robert noticed the small black eyes were clear and darted round the assembled guests rapidly, 'Assessing' was the word that came to mind as he watched.

The Rajah spoke cultured English with an accent gained at Eton and Oxford. At least that is what he claimed.

Robert was aware that he had learned his English from the master of the house in which his mother worked. As a boy he had shared her accommodation in the servant's quarters of the missionary's house, normally sleeping alone as the Missionary's wife was a frail soul and spent most of her time in the hills near Rawalpindi, leaving her husband to carry on alone in the rather more humid lowlands. The Rajah's mother was a regular and welcome visitor in the missionary's bed. The boy was the outcome of that liaison, and was an embarrassment to the missionary as the young man grew.

The boy had resented his parents who caused him to suffer the taunts of the other boys, and interfered with the achievement of his ambition.

Seated around the low tables carrying the wide assortment of food, Robert asked the Rajah about his family. He was told rather shortly that they had not survived the cholera epidemic that swept northern India 20 years ago.

Chapter twenty-two

"The ship *Rivage* I saw moored offshore when I arrived, where does she come from? I confess I did not recognize her flag.

"She is carrying my own flag at present; I have her under charter from Captain Chavez, formerly of the French Navy. It is a question of diplomacy."

"Diplomacy? There is some problem between your country and another?"

"I am afraid so, Captain, something I am sure we will clear up without too much difficulty, now you have arrived."

"Me! Is there some way that I can help in this matter?"

"Oh yes, Captain, I do think that your crew will be cooperative when they realise you are my guest."

"I am sorry, sir, I am not sure I understand what you are saying?"

"I will put it plainly, Captain. While you are my prisoner, your ship will not be inclined to attack me."

"I still do not understand why you think my men would attack you? We are not at war, sir." Robert began to rise.

"Do not force me to have you publicly restrained, Captain." The Rajah motioned him to be seated once more. "I will send your servant to inform the ship that you will be my guest tonight at least." He indicated Alan sitting between two other guests lower down the table, and snapped his fingers.

A man appeared by his side and on instruction fetched Alan to the top table.

"If you wish, I will have him killed and send my own man to the ship." The cold eyes of the Rajah left no doubt in Robert's mind that he meant exactly what he said. He turned to Alan.

"Mr. Dawson, please inform Mr. Ullyet that I will be staying here as a guest of the Rajah tonight, and that I will be in touch in the morning."

Without batting an eye, Alan took the message and saluted his captain, "Excuse me, sir."

He left the room, collecting his hat from the servant at the entry and making his way down to the quay where the captain's barge waited.

Amin Raj followed the boy down to the boat. When Alan reached the boat he carefully told the Cox'on that he had been ordered to return to the ship to tell Mr. Ullyet that the Captain would be staying as a guest at the palace tonight and that he would be in touch in the morning.

Amin Raj, hearing the message, slipped away and made his way back to the forest and passed the message to Captain Ullyet exactly as it was given.

Ullyet nodded thoughtfully and asked, "Can you get us into the grounds of the Palace quietly?"

Amin Raj nodded "Oh yes, Sahib, it is easy to get in. Getting out is not so good unless you use the gate. There is a trench around the inside of the walls that they flood at night. They release crocodiles to swim in the water; the inner rim is raised to prevent the crocodiles roaming the lawns."

Having confirmed that the Captain had been detained as expected, Captain Ullyet was now free to assault the Palace with cause.

Patrick Carter smiled happily when he heard the message from the returned Midshipman. "We can act legally now." He rubbed his hands together delightedly. "When do you think we will attack the French ship, now or in the morning?"

Billy Beaufort looked at him curiously, "When I am sure that the Captain is safe and the agent recovered."

Carter looked uncomfortable. "But we may not have a chance if we don't act quickly."

"A chance for what? My orders are to rescue the agent and if possible quell any insurrection in this area if necessary, not to have my Captain killed so that you can justify a little war of your own. Do you even know who the agent is in this area?"

"It's Charles Kay, and he is probably dead." Carter answered sulkily. "Your Captain is probably already marked for death anyway, and he was aware that he could be killed when he volunteered to act as our stalking horse in this manner. It is a small price to pay when you consider the benefits to be gained."

"Enough of this, we act as we have been ordered to act. When we receive the signal from the shore company, we will take the Frenchman, not before. Is that quite clear?" He glared at the Irishman, who shrugged sullenly.

"On your own head be it." He left the cabin in a huff.

The Palace was quiet with all the guests gone and Robert was standing beside the window, looking out at the moonlit anchorage. The ships were sitting still on the smooth water when the guards came for him. He turned and there they were. The grabbed his arms and bundled him through the doorway, down the corridor and through a dark arch into the prison behind the Palace. Passing several barred cells he was pushed into a cell next to the end wall. The next cell contained two men, both were looking the worse for wear but they were able to talk.

As soon as the guards left, Robert spoke to them. "Who are you?" he asked.

"We are buying agents for the British East India Company, sent here to purchase cotton from the local growers. We have been here many times with no problems. Yesterday we were arrested and thrown in here and questioned about some person we have never heard of, Carter?"

"Is there any other European here?" Robert asked.

"Only Wild Willie" came the reply. "He is in and out of the prison all the time. Somehow he keeps getting drunk and fighting the soldiers. They throw him in here for a week or two, beat him up a bit then throw him out again. There are no others."

Interesting, Robert thought. Where then, could the agent be? Unless he was the regular drunk he was obviously not in the prison.

"Do you know of any other Europeans in this area?"

"Only that bastard Frenchie, Chavez; but steer clear of him, he's a pal of the Rajah and a real evil bastard. I saw him gut a man in the market because he said he cheated him."

"What happened?"

"Nothing; as I said, he's a friend of the Rajah."

"Do you know where he is now?"

"He went north with the General, I don't know where but they had a lot of men with them."

Robert sat back against the wall of the cell and thought over what he had been told.

He was roused by a scratching sound from the wall beside him. He scratched back, and then moved over to the window. A dark figure rose and looked through the bars.

"Hullo, Sahib, I am here as promised. Would the Sahib please to stay in this corner of the cell for just a minute?" The figure waved to someone and ducked to one side. The crash of the field gun shattered the quiet night, followed by the almighty smash as the ball crashed through the prison wall of the cell, the mud wall shattering into a thousand pieces. Robert shook himself and stepped through the gap, brushing the dust from his coat.

Amin Raj grinned his teeth showing white against his dark skin. "Makes a pretty good doorway, I think. eh."

Ullyet appeared as a wave of riflemen with fixed bayonets swept into the prison and through to the back door of the Palace. From the anchorage came the boom of cannon fire as the two British ships attacked the Frenchman, the screams of the boarders could be heard from the Palace as they took over the frigate at sword point. In the Palace the green-jacketed riflemen gathered all the occupants into the reception room. Robert walked through and inspected them. The Rajah was standing in bitter silence on his own. Seated beside him the woman he had been with.

Elsewhere the tousled head of Wild Willie could be seen. The two buyers from the East India Company were together by the doorway.

The group assembled in the reception room at the Palace. Robert was concerned that the crew of the *Rivage* had been reduced to less than half strength. They now knew why.

The other members under the leadership of the Rajah's General and Captain Chavez had made a forced march to the town of Ahmedabad at the head of the Gulf. The taking of the family of the Rajah of Kutch had been planned and with the ransom obtained it was expected that an uprising of the entire northwest could be funded.

The Rajah was ambitious to say the least. Ullyet was even now laying an ambush for the returning party. Wild Willie it turned out was exactly what he seemed; the two buyers were also spying for the Company, but then all Company buyers were expected to spy anyway. There was no sign nor was there any record of Charles Kay.

Carter sat to one side, listening to the discussions taking place and saying nothing. Robert, having sorted the immediate problems out and given his orders, turned to Patrick Carter and fixed him with a steady look. "What have you to say for yourself?"

Carter looked startled. "What do you mean?"

"Why did you lie about an agent here in trouble? Why have we travelled several thousand miles to attack this Palace and take a French ship? What's behind it all, some devious plan of your own?"

Robert reached into the satchel on the table and retrieved the envelope marked, to be opened only at the discretion of Captain Robert Graham.

Within the packet were a chart and a number of written pages. Robert began to read. Carter stood as if to leave. "Stay!" The order was not negotionaable. Carter sat once more.

When he had read all of the orders Robert opened the chart and studied the area covered. The South China Sea covered a huge area of the world; the chart had a track marked from Ceylon through the Nicobar Islands onward through the Malacca straits between Java and Malaya then northward to Macao; the East India Company had an agent there trading with the port of Canton up river from the coast.

' The reason these orders have been issued is because someone, probably Carter has disobeyed orders and used you for his own ends. I trust your good judgement in dealing with this, hang him if you will, or not. Whatever else ensure that he does not profit from his misdeeds!

Now the purpose of your voyage was to collect, rescue if necessary the Ambassador at Large, Sir Marcus Stephen and his family, from Ceylon, where he is in residence, and transport him to Macao.

At Macao you should report to Commodore Britten, who has been instructed to assist in any way needed to refit your ships for the voyage home via Cape Horn. This return should be undertaken with all despatch. You will be required to carry such goods and personnel as may be detailed by Commodore Britten at the time'.

Robert passed the documents to Carter who sat and read them without comment.

"Wellm do I hang?" he asked.

"I'll consider it; first I would like to know why we came on this wild goose chase to Northern India. What did you expect to gain by it?"

Carter thought for a moment, then "Sir Marcus Stephen and family are in no danger whatsoever. Their transfer to Macao is a political expediency that has no serious timescale. The journey was a way of keeping your services for the department. Essentially this task was devised to keep you out of sight of the Admiralty on an apparently vital mission across the world. I became aware of this through my own contacts close to Lord Mills, and it was then that I decided to use you for an important task that I considered more urgent. Now it seems that this project had even more significance than I thought. The recovery of the family of the Rajah of Kutch will be an enormous political coup if it goes as planned. I do urge you to ensure they are promptly returned with due ceremony, always presuming they are recovered safely, that is. I think the High Commissioner in Bombay will be delighted with what has happened and I have no doubt the French frigate will be bought in by the Admiralty or indeed the Company. In the circumstances the small delay in returning the kidnapped family will pay for itself tenfold."

"Why did you not tell me in the first place?"

"Would you have believed me? I think not, and like the shadowing by the *Rivage,* it was good fortune that they were where they were, in the right place at the right time. Nothing to do with us, but it conspired in convincing you of the importance of our mission."

The silence that followed this disclosure lengthened as Robert thought about it. Eventually he decided to wait until the return of the ambushers. Meanwhile he rang his bell. When Mathews his servant answered he instructed him call the marine guard to escort Mr. Carter to the cells in the bowels of the ship. As Carter left, protesting vehemently, he chuckled quietly to himself. Perhaps it would teach a lesson to the arrogant little man.

The return of the ambush party was marked by celebration from the ship's crew. The sight of the column of green jackets, closely followed by the three carriages and a long file of prisoners was the excuse for a celebration. Robert received the family of the Rajah of Kutch in the

Palace, where accommodation was already prepared. The prisoners went directly to the prison, the wall now rebuilt ready for new occupants.

The General of the defeated army was a beaten man and the French Captain Chavez, wounded in the skirmish, was going to be bedridden for some time. His wounds included a broken leg and a chest wound that the surgeon John Sweet was unhappy with.

Lieutenant Ogilvie had his arm in a sling, after being cut in the muscle of his shoulder. Six of the men had been wounded and three killed. The enemy had suffered much greater losses, they were unknown because the force had been assembled without particular care taken to list the men involved.

Robert released Carter in time to allow him to enjoy the hospitality of the Rajah of Kutch with the others involved. He arranged for a prize crew for the *Rivage* and sailed north to Karachi, where he delivered the Rajah's family to the Palace of the Rajah.

It was impossible to escape the hospitality of the Rajah. The grateful ruler detained the rescuers for three days before it became possible for Robert to extract them from the round of entertainment and ceremony that engulfed them. When finally came the time for their departure, the entire ship's company benefitted from his generosity. Each was given a ruby in appreciation of their part in the rescue of the kidnapped family. For Captain Ullyet, the ivory and jewelled sword was a tribute to his leadership in the rescue and the order placed round his neck assured him of a welcome in Kutch as long as the family survived.

To Robert, the casket presented to him was a thing of beauty to behold, the carved and inlaid box set with ivory and ebony in rosewood appeared to be inlaid with the history of the Raja's family. The intricate puzzle lock fitted would occupy him for many days to come.

When he finally opened the 2x1 foot box it was to discover five large diamonds laid on a velvet cloth on a bed of rubies. The blaze of light and colour in the light of the sun's rays through the cabin window took his breath away. To Robert the enormity of the gift was unbelievable.

The voyage south was a relief for the entire crew. There was a limit to the amount of hot steamy air and hospitality that they could endure.

The voyage took them first to Bombay. Here, having discussed the matter with Carter; Robert decided to pay a call on Ram Das. He wanted to discuss the orders to attack Alan and Adam when they were in Bombay last.

The visit to Ram Das was enlightening as the gates were closed when the party arrived. The small keg of gunpowder opened the gates in a hurry and threat of the party's rifles opened the way to the house.

Ram Das was upset by the approach taken, "How dare you break into my home in this way, the High Commissioner will hear of this. The Governor will be informed and I will have you all flogged and imprisoned."

"Shut him up," Robert stood facing the irate Indian as Carter deliberately pushed him into a chair.

"Why did you send your thieves to attack my men?"

"I did not arrange any such thing, I know no thieves!" His reply was in a tone of injured innocence. Amin Raj stepped into the room and Ram Das paled.

"You are the son of a pig and a lying thief." The words were quietly spoken and they had an effect on the agitated Ram Das.

"I protest I am innocent, who is this man? I don't know him."

The other men sent through the house to search came in with goods of all sorts. Apart from room furniture of serious value, there were store goods obviously stolen in transit, cloth of all types and as Robert observed, the sort of booty found in a thieves' kitchen.

At this point a procession of people came through the open door and began helping themselves to the piles of goods. Ram Das screamed and cried as the booty disappeared before his eyes. Then the searchers carried in a very heavy box that brought a horrified cry from Ram Das. "No, you can't, you mustn't!" he jerked forward and grabbed the box, putting his arms round it and lifting it up as if he could carry it off. The men looked on in astonishment. It had taken two big men to carry the box in, how could this soft man pick it up and carry it?

The answer was he could not. With the box held high Ram Das cried out, his face went pale. The box dropped on the corner and the wood split. From it gushed coins of gold and silver. Ram Das fell to the floor and gasped, clutching his chest. He took two shuddering breaths and lay still. His wealth no good to him anymore.

Robert visited the High Commissioner and had a quiet word on the subject of Ram Das, who was well known in Bombay. The money was handed over to be used for helping people in trouble in the city.

In general there was no sympathy for the passing of Ram Das, he would be replaced by another to be sure, but for the present it was relief. The visit allowed the collecting of documents and packages for onwards transmission to Canton and Macao. The families of two officers on transfer were also able to be given passage to Macao in the prize, which had the space to accommodate them. The crew of the prize was made up to strength with men from Bombay who had been rescued and landed for various reasons from other ships.

It was at Bombay that Patrick Carter left the ship and disappeared into the hinterland of India on some other mission of high importance, or at least that is what he told Robert as he departed.

The voyage to Macao was an interesting one to those who had never ventured to the far eastern world. Transiting the Laccadive Islands lying like green jewels on the sunlit sea, the weather was endlessly sunny with sudden rain showers that stopped as suddenly as they began; leaving the decks steaming. The monsoon winds from the South West allowed good progress and the landfall on Ceylon was made. The three ships anchored in Colombo harbour on the west side of the island, where they were received courteously by the British authorities in the recently acquired territory.

Chapter twenty three

Sir Marcus Stephen was an uncommonly cold fish of a man with an unusually beautiful wife with a matching coolness of manner. Their daughter and son, twins, seemed to have missed the austerity of their parents and were enthusiastically exploring the ship from end to end within minutes of boarding.

At eleven years old, they became immediate favourites of the crew; their nanny was a youthful Goanese woman named Maria who appeared to have a good relationship with Jason and Jenny, the two youngsters in her charge.

Relations with the Diplomat and his wife were distant; Robert entertained them at his table for meals. Without the children to liven things up it would have been boring in the extreme. As the onward voyage progressed the Diplomat retreated more and more into the privacy of the cabin. The children were soon completely at ease throughout the ship. Their education in things nautical progressed with the assistance of the Sam Callow, the Master; they learned mathematics as seen through the eyes of the navigator. They now took most of their meals either in the Gunroom with the Midshipmen or in the cabin with Maria, the nanny. This left Robert to entertain Sir Marcus and Lady Stephen on his own.

Lady Stephen retained her aloof air until the transit of the straits of Malacca, coldly beautiful was how Robert would have described her, until Malacca that is.

Long infamous for the pirate activity, the straits lived up to their reputation and three attacks were made on the ships as they passed through.

The first was nearly the last. During the early hours of the morning a small boat hooked on to the stern of *Roister*, two men climbed up to the stern windows and climbed through the open windows. Robert, who had been on deck taking a breath of air in the heavy humidity of the night, leaned over the stern to look at the wake and saw the boat, and the first man entering the cabin below. He ran immediately below and snatched his sword from his bunk and, pushing aside the marine at the cabin door, thrust the door open and entered. The figure by the bed occupied by Sir Marcus turned with raised knife, shocked by his sudden entry. Robert lunged and skewered the would-be assassin, who dropped the knife and fell to the deck. A movement on his left caused Robert to realise the other man was there then there was a cry and a scuffle he turned to reveal the semi-nude figure of Lady Stephen grappling with a dark figure. He grabbed the man and wrenched his head back. The crack of the man's neck was loud in the dark cabin. His figure separated from his slender victim, who fell into Robert's arms, clutching him, still shaking. The scissors in her hand fell to the floor with a clatter.

"It's all right, he's done." Robert said, stroking her back through the thin silky material of her shift. He felt her calm down and realised that he had heard no sound or reaction from Sir Marcus.

"Your husband, I must check and see if he is alright, he hasn't stirred!"

"He won't, he takes a sleeping draught every night; he will not awaked until dawn at least. He will be quite unaware of the attack."

Robert examined Sir Marcus's recumbent figure to find he was in fact deeply unconscious and unstirring despite his hand on the man's shoulder.

Lady Stephen seemingly unaware of her semi-naked state stood and thanked Robert for his intrusion. He took a robe from the hook on the door and draped it round her. He indicated for the men at the door to remove the two assailants and she stood unmoved as the two bodies were carried out. Looking through the stern windows Robert saw the group of other boats apparently waiting a signal to board in their turn. Using the blade of his sword he cut the rope holding the small boat to the stern and watched it drop behind empty, rocking gently in the wake. The other boats dropped back and disappeared into the night.

"Post a watch to guard against attempts to board. And in the morning warn the other ships to keep a special lookout while we pass through the straits." Robert wiped the blade of his sword on a cloth to clean off the blood if the intruder. Sheathing it he returned to the deck to cool off once more. He was joined at the rail by Lady Stephen, now demurely clad in the robe he had placed about her shoulders earlier. He stood as she approached. "Your Ladyship." He bowed.

"Please," she said. "Call me Eve; after all, we know each other a little better now. May I call you Robert?" She looked up at him, her blue eyes seeking his approval.

"Of course, but your husband—will he approve?"

"If he notices, I shall be surprised. Since he started to use the sleeping draughts he has lost interest in me and in the children. All he seems to do is rest. It is most frustrating and worrying."

They leaned together on the rail in companionable silence for a while before she stood upright once more. "I will sleep now. Thank youm Robert, for your timely intervention and for saving the lives of my husband and I; also for your company and understanding."

When she left the night seemed empty and soon Robert descended to his berth to sleep restlessly for the remainder of the night.

While still in the Malacca Strait several suspicious boats and small craft were spotted and as Robert was pleased that he had posted lookouts to keep watch and give warning of any further attempt to board the ship. The rifles placed strategically round the deck were ready for any close action, and the swivel guns were mounted and loaded ready for action at close quarters.

Just one hour into the first dog watch on the third day the raiders came. A fleet of dark boats came to intercept *Roister,* paddling swiftly from the shore ahead.

Jaipur and *Rivage* were well astern, having been detached to collect water and provisions at Singapore, the settlement on the island at the southern end of the Malay Peninsula. They would not catch up until the morning.

The First Lieutenant was on watch and when he was informed of the boats approaching he had the Captain called and quietly called the watch to arms. The watch below were warned to stand to in case they were needed and Robert called Eve to let her know that an attack was anticipated.

The two officers peered over the bulwarks at the approaching craft. Slim catamarans, with masts stepped but no sails at present; a whole fleet of boats with maybe one hundred men poised to attack the ship.

"Rifles; the lead craft." Robert called the seven men crouched ready with their rifles cocked.

"Rapid fire, commence!"

The seven men rose and as one fired at the men in the lead craft, then they dropped behind the bulwarks and reloaded, they rose once more and fired another volley. Billy called forward a second group of riflemen. "Fire in turn target the first boat!" The second group waited until the first group were reloading and then rose in turn and fired at the first boat. When the reloaded group rose to fire once more; the lead rifleman said "Struth, what a mess, change target to the second boat, fire!"

The havoc caused by the rifles shooting had turned the first boat into a reeking horror of bleeding dead and dying men.

"Gunner, fire the swivels at any in range!" the clipped tones of the Captain broke the tension building on the quarterdeck, and the gunner leapt to the two guns mounted on the stern rail. He touched off the fuse on the starboard swivel; then over to the port swivel, aimed and set off its fuse. The first discharged its load of bits and pieces of scrap metal into the second boat then the second swivel fired it's charge of musket balls into the next boat. Seeing what had happened to the first three boats, the others slowed their approach and started to circle round. The gunner went to the bow chasers and peered through the port, cursing his gun crew he had the gun turned a little to align it with the target, at Robert's nod he touched the match to the touch hole on the cannon and stood back. The gun roared and leapt back against its stop ropes. The charge of grape shot tore the boat to pieces, smashing it and the men in it, to bloody shreds.

The waters around the boats suddenly came alive with sharks and barracuda fighting for a share of the shattered bodies scattered around the small boat fleet. At the gunner's look, Robert nodded and the gunner and his crew ran to the other bow chaser and turning the gun with spikes to line it up; the second charge this time of canister settled the issue. The charge hit the side of its target and the shattered boat tilted over and spilled the men, dead, wounded and uninjured into the shark-infested waters, adding to the screams of the other casualties already being torn to pieces by the voracious fish.

The rest of the boats were scurrying away, ignoring the cries of their unfortunate compatriots not yet found by the sharks. Robert and his First Lieutenant watched them disappear into the loom of the dark shore.

"Reload," Robert ordered, "Hopefully that will be enough to warn them off. Well done, men. Stand down the watch below, Mr. Beaufort; I'll be in my cabin if you need me. Keep a good lookout, they may have friends!"

He went below to his cabin. As he passed the great cabin door it opened and the anxious face of Eve appeared, "Is everything alright? Have they gone away?" Her blue eyes were compelling, "I've got the children back to sleep but I am unable to settle down, it's so hot. Is it safe to go on deck for a while to cool off?"

"Of course, Eve," he turned and took her arm and helped her up the steps to the quarter deck, and strolled with her arm in arm up and down on the deck while she regained her composure and cooled off.

The third attack was when they were leaving the straits and turning north to the South China Sea.

The two junks sailed into view from the direction of Java; there was nothing to indicate that the ships were pirate, just two more of the myriad of ships and boats that sailed the southern sea and across the wide Pacific Ocean.

Lieutenant Ogilvie watched the two junks with interest. They were bigger than many and they carried no flag though the big ribbed sails were painted with vivid images of Dragons and strange plants. He idly lifted the telescope and focussed on the leading junk.

There were people on deck, quite a few, more than the operation of the sails merited, perhaps she carried passengers. He shrugged and turned to look at the second junk. As he swung the telescope he caught a flash of light from the deck of the leading vessel. Curious he swung the glass back, there was nothing that he could see that could have caused the flash, then it happened again. He concentrated on the location and suddenly realised that he was looking at the reflection of the sun from a blade, a weapon.

He swung the glass to the second junk, studying the people on the deck intently, flash there it was again, another weapon? It was difficult to see, the sunlight was bright and for a moment he wondered if he was seeing things; what seemed to be a piece of cargo was a cannon. Why a cannon on a trading junk?

He snapped the telescope shut decisively and called Alan Dawson over "Ask the Captain to join me on deck, Mr. Dawson," and as Alan ran below to call the Captain, he strolled over to where Lady Stephen and Maria sat in the shade. "We may have a little excitement, ladies." he said casually I think the two junks have ideas above their station."

Robert came on deck, pleased to get away from the seemingly endless reports he was expected to make.

"Where away, Mr. Ogilvie?" Without waiting for the reply his eye's swept the horizon and fixed on the two junks. He reached for the telescope that Ogilvie held out and raised it to study the approaching ships.

"I believe you are right, Mr. Ogilvie. Please quietly call the hands to quarters, open the armoury and load the Port guns—canister, for the carronades, I think. Mr. Dawson, take the telescope to the Maintop and call down what you can see."

Ogilvie raised his voice further along the deck calling to the gunner, "Canister for the carronades." He spoke to the Bo 'sun and went to the deck lockers and opened the doors to display the rows of rifles standing in the racks.

Captain Ullyet appeared on deck, immaculate as ever. He saluted the ladies and strolled over to the Captain. "Do I smell trouble, sir?"

"I swear you must have the sight, Ullyet. You always seem to appear before you are called."

"We are trained to anticipate our leaders every wish, sir!"

Robert chuckled. "Well, my wish is for your men to discreetly come on deck hiding behind the bulwarks, to prepare to repel boarders if it becomes necessary."

"At your command, sir." Captain Ullyet tipped his hat to the ladies once more and went below only to appear almost immediately followed by his sergeant and the Company of marines all doubled over, hiding below the level of the bulwarks, to take up positions along the deck on the port side.

At Robert's raised eyebrow, Ullyet shrugged and with a smile said, "Part of the Marine culture, sir," in answer to the unasked question.

From the maintop Alan Dawson called, "Below there; armed men on deck of both junks, and to starboard three fishing boats approaching with armed men on their decks."

Ogilvie came over to the Captain and indicated without the telescope it was possible to make out the three big fishing boats approaching; through the glass it was possible to see the throng of men crowding the decks of all three craft.

"Perhaps we should also load the starboard guns, Mr. Ogilvie. What think you, Mr. Beaufort?"

The First Lieutenant had appeared on deck as the men were roused. "I think we should send a challenge, perhaps one each way just to keep things even handed."

"You think they may be rivals, do you? You could be right. Mr. Ogilvie, across their bows, if you please. Now, ladies, I think you aught to collect the twins and retire below."

"But, Captain, we can see everything from here; can we not stay?"

"Sorry, ladies. Mr. Dawson, if you please!"

Alan, having returned to the deck, collected the ladies and ushered them below, then returned and turfed out the twins who were currently hiding in the maintop.

The boom of the cannon shattered the calm of the morning causing a great flutter among the many seabirds perched in the rigging and feeding from the galley scraps on the surrounding water.

Two towers of white water rose in beautiful columns, one to port the other to starboard in front of the approaching junks and fishing craft.

Neither altered course nor did they make any attempt to slow down. On the lead junk, the cannon noticed by Ogilvie was swung round and its boom was followed by the third column of white water to scar the blue of the sunlit water.

There was no reply from the fishing craft, just the determined approach of the three craft now in line abreast.

"Very good. Mr. Ogilvie, run out the guns." With a rumble as the carriages were dragged into position in the now open ports, the Roister showed her teeth.

"Fire when you are ready Mr. Ogilvie."

"Gunners, point your pieces," when all the gun captains had their hands raised signalling ready

Ogilvie gave the order and the guns fired.

The crash of the broadside was loud on the quiet morning, the cloud of smoke blew clear and the effect of the guns could be seen. The first junk was a wreck, her masts shattered and the deck strewn with bodies and wreckage, she was down by the head and sinking steadily. The second junk had drawn alongside and was now engaged in rescuing the survivors from the devastating broadside from *Roister*.

On the other beam all three of the fishing craft had received the benefit of the *Roister's* guns; the long guns had smashed hulls and spars, and the carronades had created mayhem among the men crowded on deck.

The cries of the wounded and splashes of blood painting the planking made a pitiful picture in the otherwise tranquil scene.

"Should we stop to give assistance, sir?" Ogilvie looked pale.

"Do you understand what would happen if those men got a foothold on this ship? Against my better judgement I am not going to stop and finish them off. You may clear the guns, Mr. Ogilvie, and send the hands to routine once more."

"Yes Sir," Ogilvie turned and called to the Master gunner, "Secure the guns, Mr. Newton, and restore the armoury."

The rifles were restored to the armoury and the guns lashed, gun ports closed. Several of the gun crews gathered on the foc'sle to discuss the merits of their respective guns.

Throughout the entire action, Sir Marcus Stephens did not appear nor did he show any interest whatsoever. When Robert spoke to Eve Stephens about it, she lifted her hands in the air,

"He will not take notice of what I say. I believe he was comatose the whole time, he was certainly not awake when I went below before the action, and he showed no sign of waking when I came up afterwards."

Robert spoke of the condition of Sir Marcus to John Sweet, but was saddened to hear that John had already had words on the subject with Sir Marcus. Despite the surgeons disquiet about the use of the draught Sir Marcus was adamant that without it he could not sleep or even relax. He was therefore determined to use it whenever he felt it necessary.

Sailing north through the scattered islands of the South China Sea they were attacked by pirates on two more occasions. The pirates came from more than one direction to attempt to swamp the ship's defences. Dashing out from the concealment of the near islands gave little time to load the guns. However the rifles were placed in several places round the deck and the deadly accuracy of the marksmen dissuaded the pirates on each occasion. The softening attitude of Lady Stephen towards Robert and indeed the other officers on the ship made the voyage much more congenial. The absence of Sir Marcus ceased to be a topic of conversation or conjecture, and Adam Tamar fell in love.

It was not surprising that in a ship full of men even a plain woman would be popular, and the pretty Maria, nanny to the twins, could have been the cause of mayhem had she chosen to. As it was she had seen Adam Tamar and for her there was no other on the ship. For Adam it was a total surprise to discover that this seventeen-year-old girl could captivate him in such a complete way.

He confided in Alan Dawson that he wished to marry Maria, and when Alan pointed out he had never even spoken to her, he brushed this aside as incidental since he knew. Alan was mystified by this strange fixation that seemed to affect people when they grew up, he was made aware of the fact that he and Adam were years apart in age, a fact that had not been obvious up to now, and it saddened him.

It was Eve who broke the news to Robert as they sat on the quarter deck in the shade of the Spanker sail.

"You realise, Robert, that your masters mate, Adam Tamar, is in love with Maria?"

"I realise that most of the crew are in love with Maria." he replied with gentle irony.

"True indeed, but in this case Maria returns his affection, and I think the situation is beyond curing. The twins have actually arranged for them to meet and talk for the first time this afternoon."

Robert looked at her in astonishment. "You say that they are in love and they haven't even spoken. How can that be?"

She looked about to see if anyone was near.

"Dear Robert, how innocent you can be. It is in their eyes as they look. It shows in their manner when they are near. You will see I am right."

She sat back and sighed, her own feelings for Robert were, she guessed, equally obvious to all but the man himself. She was aware that there could be no future in it but she had suffered from her husband's lack of attention for many months now and she was a woman of normal needs. With a shiver she chided herself for thinking such thoughts in the presence of a man who could never be hers.

Thinking of her husband, she was becoming seriously worried at his increasing dependence on the draughts that he was taking increasingly these days. He was eating less and less and it was affecting his health adversely.

She had spoken to the surgeon John Sweet who had already tried to get him to stop using the draught but there was little either could do without the cooperation of Sir Marcus himself.

She sat back and closed her eyes ,the sewing sampler dropped unheeded into her lap as she dozed off. Robert looked at her with a smile. He was seriously attracted to the lady, in other circumstances he felt he would have fallen in love with her, but just as well she was married and therefore beyond reach. He stood and walked over to the binnacle to check the course.

Robert's good intentions were overcome two nights before they arrived at Macao. They had met on deck during the night as they had habitually done since the pirate attacks, this time the imminence of their separation lent urgency almost an impatience, to their conversation. Words took on meaning. As they descended to their cabins to go to bed they touched, and before they realised it they were in each other's arms, kissing. Robert carried her into his cabin and laid her on the bed. Impatiently he had opened her wrap to find her naked beneath; she wrenched and tore at his clothes until both were wrapped in each other's arms. They made love with abandon, the frustration of the past month behind them. As if, Robert afterwards thought, it was for the last time.

In fact it was the first and last time, but it was a time that neither would ever forget, and it marked a voyage that would live for them both thereafter. He felt guilty afterward and could find no excuse for his behaviour, he loved Barbara and missed her terribly, but he could not undo what had been done, and he decided it would not occur again.

At Macao Adam Tamar requested permission to marry Maria. With the cooperation of Eve it became possible, and before *Roister* left for the next stage of her journey round the world, the wedding took place in the English Church in Macao.

Chapter twenty four

Sir Marcus Stephen collapsed as he stepped ashore in Macao; he died one week later in the hospital run by the Sisters of Mercy. The Doctor diagnosed death from a tropical seizure. Privately John Sweet confided in Robert that the death was from starvation due to overuse of Opium, the substance which was being supplied to the Chinese people by the East India Company.

In the circumstances, Lady Stephens and her children were required to take passage home in the packet ship departing for England three weeks after the funeral. Her children were accompanied by the newlywed Mrs. Tamar after a tearful separation from her new husband who sailed on the *Roister* in the opposite direction.

Commodore Britten was helpful in getting the ships fitted out for the long voyage home; luckily all carried spare spars, as the supply of timber available in Macao was limited. The Chinese labour proved adept and efficient, considering the time available if they were going to avoid the worst of the weather en route.

The short, irascible Commodore was one of the no-nonsense officers who got things done. He had been advised of the current situation in Europe, and was frustrated to be so far away when great events were occurring on the other side of the world. Hearing of the conquest of the Middle East by Napoleon despite the defeat of his fleet at Abukir was not good for his temper or his blood pressure. Even the fact that Napoleon seemed to have abandoned the sea to settle for land conquests at present was no compensation, he was still frustrated by his far eastern posting.

Additional crew for the prize were found from the survivors of several skirmishes between Chinese and English ships in the river on the way to Canton. The Commodore commandeered the frigate *Rivage* giving Robert a note of hand for the purchase based on a value mutually agreed. He also provided a Captain and officers from his own local sources which permitted *Roister* and *Jaipur* to sail with their own crews once more.

The two officers who had taken passage with the prize were accommodated in *Roister* and *Jaipur* for the final stages of their journey, despite causing a certain amount of congestion among the officers in the wardrooms of the ships.

The Mail Packet *Mercury* sailed two days before the return voyage began and the departure of the twins had caused considerable sadness among the crew who had adopted the pair since their appearance on board in India.

So it was a surprise for Robert when the lookout reported her emerging—hull up—from a mist bank, sailing towards the Philippines. The two ships gave chase, and despite the Mail Packet's sailing capabilities, the inept handling by her crew enabled them to catch the ship before evening.

The *Mercury* was armed but faced with the overwhelming force offered by the two warships, the pirates who had captured her took to their boats. *Jaipur* was there to herd them back under the guns while the boarding parties took over the ship and searched for survivors. The twins were found with Maria looking after their mother who had been wounded in the fight with the pirates.

Of the crew there was one officer and seven men still alive. The others had been thrown to the sharks. The ship had been attacked off Hainan Island by a group of boats disguised as fishermen. The crew had no real chance to do much, the odds were too great. Lady Stephen had been injured when she had shot one of the pirates attacking Maria; the pirate's Kris had cut her upper arm raised to fend him off. The leader had ordered the others to leave them alone for ransoming.

Her wound, received two days ago, was looking angry and she was feverish, in considerable pain. The surgeon John Sweet had her carried into *Roister* so that she could be looked after personally, Maria and the twins accompanied her on board. Robert then made a decision after consultation with Captain Keith, to send *Jaipur* back to Macao with *Mercury* and his report. He arranged to meet *Jaipur* at Rarotonga, in the Cook Islands where he would collect water and wait for her to catch up. *Roister* would take Lady Stephen and her family with them so that the surgeon could look after her wound. She would have a better chance of complete recovery at sea away from the fever climate of Macao.

Mercury and *Jaipur* departed carrying between them the pirates taken with *Mercury*. *Roister* carried on alone across the broad Pacific.

Eve was cared for in the Great Cabin, the fanlight and the windows open to produce a breeze. John Sweet was not happy with her condition. Robert sat with her holding her hand as she tossed and turned while the fever raged through her. After three days it began to abate.

"Tell me, John, is it over. Will she recover now?" Robert was concerned since Eve was looking thin and wasted.

"I cannot promise anything, she has had blood poisoning, probably from the blade of the knife. It is often fatal in a cold climate, Here? Who knows? Now the fever has broken perhaps, but I make no promises."

In the great cabin Eve, conscious once more, grasped Robert's hand. "Please, Robert, keep my children safe. They have no relations in England. We, Marcus and I were both orphans and though there is plenty of money for them I would like them cared for by someone I know and trust. Promise you will look after their care, promise?"

"You will be able to do that yourself, but of course if anything happens, I would be proud to take care of them. Now concentrate on getting better and look forward to enjoying them yourself."

Over the next few days Eve's condition improved and she was soon able to join them on deck, resting in a chair and chatting to the midshipmen and other officers on the quarterdeck. The crew had taken the twins in hand and they were running through the rigging once more. Sam Callow had resumed his lessons in Mathematics whilst Billy Beaufort undertook their reading and writing. Maria saw her Adam every day and looked after Eve and the children when needed.

The weather was kind for the next week, no sail sighted though the bo'sun caught a shark, much to the excitement of the twins. It was brought on deck thrashing about causing all sorts of problems until Hanson clouted it with the carpenter's maul. The cook made sharksfin soup and Hanson removed the jaws of the shark and boiled off the flesh, he polished the result and presented it to the twins as a memento of their voyage.

It seemed sometimes that the voyage would go on forever the horizon stretching away to the east with the occasional sighting of an Island to break up the journey. It came as a complete shock when Maria went to call Eve one morning and she could not wake her. John Sweet came and examined her and shook his head sadly, "I'm afraid there is nothing I can do, Lady Stephen is dying!"

Robert came and was holding her hand when her eyes opened, she gripped his fingers fiercely.

"Robert, you promised; look after them." Lady Eve Stephen died.

Robert bowed his head and laid the lifeless hand on the sheet; he rose to his feet and went on deck, leaving the sobbing Maria, with her mistress. He called for the twins and sat in the chair that was placed already for their mother, and broke the news to them, putting his arms round them both as they sobbed their hearts out.

The entry in the log book recorded that Lady Eve Stephen died from blood poisoning and was buried at sea on the 12th of July 1801 at 08 degrees N, 176 degrees W at twelve noon.

***

They made the rendezvous at Rarotonga Island with time to spare, and despite the gloom created by the loss of Eve, the golden beach and the break in routine entailed in fetching the water butts ashore lightened the atmosphere a little.

Scrubbing and refilling them from the fresh water stream coming down from the hillside was hard work but the men were happy to get off the ship and stretch their legs on shore.

Robert allowed groups of the crew to go ashore hunting and gave them the chance to frolic in the water from the beach. The people of the island were friendly and happy to trade for food and cheerfully helped with the water.

There was a whaling ship anchored in the lagoon and the crew of Americans brought news of increasing frustration among the former colonists over interference with their shipping by British ships. Although there was no conflict locally as Robert pointed out there was a lot of support for the French among Americans which did cause resentment in Britain.

The twins enjoyed the break immensely and had a great time exploring the island and the whaling ship poking their noses through the nooks and crannies under the supervision of the bo'sun. All in all it was a more cheerful group that greeted the eventual arrival of *Jaipur* three days later.

John Keith brought revised orders from the Commodore covering the change of plans due to the pirate attack. After a further two day break the ships set sail once more South of East for the passage of Cape Horn.

Rounding the Horn from west to east is not quite the same as rounding from east to west. The prevailing winds blow from west to east so that the transit is at least with the wind. In addition, the Cape Horn current flows in the same direction so that ships are not fighting the current and the wind as they do in the other direction.

Nonetheless, going either way is no picnic and it is always a relief when the ship turns north after the passage has been made. Both ships rounded the Horn without too much difficulty, the weather could not be described as kind but it could have been much worse.

Once round, they were soon set safely on the northern course and the crews felt that they were really on their way home at last. The weather began to improve and the spirits of both crews lifted the further north the ships sailed. The weather warmed day by day and the clothing became less and less with the increasing warmth of the sun. Days of wind and sun were succeeded by days of sun and calm as they entered the doldrums.

The crew and passengers found the calm waters of the doldrums a relief at first after the tossing about that had been seemingly endless since the departure from Macao. The long Atlantic swells lifted and lowered the ships smoothly. Swimming groups went overboard; the twins quickly grasping the elements of swimming and taking to the water like a pair of dolphins. Watch was kept for sharks of course but generally the swimming went untroubled by incident.

The novelty soon began to wear off, as the heat, untempered by wind, became a live thing and tempers began to fray. Robert ordered the boats launched, initially to keep the wood from shrinking, but he soon decided that towing the ships using the boats would be useful. It would occupy the men and tire them. In addition, it could bring them into range of a breeze; and finally it would also make some progress towards the homeward journey.

Six windless days passed before relief came and the first small gust of moving air reached the becalmed ships. Within four hours the ships were being battered by the northeast Trade winds and they were plunging through the waves while the wind shrieked in the rigging, both ships under storm foresails only scudding north, logging a steady 8 knots through the long waves that had been building unchecked for over one thousand miles.

The weather calmed as they approached the Azores and the break to water and provision was a welcome relief for all.

From the Azores north the sailing was easy, they had been informed that a truce existed between Britain and France so there should be no problems with encounters with the French en-route. The passage through the Bay of Biscay was no worse than usual, though Robert found it strange to pass up Channel without encountering the blockade fleet off Ushant.

The approach to the end of the long voyage was welcomed by most though for some there were mixed feelings. After nearly one year away, some found the idea of living away from the closed community of the ship a daunting prospect.

For the twins the thought of life with strangers in a country they hardly knew was worrying. They had left England when they were three years old; over seven years ago, and without their mother or father they were apprehensive, entering the strictures of a strange society was not easy.

Robert called them to his cabin and seated them on the bench beneath the stern windows; the sun was breaking through the broken clouds revealing patches of blue sky.

"Before she died your mother asked me to look after you both. I am very happy to do that, and if you do not object I will make proper arrangements to become your legal guardian at least. That means I will be responsible for your education and welfare until you become of age to take over your own lives. I am saying this to you now before we land at Plymouth. If you have objection to this I would like to know before we arrive?"

Peter Stephens spoke, sounding very responsible and grown up. "Sir, my sister Jenny and I would be obliged if you would look after us as you suggest, we know no one in England and we would rather not be placed with strangers."

"You are, since the death of your father, Sir Peter Stephens, and you Jenny, are Lady Stephens. However I hope you understand that within my household you will continue to be Peter and Jenny to the family?"

"Oh, I hadn't realised; please, we would both prefer to stay as we are at present, be as our friends know us now if you don't mind." Peter said anxiously.

Robert was pleased. "Good! Well, I'm pleased that's over, off you go and start packing. We will be arriving in Plymouth tomorrow and you will need to be ready to go ashore."

HMS Roister returned to Plymouth to a flurry of salutes and the sight of many ships crowding the anchorage. Robert was ordered to report to the Port Admiral and was met at the quay by Barbara, with little David in the carriage. Peter and Jenny who had come ashore with him hung back while the couple hugged each other with joy at their reunion. Robert stood back and examined his wife with admiration and pride. "You are more beautiful than ever, my love and David is so big and strong." The baby was gripping his finger in that serious interested way that babies do.

"But here may I introduce two friends of mine whom will be our guests. Barbara, please greet Sir Peter and Lady Jennifer Stephens."

Peter stepped forward and bowed while Jenny curtsied to Barbara. Barbara nodded to the two children and looked a question at her husband, Robert answered the unasked question. "Their parents both died during the passage from India, I made a promise…." Barbara held up her hand and stopped him. She reached out and swept the two children into her arms and said, "I just knew we would be friends as soon as I saw you. Come into the carriage with me while the Captain goes and sees the Admiral. We will see him later at home, I'm sure. Meanwhile I would like to introduce you to my horses. You do you like horses, don't you?"

As the three boarded the carriage and Barbara turned to Robert and kissed him, "Please don't take too long. Bring Alan if he is permitted, we need some life about the place it's been too long without you both; it has been an eternity."

Chapter twenty five

The Treaty of Amiens between England and France gave both countries breathing space; though in England, politics ruled. Despite cynical disbelief of the majority of the general public; the government used it as an excuse to divert funds from the maintenance of the navy and the army. It was only when it became obvious that recently elected First Consul of France had no intention of giving up his ambitions of including Britain in his European Empire, that the refitting of the fleet and the re-expansion of the army was undertaken. As ever, too little too late. leaving the services expected to defend the nation to perform miracles with inadequate provisions and resources.

The Treaty was not dissolved until 1803 but by that time many of the beached officers, on half pay, had been recalled to man the hastily refurbished fleet, though many others disillusioned had turned to the merchant trade to keep their families fed.

In Plymouth, Robert and *HMS Roister* had been returned to the control of the Preventive Service to the duty of stopping the smuggling which had become more prevalent since the treaty had been signed. With the completion of *Roister's* refurbishment in the dockyard after her circumnavigation of the globe, the frigate had once more become a regular part of the scene along the south coast.

Lord Mills expected and used the services of *Roister* and her crew, and the fact that the war had ostensibly ended did not interfere with the gathering of information in any way.

The visit to Dublin was a case in point. Once more it was required that he arrange the safe conduct of one of Lord Mills most important agents to travel through Ireland, assessing the possible support for a French invasion. While it seemed a ridiculous task to many, underlying it was a very serious suspicion that there were people in Ireland who would willingly replace an English yoke with a French one. There was also the suspicion that a French army could be landed in Ireland as an alternative to England.

The resultant journey of Alastair Walker and Amelie Parker became part of the history of the Secret Service.

The choosing of Alastair rather than of young Ogilvie was a matter of pure sense; Amelie and Alastair were a matched couple, much to the disgust of Ogilvie. The first choice would have been Robert, which would also have been a match, but as Lord Mills had to accept, Robert was now a well-known figure, and likely to be recognised wherever he went. It was also known that he was married, the wedding had been a much publicised event, so—to his relief—he was ruled out.

Thus Alastair Walker was reunited with Amelie, whom he had known first on the voyage to Gibraltar in '98. Such are the demands of the service that the travelling arrangements were made for them to appear to be a married couple and conduct themselves in public accordingly. This of course did not mean the subterfuge needed to continue in private.

The couple set off from Dublin in a carriage for the trip to Limerick on the west coast where the river Shannon flowed down to the Atlantic. The journey through Ireland seemed to be an endless succession of small stone-wall fringed fields, often containing one animal or, more often, no animals. The general air of poverty was everywhere. As Alastair remarked it was little wonder that the people here might consider any change better than this.

They stayed the first night in Johnstown, after an uncomfortable journey from Dublin.

Both were tired and the fact that they shared a room did not interfere with a good night's sleep for either of them. At Tullamore the following night they were less tired and they spent time entertaining and being entertained in the bar of the Tullamore Hotel where they lodged for the night.

Alastair was beginning to enjoy the trade of secret agent, not having realised that it entailed entertainment and being entertained with good food and wine. He had also noticed that being accompanied by a good-looking lady gave the whole business an extra fillip. Amelie was also enjoying herself; she had remembered the rather serious Lieutenant from the voyage to Gibraltar and also remembered liking his polite, rather withdrawn manner.

Being unaware of the circumstances at the time she took his withdrawn manner for lack of interest and it was nice to discover that she had actually been mistaken in this. During the long journey in the carriage she had teased the story of his career and capture; of his shock discovery of his wife's remarriage and the loss, in effect of his son.

The decision to keep away from the boy so that he would not be upset by having two fathers touched her especially, confirming her feeling for the sensitivity of this man.

That night in the bedroom the atmosphere was spiced with the realisation that they could not just be impersonal as it was clear that they liked each other. In practice they had physically to sleep together, there was only one bed, and it was Alastair that suggested the solution.

The bolster was laid down the middle of the bed between them, each turned their back while the other undressed and donned their night clothes. For the period of this journey they would settle for being friends, if afterwards they agreed; they could, perhaps should, take things further.

As the journey through Ireland progressed their friendship blossomed, they found mutual interest in many things and as his knowledge of this talented lady grew, so did his determination to extend their friendship beyond the bounds of Ireland.

It's perhaps one of the facts of life that through restraint the two people found a friendship and forged a bond that lasted for life. By the time they reached Cork both were comfortable enough with each other to be honest and admit that they both wished to continue what had begun in Tullamore. With the report on the survey sent to Lord Mills went the resignation of Amelie Parker from the employment that she had enjoyed since the death of her husband in 1789 during the suppression of a street riot in the Potteries.

The wedding of Lieutenant Walker and Amelie took place at the Naval Chapel in Plymouth in February 1804; the reception in Tamar House was the wedding gift of Robert and Barbara. Lotte was present, as was the ubiquitous Lord Mill,s who provided the use of his townhouse in London for their honeymoon.

***

The rubies from Kutch presented to Robert by the Sultan had been mounted in a magnificent necklace, brooch, and earring set, for Barbara. His return to the Preventive duties allowed a renewal of the social life for Robert, and the adoption of the two Stephens children had been a success they had neither of them anticipated. Jenny and Barbara had the close relationship not always enjoyed by mother and daughter. Peter adored Barbara, who treated him with a happy relaxed manner that made him feel he belonged, and the joyful happy household where laughter prevailed was the result.

Alan Dawson turned out to be the big brother to them both and, though the youngsters delighted to play tricks on him, it was to Alan they turned when Robert and Barbara were not about. To Alan the entire household was a revelation, his own home when his parents were alive had been fine, but after the death of his stepfather and mother, the grandparents had done their best, but his uncle had far too much to say about what went on and had made life miserable for them all.

Since arriving here when he came with the Captain to join *Roister* for the first time, the welcome he had received had begun a relationship that had never failed him. He adored Barbara and admired and regarded Robert like a father. Here he was home.

To Peter, Robert had become the father that he had never really had and it was not surprising that when the question of Peter's future began to loom large within the happy group it was to Robert he turned for advice. The tutor who had been retained to complete the education of the twins had been in favour of Peter following his father's career in the Foreign Office. Not surprisingly, Robert was in favour of a more active career in the Navy or Army.

Lord Mills had suggested he could assist with Peter's cause in the Foreign Office, but in the end it was Peter himself who made the decision.

The acceptance of Peter into the sloop *Jaipur* as midshipman was a moment of great pride to Robert and Barbara. Captain Keith had become a friend of the family since those years ago when *Roister* had been in the Mediterranean.

Jaipur's home port was Plymouth and John Keith had been a regular and welcome guest at Tamar House whenever he had been in port. The interaction between the two ships on the voyage from India had meant that Peter had made friends on *Jaipur* as well as *Roister,* so his welcome was assured on either ship.

Jenny, whilst remaining very close to her brother, had also taken to the life of the big houses of the area. A regular visitor to Hartwell Hall, her adoptive grandfather took to her and found a ready student to share his love of the countryside and his ideas on the running of the estate. She rode to hounds with courage and skill and was soon at ease with the young people of the county.

It was with interest that Barbara noticed that Alan Dawson, who she regarded as a member of the family since his arrival as an embryo midshipman three years ago; seemed to be becoming more than interested in the activities of Jenny. Their friendship was just that, and in the absence of Peter, it was Alan that filled the gap when he was available. It was with some amusement that she noticed that Jenny was comfortable with this, and importantly did not seem unhappy about it. Barbara was aware of the growing interest of the other young men in Jenny and had noticed that Jenny, while aware of the effect she was having, took no real interest in their attention.

Being fond of both youngsters Barbara was quite happy to throw the two together whenever the opportunity occurred.

For Robert the false peace had been irritating and a waste of time. The signs from Europe of the build up of Napoleon's army and the refurbishment of his fleet merely indicated the transparency of the motives for the temporary truce. His beloved *Roister* was passed on to Captain Keith, ex the *Jaipur*. Robert was pleased to see that young Peter Stephens had been taken into *Roister* to join Alan Dawson in the gunroom.

The New year of 1803 had been celebrated two months ago when Robert was coming up for appointment in the 38 gun frigate *HMS Furious* as befitted his acquiring his second epaulette as a Captain on the list to eventual more exalted rank. Rear Admiral at least, according to Barbara.

His conduct over the past four years had not gone unnoticed by others, though it had been a frustrating period; dissatisfying in many ways to Robert. So it was an uneasy man who attended the Admiralty by appointment.

The arrival of a Captain at the Admiralty was a much more important affair than that of a humble Lieutenant. The servant who met him not only greeted him by name, but seated him in a comfortable chair, apologised for keeping him waiting and offered him coffee. He refused the coffee and it was as well since he was called a few moments after he had been seated. The room was the same and the secretary was the same. To his surprise, Nelson was present once more, though the other Admiral was Keith, who advanced on him with a broad smile and his hand out in welcome.

"My dear fellow, how good to see you looking so well; do you know Admiral Nelson?"

Keith's effusive welcome was daunting but well meant, and as he went to answer, the clear voice of Admiral Nelson cut in. "We are well met once more, Graham; did I not say we would meet again?" The rather languid slim hand clasped his as Nelson smiled and greeted him.

With a cough the civilian spoke "If I may, gentlemen?" He did not wait for an answer but carried on with his task. "Captain Graham, I have been instructed by their lordships to inform you of your appointment to the 38 gun frigate *Furious*, the usual rules apply. She lies at Chatham and is refitting at present. I am informed that collecting a crew will not be a problem. The appointment and your orders will follow within the next few days to your London address. My congratulations, sir! Thank you gentlemen!" and with that, he collected his papers and left the room to the three officers.

"May I congratulate you on your victory at Copenhagen, my Lord? The Gazette was full of the report when I reached Macao. I fear I have missed out on great events while I have been sailing round the world."

Keith smiled "There are few indeed that can claim to have done what you have done. I myself have never sailed beyond the Atlantic on one side and the North Sea on the other. Have you, Horatio?"

"I admit I have not! Mainly it has been the home waters and the Mediterranean, of course the Baltic also." He added with a smile. "But do not presume you have missed out on all the action; there will be plenty of opportunities during the next few years, depend on it.

"For the moment you will be under the flag of Keith here, but we will soon need to finish off the job we started with the French fleet. When the time comes, I promise you will be called to join me. You can take your frustrations out on Boney's ships, d'ye agree?" He looked at Robert with his good right eye."

"I would be proud, Sir!" Robert was overcome and he shook the hand of the little Admiral once more, then Nelson left.

"Now, Graham, let's be off to the Cock Inn for a jar, we can have a yarn about plans for the future."

As the pair left the Admiralty a messenger ran up to the Admiral. "Admiral Keith, Sir?"

"Yes, what do you want man?"

"Message from Lord Mills, sir." The man thrust the note in the Admiral's hand and ran off,

"What the devil? Dratted man, what can he want?" he tore open the note and studied it for a moment, he smiled. "Not before time," he muttered, "Come; Robert, isn't it? Qe must hurry." Mystified Robert followed. The Admiral called a passing cab and hauled himself in, "Come on, man; we don't have much time. Buck House, cabby and get a move on; we're late."

The cab sprang off with a jerk that nearly knocked Robert's hat off. "What is all this about?" he cried.

"You'll find out soon enough," was the enigmatic reply. And the Admiral sat back with a satisfied smile on his face. Nor could Robert get a word out of him for the entire journey to the Palace.

The quadrangle in front of the Palace was busy with people going back and forth, but Keith walked straight through the crowd and into the Palace itself, with Robert following. There they were met by a harassed little man who unlaced Robert's cloak and took his hat; a footman dusted Robert]s buckled shoes and straightened his jacket.

He lifted each epaulette in turn and straightened the hanging gold cords. Then he stood back. "You'll do!" he said and then "Follow me." As he walked he gave instructions to the bemused Robert. "Call him Your Majesty, afterwards remember to bow and walk backwards until you come to where I am, then turn and walk out."

They entered a long room with a red carpet. There were three men lined up in front of them. As they joined the line, the first man walked forward to where the King stood. The man bowed and dropped to one knee. The King took the sword from the Aide beside him and tapped the kneeling man on both shoulders with the blade; there was a murmur of voices and the man rose, bowed and retreated down the carpet; stopped turned and walked out of the room. This procedure was followed by the next in line, and the next. It was now Robert's turn and he set off down the carpet and bowed to his sovereign. As he straightened, the King spoke, "We are informed that you have performed diverse services for us without hesitating, regardless of risk to your life or person. It is our pleasure. Kneel, Captain Graham." The tap of the blade on each shoulder was followed by the instruction. "Rise, Captain Sir Robert Graham, Baronet."

In a daze Robert rose, bowed and retreated down the red carpet until he heard the hissed order, "Stand and turn."

Outside the Palace Admiral Keith pounded him on the back. "Well done, young man; you deserve it. Now come and wet the Parchment."

For the first time Robert noticed the roll of Parchment carried by the Admiral. "May I?" he reached out and slipped the ribbon from the roll, *'Captain Robert Graham, Royal Navy, is by order of the King appointed Baronet for services in the protection of the King and his Dominions.'*

The signature was of the King and the Royal Seal was appended.

Countess Dorothy Beaufort-Robinson was at home to the two officers when Robert and Admiral Keith presented themselves.

The Countess had taken to Robert when they had first met and was always pleased to see him. Introduced to the Admiral, she made him welcome and assured him he was not intruding at all. They sat and she called for tea. Without a word Robert handed over the Parchment. She opened it and a smile lit up her face, "Why did you not tell us?" she cried, "We could have attended the investiture."

"I did not know; I was taken there today without notice." Robert was still dazed at the whole affair.

"So Barbara doesn't know?"

"No one else but we three know and, of course, the King!" The Admiral grinned. "Perhaps we ought to send a message to your wife and bring her here to celebrate; after all you must be in London to receive your orders."

"Of course," he turned to Dorothy, who was already ringing the bell. When the butler appeared, she told him to get the stable boy to saddle up and prepare to post to Devon with an urgent message immediately.

Chapter twenty six

The arrival of Barbara and Jenny from Devon brought sanity to the turbulent life in the London home of the Graham family, after the initial excitement of the investiture. Robert visited the ongoing fitting out of the *Furious*, ensuring that his new First Lieutenant Alastair Walker, transferred from *Roister,* was settled in and in control of the fitting out in Chatham.

Since it was taking longer than expected, Captain Graham's services were gratefully accepted by Captain Leclerc in the ongoing pursuit of the elusive smugglers.

In the world of the Free Trade, there is no boundary between greed and need. In the trade between importer and the consumer, supply must keep up with demand, and the demands of the customers were insatiable. It seemed that for every smuggler captured, two more would take their place.

Between the two men, a system was devised using watchers along the coast. Men stationed at strategic points keeping watch; depending not so much on gathering information, but observation, catching the boats as they approach the coast, then, signalling between positions with lights, passing messages along the coast far more rapidly than a man could gallop or a ship sail. With parties of men on duty, each supplied with a mount, ready to ride in answer to the signal.

The system was started and the watchers installed, now they had to wait and see what happened.

Meanwhile the situation between Leclerc and Margaret Yorke had stalled largely because of the need for Leclerc's attendance to the smuggling problems.

Barbara vowed to set things right and arranged for a party for them both. The setting was the Knightsbridge house, and the guest list was minimal; just two, plus of course Robert, Barbara, Jenny and briefly little David. The arrangement was simple and effective. Before dinner Jenny and David were introduced to the guests and whisked off upstairs while the adults had drinks and sat down to eat. The leisurely and homely atmosphere after dinner encouraged the sort of relaxed conversation that Barbara had anticipated.

Robert was called away first by a message leaving Barbara to make excuses for his absence. Then the nanny came for Barbara, Margaret and Jean both rose to leave but Barbara would nor hear of it and sent Margaret to show Jean the newly created garden, while she dealt with the emergency.

The two wandered round the garden chatting in the idle way of friends exchanging comments on the world and the garden and everything other than what really occupied both minds.

Then Margaret stumbled and Jean's hand was there to catch and save her from falling. She caught her breath and Jean put his arm around her waist to support her, it seemed that for both, time stood still. The moment stretched until it seemed it would never end, as Margaret looked up at her saviour Jean leaned down and kissed her on the lips, lightly. They both smiled, straightened, and arm in arm went back into the house. When Barbara came down she found them both chatting quietly as if they had been friends for years rather than only having seen each other on two occasions before.

They made their excuses and left shortly after with Jean promising to see Margaret home in his carriage.

Margaret lived in a cottage in Chelsea, a village west of Knightsbridge bordering the river; the accommodation used by the Captain when in London was across the river at Southwark.

Rather than keep the carriage, he sent it off when he dropped Margaret at her house, intending to walk to Chelsea pier and take a boat from there to Southwark.

As the carriage left, Margaret suggested he might like a warn drink before he took the walk in the fresh night air.

The cottage shared by Margaret and her son Michael, age seven, was comfortable and reflected the gentle nature of its owner. Margaret prepared the posset of rum herself and seated herself while he drank. In the carriage conversation had been stilted, both on the edge of their seats hesitating because of the warmth earlier between them, neither trusting their feelings. Whether it was the rum or perhaps it would have happened anyway, Jean leaned forward and spoke directly to Margaret, "When I kissed you this evening I did not wish you to think me forward." He stopped not sure how to go on. She put her finger to his lips "When we kissed," she corrected him. "I think something happened?"

The directness of her remark took him aback, then emboldened by her frankness "For me it certainly did, I did not wish to stop. I wanted the moment to go on forever!"

"So did I. I prayed you would continue holding me, and that time would stand still. I confess to having the feeling that I have found a new love in you, sir." She sounded flustered and confused as she spoke.

"Oh, Margaret, please I could not be happier. I will try to demonstrate my love for you every day of my life, if you will but give me the chance."

They kissed and held each other for what seemed ages but was in fact just a few minutes before he rose. "I must leave, but if I may, I will call tomorrow, for we need to tell our friends so they may join us in our happiness."

Margaret smiled, "Barbara knows already, I could tell she knew and I believe we can thank her for our meeting in the first place, do you not agree?"

After a few moments Jean smiled ruefully, "Gulled. We were gulled. Thank the lord for our friends."

He kissed her once more and left to pace along the embankment path to Chelsea Pier.

HMS Furious was finished at last, at least with the Chatham yard, and Robert had her sailed round to Plymouth by his First Lieutenant Martin Walker. At Plymouth, Walker found a strange situation, the crew of *Roister* had been replaced almost entirely with men from other ships, mainly from the returned galley slaves from Bone. The bulk of the crew including the Master, Sam Callow, and the Purser, Abel Jackson, had been reassigned to *Furious* along with Captain Ullyet and his reinforced number of marines. The rifles, uniforms and field gun had followed, so the Captain had found familiar faces on all sides when he boarded at Plymouth to accept his command.

The three Captains sat at the table in the Angel Inn. Having dined earlier, they were enjoying their pipes and discussing the possibilities of action against the French. Robert casually glanced around the room and realised that they were being observed. The bearded man watching the three had grey hair and the look of a parson. Then he realised he knew him. Excusing himself, he rose nodded to the parson and went out to the yard. After a moment the parson followed. "You took a risk being here, you know. They will still hang you if you are caught?"

Peter Tregarth, for that was who it was, smiled grimly, "I'll not be caught, and I needed to know Adam was alright."

"My wife told you we would look after him, he is safe and doing well, soon he will qualify as Master and at his age could well become a Commander in due time."

"I understand he is on your ship, and that's why I came to see you. You kept your word to me and the boy, so I've come to warn you. I'm just come in from New York. I return in two days, on the schooner *Abigail Morrow*, lying at Falmouth, taking cargo." He coughed and cleared his throat and continued. "The word is murder; you are marked for death by the Whinns family, headquartered at Marazion. They're serious folk and they will take you or your family. I reckoned I owed you and your lady. Now I feel better, you may tell the boy I'll write when I can, if you will."

As he turned to go Robert held out his hand, after a moment Peter grinned and took it "Why not?" he said.

"Why not indeed?" Robert watched him leave the yard and walked back into the Inn deep in thought.

The three Captains discussed the warning given by Adam's brother. John Keith suggested that Barbara and the children spend time in London until the danger was over. Captain Beaufort was in agreement but as an alternative suggested perhaps moving to Harwell Hall might be the answer.

Captain Willets came in and joined them. After he had settled down with a drink in his hand, Robert asked him about the Whinns family.

"Yes I know of them, a nasty bunch and frustrated at the moment by your coast watcher program. The way it is set up it means they can't make forward plans. It seems their only way to avoid capture is to wait for a foggy night, and they are few enough at this time of year."

Robert told him of the threat, "I wouldn't worry too much about that, smugglers are always making threats but they seldom carry them out."

"What if the warning comes from a source I trust?"

"Well that could be different; I suspect the Whinns have already killed several people within the county. No proof mind you, but they are a rough lot. It might be an idea to send the family away for a while and we'll see if we can sort out the Whinns meantime."

All four thought about this for some time then John Keith suggested that a visit to the family might be worthwhile. They discussed things back and forth for a while before they went their separate ways.

It was two days later that Barbara shot the footpad. While returning home from a ride along the river with Jenny, two men sprang from the trees and grabbed the headstalls of the two horses, nearly causing Jenny to come off.

Both ladies, whilst taken aback, maintained a calm attitude causing one of the men to call to the other, "We got a cool pair of damsels here. Fred; they'll not go to waste neither." He leered at the two women. "Your young 'un looks a bit of all right, mine'll do me well."

"Just what have you two louts got in mind?" Barbara's voice was cool and she showed no sign of fear despite the coarse attitudes of the men.

The first man produced a pistol and waved it at Barbara, "Just step down, ladies, and we'll talk down here on the ground like."

"No!" Barbara's voice cracked like a whip. "Who has paid you to harass us like this?"

"Saucy, aren't you, lady. Suppose I say it's my own idea?"

"Suppose I say you're a liar?" Barbara was keeping him talking—praying someone else would appear along the path.

Jenny kept nudging her horse, making the man at his head have to adjust his position and hold to keep the horse under control. In the struggle to keep the horse controlled he bumped into Barbara's horse causing it to plunge against the hand holding its head.

"Barbara reached down while the man was occupied and drew and cocked the small pistol kept in the pouch by the saddle. Jenny who was watching lashed the face of the man at her horses head with her crop, drawing a red line across his right cheek. He screamed and let go of the horse. Jenny slashed him again as he stood holding his face. Her horse was rearing and lashing out with its hooves. Barbara's assailant was trying to hold the horse and his pistol. He lifted it and aimed at Jenny. Before he could fire Barbara shot him. He fell to the ground gasping blood spilling down his front from the wound high in his chest.

The second man, half-blind from the blows of the riding crop, stepped into a kick from the horse that took him in the knee and he fell screaming to the ground beside his partner.

"Jenny, fetch the grooms!" Barbara swung down to the ground and hitched her horse to a tree branch. Then she reloaded her pistol and recovered that of her attacker.

She turned to the two men on the ground, "Right. Whose idea was this? Who paid you to attack us? Out with it, I can shoot you both and no one would say a word. Well, perhaps they might say what a brave person I am, tackling two footpads and killing them both. I would willingly shoot you both dead. You threatened unspeakable things to my ward."

The whipped man said "Please don't shoot, Missis, we was told to rough you up a bit, maybe hurt you a little."

"With a pistol?" Barbara was unconvinced.

"The wounded man spoke. "We were told to kill you both and use you as we will before we finish, to punish Sir Robert. I would not of killed you, honest' I couldn't."

"Who told you to do this?" Barbara cocked her pistol.

"John Whinn from Marazion." he said finally. "Now, you might as well pull the trigger for we are both already as good as dead." He fell back, still bleeding.

Jenny returned with two of the grooms from the house, with the gig. They loaded the two men on the carriage and the little group went up to Tamar House, led by the ladies on horseback.

Later that day Captain Willet looked sadly at the bandaged figure on the bunk. "You'll suffer when you hang," he said sadly. "Pity you have to take the blame for someone else. Still, it's your funeral." He turned and started to leave the cell.

"Wait!" The voice was panicky. "Is there any way......?" the words trailed off.

"Of saving your worthless necks?" Willet finished for him. "Well, yes I suppose there would be a chance if you gave Kings Evidence."

"Would I have to speak in court?"

"You would, but if the evidence can be proved; the Whinns will go to the gibbet, not you. Otherwise you will surely hang."

He turned to leave once more, but as the door closed he heard the cry once more.

"Wait, please wait."

He re-entered looking weary "What now, more questions?"

"My name is Corbett, and my family mined tin and copper for generations in the county. The Whinns arrived ten years ago and started smuggling, I got the feeling they come from Dorset way, maybe Hampshire. The mines have been failing for years with fewer jobs to be had, so my dad told me to leave home and find work.

"I was up and down the county looking, getting some pickings here, and chopping wood there, but no real job. I met John Whinn in Boscastle, he was looking for a new boat and he found one but he needed a crew to take her round to St Mawes. I've done a bit on the boats so I signed on for the trip. When we arrived he had no job on the boat but he said he'd give me work on the shore. I been humping ever since.

"This job was the first I had like this I thought the ladies were doxies putting on flash style. We were trying to scare them while we had some fun." His voice droned to a halt.

"Who told you to attack the ladies?"

"Why that was John Whinn himself, he gives the orders, though I do believe Ma Whinn tells him what to do.

'Finish them', he said, 'make a real mess of them'. I couldn't do that I'm no killer. I would have told him they got away but I would have had my fun first, she was a beauty."

"How many Whinns are there?" Willet was interested.

"There's John, Joel and the youngster Michael, though he doesn't count; he knows naught of what happens. Then there's Mary, John's wife, she's a beauty but vicious, enjoys hurting folk. And last there's Ma. As I say, she's worst of the lot. I'm sure she gives the orders. You want to catch one, catch them all—otherwise you'll regret it."

He stopped and took a drink of water then, "There is a run being made to Mousehole in three days, six ponies at the quay; the rest goes by boat across Mounts Bay to Marazion. The Whinns will be on the boat. If you meet them and follow them home you'll get the lot." He stopped, breathing hard still suffering from his wound. "Will that make a difference?"

Willets stared at him for a moment. "If what you say is true, I'll see what I can do. I should save you from the rope, but only if this is all true." He turned and left the cell, and went seeking Captain Graham.

Robert and Captain Willet got together that evening to discuss the plans for taking the Whinns. The problem would be following without being seen. The watch system was working well and it was difficult to accept that the delivery could be undertaken without being reported in the normal way.

They decided to take the Schooner *Amy*, because of her speed and also because she was similar to the other runners in use at the time. They sailed before midnight for Falmouth with thirty men aboard, mainly from the crew of the *Furious*, armed with their rifles as well as swords and pistols.

By morning the party of ten men under Robert were put ashore at Helford River, the ship left for the ambush at Mounts Bay. Robert and his party took horses with the local Preventive men and rode for Marazion via Helston.

Changing horses in the town, and then riding on through the afternoon to the hills around Marazion, the group rested after their tiring journey, and having identified the house through Robert's telescope, they settled down to wait for nightfall when they could close up to the house for the final ambush.

On the Amy, Captain Willet launched the longboat and landed the other riflemen at Lamorna Cove. The local watcher met them and steered them on the right road for Mousehole, north along the coast, just two miles away. They settled down out of sight and waited for dark.

The farmer on whose land they stayed found he was being held captive in his own house, but on being paid for it, he happily arranged for food for the party and waited with them to see what would happen. Willet was intrigued to discover that the Whinns were feared and disliked all along the coast around Mounts Bay.

John Whinn had hurt several of the local lads who did a little smuggling on the side. This had stopped the local enterprise but caused him to be resented, and in some cases, hated.

The cutter crept into the Bay from the south, no lights showing and the only indication that she was on the way was the jingle of the harness as the ponies were brought to the quay.

Captain Willet and his men had moved into the village and were waiting for the pack train to leave. The boat was going on to Marazion when it left the quay but he did not want to alarm the Whinns.

The jingle of the bit chains and the clop of the hooves signalled the approach of the pack train, up the steep hill, no lights showing, no sign that the village was aware of the night visit.

As the train came over the brow of the hill the ambushers appeared and the smugglers found themselves hemmed in with rifles aimed. None had the nerve to protest, they were completely surprised.

The cutter sailed across the Bay to the other shore, followed by the Preventive longboat with muffled oars. They lay off watching the transfer of goods from the cutter to a wagon, and only when the wagon and men departed did they pull in and land. Five men took the cutter, the other ten followed the sounds of the wagon through the village to the big stone house that was once the Rectory but now owned by the Whinn family.

The longboat men were stopped by Robert's lookout who had been sent to meet them. When the wagon was unloaded and the goods taken within the house the signal was given; and Robert and his men moved in.

The knock on the door was answered by an impatient man who demanded to know who it was at this time of night. He was thrust aside and the men pushed into the house to find the family gathered in the main room. A fresh barrel of Brandy stood in the centre of the floor and two bolts of silk lay in the chair beside the old woman.

Robert guessed the old woman was the mother, and her shrill voice demanded to know what was happening. A pistol shot brought one of the men of the family down as he lashed out with a knife at Robert who was in the forefront of the intruders.

"You are all under arrest for importing goods on which duty has not been paid. As he spoke there came a thunderous knocking at the door, which burst open under the assault. There was a flash and bang as guns fired in the confined space and the room became a melee of fighting men and women. Robert was attacked by a woman with a knife. She was a shapely, dark-haired woman of middle height, though Robert was not seriously interested in her looks, the surprise and the viciousness of her attack were taking him all his time to fend her off. She slashed at his face with the knife that cut the cloth of his collar. He struck her with the hilt of his sword, stunning her. The man behind her pulled her back out of the way to receive Robert's blade in his neck. The man desperately tried to reach Robert with the club in his hand but he subsided with a sigh in a heap on the floor. The woman screamed and returned to the attack crying "You killed my John; die, you bastard, die." A back swung sword caught her across the throat and she stopped as it drew a reddening line across her neck. The wound had been inflicted without the swordsman knowing, he being busy with another hand to hand struggle. She folded and fell across her man her blood mixing with the pool of blood from the dead man.

The fight was over quickly after the deaths of the man and woman;\. Ma Whinn was gasping and wheezing on her knees beside her dead son, and as they watched she went white and collapsed across the woman's body. There were six prisoners, three of them wounded; and four of Robert's men were hurt, one badly. The dead: John Whinn, his wife and his mother—who they found had died when she collapsed over her son and daughter-in-law—were all formally identified and laid out for burial. The prisoners included the two brothers Whinn; Michael having been embroiled in the fight will ye nil ye.

Robert reserved his opinion on the guilt of the young man, keeping in mind the report of the informants prior to the raid. The elder brother was charged with murder and smuggling and sent with the other captives to the Assizes for trial.

The Whinn house was left empty when the Preventive men withdrew, the barrels and other goods in the cellar as well as the new consignment all contributing to the extensive haul as a result of the raid. The goods from Mousehole were all put up for sale to cover the taxes and the impact on the local smuggling was dramatic. Captain Willet reckoned that the smuggling in the area would revert to the small scale level that was once the feature of the West Cornwall.

Chapter twenty seven

Michael Whinn was spared the noose; even the other members of the Whinn gang swore he had always refused to take part in the smuggling and that he was there visiting his mother when the raid occurred. The result for him was the choice between serving in the Army or Navy or a several years prison—not for being a smuggler but for not reporting his family. He chose the Army, and was immediately recruited by Lord Mills for his secret service, a well-educated agent who could be trusted to use his head in an emergency; he obviously decided that Michael Whinn filled the bill.

Robert suspected that Barbara had suggested the employment when Lord Mills visited Tamar House on his last visit to the area.

The call to visit the Admiralty was not unexpected, the activity a sea had been gradually building over the past few months, and Robert had been getting more restless as the reports of sea actions became more and more regular.

He was greeted by a younger man on this occasion; his deference made Robert feel older than his thirty-five years. The waiting room was warm and he allowed the young man to take his cloak and stamped the snow off his shoes.

The door opened to the inner room and a wash of voices flooded out and he found himself gathered into the company of several of his acquaintances, Captains and

Commanders, including his friend Captain Keith, of the *Roister*. All were drinking coffee and renewing friendships; the buzz of conversation with the warmth of the fire made the gathering appear to be a levee rather than a council of war.

The entry of two men heavily decorated with the insignia of their rank and position stopped the chatting as if a knife had sliced the air. In silence, the two men took chairs beside the large table beneath the tall window. The senior of the two, Admiral Keith—recalled to the Admiralty in the current crisis—spoke.

"Gentlemen, you have been called here to be given your tasks in the present situation. As you are aware, Napoleon has been assembling barges and other craft along the coast at Boulogne with the intention of mounting an invasion of this country. He has an army of 150,000 men and I am informed that if he succeeds in landing his troops here it will be difficult to stop him on land. It is our intention therefore to stop him at sea. He has been heard to say that if he can keep the seas clear for six hours he will achieve his ambition and invade England.

I do not intend to allow that to happen; you gentlemen are given the task of dissuading Boney and showing him that he cannot expect to cross the channel without invitation."

He held up his hand to stem the immediate rush of questions. "I am aware that many of you feel you should be with the fleet under Admiral Nelson. Well, I can say some of you will be, but first we have the invasion to stop.

Sir Robert, Captain Graham?" Robert looked up, "Ah there you are, come forward, please. Your experience of action in the Boulogne area will be of use in your task of destroying the craft assembled there. You will be in command of three frigates, *Furious*, your own command, *Roister* under Captain Keith and *Pharos* under Captain Archer, in addition the sloop *Delft*, Captain Leclerc will be attached for specific duties, I understand that her draught gives her the advantage in shoal waters. Captain Leclerc, I understand your duties with the smugglers have made you familiar with the disposition of the boats kept in the area?"

Leclerc, who had slipped in unnoticed by Robert, stood up and nodded to the Admiral. "As you say, sir, I have visited the area several times and watched the build up of boats. My ship and crew stand ready to support Sir Robert, with whom we are well acquainted."

"Captain Graham, for the task you will carry the rank of Commodore; strictly for the task in hand.

"I suggest the Captains mentioned withdraw from this assembly to arrange their plans for their task."

As he left the room Robert heard the Admiral address the others on the subject of diversionary raids on the coast of France, and the Low Countries.

"Gentlemen, I welcome Captain Archer of *Pharos*. Richard, I am pleased to see you and welcome you to our group." He shook Archer's hand and informed the others of his service with Richard Archer on the *Witch*, under Captain Dawson. Introductions over, they got down to the planning of the raid.

The Captains all had their input to the discussion but it was Leclerc who put his finger on the main problem; getting boats and men close enough to burn or blow up the closely packed craft.

He also suggested the answer.

"When we cut out the Corbeau in Calais, we managed it by seizing the forts on the quay and sailing in with the

Delft and offloading the men on the outer quay itself. Of course, the Militia manning the defences were badly trained. I think we can expect better trained troops and more sophisticated batteries on the quay."

"I agree!" said Robert. "But we will still be unexpected and with a little subterfuge—the *Roister* is French built. And the *Delft* is Dutch. We can draw the parties for the burning from the ships' crews in general, the *Furious* can provide covering land forces plus the marines from the other ships. Between them they comprise a formidable army."

"What about fire boats? Surely it would be an idea to use boats to burn the moored craft?"

Archer's clear measured accent added another aspect to the task, but the final suggestion was from Billy Beaufort who came up with the suggestion of Greek fire. "Using a bomb vessel! It can fire incendiary shells into the packed boats within the inner harbour. The outer harbour would be accessible to the raiding parties but the inner harbour could be a problem. A mortar would make all the difference."

Time was a problem; the Admiralty had been dilatory in recognising the problem of the invasion fleet and it was reported that the boats were already being manned and readied for the invasion. The attack needed to be mounted within the next 36 hours.

A bomb vessel, *HMS Badger* was supplied and armed with extra Incendiary shells for the purpose. Based on a collier built in Newcastle, the *Badger* had been converted from her life as a sloop to her present role by the removal of her foremast and the re-rigging to brig rig. The reinforced deck carried the mortar which could fire 200lbs missiles that burst in the air, showering burning material on the boats below with dramatic effect. The mortar had the advantage of being fairly accurate so fire could be directed to specific areas. She was at Deptford, and available immediately.

The hastily conceived plans were put into action, the ships assembled off Folkestone, from where they set sail for Boulogne arriving at safe distance after dark.

The Sloop *Delft* took aboard over one hundred riflemen in their Green, the recently promoted Acting/Major Ullyet in command; she was trailed by *Roister* carrying parties of gunners mates under charge of Roisters Chief Gunner, the men split into sections under the command of Midshipmen all directed by Lieutenant Ogilvie.

The two ships, under French colours. crept into the entrance to Boulogne Harbour, *Badger* followed at a safe distance. The harbour was a hive of activity with soldiers and sailors marching to and fro in the light of the lanterns and flambeau. Within the entrance channel boats went this way and that the occasional challenge ringing out sometimes answered with just a curse, sometimes ignored. Into the general confusion the two ships drifted quietly.

Delft reached the end of the quay and set ashore her landing party of riflemen and arsonists. The riflemen immediately formed ranks and marched down the quay to the nearest Battery. The arsonists from the *Delft* had the furthest to go and they set out over the wall and across the moored boats for the other side of the harbour.

Roister touched shore and dropped a party of arsonists before swinging across the water to the outer quay where she dropped her marines and a second party of arsonists. The marines immediately entered the unguarded gate of the defence Battery, and in their disciplined manner took the garrison prisoner. From the other quay the sound of firing broke out as the green-clad Riflemen, as expected, encountered resistance.

The parties of arsonists went about their business with a will and as swiftly as possible. Alan Dawson had already led his men over to the other side of the harbour to the lines of boats moored alongside the far wall. The boats formed a carpet of bobbing decks covering the water completely to the wall of the inner harbour, where other craft were similarly moored.

"Quickly nowm lads, let's get started. Take the cans of pitch and pour it wherever you can on the way back here, now let's get going!" He picked up his pack of combustibles and a bucket of pitch and began. He stooped and wedged a small bag of powder under the stern seat of the first boat and hauled the provision box on top of it, leaving the long fuse out he jumped into the second boat and performed the same service, then a third, fourth and fifth in all fifteen boats were prepared in this way before he ran out of powder. As he started to pour the pitch into a further line of boats a head appeared over the wall of the inner quay. The man shouted a challenge.

Without thinking Alan jumped up onto the thwarts of the boat and hopped from boat to boar until at the quay he leapt up onto the stone surface. He pulled out his hanger and slashed at the soldier who was standing aghast at the sight of the men all over the boats where no one should be. Gathering his wits he raised his musket to fire a warning shot; too late—the blade cut his wrist before he could pull the trigger, and the musket fell with the man himself looking at his severed hand in astonishment. Alan was turning to return to his fuses, almost without thinking his sword swiped the soldier across the back of his neck and he died on the spot. Other soldiers appeared and Alan found himself beset on both sides by soldiers armed with bayonets attached to their muskets. A spatter of shots from the inner quay ripped through the increasing band of French soldiers mounting the quay

Alan leaped down into the nearest boat and set out for the craft with the gathered fuses. As the soldiers followed him he realised it would be difficult to light the fuses with a flint and steel, drawing his pistol he took a risk and bent to the fuses. Firing the pistol with the pan rammed close to the clustered fuses caused the flash from the pistol to ignite one fuse and this caught the others in the bunch. Alan ran for his life, clearing the last boat in his group just ahead of the first explosion.

Alan yelled to the men to get going as he ran back across the boats. Catching up the can of pitch he started pouring the liquid in the boats as he left his collection of exploding boats behind. He estimated at least twenty boats had a dose of pitch. Looking around he could see his men, now all moving, not waiting for the signal to light the fuses. The pattern of explosions spread across the inner harbour, creating fire and smoke that obscured the scene for friend and foe alike.

Three soldiers appeared, the first catching Alan in the arm with his bayonet, Alan threw his pistol at the man who fell back. Wwinging his hanger he caught the second man with the hilt, crushing the man's hand against the stock of his musket causing him to howl in agony. The third man had stayed back and was aiming his musket at Alan, when he collapsed with a sigh, as Adam Tamar ran him through from behind with his sword.

Badger had arrived within the channel between the quays and in sight of the inner harbour. She opened fire on the boats within, giving the signal for the men to light fuses. All over the outer harbour similar groups were striking flint and lighting fuses. As soon as the fuses were lit the men raced back to the quay and reformed to board the waiting *Delft*. The bombs from *Badger* created mayhem in the inner harbour, the exploding incendiaries caused the boats, many already loaded with soldiers, to burst into flames accompanied by the screams of the trapped men. The ammunition of the soldiers added to the confusion and conflagration. The fuses of the arsonists began to go off, the sharp crack of the exploding powder splitting the strakes and bottom planks of the moored boats. The pitch catching alight illuminated the horrific scene.

Parties of soldiers ran onto the quay to help quench the flames unaware of the cause, volleys of rifle fire swiftly dissuaded even the boldest from the task. The batteries on the inshore quay manned by the raiders opened fire with canister shot on boats surviving the holocaust; smashing planks and shattering boats at their moorings.

Captain Ullyet, using two fishing boats found at the quay, loaded them with all the rest of the powder from the magazine, and had them rowed into the harbour, where they drifted bumping into the moored boats. The rowers lit fuses and were collected in two dinghies sent to bring the rowers back to safety. The fuses reached the powder barrels and both craft exploded in flames and sent burning debris showering over the other craft around them.

Lit by the menacing flames of the burning harbour the raiders began their retreat, the red stained sky and rolling clouds of smoke a testament to the effectiveness of the raiding parties.

The sound of gunfire was heard as the other ships in the little fleet fired at the quay forts, the guns of the batteries had been shattered by firing charges with the barrels plugged with mud. The ships guns destroyed the walls, embrasures and buildings.

Badger retreated, still in action but now dropping her mortar shells wherever she could. As the ships withdrew the cost was being assessed. Alan had lost one of his men, killed while they were boarding *Delft;* he had himself suffered a wound in his arm. The man had been struck by flying debris from their own handiwork.

The riflemen had suffered seven injured and three killed, elsewhere the party had lost eighteen injured and seven killed, four of them marines.

As *Badger* retired, a piece of hot metal flung high in the air from the inferno ashore landed on a shell about to be loaded into the mortar. The hot metal ignited the incendiaries in the broken shell which exploded engulfing the ship in a mass of flame. Only the men on the quarter deck survived the initial explosion and of them two drowned, the remaining four were rescued by the other ships. The grand total of 91 dead, 25 injured, and one bomb vessel, was regarded as small price for the damage they had caused. The raid would be measured as a complete success, without a doubt. The raiding parties rejoined their ships and the fleet turned to return to England. *Roister* leading the ships staggered as she was hit by several cannon shot, and out of the darkness came a French ship, guns run out and flags flying.

The frigates were still at their action stations *Roister* swung to bring her broadside guns to bear as the other ship fired again causing the frigate to reel at the impact of shot. By now her guns were manned and the *Roister* luffed, as her head fell off the wind her guns bore and the full weight of her broadside lashed out at the enemy ship. The *Furious* had come about and cleared for action her broadside was added to that of *Roister*.

Delft had run inshore at the first sight of the French ship and she was the only one in position to fire on the second Frenchman following the first out of the darkness. Her guns caught the second ship by surprise coming as it did from the shoal waters so near the French shore, unprepared as she was the second French ship, was still more powerful than the little *Delft* and she swung shoreward to bring her bow guns into action while the Port broadside was loaded and run out.

Delft sailed even closer to the shoals and having reloaded was able to get of a second broadside before the French ship was ready for action. A lucky ball from the *Delft* smashed the steering wheel and binnacle and the ships head dropped off to Port causing the bow to plunge into the sand bank of the shoal bringing her masts down with a crash. *Delft* clawed off from the shoal waters reaching for the open waters beyond, following the other ships of the little fleet as they broke off the action. Two French ships of the line loomed up into view lit by the fires of Boulogne.

The British ships crossed the bows of the big battleships and each fired their starboard broadside into the bows of the French ships only causing real damage to the rigging and the bowsprit of the leading ship.

The report of the action was passed to the Admiralty and duly reported in the Gazette. Captain Leclerc was raised to the rank of Post Captain and Richard Archer also. Alan Dawson was rated Acting Lieutenant pending a board.

Major Ullyet in response to the urgent recommendations of Commodore Graham was raised to the substantive rank of Major.

The threat of invasion effectively past, the frigates *HMS Furious, Roister* and *Pharos* were detached to join the frigate-starved fleet of Vice Admiral Nelson, currently seeking the French fleet that had escaped from Toulon under Vice Admiral Villeneuve. Under the command of Robert, the three frigates departed for Gibraltar and the search for the French fleet.

The situation between the newly promoted Captain Jean Leclerc and Mr.s Margaret Yorke had progressed to the point of the announcement of their engagement.

Captain Leclerc had already decided that the cottage currently owned by Margaret would be too small to accommodate them when married and he had found an attractive three-story house in a square in Knightsbridge which he was hoping would be agreeable to his new fiancé. They were accompanied to the viewing by Barbara who had found the house in the first place. Both Margaret and Jean were delighted with the property and since it was well within his pocket, Jean bought the house on the spot. It was then the self imposed task of Barbara to arrange the wedding. Neither was interested in a grand ceremony, both having been through the process before, and the resultant quiet marriage conducted by the Parish Priest from Tamar House was attended only by the close friends and relatives of the happy couple.

It was at serious meeting with Captain Willet that Jean found he was expected to give up his beloved sloop *Delft* to command a new frigate *Hebe* building in Deptford at the moment. Willet had been given the rank of Commodore and taken overall control of the Preventive service. Admiral Keith had been posted back to active rank in the Admiralty.

For Jean and Margaret Leclerc the time taken for the new ship to be completed was just what they needed to learn to live together, David Yorke was a quiet friendly lad and he took to the thoughtful warmth of his new father, who was delighted to accept his readymade family.

The appointment of his First Lieutenant gave them the freedom to explore their new relationship fully and the as the building of the *Hebe* progressed they settled into an acceptable routine that suited them both.

The news from the fleet was sparse, letters brought by the swift sailing sloops had been collected at different times, and sometimes they were intercepted by enemy action.

For Robert the search for Nelson was frustrating. The frigates had been intercepted by a Spanish ship in their travels, the declaration of war was only three months old and the Spanish ship was clearly not enthusiastic about the conflict because she immediately demonstrated her superior sailing capabilities by turning and running for the Spanish coast. Although *Furious* and *Roister* gave chase, the Spaniard was too fast for them and they were obliged to break off the chase before they ran under the guns of the fort at the entrance to Cadiz. As they beat to windward once more *HMS Pharos* signalled three ship sailing south. She followed her signal with a second identifying the ships as French of the line. Robert ordered the frigate to give chase and shadow the enemy ships, hoping that they will lead him to the main French/Spanish Fleet. *Furious* and *Roister* gradually caught *Pharos* only to be frustrated by sea mist that persisted most of the day, causing them to lose contact with the French ships. When they finally caught up with the fleet, Admiral Nelson called all three frigate Captains to attend him on the flagship. The Captains were piped on board the Victory and greeted by Nelson's Flag Captain Thomas Hardy who conducted them below to the great cabin.

Nelson greeted Robert with a smile. "Delighted to see you, Graham; please introduce your companions?"

Robert managed the introductions and turned to the little Admiral. "Sirm I am happy to be here and hope to be a part of the forthcoming conflict when we find Villeneuve. I understand that the Spanish have joined forces with the French and confess a Spanish frigate we encountered showed us a clean pair of heels. We did in fact contact three French ships of the line but sadly lost them again in the sea mist that hung around for most of yesterday"

Nelson commented, "We have actually been lucky in the capture of three Spanish frigates which proved to be excellent sailors and a welcome addition to the fleet. I understand it was probably the reason for the declaration of war in December. Mind you, I have no doubt they would have declared war anyway, it has been threatened for some months. Now, gentlemen, here is what we are doing and I wish you to screen the fleet between here and the Spanish coast. I need time to form lines of battle and it is up to the frigates to give me the time.

"Once the fleet is in contact with the enemy I expect you to stand off and let us do our work. You will be free to tackle the enemy frigates if the chance arises.

"Are we all clear gentlemen, I do not deny any of my Captains the opportunity place his ship in harm's way, I only expect it not to be a foolish or pointless action!"

The three Captains made their farewells and left the Admiral poring over the chart on his desk.

Graham did not realise that this was the last time he was to see Nelson alive.

The three frigates covered a considerable area of sea as they sailed spread out in line abreast. They had been spared the frustrations of the fleet that for months had been forced to wait and watch and sail back and forth seeking the opportunity to bring the enemy to battle. For Robert the sight of the massive ships of the line sailing in close order was inspiring, though he would not have exchanged his *Furious* for the Victory for a step in rank. They were apparently pursuing the combined fleet under Villeneuve southwards though they had not sighted a ship for days. It was on the 21st October that the first sighting of the returning enemy fleet was made by Pharos. Archer's signal was passed as the frigate came about to reverse her course, *Furious* maintained her heading to establish that it was the full fleet approaching before he reversed course and joined the others racing back to warn the British fleet.

Chapter twenty eight

From the sidelines it was an impressive sight; seeing the two fleets coming together. Once the battle had commenced, however, the smoke and viewpoint made the battle one of complete confusion for the watchers in the frigates, the general situation with guns firing and smoke billowing made Robert restless and seeing the enemy frigates hovering around the fringes of the battle was enough to cause Richard to decide to take action himself. Signalling his two consorts to follow him he turned *Furious* towards the nearest French frigate. Ordering the battle ensigns to be raised, he had the drummer beat to quarters and with all guns loaded and ready to run out, he sailed into battle. The Frenchman turned to face him and the two ships manoeuvred to take the best advantage. *Furious* had the weather gauge and was best placed to fire first; the French had to endure the first broadside before having the chance to reply. The three other enemy frigates, seeing the action beginning, came to support their ally. Seeing this, Robert—rather than concentrating on the first frigate—ran down the line and fired her reloaded guns into the next frigate in line.

"Oh, well done, Billy!" Lieutenant Walker cried as the *Roister* followed suit and fired her first broadside into the first frigate, which had commenced turning to re-engage the *Furious*. Captain Archer in the *Pharos*, seeing what was happening, followed suit and, despite taking the remnants of the broadside from the first ship, put the whole of her broadside into the shattered ship, that was now contending with a broken mainmast and several dismounted guns, her ensign was lying hanging over the side to the remnants of the mizzen mast; effectively out of the battle. The second was already suffering a similar fate as all three British frigates poured their fire successively into her. The last in range was a 44 gun frigate, the Captain of which seemed undecided whether to take part in the action or not. The sight of the three British ships descending on him bristling with guns made up his mind for him; the British ships all had the weather, making it a case of fight to the death, or yield. She fired her bow chaser, the ball skipping across the water across the bow of *Roister*. She then struck her colours. The other two French ships were still reeling from the hammering they had received and when the *Furious* and *Roister* came about to renew the attack, the two ships—one dismasted, the other trying to make sail for the bulk of the enemy fleet—the fugitive was caught by *Phoebe* and struck her colours thus the captives plus the dismasted French ship were all secured as prizes.

The casualties on the Frenchman were horrific, she had lost half her complement and, being undermanned to start with, was very poorly off. Leaving prize crews aboard the three frigates, Robert returned to the main battle area, trying to see what was happening. *Furious* came up with the battle between a British 74 lying between two enemy battle ships Sending as many riflemen as he could into the tops, Robert ordered them to clear the Quarterdeck of the nearest ship. The withering fire put up by the riflemen was sufficient for the battle ship to pay attention to the little frigate lying off her stern. The stern windows opened and two guns were run out preparing to fire upon the annoying ship, however the guns could not be depressed enough to effectively harm the frigate. Then a group of men armed with muskets appeared and were promptly shot by the riflemen. With men keeping the stern windows clear, a group of men under Lieutenant Ogilvie ran along the main yard and jumped aboard the French ship. Grapples were hooked on and more men boarded, the stern rail had been swept with fire from the swivel guns mounted in the tops, so a party of riflemen made the climb up ropes to the stern rail where they crouched and slipped their rifles through the rails made sure the quarterdeck was clear before climbing over the rail and securing the wheel. The balance of the rifles went to the break of the poop where they lay down to open a withering fire on the gunners serving the guns along the main deck. The party within the main cabin below seeing the deck being cleared came out from the cabin and joined with the Quarterdeck party in shooting at anyone that moved. The survivors from the main deck ran below to escape the deadly fire. Ogilvie called down to the *Furious* below, "We have secured the deck, boarders away?"

Robert turned. "Signal *Roister,* close and assist! Away boarders," He ran to the shrouds where he climbed to the main yard and boarded the ship through the stern windows. Rallying the boarders, he went through to the main deck. The dead and injured were piled everywhere. The boarders went to the main hatch to the gun deck, and two bold souls leaped down the stairs into the inferno of noise and confusion of guns being run out and fired, withdrawn and reloaded. A group of men followed the first two down, and then Robert appeared. "Take aim!" He called "Fire!" and the collection of rifles and his own pistol cleared two guns of their crews. The officers in charge of the guns realised something was wrong at that point, and turned to organise resistance. Effectively it was too late as more men had boarded the ship and joined the boarders below deck swords swinging, pistols firing. The boarders on deck had already begun the process of extracting the ship from her position broadside to the British ship. The French flag was cut down and the union flag was raised.

The combined efforts of *Furious* and *Roister* had taken a French 74 gun line of battle ship. Importantly, the Frenchman had been plucked from occupying its place in the line and the gap made allowed more room for manoeuvre for the British ships. The need for prize crews caused Robert to stand off from the immediate action once more, allowing temporary repairs to be made and permitting the surgeons to work on the wounded. By transferring the prisoners to the dismasted frigate, it allowed the captive 74 gun *Agen* to be used for the care and treatment of the bulk of the casualties both French and British, the four surviving surgeons working together.

By the evening, all six ships had worked clear of the battle that was still raging. From the maintop Robert was able to see many of the ships in sight were without masts, the smoke from the guns was creating a huge cloud rolling across the surface of the water obscuring many of the ships. The crash of guns was followed by red highlights in the smoke. It was impossible to tell who was winning, the flags of many of the ships were tangled and wrapped around the rigging. He could just make out the string of signal flags which indicated the position of the Victory, though it was too far away to read what it said.

The dismasted frigate was jury rigged with some sail giving her steerage way. The others were all able to sail, so the *Phoebe* was left to escort the damaged frigate, while Robert sought to give assistance where he could to the other ships in the fleet.

They learned of the death of Nelson from Captain Rutherford of the 74 gun *Swiftsure.*

The voyage home was a sombre affair, the people stunned by the loss of their little Admiral, the atmosphere in Plymouth affected everyone and despite the resounding victory there was little celebration. For the navy the war went on. Although Napoleon appeared to have ignored his fleet, the ships of the British fleet continued with the daily grind of the blockades mounted at the various ports that still sheltered French warships. The escape of the Brest fleet in December that year with its five ships of the line made it clear that while threat of invasion was over, there was still work to be done.

For Robert, the return home and seeing his family was everything, Tamar House was alive with the sound of young people, Jenny and Peter Stephens were renewing their acquaintance, and newly promoted Lieutenant Alan Dawson who spent most of his time with the Grahams, was also to be heard as he carried a struggling David Graham on his shoulder through to the Garden room where he dumped him on the settee. "That will be enough out of you, young man, just you wait until I get you on the deck of my ship, your feet won't touch the ground!"

"You're a bully, Alan Dawson," said a soft voice from the door.

"Oh, am I? I'll show you a bully." He turned and ran to the door while Jenny Stephens ran, skirts flying, down the garden with Alan in pursuit.

Barbara smiled to herself as she heard the exchange; it was as she had thought, Alan and Jenny were getting on nicely, they were good for each other. She had been told by the doctor that David would be her only child, but looking and hearing the noises through the house, she considered herself blessed.

In the garden, Alan caught Jenny in the copse of trees at the far end. He did not realise that she had allowed him to catch her. Having caught her he was at a loss with what to do with her.

"Let me go, bully!" She laughed he held her in his arms.

Without thinking, he laughed and said, "I demand a forfeit; an apology and a kiss!" He almost let go as he realised that he may have spoiled everything, gone too far.

"Very well then," she said seriously, "I'm sorry." She leaned forward and kissed him carefully on the lips, melting against him and slipping her arms round his neck. They stood seemingly for a long time. He could feel her body trembling up against him; neither seemed to want to stop. Then a voice from the trees called "I see you. You're kissing." There was a peal of laughter and David ran up the garden shouting that Alan and Jenny were in love.

In the trees Alan uncertain stood back. "Well we've been found out."

Jenny replied, to his surprise, "It was bound to come out sooner or later. Let's face the music together." She took his hand and together they walked up the garden to face the rest of the family.

For Alan it was a complete revelation, he had not realised that Jenny felt as he did. Looking back, he could see it had always been there, when there were problems they always sought each other out to discuss them. It was with a full heart that he endured the teasing of the others in the family, openly holding Jenny by the hand in public.

Robert, at thirty-six, was now a full captain for over two years and on the list for promotion to Flag rank, though with the war now largely confined to the land he considered the prospect distant. *Furious* was in the dockyard getting yet another few replacement timbers, the frigate was not the most well-constructed ship in the fleet. *Jaipur* was also in Plymouth, which was why Peter was at Tamar House with Jenny, Alan and David.

Adam Tamar had been invited to join Sam Callow and Abel Jackson at the Half Moon for a few days. Martin Walker had been reported in the company of, of all people, Amelie Porter, who was staying with friends in Plimpton, just over a mile along the coast. Lieutenant Ogilvie had charge of the ship while she was under repair.

Robert and Barbara went with the family to London for the funeral of Lord Nelson after the subdued celebration of Christmas and the New Year.

They stayed at the house in Knightsbridge and prepared for the ceremony in two days time. As one of the Captains under command at Trafalgar Robert would walk behind the carriage, after the crew of the Victory who would follow the coffin.

The two days in London were overshadowed by the occasion, and despite the appearance of Billy and his wife and son, Mathew, were staying with his aunt the Countess, it was no time for good cheer.

The occasion of the funeral was a time of extraordinary preparation and the crowds started to gather in the streets during the night, gathering together for warmth and comfort. Wherever the procession was due to pass the streets filled with people, but it was the quiet that impressed Robert most, as he returned from a meeting at the Admiralty, he was astounded by the behaviour and the discipline of the silent crowd.

The cortege travelled through the streets of London from its resting place in the Painted Hall at Westminster where it had lain for three days. Robert was filled with pride as he walked through the streets in the train of his hero.

During the week that followed Robert and Barbara stayed close to home with their family, the pall of gloom that hung over London seemed to them to have stopped all normal social life.

For Robert it was the realisation that their family so recently brought together was now about to separate once more. Alan now a Lieutenant would soon be off to sea once more, Jenny would be here but Peter her brother would also be off to sea.

As for himself, he had no idea at present what he would be doing; the path his career had followed had been completely unpredictable. Where it would lead in the future was anyone's guess.

He sighed; Barbara still had David at home, but for how long?

Barbara came into his study and joined him; slipping onto his knee she put her arms around his neck and kissed him. "You are looking tired and troubled, my love, what's wrong?"

He explained about his feelings, about the family splitting up……!"

"Shush." Barbara said putting her finger to his lips. "They are our family, and they will always be our family, whether they are in Rangoon, Macao or London. Don't ever forget it. Now come to bed and let me enjoy my husband while I may, for you will be off again without doubt and it is for us to live our time together as best we can."

She kissed him and rose from his lap leaving the room swiftly so that he would not see her tears as she went.

Counterstroke # 1....Exciting, Isn't It?

O'Neil's initial entry into the world of action adventure romance thriller is filled with mystery and suspense, thrills and chills as *Counterstroke* finds it seeds of Genesis, and springs full blown onto the scene with action, adventure and romance galore.

John Murray, ex-Police, ex-MI6, ex management consultant, 49 and widowed, is ready to make a new start. Having sold off everything, he sets out on a lazy journey by barge through the waterways of France to collect his yacht at a yard in Grasse. En route he will decide what to do with the rest of his life

He picks up a female hitch-hiker Gabrielle, a frustrated author running from Paris after a confrontation with a lascivious would-be publisher Mathieu. She had unknowingly picked up some of Mathieu's secret documents with her manuscript. Although not looking for action, adventure or romance, still a connection is made.

An encounter with Pierre, an unpleasant former acquaintance from Paris who is chasing Gabrielle, is followed by a series of events that make John call on all his old skills of survival to keep them both alive over the next few days. Mystery and suspense shroud the secret documents that disclose the real background of the so called publisher who is in fact a high level international crook.

To survive, the pair become convinced they must take the fight to the enemy but they have no illusions; their chances of survival are slim. But with the help of some of John's old contacts, things start to become... exciting.

Counterstroke # 2....Market Forces

Market Forces, Volume Two of the Counterstroke action adventure romance thriller series by David O'Neil introduces Katherine (Katt) Percival, tasked with the assassination of Mark Parnell in a hurried, last-minute attempt to stop his interference with the success of the Organization in Europe. As a skilled terminator for the CIA, Katt is accustomed to proper briefing. On this occasion she disobeys her orders, convinced it's a mistake. She joins forces with Mark to foil an attempt on his life.

Parnell works for John Murray, who created Secure Inc that caused the collapse of an International US criminal organisation's operation in Europe, forcing the disbanding of the US Company COMCO. Set up as a cover for money-laundering and other operations designed to control from within the political and financial administration, they had already been partially successful. Especially within the administrative sectors of the EU.

Katt goes on the run, she has been targeted and her Director sidelined by rogue interests in the CIA. She finds proof of conspiracy. She passes it on to Secure Inc who can use it to attack the Organization. She joins forces with Mark Parnell and Secure Inc. Mark and Katt and their colleagues risk their lives as they set out to foil the Organization once again.

Counterstroke # 3....When Needs Must...

The latest action adventure thriller in the Counterstroke series opens with a new character Major Teddy Robertson–Steel fighting for survival in Africa. Mark Parnell and Katt Percival now working together for Secure Inc. are joined by Captain Libby 'Carter' Barr, now in plain clothes, well mostly, and her new partner James Wallace. They are tasked with locating and thwarting the efforts of three separate menaces from the European scene that threaten the separation of the United Kingdom from the political clutches of Brussels, by using terrorism to create wealth by a group of billionaires, and the continuing presence of the Mob, bankrolled from USA. An action adventure thriller filled with romance, mystery and suspense. With the appearance of a much needed new team, Dan and Reba, and the welcome return of Peter Maddox, Dublo Bond and Tiny Lewis, there is action and adventure throughout. Change will happen, it just takes the right people, at the right time, in the right place.

Donny Weston & Abby Marshall # 1 – Fatal Meeting

A captivating new series of young adult action, romance, adventure and mystery.

For two young teens, Donny and Abby, who have just found each other, sailing the 40 ft ketch across the English Channel to Cherbourg is supposed to be a light-hearted adventure.

The third member of the crew turns out to be a smuggler, and he attempts to kill them both before they reach France. The romance adventure. now filled with action, mystery and suspense, suddenly becomes deadly serious when the man's employers try to recover smuggled items from the boat. The action gets more and more hectic as the motive becomes personal

Donny and Abby are plunged into a series of events that force them to protect themselves. Donny's parents become involved so with the help of a friend of the family, Jonathon Glynn, they take the offensive against the gang who are trying to kill them.

The action adventure thriller ranges from the Mediterranean to Paris and the final scene is played out in the shadow of the Eiffel Tower in the city of romance and lights; Paris France..

Donny Weston & Abby Marshall # 2 — Lethal Complications

Eighteen year olds Donny and Abby take a year out from their studies to clear up problems that had escalated over the past three years. They succeed in closing the book on the past during the first months of the year, now they are looking forward to nine months relaxation, romance and fun, when old friend of the family, mystery man Jonathon Glynn, drops in to visit as they moor at Boulogne, bringing action and adventure into their lives once again.

Jonathon was followed and an attempt to kill them happens immediately after his visit. They leave their boat and pick up the RV they have left in France, hoping to avoid further conflict. They are attacked in the Camargue, but fast and accurate shooting keeps them alive. They find themselves mixed up in a treacherous scheme by a rogue Chinese gang to defame a Chinese moderate, in an attempt to stall the Democratic process in China.

The two young lovers, becoming addicted to action and adventure, link up with Isobel, a person of mystery who has acquired a reputation without earning it. Between them they manage to keep the Chinese target and his girlfriend out of the rogue Chinese group's hands.

Tired of reacting to attack, and now looking for action and adventure, they set up an ambush of their own, effectively checkmating the rogue Chinese plans. The leader of the rogues, having lost face and position in the Chinese hierarchy, plans a personal coup using former Spetsnaz mercenaries. With the help of a former SBS man Adam, who had worked with and against Spetsnaz forces, the friends survive and Lin Hang the Chinese leader suffers defeat.

Donny Weson & Abby Marshall # 3....A Thrill A Minute

They are back! Fresh from their drama-filled action adventure excursion to the United States, Abby Marshall and Donny Weston look forward to once again taking up their studies at the University. Each of them is looking forward to the calm life of a University student without the threat of being murdered. Ah, the serene life.... that is the thing. But that doesn't last long. It is only a few weeks before our adventuresome young lovers find that the calm, quiet routine of University life is boring beyond belief and both are filled with yearning for the fast-paced action adventure of their prior experiences. It isn't long before trouble finds the couple and they welcome it with open arms, but perhaps this time they have underestimated the opposition. Feeling excitement once again, the two youths arm themselves and leapt into the fray. The fight was on and no holds barred!

Once again O'Neil takes us into the action filled world of mystery and suspense, action and adventure, romance and peril.

Donny Weston & Abby Marshall # 4....It's Just One Thing After Another

Fresh from their victory over the European Mafia, our two young adults in love, Abby Marshall and Donny Weston, are rewarded with an all-expense-paid trip to the United States.

But, as our young couple discover, there is no free lunch and the price they will have to pay for their "free" tour may be more than they can afford to pay, in this action adventure thriller. Even so, with the help of a few friends and some former enemies, the valiant young duo face danger once again with firm resolve and iron spirit, but will that be sufficient in face of the odds that are stacked against them?

And is their friend and benefactor actually a friend or is he on the other side? The two young adults look at this man of mystery and suspense with a bit of caution. Action, adventure and romance abound in this, the latest escapades of Britain's dynamic young couple.

Donny Weston & Abby Marshall # 5....What Goes Around...

Just when it seems that our two young heroes, Donny Weston and Abby Marshall are able to return to the University to complete their studies, fate decides to play another turn as once again the two young lovers come under attack, this time from a most unsuspected source. It appears that not even the majestic powers of the British Intelligence Service will be enough to rescue the beleaguered duo and they will have to survive through their own skills. In the continuing action adventure thriller, two young adults must solve the mystery that faces them to determine who is trying to kill them. The suspense is chilling, the action and adventure stimulating. Finding togetherness even among the onslaughts, Donny and Abby also find remarkable friends who offer their assistance; but will even that be enough to overcome the determined enemy?

Better The Day

From the W.E.B. Griffin of the United Kingdom, David O'Neil, a exciting saga of romance, action, adventure, mystery and suspense as Peter Murray and his brother officers in Coastal Forces face overwhelming odds fighting German E-boats, the German Navy and the Luftwaffe in action in the Channel, the Mediterranean, Norway and the Baltic – where there is conflict with the Soviet Allies. This action-packed story of daring and adventure finally follows Peter Murray to the Pacific where he faces Kamikaze action with the U.S. Fleet.

The Mercy Run

O'Neil's thrilling action adventure saga of Africa: the story of Tom Merrick, Charlie Hammond and Brenda Cox; a man and two women who fight and risk their lives to keep supplies rolling into the U.N. refugee camps in Ethiopia. Their adversaries: the scorching heat, the dirt roads and the ever present hazards of bandit gangs and corrupt government officials. Despite tragedy and treachery, mystery and suspense while combating the efforts of Colonel Gonbera, who hopes to turn the province into his personal domain, Merrick and his friends manage to block the diabolical Colonel at every turn.

Frustrated by Merrick's success against him, there seems to be no depths to which the Colonel would not descend to achieve his aim. The prospect of a lucrative diamond strike comes into the game, and so do the Russians and Chinese. But, as Merrick knows, there will be no peace while the Colonel remains the greatest threat to success and peace.

Available at A-Argus Books
www.a-argusbooks.com

Made in the USA
San Bernardino, CA
22 April 2014